DOC AND
THE PRINCESS

David K. Siegle

ISBN 978-1-64191-641-7 (paperback)
ISBN 978-1-64191-643-1 (digital)

Christian Faith Publishing, Inc.
832 Park Avenue
Meadville, PA 16335
www.christianfaithpublishing.com

Printed in the United States of America

This book is dedicated with love,
affection, and gratitude to my wife, Leslie.

Her faith, love, and encouragement inspired me to write
this book, in order to share my story with you, the reader.

CHAPTER 1

The Welcome!

It was a splendid, warm summer afternoon in July 1966. A calm breeze rustled the leaves of the maple trees beneath white puffy clouds floating under a backdrop of blue sky. Hidden in a cove near the shores of Jervis Inlet, a beautiful spot one hundred miles north of Vancouver British Columbia, sat a twenty-six-foot open freight boat, the *Nefertiti*. It was silent and peaceful along Queens Reach, with no sign of civilation, only the natural sounds of wind, water, and songbirds.

The *Nefertiti*'s engine was silent as the craft drifted along the shoreline. Inside the boat was Vic Hookums and his crew. In his forties, Vic had a rugged look and a deep voice. His husky build forced his khaki shirt to bulge around the chest and lay tightly around his muscular upper arms. A burly, six-foot-tall man with weathered skin and calloused hands, he was the quintessential outdoorsman.

"Shh!" he said as he intently listened for the sound of a ship moving up the inlet, "Do you hear her, mates? She's fast approaching. It won't be long now. Woody, is the cannon in place?" he asked in his thick English accent.

"She's set to go, Vic," said Woody, a lanky young teenager. "She's loaded and primed."

"Errr!" said Vic, sounding like a pirate anxiously awaiting an assault. "Doc, you'd better turn the wheel over to Woody and man your piece."

Doc is a handsome young man in his late teens. He'd been at camp for over sixty days now.

"Aye aye, sir!" Doc exclaimed in mock military style. He jumped down from the wheel mount leaving the helm to Woody and then reached into a box sitting on the deck and pulled out a trumpet. "Who's got my uni?"

"Right here, Doc," answered Ryan.

"Oh, thanks. Here, hold this while I get my uni on," said Doc. He handed Ryan his trumpet and put on his hat and jacket, which resembled those of a navy officer's uniform. Ryan took the trumpet from Doc, careful not to drop it. There were four other band members in the boat, all with different instruments: a bass drum, trombone, saxaphone, and whistle. Vic's wife, Edna, the drum majorette, sported a toilet plunger for a baton.

Doc leaned over and whispered to Woody, "Remember, keep ahead of the ship's wake or we're all going to be bouncing around in here like toy soldiers!"

"Gotcha!" replied Woody with a determined look.

"Set for a new week, Vic?" Edna inquired, flashing a smile, her short dark hair blowing in the breeze.

"Ready, my love," Vic responded, with a smile so big it almost made Edna's look like a frown.

A thousand yards from the *Nefertiti*, the white-and-blue *Malibu Princess* sliced through the deep blue waters of Queens Reach, at twenty-two knots, on her way toward the entrance to Princess Louisa Inlet. At one hundred and twenty-six feet with a wide beam and three spacious decks, she could easily transport more than three hundred people to Young Life's famed Malibu Club. The *Princess* had embarked on an eight-hour voyage through the scenic waterways of the Canadian coast from Vancouver at 6:00 a.m., with a full load of teenage passengers on board. Panoramic views of majestic mountains and lush scenery could be seen from every deck of the *Princess*, making for an impressive journey.

Set among the spectacular scenic beauty of coastal British Columbia, the Malibu Club was built in the late 1930s by an American industrialist, as a resort for the rich and famous. Now owned by Young Life, a nondenominational Christian organization, it is the perfect playground for high school kids, offering them a variety of activities and the opportunity to hear the message of Christianity. The *Malibu Princess*'s young passengers would be spending a week of their summer vacation there.

The *Princess* navigated the final arm of the Jervis Inlet as she made her way to a peninsula that jetted out between Jervis and another, narrower inlet called Princess Louisa. The Malibu Club spanned the entire center of the peninsula, perfectly positioned under the majestic snowcapped mountains, which loomed magically over the placid water.

Meanwhile, a four-seat Cessna floatplane was drifting in the middle of the Princess Louisa Inlet preparing for takeoff. The red-and-white aircraft started its single engine, its propeller spinning faster and faster as it headed down the inlet, as its floats skimmed across the water. The sound of the engine echoed off the granite walls of the mountainside that could be heard throughout the inlet. Finally, after gliding through an expanse of flat water that stretched the length of a football field, the plane lifted off and approached the inner dock area of the Malibu Club. Mr. Campbell, the owner and pilot of the craft, immediately picked up his handheld radio microphone and began speaking over the sound of the engine.

"Chuck, this is Seagull. Come in."

"I hear you, Mr. Campbell," Chuck answered. "In fact, I can hear the plane coming down the inlet toward me."

"I'm about to make my final approach over Malibu. Signal the skiers!"

"You got it," said Chuck excitedly. He picked up a large Canadian flag and began to wave it with excitement. Three ski boats, each with a water-skier connected to it, saw the signal from where they were sitting in a different cove between Chuck and the *Nefertiti*. The boat drivers started their engines and accelerated away, pulling the skiers out of the cold water, as they headed toward the *Malibu Princess*. Campbell's Cessna came flying out, wing tip down, through the narrows and past Forbidden Island. Popeye, the cook, stood on the deck in front of the camp's dining room watching the dramatic display unfold, waving and smiling with other members of the kitchen crew.

The Cessna headed for the ship, swooping down over the *Princess*, out of the clear blue sky. Scores of teenagers were on the ship's top deck, shouting, waving and pointing with excitement. The ski boats were next. They approached the *Princess* with the water-skiers gripping their ropes while they swiftly and skillfully crossed back and forth across their boat's wake. The band on the *Nefertiti* followed behind. On the top deck of the *Princess*, a small group of friends were talking enthusiastically about the spectacle they were witnessing.

"Wow!

Did you see that, Julie?" said Diane, a cute brunette teenager.

"Talk about a welcome committee. That was super!" Julie responded with a smile. Julie, an attractive young lady of eighteen, combed her fingers through her long, golden blond hair trying to untangle it.

"I could fly that plane. Back home I fly my uncle's all the time," said Rusty, who was trying to impress her. He already had a crush on Julie, even though they had just met earlier that morning, when they both boarded the small ship in Vancouver.

Chris, a tall sixteen-year-old, with a slender physique, curly light brown hair, and blue eyes quickly jumped in, "You mean he lets you *steer* it at a safe altitude? Come on, Rusty!"

Just then a boy from the other side of the deck yelled out, "Hey you guys, check out the skiers!" Julie, Chris, and Diane immediately hurried over to the portside railing. The skiers were soaring past the side of the ship carrying colorful Canadian flags. One of them was a girl who expertly jumped the wake of the boat pulling her.

Rusty sauntered over, unimpressed. "I'd laugh if she fell," he said obnoxiously.

Chris slapped him on the shoulder. "Don't be such a jerk!"

"Oh, Mister Perfect all of a sudden, huh?" Rusty barked back. "Just because you're going to be on work crew, and I'm a flunky camper."

"Hey! I never said you were a flunky —"

"I'm glad I'm a camper," interrupted Rusty, "I can loaf around and screw off. You've gotta work and follow orders. What a drag!"

Chris just shrugged his shoulders. "You're too much, Rus."

Rusty turned to walk away. "Besides," he said, turning back to Chris, "I know how you got chosen for work crew. I'm sure your dad had something to do with it."

"Thanks a lot, Rusty," said Chris, obviously upset by Rusty's comment. Julie, overhearing their little spat, looked embarrassed. She felt bad for Chris, who on more than one occasion had to deal with being the son of a celebrity.

Before they could continue, one of the passengers on the opposite side of the deck shouted, "There's Malibu!"

Everyone looked in the direction of the camp. They were thrilled with excitement over what they saw. Constructed in the late 1930s, Malibu was built on granite slabs that formed the entranceway to Princess Louisa Inlet. The entire property was dotted with rustic log buildings and a couple of dozen colorful totem poles. The buildings were connected by walkways built from locally cut cedar. Apart from a boat, the only way to reach this secluded piece of land was by seaplane. There were no roads to, or on, Malibu, thus the absence of cars and vehicle noise.

Malibu's dining room was at the very tip of the peninsula overlooking the swimming pool and the narrow channel that connected the two inlets. The pool, an iconic feature of Malibu, was unique in that it was blasted out of solid granite. Near the high tide mark in the far west corner of the pool was a steel gate that could be raised and lowered, allowing the swimming pool to be emptied and filled with cold fresh saltwater from the inlet.

The attention of those aboard the *Malibu Princess* was suddenly diverted amidship where the *Nefertiti* had pulled up alongside. Inside, the band was playing Malibu's unofficial theme song of the New Ashmolean Marching Society and Students Conservatory Marching Band from the 1948 play entitled *Where's Charley?* Just as the band was entering the climactic part of the piece, Vic swung a three-and-a-half-foot, red cast-iron cannon around in the direction of the ship.

With sinister excitement, Vic hollered at the band members and Woody. "Hey, gang! Let's start this new week with a *big bang*! I'm going to do a double load, so I suggest you cover your ears." The music suddenly stopped, as everyone was scrambling to put down their instruments so that they could protect their ears with the palms of their hands. They knew that the noise from this blast was going to be extra significant, since it was a double load. In an instant, as the workboat was swiftly moving through the inlet waters and keeping pace with the ship, Vic reached down and slightly opened the top of a wooden crate, the size of an old travel trunk. He quickly grabbed out what looked like an inflated clear plastic bag, about the size of a small watermelon. As the lid to the crate dropped back down on its own, Vic swiftly jammed the bag into the muzzle of the cannon and shoved it down inside.

Just then, the *Nefertiti*'s hull slipped into the lofty wake of the ship, and all aboard took their focus off the cannon as they immediately grabbed on to the curved gunnel. The boat suddenly tilted heavily toward the port side. Woody was struggling at the helm, as he was trying to steer the boat back into smoother water. The band members were also distracted, as they continued to hold on the inside of the rocky craft, with fear of falling down.

Woody had just then successfully guided the workboat back into smoother waters, as Vic was on his knees, below the gunnels, and away from the wind gusts. Next to the cannon, he was in position to strike a wooden match. The band members, who once again saw Vic preparing to light the cannon, covered their ears from the blast.

Vic shouted out instructions to Woody, "Slow her down, Woody, bring her around." He then struck the match and placed it in a small hole on the top of the breach. *Boom!*

The cannon loudly ignited.

One of the adult guests, shaken by the cannon fire, blurted out, "What was that?"

"Don't worry, that was just Vic and his cannon," answered a seasoned counselor. "It's only a noisemaker."

"Who's Vic?" asked the guest. The counselor smiled. "He's Malibu's caretaker, a real character! He and his wife moved here five years ago from England."

Startled by the blast, the teens on the top deck of the *Princess* were speechless. Some were laughing while others weren't quite sure how to react. Diane, obviously impressed by the band's welcome, quickly dismissed the cannon shot and said to Julie with enthusiasm, "I can't believe it! A band!" Julie, reflecting her enthusiasm, smiled in return. As the *Nefertiti* cruised parallel to the *Princess*, Vic prepared the cannon for another blast, shoving another inflated bag into the barrel. He yelled out to the band with a mischievous grin, "Everyone ready? It's another double load!"

"Fire at will!" shouted Ryan.

Without hesitation, Doc said, "Which one's Will?"

Ryan gave Doc a wry smile. The band members cringed when Vic, with a glint in his eye, reached over to light the cannon again. Back on the *Princess*'s deck, Julie, Chris, and Diane covered their ears with their hands. Rusty, trying to play it cool, didn't bother.

Boom! Rusty, whose smile had transformed into a painful frown, wished he had followed the others. His ears were ringing from the blast.

Woody steered the *Nefertiti* away from the ship and headed for the outside dock on the east shore of the Jervis Inlet. At eighty feet long and fifty feet wide, the floating dock was large enough to moor the *Princess* and had more than enough room to unload a week's supply of food and materials. This is where the passengers and crew would disembark. The captain slowed the ship to where it was barely advancing through the calm water. With great skill, he brought the ship to a stop along the port side of the dock.

Several work crew boys from the camp assisted the ship's crew in securing the boat to the float. Once the ship was secured to the dock, with its lines tied to the large cleats along the dock's outer edge, several more work crew boys began moving the portable metal stairs into position. On a large flat rock on the shore above the float stood about twenty work crew girls, who were sporting bright-red golf-style shirts with white shorts and white hats. They were singing the Malibu work crew song:

We are the work crew, we work at Malibu,
Love it, you bet we do, we're telling you ou ou ou,
And in our memories, dear to our God to Thee,
Malibu Canada sure does shine, all of the time, hey!

Mounted on the boardwalk near where the girls were standing was a large carved wood sign that read:

WELCOME TO YOUNG LIFE'S MALIBU CLUB, B.C., CANADA

Once the *Nefertiti* was secured to the float, the band disembarked and moved into place on the corner of the dock where they continued to play the work crew song.

The passengers, who were eager to get off the *Princess* so they could begin exploring Malibu, started pouring down the portable stairs. The newcomers walked past the work crew boys, who sang and welcomed them with handshakes and shoulder pats. They made their way up the dock's long gangplank, through scores of other teenagers who were waiting on the wooden walkway. These teens had just completed their week at Malibu as campers and were preparing to board the *Princess* and head back to Vancouver and home. They greeted the new arrivals with enthusiasm, some shouting out the names of activities for them to try.

"Check out the cool golf course!" a tall kid said, with some inflammation of pimples on his forehead. "But be careful of the Rough . . . it's like a jungle out there!"

"Definitely go on the Inspiration Point Hike!" said a dark-haired girl who couldn't believe she was going back home. "It's challenging, but totally worth it!"

Vic walked to the work crew boys who were standing by ready to work. "Okay, men, let's go to work on the luggage," he said in a commanding voice. He began to direct them to unload the ship's cargo into the *Nefertiti*, which was now floating along the starboard side of the ship while the remaining passengers disembarked. Once the work was underway, Vic whistled at Doc, motioning him over. Doc handed Ryan his trumpet, removed his jacket and hat, and also gave them to Ryan.

"You're going to have to take the luggage to the inner dock," Vic said. "I need to run up and check the waterline one more time."

"No problem," assured Doc.

"Ron, you're with me!" said Vic authoritatively.

"Gotcha!" said Ron.

"And, Doc, be sure you get *all* the food crates this time!"

"Don't worry, I will," Doc replied. "All right, guys, let's do it. Keep the heavier weight midship—that's in the middle for you, Chuck!" Chuck gave Doc a smirk.

Doc's six-foot frame was bronzed from working under the hot sun most days. His wavy brown hair, which flopped just over his ears, was usually on the messy side, giving him an outdoorsy look many girls found attractive. He was dressed in his normal wear, jeans and a Malibu sweatshirt with the sleeves cut short. As usual, he was barefoot.

While Doc's back was to the ship's temporary stairs, Julie, Diane, Chris, and Rusty came ashore along with several adult guests. Together they climbed up the steep gangplank, holding on to the railings as they hiked through the crowd of welcoming teenagers. When they reached the end of the line of campers, a work crew girl stepped out to greet them.

"Are you Julie Copeland?" she asked, Julie being the only blonde in the group.

"Yes, and you are . . . ?" Julie replied.

"I'm Beth Collins. I'm on work crew, and I've been assigned to show you to your quarters and stuff. You know, kind of help you get started on your first day."

"Great!" Julie said with a thankful smile. "Oh, these are my friends Diane and Chris. And this is Rusty."

Rusty interrupted and asked Beth, "So, this path will take us to Malibu?"

"Well, actually this is all Malibu, but yes, this will take you to the Malibu Village, the main part of Malibu," she replied.

"Okay! Well, let's go!" said Rusty. "Come on, Chris. We'll catch you girls later."

Before they walked away, Beth turned to Chris and said, "You're Chris Van Heuson, right?"

"Yes, that's right."

"And you're going to be on work crew?"

"Uh-huh."

"After you get your suitcase, you need to report to the guys' work crew quarters."

"Where's that?" Chris asked.

"Just ask someone with a red Malibu shirt, they'll point it out to you. Ask for Bob Rawlings, he's the boys work crew boss," answered Beth.

Chris nodded in understanding as he and Rusty turned and headed down the path. "By the way, Chris," Beth called out to him. "Your dad's great. He's really funny!"

"Thanks," he replied over his shoulder.

As Chris and Rusty walked down the cedar-planked path, Rusty leaned over to Chris and whispered, "Here we go again. The girls are going to be swarming at your feet, Chrisy Boy!"

"Give me a break, Rus!" Chris said, giving him a stern look, clearly offended by Rusty's comment. "I thought you were my friend. I don't need my dad to help me meet girls."

A few dozen feet behind them, the three girls were walking down the path to Malibu Village at a much slower pace than the boys. "So he's really Dick Van Heuson's son?" Beth asked Julie.

"That's right," answered Julie.

"How did you meet him? Doesn't he live down in LA? You're from Spokane, Washington, right?" said Beth, trying to understand the connection.

"Actually, he lives in Sherman Oaks near North Hollywood. We met at Frontier Ranch Camp last summer."

"That's the Young Life ranch in Colorado, right?"

"Yes. It's a really neat place. We had a blast there."

"I'm from Spokane too," chimed in Diane, seeking to be included into the conversation.

"Neat. So what grade are you in, Diane?" asked Beth.

"I'm going to be a junior. Julie just graduated."

Beth looked at Julie. "Congratulations! I'll be a senior this year myself. We'd better get moving," said Beth. "And by the way, machine guns aren't allowed at Malibu!" She giggled, pointing to Julie's violin case.

Julie laughed. "Oh, no, this is just my fiddle."

"Fiddle? As in country and western?" asked Beth.

"Yes, that's right. I was asked to bring it for entertainment night."

"Right on!" They continued along the dirt trail, hiking between lush green trees and dense foliage.

"It's so beautiful here," Julie said as she admired the multicolored flowers that lined the pathways.

"Wait until you see the rest of it." Beth smiled, eager for the girls to experience the wonder of Malibu.

On the outer dock, the work crew boys were unloading food crates on to the deck while the outgoing campers began to board the boat. The teens, sad to leave Malibu, were mostly quiet. There were lots of goodbyes, hugs, and kisses.

Woody, who was on the dock near the bottom step of the movable stairs, called out to Doc that he was leaving. "Hey, guys, keep unloading the supplies," said Doc to his crew. "I need to say goodbye to Woody. And don't miss anything, or Vic will have my head!"

He strode over to Woody. "Well, pal, this is it," said Doc. "Time to head home and get civilized again."

"Yeah, I'm sure going to miss this place," said Woody. "And I'm going to miss you especially, Doc. You've been really nice to me. You taught me a lot."

"Thanks, Woody. You did a terrific job as my assistant. I appreciate it. And when I get back to the Bay Area in September, we'll get together and talk about old times. I promise."

"You mean like the 'far-flung flying Garbonzo brothers'?" Woody said with a laugh.

"You got it! Take care of yourself, Woody."

"You too, Doc."

Woody stepped on to the sturdy steps that led up to the ship's middle deck. "Remember, keep the faith!" Doc called to Woody as he began to climb the short distance to board the ship. Woody turned his head and gave Doc an affirmative nod and a salute.

Meanwhile, Julie, Diane, and Beth were passing Malibu's eighteen-hole golf course. They were getting closer to the village and had been walking in silence for the last few minutes. Julie stopped and admired the course, which amazingly was constructed on the side of a mountain. She broke the silence. "I've never seen a golf course built on a hill in the middle of a forest! Wow!"

"Pretty neat, huh?" Beth responded. "It's just a pitch and putt, but it's superfun! You girls are going to have a great time. There are so many things to do here: waterskiing, swimming, boating, volleyball, golf, fishing . . . if you like that kind of thing? There's also some fun organized stuff too, you'll see. Wait until our regatta!"

As the girls neared the village, the *Malibu Princess* had begun to pull away from the outer dock, brimming with sad campers heading back to Vancouver. The *Princess*'s hull was slightly leaning over onto its port side where most of the passengers were gathering to call their goodbyes to the work crew and staff. Some of the girls were so emotional about having to leave, that they were crying.

"Bye, Doc!" shouted one of the girls as the ship began to pick up speed. "We'll miss you! We'll send you some cookies!" Tears began to well in her eyes as the *Princess* backed away from the float. Doc smiled back at her and waved goodbye. *The Princess* left a trail of white froth in its wake as it slid through the waters of Jervis Inlet, away from Malibu toward Vancouver.

After leaving the forest behind, the girls walked into an open area where they could see Jervis Inlet once again. As they walked near the water's edge, they spotted a nearby cabin on the hillside of the trail. It was a rustic one-story structure named Haida, after one of the region's Canadian Indian tribes. The cabin paid them tribute with a colorful totem pole of red, blue, yellow, and white, mounted on the front of the cabin. Haida's bay windows and deck had spectacular views over Jervis Inlet and the surrounding mountains.

"So who lives here?" Julie asked Beth.

"Vic and Edna. They're the caretakers for Malibu. They live here year-round. Can you imagine? They're here alone eight to nine months out of the year!"

Julie stopped dead in her tracks with her eyes focused on the central part of Malibu, just ahead of them. "Golly! That is magnificent!" she exclaimed with wonder.

"That's what we call Malibu Village," explained Beth. "It's the main area of the camp, where the dining room and pool are and Main Street, with all the different shops and several offices. It's also where most of the living quarters are. It's gorgeous—just wait!" Beth was bubbling over with excitement.

"Diane, see over there? That's Nootka," Beth said as she pointed toward a large two-story log building with two large decks at its front. The surrounding area was dotted with a handful of totem poles adding color and character to the buildings. "The girl campers stay there."

Suddenly, there was a horn blast from the *Malibu Princess*. The girls turned around quickly to see the *Princess* heading farther down the inlet. It got smaller and smaller as it sailed away.

"Well, there they go, back to Vancouver," said Beth.

As the girls turned their heads away from the ship, they couldn't help but notice a tiny island just off Malibu Village. "That's Forbidden Island," said Beth.

This small island was once a burial ground for Sechelt Indian chiefs, a prominent tribe of the British Columbia coast. The oblong island was only about four times the size of the outer dock and sat a hundred yards from Nootka. With its picturesque beauty and tall pine trees, it was a natural navigational point to help yachtsmen negotiate the narrows, a one-hundred-fifty-foot-wide waterway between the end of Malibu's peninsula and the other side of the inlet. The girls' eyes were fixed on Forbidden Island when the *Nefertiti* came past on its way through the narrows. The sound of the boat's engine drew their attention. Doc was at the helm, his eyes focused solely on the narrow gap that led to the inner dock.

"There goes the work crew boys with the luggage," Beth told the girls. "They're heading for the inner dock."

"The inner dock?" Julie said with a puzzled look.

"It's just inside the Princess Louisa Inlet, on the other side of Malibu. Speaking of docks, wait till you meet Doc."

"Doc? Who's he? The camp's doctor?" asked Julie.

"No, just the number one dreamboat of Malibu. That's him driving the workboat, the *Nefertiti*. He's Malibu's harbormaster. This is his second summer here. I wouldn't mind tying up to his dock!" Beth whispered to Julie, pointing to her lips, as if she imagined pressing her lips against Doc's in a kiss. "If you know what I mean?" she said with a wink. "You didn't hear that, Diane. Julie, the number one rule for work crew and summer staff: no frat! Bummer, I know!"

"No frat?" Julie asked. She had no idea what Beth meant.

"You know, no fraternizing with work crew guys, or staff guys, and, of course, campers. I mean, we can be friends, but no romances. You know . . . no relationships."

"So why do they call him Doc?" asked Julie. "Is he studying to be a doctor?"

"Oh, no!" Beth laughed. "He just graduated from high school too. He's your age. They call him Doc because he runs the dock. You know, he's the harbormaster."

Diane was impressed. "That's cool."

"His real name is Joe, but everyone here calls him Doc. He's from California, near San Francisco. All the staff guys have nicknames," she continued. "There's Larry Lawnmower. He's in charge of the golf course. Turtle is the lifeguard. The cook's name is Popeye."

"As in Popeye the Sailor?" Julie interrupted.

"No, that's not it. He wears these really thick glasses, and his eyes kind of bug out. Hence, Popeye!" she explained as she opened her eyes really wide to show them what she meant. The three girls could not help but slightly giggle together. "Let's head over to the girls' work crew quarters first. Diane, you can come with us for now, and then we'll get your luggage."

"Do you know what they're going to have me doing?" asked Julie with anticipation.

"I think you're going to be the new head-table, adult-guest waitress."

"Really?"

"Yes, that's because Jill, the girl who's been doing it up to now, had to leave today," said Beth. "It's a very prestigious job." Julie beamed with pride.

Meanwhile, Vic and Ron had spent the past half hour climbing wooden ladders along the side of a waterfall and creek so that they could inspect the waterline filter box. They wanted to make sure that there wast't any debri, such as falling branches, blocking the flow. This pipeline was located fifty yards past the outer dock and provided all the fresh water for the camp. Once they discovered that the box was clean and operating correctly, they returned to the ski boat and headed back toward Malibu.

The inner dock area, located on the Princess Louisa Inlet side of the peninsula, was crowded with campers who were there collecting their luggage. The work crew boys, who were unloading the luggage, passed every bag from the *Nefertiti* up the gangplank before placing it onto the upper deck. Doc was nearby directing the work crew boys' efforts.

Just then, a speedboat emerged from the narrows and tied up next to the *Nefertiti* with Vic and Ron aboard. "How's the waterline holding up?" asked Doc as he watched Vic climb out of the boat.

"The flow looks good. Now I just need to check the tank. So have you done it yet?" asked Vic.

"You mean . . . ," Doc said with a little smirk. Vic nodded his head and smiled. They both knew what the other one was thinking.

Doc whispered to Vic, "No. I was waiting for you. I know how much you enjoy these little pranks."

"You have to keep them guessing, mate," Vic said with a mischievous look on his face. "Besides, a little humorous prank won't hurt anyone. Where is it? I'll set the bait."

Doc pointed inside the *Nefertiti*. "Next to the battery housing."

Vic glanced over into the boat. "I see it. Go ahead and motion Chuck to be ready for the prank."

"Hey, Chuck!" Doc called out. Standing at the bottom of the gangplank, Chuck turned and nodded when Doc gave him the high sign. Vic now had a large brown suitcase in his hand. He quickly walked it over to Chuck and sat it down at his feet next to other pieces of luggage that were beginning to stack up. Vic headed up the gangplank in a hurry.

"Coming through! Coming through!" Vic shouted loudly.

Then he whispered to the crew, "The fish is in the pan," as he slithered past them on his way up the gangplank.

Chuck picked up the marked suitcase and handed it to the next worker in line. "Special delivery," he whispered. The suitcase passed up the line until it got to two luggage handlers in the middle of the gangplank who, making it look like an accident, lost their grip on the suitcase, causing it to slip from their hands. The brown bag fell directly into the water below. As it hit the salty water, the lid popped open.

Many of the new campers watched the staged mishap unfold from the upper deck. Some laughed, others looked genuinley distressed.

Rusty, who was standing in the crowd of new campers, shouted, "Check it out! They dropped a suitcase in the drink! Sure glad I got mine," he annouced proudly.

Clothes were beginning to float out of the case, including a girl's bra and underwear. A camper girl whispered to a friend in a panic, "Oh my God! I think that's my suitcase." The suitcase was now beginning to drift away from the dock with the tide. Doc came running up to the bottom of the gangplank, pretending to be angry.

"Come on, guys. We need to be more careful," he said with feigned anger. "This is the second one we've lost in three weeks!" He looked over at the suitcase as more and more of its contents floated out of the bag and into the water. "Keep working," Doc said sternly. "I'll pluck that stuff out of the water in a bit."

The girl on the deck was about to faint with disbelief. Vic spotted her and chuckled under his breath. He looked at Doc, gave him a thumbs-up, and then left.

The work crew, trying not to laugh, resumed their work. Feigning anger, Doc jumped in the ski boat and headed to the floating suitcase, then pulled it and the clothing out of the water. At that moment, the girl who believed her bag to be the one that flopped open in the water spotted her real suitcase up on the deck. She sighed with relief.

Doc tied the speedboat to the end of the dock and promptly made his way up the gangplank to the upper deck. The camper girl quickly walked over to him. She wasn't impressed by what she had now determined was a prank. "Ha ha," she said icily, "that wasn't funny!"

"What?" Doc responded, flashing a smile. He didn't want to admit his guilt.

"You know what I'm talking about", she snapped back at him.

Trying to calm the situation, Doc casually asks her, "What's your name?"

"Tracey", she answers.

"Well, Tracey, my name is Doc, and I truly apologize." He places his hands in a prayer-like position, and slightly nods. "We will make it up to you, okay? Trust me."

Tracey, feeling his sincere apology, responds with, "Okay. Well then, I accept your…regret, I guess?"

The girl just shook her head and turned back toward her suitcase. Doc immediately began instructing the work crew boys how to organize the luggage on the deck. After he explained the process, he headed back down to the lower dock to his floating harbormaster's office, which was attached to the inner side of the long float. He heard someone inside. "Ken, is that you?" he called out.

"Yes, I'm just trying to finish repairing this 150 Merc," Ken answered.

Doc called over to the work crew boys, "Hey, guys! Finish up. I'll be in the shack for a few minutes. Then we've got to get back out to the outer dock and pick up the rest of the food."

Doc entered his office, which was also the storage area for harbor equipment. The shack was full of tools, pumps, oars, ropes, anchors, fishing gear, outboard fuel tanks, life preservers, first-aid kits, and other bits and pieces. Behind the large service counter was a mounted board describing harbor rules and times. On the counter were sign-in and sign-out clipboards used to track boat use. In one corner was a repair workstation where Ken was working on the outboard motor. His ears were big, and his eyes were slightly sunken into his face. He was a skinny young man in his early twenties with light-colored hair.

"So how's it going?" Ken asked Doc.

"Not too bad actually. Still working on that 150?"

"I think I've just about got it. I missed playing the snare drum with you guys, but I really had to get this motor fixed this morning. How was the welcome?"

"Oh, it was great! Vic did a double load on the first blast. You should have seen everyone aboard the *Princess* grab their ears."

"So, did you . . . ?"

"Dump the suitcase?" Doc said eagerly, with a look of satisfaction smeared across his face. "Oh, yeah, it was great. I just pulled it out of the inlet. In fact, I just had a girl camper challenge me about it—she wasn't very happy!"

"No! Not the suitcase! Any luck with the new arrivals? Any possible 'princess' on the horizon?"

"Are you kidding? They're all campers—too young, pal," said Doc. "Besides, you know the frat rule. I really need to force myself away from any potential relationship, especially with campers!"

"It's never stopped you before," Ken said to him with smug confidence. "What about last year with Suzanne?"

"Yeah, but Suzanne was on work crew, remember? She was a great gal. I really did like her and cared about her a lot, but it just wasn't true love for me. She wasn't like the 'princess' of my life, or anything. It was just a young attraction. We were just good friends."

"Oh, come on, Doc. Wh
live together, remember? Wha
Suzanne?"

"I swear ---- we played a litt
in a defensive voice.

"Well, that would have beer
You're right, you'd better cool it,"
an older brother.

"Hey! Have you heard yet w
to be?" asked Doc. "Is it going to b
think it's going to be the new kid wl

Los Angeles. He was a camper a

"Really?" Doc said with a puzzle ... well, I hope he knows
something about boats and waterskiing. Why him? I don't get it! I
thought Mitch."

"Hey, Doc!" shouted Chuck from outside the shack. "We're
ready to go!"

"Okay, I'll be right there!" Doc hollered back. He started to
leave, heading toward the door. "I'd better go."

"Doc!" Ken said hastily. "This kid from LA . . ."

"Yeah?"

"He's Dick Van Heuson's oldest son."

"Dick Van Heuson, of the *Dick Van Heuson Show* on television?"

"Yes."

"No way! Are you serious?" Doc said, clearly amazed by the
news.

"I'm serious."

"Interesting. He's one of my very favorite comedians. Hmmm,
I'll tell you what though . . . what's this kid's name?"

"I don't know," Ken answered.

"Well, anyway, he's not getting any special treatment from me.
And you can be sure Vic won't cut him any slack!"

"That's for sure," Ken agreed.

were walking down the sloped wooden board-
Main Street toward the large upper deck above
where all the suitcases had been placed for collection.
last remaining suitcases to be claimed sat next to the base
redibly tall totem pole. Standing sixty-five feet tall, with a
ve base, the pole was an original hand-carved totem. The rich
olors of red, yellow, blue, white, green, and black looked as if they
had recently been repainted.

"Here they are," Julie announced, pointing at their bags. Her
eyes slowly scanned from the base of the totem pole, all the way to
the top. "That's incredible!"

"You'd better hurry on over to Nootka and find your room,"
Beth said to Diane in an anxious tone. "Remember I showed you
where it was?"

"I remember," Diane answered, then gave Julie an uncomfortable look.

"It's going to be fine, Diane," Julie said, hoping to give her some
encouragement.

"I'll be right back," Beth said before walking over to the deck
railing. She looked down at the long floating dock area as if trying to
locate someone.

Julie continued to reassure Diane, "I'm sure you're going to
meet some great new friends. And I'll be around, okay?"

"Okay," she answered, slightly skeptical, as she began to walk up
the walkway toward Nootka with her suitcase.

Meanwhile, Beth spotted the target of her search. "Doc!" she
called as he turned toward the freight boat.

"Hey, Beth! How's it going?" Doc called back. "Another new
week, huh?" Beth turned her head and looked over at Julie.

"Julie, come here, hurry!" she said to her new friend. She turned
back to Doc and said, "There's someone I want you to meet."

"Later, Beth!" he shouted back. "We really need to get out to
the outer dock."

He turned and climbed aboard the boat where the crew was
waiting for him to take them out to the outer dock, where the

remainder of the freight waited. Julie had joined Beth at the railing and was following her gaze.

Just as he begun to ease the boat away from the dock, Doc looked back just in time to catch a glimpse of Julie's golden hair. He did a visible double take and immediately steered the boat back around to pass in front of Beth and Julie again. He could not believe his eyes. He had never seen such a beautiful girl!

"This is Julie Copeland," Beth called as Doc idled past. "She's our new work crew girl, to replace Jill."

Doc was in a bit of a daze. A couple of seconds passed before he finally regained control. "Hi!" he called up to Julie with a broad smile.

"Hi! Nice to meet you," Julie responded, her interest obvious.

The *Nefertiti* was idling toward the shoreline rocks while Doc and Julie continued to stare at each other in silence.

"Doc!" Chuck suddenly called out. Doc turned around and saw the upcoming shore. He quickly swung the boat to the left, barely missing the rocks.

"Are you okay?" asked Chuck.

"Yeah, sure," Doc said nervously.

"Not bad, huh?" Chuck said quietly to Doc.

Doc quickly looked back at Julie and Beth, gave them a brief wave, and then returned his attention to the task at hand as the boat began to head toward the narrows once again. "That, my friends, is a total knockout," Doc said to his crew. "An absolute 'stone fox'! But that's between us guys, right?" They all agreed.

Before walking back to the suitcases, Beth said to Julie, "So what did you think?"

"He's really cute. What's he like?" Julie asked.

"He's nice, really nice," Beth said empathetically. "You'll see. But just remember . . ."

"I know."

They both said together out loud, "No frat!"

CHAPTER 2

First Day in Camp

An hour after arriving on the peninsula, Chris was strolling along a wooden planked walkway that led to Malibu's dining room. Every meal served in the dining room came with breathtaking views, thanks to the large bay windows that extended from the floor to the ceiling and wrapped around the entire space. Malibu's diners could look down to the pool or out to the inlet and mountains while they enjoyed their meal.

Rusty hadn't wasted any time acquainting himself with the pool. His long, surfer-style red swim trunks were dripping wet from the laps he'd been doing in the cool water. He was standing on the pool deck when he looked up toward the dining room and spotted Chris on the walkway.

"Hey, Chris, down here!" Rusty yelled, motioning him to join him down on the pool deck. Chris hurried down the large granite rock flow that separated him from Rusty. He took each step carefully so as not to slip and fall.

"So, where were you going?" asked Rusty, as he brushed his long, wet wavy red hair away from his face with his fingers.

"My work crew boss sent me to the harbormaster's office, down on the lower dock. I'm going to be the harbormaster's new assistant."

"No kidding?" Rusty responded with enthusiasm. "Does that mean you can get me some extra ski rides?" He then gave Chris a look that was more of a smirk than a smile.

"Rusty, listen to me. Don't be asking me for favors. I do enough of that at home for you. I don't want to get in any kind of trouble here. Do you understand?"

"Okay, okay. I don't know what the big deal is. By the way, see those two guys over by the diving board?"

Chris nodded.

"They're a couple of my roommates from Portland. The guy on the left, in the green trunks, said he brought some grass with him. He said he'd give me some later."

"Rusty, jeez! Weed?" Chris uttered angrily. "You don't need that stuff. It's just going to get you in trouble. I thought we both agreed to stop doing that kind of crap! You'd better stay away from those guys."

"Give me a break, Chris. I'm on summer vacation. I'll do what I want to do. And I'll be careful, trust me. It's no big deal. Just a little added fun is all."

"That's not the kind of so-called fun you need up here. It's just going to screw you up. There's plenty to do up here without using that stuff! Besides, if you get caught, you'll be out of here so fast you won't believe it. Plus, I'm the one who recommended you for this trip, and—"

Rusty interrupted him before he could finish his train of thought. "I get it. If I get in trouble, you're in trouble. Is that what you're saying, Chris?" Rusty barked back, clearly annoyed. He folded his arms across his chest; his five-foot, nine-inch stocky build showed signs of irritation. "Look, they're not going to do anything to you. You're a Van Heuson, remember?"

Chris snapped back, "I'm really getting tired of you always—"

"Oh, go on to your harbor office. You know, ever since you started going to Young Life Club, and even church, you've really changed. You're not the same ol' Chris. In fact, you really tick me off sometimes!"

Chris paused a moment, took a deep breath, and then calmly said to Rusty, "You're right, Rus, I'm not the same person. Listen, just be careful, will you?" Chris turned and walked back up the large rock flow toward the dining room.

Meanwhile, in the harbormaster's office, Doc and Vic were discussing the new assistant harbormaster.

"So what about Mitch, was he upset?" Doc asked Vic.

"No. You know Mitchell, he's very easygoing. The fact is, this new kid, Chris Van Heuson, has some experience with boats and skiing. It's a hobby he and his dad share, and as you know, Mitch really doesn't know much about boats or the harbor. He doesn't even ski. I know he was willing to learn, but I think it makes more sense for Chris to become your new assistant under the circumstances. It's more realistic. You know me . . . Mister Practical."

"That's true," Doc said. "I mean, it is logical, and you're always teaching me the value of common sense. I understand. I'm just glad Mitch does too. It's just that I've been praying that Mitch would become my next—"

"You know, Joe," Vic interrupted, "even though we're Christians, and believe in the power of prayer, you need to remember that God didn't design us to sit back and expect Him to make all the moves or to answer all our prayers in our favor. We need to be assertive in our actions, and that means making decisions on what we think is best for a given situation. Do you understand?"

"Yes, I do. I really do. So do we know anything about this kid, other than his dad is Dick Van Heuson?"

"My understanding is that he's a nice kid and well-liked, but obviously I don't know much about him," Vic admitted.

"So what do you think? Should we give him our 'instant personality test' right off the bat?" asked Doc in a slightly devious voice.

"Sure, why not? We might as well find out who we're dealing with. There's no better time than the present. Where is it?" he asked, looking eagerly around the shack.

"Right here," Doc replied.

Doc turned around and took a small black box, about six inches long, off the shelf. On top of the wooden box, sitting above an obvious hole, was a small four-paddle windmill. Another hole had been drilled into each end of the box. On the side, in white letters, it read: Breath Tester. Above the hole on the right hand end, Average Lungs had been lettered. On the other end, Strong Lungs had been lettered. Doc set the small contraption on the broad counter.

"Loaded and ready to go," Doc said.

Just then, Chris appeared in the doorway of the shack. *Perfect timing*, thought Doc. When he stepped through the open door, he looked curiosly around the room and then settled his eyes on Vic.

"Excuse me, are you Vic?" he asked.

"Yes, that's me, mate," Vic answered in his deep, brawny British accent. "You must be Chris."

"That's right," Chris said, extending his hand out to Vic.

Vic gave the teenager's hand a firm shake. "This is Joe, otherwise known as Doc, our harbormaster. You'll be working for him."

"Nice to meet you, Doc," Chis said as he politely shook Doc's hand. The introductions completed, Chris glanced around the shack. "Wow! This is a pretty cool place. You sure have a lot of stuff in here. Is that a portable bilge pump?"

"Yeah, a very important tool for us," Doc replied. "So, I understand you know quite a lot about boats?"

"Well . . . to some degree. My dad has a forty-one-foot motor yacht. We moor it down at Malibu—the Malibu in Southern California that is. And I've been skiing since I was eight. So yes, I've been around boats for quite some time. I surf too."

"That's a start," interjected Vic. "When you leave here next month, you'll know a lot more about boats and running a harbor. This is Doc's second year. He was my assistant in '65, before my wife and I became Malibu's caretakers. Doc will teach you everything you'll need to know."

"Will I be able to drive all of Malibu's boats?" Chris asked eagerly.

"Pilot them, yes. But one step at a time, son. You need to be patient learning the basics." He turned to Doc and said, "I've got to run over to the lumber mill. Hand me that tester please, I need to check Ron out." He purposely flashed the little black box in front of Chris as he started to leave.

The box caught Chris's eye, and pointing at it, he asked, "What is that, Vic?"

"Oh, this thing? It's a lung tester," Vic answered nonchalantly.

"What's it for?" Chris pressed on with obvious curiosity.

"When you're around saltwater up this far north, you have to make sure your lungs don't get clogged up. We use this tester to ensure that our new workers are at least at the normal level. Let me show you." He blew into the side that said Average, and the windmill started spinning. "That's all there is to it." He started to walk away, but Chris stopped him again.

"What's that other end for?" he asked.

Doc and Vic made quick eye contact. They both knew that Chris's curiosity was about to get the best of him. *Fish on,* Doc thought, laughing to himself when Vic quickly answered Chris.

"That side is if you have really strong, healthy lungs. You should be able to blow hard enough to make the windmill turn. Do you smoke?"

"No. Can I try?" Chris asked as he reached for the box.

"Sure, but you need to get a lot of air in your lungs, so take a deep breath and then blow as hard as you can."

Vic handed him the box. Chris took a deep breath, stuck the Strong Lung side of the device into his mouth, and gave it a powerful blow. Instantly, and without warning, dark soot was released through two tiny hidden holes, which were on either side of the main blowhole. The soot blackened Chris's entire face. The dry flowerlike powder was harmless, but it was all over him, mostly in his eyes and all over his cheeks.

"Gotcha!" Vic exclaimed with a broad smile, then joined by Doc, started howling with laughter.

They both turned toward Chris to get his reaction. Chris, still in shock, paused for a brief moment and then started laughing with them.

"You're a good sport, mate," Vic said, happy to know Chris could take a joke.

"I can't believe you guys just did that. You really suckered me in, didn't you?"

Doc smiled. "I'm afraid we did, Chris, but we're happy to see that you took it like a man. That tells us a lot about you."

Vic handed Chris a towel off the workbench. "Here, wipe off your face," he said. "There's something we want to loan you. It's a tradition of ours."

Doc reached around to the back of the counter and grabbed a Buck knife that was protected by a black sheath. He handed it to Vic, who passed it to Chris. "Go ahead, take a look."

Chris carefully removed the knife from the sheath. The four-and-a-half-inch stainless steel blade was topped by a handsome zebra-wood handle. Engraved on the handle was: Assistant Harbormaster—Malibu, Canada.

Elated, Chris asked, "Wow! I can keep this?"

"I said loan, not keep," Vic reminded him. "This is not just an important harbor tool, but it's a symbol of our friendship and respect for each other. We must have trust and reliability among ourselves to perform the daily tasks required to make this harbor function efficiently and safely. Do you understand?"

"Sure."

"I'm off to the sawmill," said Vic as he headed out of the shack.

Once Vic was gone, Doc explained an important detail about the knife to Chris. "There's one other thing about this knife. Whatever you do, don't lose it! Not only will I be unhappy, but you'll be in big trouble with Vic."

"I understand," said Chris earnestly. "I wouldn't want to cross him. He's about the toughest and most rugged person I've ever met. He's English, right?"

"Yes, he spent eight years in the British Navy. He and Edna, his wife, have traveled around the world twice. They've lived in Australia, New Zealand . . . Vic was even a bush pilot in Yellowknife, Alaska."

"Really? How long has he been here?" inquired Chris.

"Five years."

"So what would he have done if I'd gotten all bent out of shape and upset about the soot box?"

"To be honest," Doc said with a somber look, "you probably would have been reassigned to kitchen duty washing dishes and scrubbing pots."

Just then Kyle Schimmel—a tall, blond-haired, blue-eyed twenty-something with a dark tan—stuck his head inside the door.

"Hey, Doc! Are we still starting up at three?"

"Yes! Oh! And by the way, this is Chris, my new assistant." Kyle and Chris greeted each other and shook hands.

"Kyle is our ski instructor," Doc pointed out. "You'll be working with him some. We'd better assemble the drivers down here by 2:45 so we can have the weekly chalk talk about safety and so on," Doc said to Kyle.

"Got it," replied Kyle. "I'll see you then. See you around, Chris."

When he left, Chris turned to Doc. "Who drives the ski boats?" he asked.

"We have four staff guys designated as our ski boat drivers. They're normally here one month, just like the work crew. However, there is one new guy who came in today on the *Princess*, because one of our drivers had to leave early. We'll just stick him with one of our experienced drivers for a while, he'll be fine. Like I said, Chris, there will be times that you'll be helping Kyle, but I first want to get you started on how to check out the rowboats, canoes, and sailboats. You'll be doing that this afternoon. It's real easy."

"So what other things do we do?"

"Other responsibilities include tying up and greeting the yacht guests from Vancouver and Seattle, or wherever. Our yacht hostess usually gives them a short tour before they head back out. And of course we have to fuel the boats, keep them clean, keep the dock clean, clean fish, run the regatta, and . . . oh, we also run the inlet tours down to Chatterbox Falls."

"Chatterbox Falls?"

"It's the waterfall down at the end of Princess Louisa. It's really spectacular."

"So, how did you get the name, Doc?" Chris asked. The strange nickname had piqued his curiosity.

"I'll explain that in a minute, but first I want to know some things about you."

"Well, I'm sure you've already heard who my dad is?" Chris said with a mixture of pride and reluctance.

"I do know, he's Dick Van Heuson. I see the chin." Doc pointed at Chris's long chin and grinned.

"A gift from my dad," Chris acknowledged with a tinge of resentment.

"But honestly, I don't want to hear about your dad, or your mom, or your Uncle Louie—if you have an Uncle Louie?" he said, cracking a slight smile, which quickly faded to make way for a more serious expression. "I want to hear about you. How old are you? What grade are you in? What are your interests? What are your likes? What are your dislikes? How are you doing in school? Who do you hang out with? How long have you been going to Young Life Club? How does Christianity fit into your life? And what are your expectations here at Malibu?" When he finished, he took in a deep breath and exhaled; he hadn't planned on listing all the questions at once.

With a bewildered look on his face, Chris said, "Gee, I'm not sure where to start."

"How 'bout with where do you live?" Doc said calmly to reassure Chris.

"Okay," Chris said with a little relief in his voice, "I live in Sherman Oaks, California, over the hill from Hollywood. We've lived there since I was in junior high."

While Doc continued to pepper Chris with questions inside the harbormaster shack, Kyle was assembling the ski boat drivers just outside, at the end of the long floating dock. The new campers who had signed up (aboard the *Malibu Princess*) to ski that afternoon were also gathering, in anticipation of a quick, but thorough, safety meeting. Minutes later, Doc and Chris joined Kyle and the group of drivers and skiers to participate in the important talk regarding procedure and water safety. After the quick ten-minute meeting, campers were beginning to spend the warm afternoon waterskiing while others were milling aimlessly about the bay in rowboats. Many were lounging by the pool while other groups of teenagers could be seen playing volleyball in the sand and swinging clubs out at the miniature golf course. And others, seeking a more relaxing time, were fishing by the shore, basking in the sun reading a book, or simply hanging out with new friends.

Back at the dock, ski boats pulled water-skiers back and forth across their wakes crisscrossing Princess Louisa. Some of the kids watched from the dock, smiling and laughing as they spotted their friends gliding across the waves behind the speeding boats. At the end of the inner dock, a ski boat, with its towrope in the hands of a young beginning skier with a ski on each foot, was idling slowly away from the dock. When the skier yelled, "Hit it!" the driver of the boat pushed the throttle forward, and the boat instantly surged ahead, pulling the excited skier off the end of the dock and up on the water, zooming across the waves. It was his first successful trip on skis, and his whoops of excitement could be heard from across the water. Dozens of other campers were in the area either waiting for their turn to ski or just watching the fun.

Nearby, Chris was helping some kids with a small sailboat while Kyle was giving final instructions to yet another new skier. A private yacht had arrived, and Doc was busy tying the thirty-five-foot craft to the outside of the inner dock. As he secured the boat's stern line to a cleat mounted on the dock, he greeted the yachtsmen with a friendly smile and offered to introduce them to the yacht hostess for a tour of Malibu.

Meanwhile inside the camp's kitchen, Beth was teaching Julie about her duties as a waitress. The commercial-style kitchen was well organized and spotless. Cooking appliances were installed along the walls, and various utensils hung over the countertops, which provided space to prepare the food. There were several deep sinks, with large aluminum pots stacked on the shelving above. The cramped room was painted white to help illuminate the area, since there were no windows to give the kitchen some natural light.

Beyond the wide swinging kitchen doors that led into the main dining room area was a superb split-level large eating area, with wraparound bay windows, providing spectacular views of the rugged region. Several colorful totem poles and other authentic northern Indian artifacts were on display in the room. In the far right corner of this unique dining room were Beth and Julie standing and talking alongside several round dining tables. This front corner section was part of the structure that was cleverly built on stilts, which caused this lower area of the room to jut out above the swimming pool. As they stood near one of the bay windows, which overlooked Forbidden Island, Beth was instructing her newest waitress, Julie, about which tables she would be serving daily. After a short period of discussing the serving procedure, Beth guided Julie away from her assigned duty area and walked her over toward the beverage station, which was located on the back side of an oversized stone fireplace, adjacent to the kitchen doors. She then continued to instruct and explain the waitress self-serve process of operating the multibeverage dispensers. Afterward, she turned around and faced the two wooden wide kitchen doors that easily swung in or out.

"Be sure to use the right door as you enter the kitchen, and the left door as you exit. Got it?" Julie nodded yes to Beth, understanding the logic behind the directive.

While Julie and the rest of the work crew went about their jobs, the remainder of the afternoon was busy with activity and fun for the campers and guests. All in all, it was a perfect first day for the new campers and guests, who would be at Malibu for an entire week.

Late in the afternoon, a staff member entered the kitchen, not to prepare food, but to announce the end of the day's recreational activities. He walked to the far corner of the bustling room, which was now occupied by a dozen kitchen prep-cooks who were diligently preparing the camp's dinner. In a dark corner dangling from the ceiling was a section of yellow ski rope that hung about six feet off the floor with a small wooden knob attached to the end. The man reached up and pulled it straight down. In an instant, a blaring air horn blast penetrated the entire peninsula with a loud train-horn–like sound. Even those golfing out toward the outer dock could hear the signal, which indicated the end of outdoor activities for the day. He pulled the cord twice, holding the line down for several seconds with each pull. Everyone now knew that they had an hour to get ready for dinner at six.

Fifty-five minutes later, the air horn blasted a three-second burst, signaling everyone that dinner was in five minutes. The guests began gathering outside three sides of the dining room on the wooden walkway high above the swimming pool and waters of the narrows.

There was a great deal of chatter with everyone excited to share their experiences of their first afternoon at Malibu. At precisely six o'clock, the three main doors to the dining room swung open. Inside, a nautical brass bell, which was mounted near the stage along the front windows of the restaurant, was rung by a work crew girl. Everyone began pouring through the doors searching for a table to share with their friends. The forty round tables, which sat six and were decorated with forest-green tablecloths, filled quickly as everyone was anxious to visit and eat. A dozen work crew waiters and waitresses materialized scrambling to serve beverages to the new arrivals.

A large rectagular table, which seated ten, was situated in the far left corner of the sizable room, in front of the big bay windows, which—overlooked the swimming pool and Forbidden Island. It was reserved for Malibu management and the adult guests. On this particular night, three adult guest couples and one other older couple sat at the table, along with Chet Raley, Malibu's camp manager and speaker. Chet was in his early forties and was well-groomed, of medium height and build with an easy smile. Julie was busy serving the long table their salad plates when she sat one in front of Chet.

"So you must be Julie Copeland, our new work crew girl?" Chet said with a smile.

When Julie nodded in reply, he said, "It's great to have you here. This is Helen Campbell, Malibu's hostess, and her husband, Bob. Bob's our pilot. You most likely met some of our new adult guests on the boat today. These are Dale and Jeannie Fredericks, from Salem, Oregon. Over here are Jim and Vickie Shepard from Seattle, and these folks are Rick and Judy Hammel from—"

"Oh, we know Julie," Judy interrupted.

"Oh, that's right. You're from Spokane as well," Chet responded.

"Yes," Julie politely said. "Hi, Mrs. Hammel, Mr. Hammel."

"Hi, Julie. So you're going to be our waitress? How lovely," Judy said, obviously pleased.

Turning to Chet, she said, "Our oldest daughter used to babysit Julie when she was just a little girl—she was a cute little thing I might add—and now look at you. All grown-up and as pretty as ever."

Julie blushed. "Thank you, Mrs. Hammel. I'll be back with some beverages," she said, heading off toward the kitchen.

"She is the sweetest girl," Judy continued. "And smart too. I know she did well in school. I've known her mother for a number of years. She's also a very talented musician and plays piano for our church."

"What does her father do?" Chet asked. "Do you know?"

"He's a drama professor at the university, a very pleasant person."

"Does she have any siblings?"

"Yes, she has a sister who's quite a bit younger."

Julie returned to the table with a pitcher of water and a pitcher of milk.

Meanwhile, on the cedar walkway outside the dining room, high above the inlet, Edna Hookums was wearing her majorette hat, along with her navy-blue band uniform. A police-style whistle was in her mouth, ready to be blown and heard. Like her husband, Vic, she too was born and raised in England. Suddenly, she blew the whistle loudly several times, and without a doubt, it was heard by all those in the dining room. With the band that had performed the welcome lined up behind her tiny frame, she stepped forward and led them down the wooden passage. As she pumped her toilet plunger-baton up and down with her right arm, the seemingly clumsy group of silly musicians behind her began playing their theme song as they began their march toward a side door that led them into the dining room. Their music was purposely a bit off-key for effect, and their misfit uniforms only added to their absurd performance. As they entered the packed room, they marched around various tables of campers and staff, entertaining them with ridiculous music and comical moves. Eventually they found their way to the stage along the front bay windows to the amusement of the campers and guests alike.

Acting silly, the band members lined up across the middle of the stage and finished their song. The trombone player, Jake Costa, who was also Malibu's program director, stepped up to the microphone. Jake was in his early thirties, thin, and stood five feet six inches tall. He had a flattop 1950s haircut. Taking the microphone and making a silly face, he confidently said, "As leader of the New

Ashmolean Marching Society and Students Conservatory Marching Band, I welcome you to the Malibu Club. Please stand to sing the Malibu National Anthem."

Laughing at his antics, everyone in the dining room stood as the band played the theme song from *The Mickey Mouse Club*, a Walt Disney television show. The work crew girls and staff began singing along, and soon smiling and laughing, many of the campers joined in as well.

"Who's the leader of the band that's made for you and me?" everyone sang. "M-I-C . . . K-E-Y . . . M-O-U-S-E, Mickey Mouse."

"Donald Duck!" the work crew girls yelled, adding to the frivolity.

While the band continued to play, Diane and her new friends from Nootka Cabin Twelve were near the stage singing along, smiling and laughing at the performance. At a different table, even Rusty was laughing along with some of the new friends he made from Oregon who were sharing the same cabin, Sitka Seven, with him.

Doc, who was standing next to Jake on the stage, was playing his trumpet and making funny faces. He reached up and pulled off his band hat to reveal an actual Disneyland Mickey Mouse hat hidden underneath. As if spring-loaded, large, rounded black mouse ears popped straight up! Everyone, including Julie, got a real laugh out of it. Doc crossed his eyes and made even more silly faces, putting on a goofy look, which everyone found quite hilarious. Julie in particular appreciated his sense of humor and his willingness to appear foolish for entertainment purposes.

While the performance continued, Jeannie tapped Chet on the shoulder and, speaking loud enough to be heard over all the laughter, said to him, "That trumpet player is so funny!"

"Believe it or not, that's our harbormaster, Doc," Chet responded with a grin. "He doubles in our program as one of the funniest comics we've ever had. As the week goes on, you'll see that he's quite amusing and very popular."

Julie, who was standing behind Chet, happened to overhear his comment to Jeannie. She immediately fixed her gaze on Doc, intrigued by Chet's remark. *He sure is funny,* she thought with a smile, *I wonder what he's like.*

The song ended, and Doc put his band hat back on, covering up the Mickey Mouse ears. Jake once again took the microphone. "Take your seats please. Okay, first things first. Time to say grace. Lord, we're thankful for this beautiful place, Malibu. And we thank You for this meal that we're about to eat. Amen. And now, ladies and gentlemen, I want you to take your fork in your right hand, and your spoon in your left hand." He paused for effect, looking around the room as if to ensure that everyone had complied. "On your mark. Get set. Eat!"

As Jake stepped back from the microphone, the band members began playing their theme song again while they marched off the stage and wound their way through at least a dozen tables of teens who were all watching them with glee as they headed out the main doors toward Main Street. As the band disappeared around the corner, the dining room was buzzing with excitement and chatter.

Once the guests finished dinner, they moved on to a nice dessert of cherry pie and vanilla ice cream. Chet had already taken the stage and was at the microphone welcoming everyone to Malibu and speaking about the property and the week ahead.

"That's right, everybody, double-daylight savings time. Since we're a self-contained city, completely isolated, without roads or even telephones, we're allowed to set our own time zone. So we decided that by moving our clocks forward two hours instead of just one, we get one more hour of daylight. Since we're so far north to begin with, according to 'Malibu time,' it doesn't get dark until 11:00 p.m.! That gives us more playtime. So what do you think about that gang?" Everyone in the dining room cheered.

"Another thing I want to mention," Chet continued, "is for you 'puffheads'—you know, those of you who suck on those coffin nails otherwise known as cigarettes. I've always said, while here at Malibu, 'sail them, don't inhale them.' Float those babies out into the inlet, instead of turning your lungs black! That's my advice of the day. Anyway, right out here"—he turned and pointed out the main door—"there's this big slab of granite leading down to the pool, which is the designated smoking area. We call it Smoker's Rock, and it's the only place where you're allowed to smoke at Malibu. As you know, everything around here is built of wood, so we're extremely fire-conscious! Please help us out, okay?" said Chet, hoping the campers understood how important this rule was. "Oh, and you'll notice there's a small, round, rock structure that looks like a wishing well, built on the granite slab out there. Don't toss coins into it or sit on it. It's for your cigarette *butts*, not for your bottoms! Got it? Thank you." Many of the campers looked at one another and laughed.

Chet continued, "The way we communicate to the entire camp is with our loud Malibu air horn. I'm sure you heard it earlier today. The way it works is you'll hear two, two-second bursts one hour before dinner, and one short burst five minutes before each meal. A bunch of short bursts in a row means there's an emergency and we need the doctor. By the way, if you go on a tour of camp after dinner, you'll get a chance to meet our camp doctor. He's a very colorful person. Now, if we should have a fire—God forbid—you'll hear a continuous blast, which means everyone should jump in the inlet. I sure hope you all can tread water! Just kidding! Don't jump in the inlet," he added with a laugh.

"Actually, we have assigned areas for you to go to, depending where you are at the time of the alarm. We'll be performing a fire drill later this evening. Oh, and then before we go to bed, the horn will blow again, and we'll all have a blast!" He had a broad smile on his face, and everyone was cheering and laughing. (Having a 'blast' was a 60s term, meaning: having an exceptional great time.)

In the back of the room, behind the fireplace, Doc and some of the resident staff members were sitting at their assigned table, finishing dinner. Ken leaned over and whispered to Doc, "Are you ready for your 'colorful' performance, Doc?"

"Sure, why not?" he said, as his eyes darted around the room. He was trying to spot Julie.

"Who are you looking for?" Ken asked inquistively.

"Oh, nobody in particular. I was just checking out the new group," Doc didn't want Ken to know the truth.

Back on stage, Chet was still at the microphone. "At this time I want to introduce to you a buddy of mine. He's already been up here once this evening leading our fine Malibu band. The July 1966 Malibu program director. The only guy I know who is a reformed school dropout. Please welcome Mr. Jake Costa!"

Chet reached over and rang the brass bell mounted behind him. Jake, who had changed out of his band uniform, came running up on stage. Grinning, Chet turned to him and asked, "Hey, pal, is this going to be a great week or what? Did you see that sun shining out there today?"

"Yeah, the weather wasn't bad either," Jake said with a dopey look on his face.

"Tell us, Jake—folks, this is so exciting—what do you have planned for us this week? I mean, with all the great activities we have here: skiing, boating, fishing, swimming?"

"No swimming this week, Chet," said Jake with a loud sigh and a frown, "gotta drain the pool. Might be able to use it as a handball court, but that's about it."

"Okay, then tell them about the waterskiing," Chet said enthusiastically. "We've got the fastest boats and the best skis."

"Killer whales are back. We're going to have to shut the ski program down all week. It's pretty ugly out there. Besides, the boats are all out of gas."

"Golfing then! What about our great golf course?"

"Remember those man-eating plants that ate a camper last week? No, that's going to be off-limits to everyone," said Jake, looking more gloomy than ever.

Clearly let down by the news, Chet asked, "Well, what *are* we going to do all week?"

"Hey, don't worry about a thing," said Jake as his face turned from solemn to excited. "Ol' Jake has got a plan. Forget about all that other dumb stuff. You know what we're going to do? This is so exciting! What is the most favorite pastime of teenagers?"

"Watching the submarine races?" asked Chet.

"No! Charades, of course! We're going to play charades all week long. Isn't that great?"

"Charades? Are you crazy? That's about as exciting as watching one wrestler in the ring. Jake, have you lost your mind?"

Apparently wound up with excitement, Jake continued, "Think of it, Chet, it's perfect. We can break into teams—guys against the girls, campers against the work crew." Meanwhile, wise to the two men's comedy routine, everyone in the room was cracking up with laughter.

Doc leaned over to Ken. "This is such a funny routine," he whispered, "I wish I could stay and watch it again, but I've got to get some things together. I'll see you later."

Doc left through the kitchen, which was still bustling with activity. The work crew boys were busy scrubbing pots and pans, utensils, and kitchenware. Popeye was supervising and giving orders. It was a noisy scene. Several of the boys called out a hello to Doc as he walked through the room. It was obvious that they respected and admired him; he had a reputation for being a kindhearted, jocular, and a caring friend to everyone.

"How's it going?" Doc said, smiling, as he addressed the kitchen staff. "Hey, Popeye!" he said. "The dinner was excellent, my man, thanks!" Popeye—a tall, thin black man in his early thirties—wore thick glasses that made his eyes appear larger than they actually were. His head was shaved bald. He never explained why he shaved his head. Some guessed that he was beginning to go bald, or perhaps he didn't like carrying around a comb! The truth was he liked the look.

"I appreciate that," he said to Doc, clearly pleased by the compliment. Just then, a busboy walked in from the dining room with a large tray of dirty dishes. Right behind him was Beth holding several empty beverage pitchers. They both unloaded the dirty dishes onto the counter. Doc stepped over toward Beth.

"Hi, Beth!"

"Oh, hi, Doc." With an abrupt hand motion, Doc signaled her to follow him out the back kitchen door. She was confused, but followed him anyway. They came out to a narrow alleyway. One way led to a small storage building for nonperishables and supplies, the other direction led to Main Street. Standing there, waiting for the door to the kitchen to close, Doc looked over at Beth.

"The new work crew girl Julie, was she a camper here last year? I don't remember seeing her."

"No, she was a camper at Frontier Ranch," Beth answered, curious where the conversation was going.

"Where's she from?"

"She's from Spokane, Washington. Did you know that she's friends with your new assistant, Chris Van Heuson? That's pretty cool about his dad being Dick Van Heuson, the actor, huh?"

"Yes, it is. So, obviously they became friends at Frontier."

"That's right. Did you want to talk to her? I could maybe see if she's—"

"Oh, no, that's okay," interrupted Doc. "Is she going on the Malibu Tour in a few minutes?"

"I don't know."

"Well, you might encourage her to do so since she's new and all. It'd probably be good for her." Doc obviously had his own agenda.

"You're right. I'll tell her. See you later, I gotta get back to work." She turned and headed back to the kitchen.

Doc hurried down the narrow alleyway, toward Main Street. The wide wooden boardwalk was located in the center of Malibu. It was lined with several stores and offices, including a souvenier shop, the camp office, and a medical infirmary. The Malibu Office was located at the far end of Main Street, toward the boardwalk leading to the golf course and outer dock. Being a large camp, operating Malibu required great amounts of paperwork and administrative duties. The office was always busy.

The Totem Trader—a store filled with clothing, books, gifts, photo supplies, and toiletries—operated in the center of the street. A short alley separated the Trader from the Totem Inn, a camp favorite. Campers and staff could frequently pop inside for a scoop of ice cream or a refreshing soft drink. It also served up frozen desserts, all of which were made with fresh ingredients.

On the other side of Main Street, overlooking Princess Louisa Inlet, was Big Squawka, a sizeable meeting room, which was also used as a recreational space during the day for playing the ball game Four Square. Unlike the classic children's game though, Malibu's

Four Square was fast, furious, and extremely competitive. Vic, Ken, and Doc were the three best players in camp.

About fifteen minutes after Doc had spoken with Beth, Chet led a large group of campers, adult guests, and counselors down Main Street on the camp tour. He stopped in the center of the boardwalk and turned back to the crowd.

"So now you've seen the Totem Inn and Totem Trader. Next, I want to introduce you to our camp doctor. If you should get sick or hurt while at Malibu, he's the one to see."

The group gathered around the front of the office. A sign hung over the door that read: The Medicine Man. Julie and Chris were part of the crowd along with Diane, Rusty, and a few new friends.

"Let me just see if he's in," Chet said to the assembly. He knocked on the door. "Doctor, are you there? Doctor?" he said a bit louder.

Doc opened the door and stepped out on to the small porch next to Chet. He was dressed in a white smock with what appeared to be blood smeared on the front. He had a stethoscope around his neck and was wearing black horn-rimmed glasses, which had slipped down his nose. In his hand was a medium-size aluminum bowl, which he placed on the porch railing. He put his hands in the bowl and scrubbed them in the soapy water.

"Can I help you, Mr. Chet?" he asked. He looked out at the group. "And who are all these people here?"

"This is our new group of campers, Doctor. I wanted them to get to meet you. Everyone," Chet said loudly, "this is Dr. Delbert Suggins, our camp doctor."

Still looking out over the new guests, Doc commented, "Golly! The groups get uglier each week, don't they?" Everyone laughed.

"So, Dr. Suggins, we're not keeping you from anything important, are we?" asked Chet.

"No, I was just taking an ax out of a logger's spleen," Doc said casually.

"Gee, that's sounds awful! Listen, why don't you tell everyone about your background."

"Well, I'm an MD, DM, AM, even an FM sometimes! When I'm not here, I'm working in a regular doctor place. You know, a hospital?"

"What field are you in?"

"Oh, I'm not in a field. We have a building. You see, the nurses started complaining about grass stains." At this, everyone laughed even louder.

"I hear a woman has a baby every three seconds. Is that true?" Chet asked the doctor.

"Yeah, and we're still looking for her!" Now the group was laughing hysterically, including Julie, Chris, Diane, and Rusty.

Chet kept on with his questions. "This is kind of a personal question, but does the population explosion bother you?"

"Not at all. I wear earplugs!"

"Tell me, Doctor, could you give me a quick checkup?"

"Sure. Stick your tongue out." Chet immediately stuck his tongue straight out at the crowd. "No, over there." Doc pointed down the street.

"Why over there?" Chet asked in apparent confusion.

"'Cause I don't like the girl who works in the Totem Trader, that's why!" The group continued laughing at the skit.

"Well, I guess we'd better let you go, Doctor. Tell me, I notice you've been scrubbing your hands in that basin there. Are you getting ready for another surgery?"

"Oh, no. I'm just washing out an old pair of underwear!" He pulled a pair of white faded shorts out of the bowl, which dripped all over the porch. Julie had focused on Doc, nearly breathless from laughing so hard.

Minutes later, the tour group made their way down a walkway that led to the large deck above the inner dock area. The same deck that all the suitcases had been placed earlier in the day. They all gathered around the base of the tall totem pole. The lofty, bright-colored totem pole sixty-five feet straight in the air. The intricate carvings on the front of it told the story of Tom Hamilton, who built the Malibu Club just before World War II. At the base of the pole was a carved airplane propeller, denoting Mr. Hamilton's association to the variable-pitch propeller for airplanes. Two multicolored carved bird wings stuck out near the top of the pole. Each carving was painted in red, blue, yellow, white, and black and displayed the faces and bodies of Sechelt Indians in their native art form.

Doc, who had quickly changed out of his doctor costume, stood on the stone base of the pole and was explaining the harbor and ski program.

"So you should be able to ski about twice a day. Keep track of your number. And don't forget, we'll start the Princess Tours to Chatterbox Falls tomorrow at 10:00 a.m. Let me introduce you to my assistant. Some of you probably met him on the boat on the way up. This is Chris Van Heuson." Chris waved at the group. He was very proud of his new position, as was Julie, who was standing next to him. She was happy that Chris was excited about his new job on the harbor.

"And over here is our ski instructor, Kyle Schimmel," Doc announced as he pointed over to Kyle. Kyle waved and smiled to the crowd. "That's about it. Oh, one more thing." He threw his head back and looked straight up at the top of the carved pole and placed his right open hand on it. "This totem pole here, it's the tallest totem pole in BC, carved by the tallest Indian in BC!" The group broke out in laughter. Even Tracey, the camper girl who had challenged Doc earlier about the suitcase prank, was grinning from ear to ear. "Enjoy your time here and enjoy the water sports. Just please follow the rules." Doc jumped off the base of the totem pole and immediately walked toward Chris and Julie. As the crowd disbursed in numerous directions, Doc turned to Julie.

"Hi again," he said with a smile.

She returned his smile.

"So, I understand you two know each other."

Yes," Julie said. "Chris is my Frontier friend. I certainly see why they call you Doc now, Doc." She giggled.

"Oh, you mean the doctor routine? Actually, it's because—"

"Because of the harbor, the dock," Julie interrupted. "I know, Beth filled me in."

"Oh, she did, huh? Do I understand you're from Spokane."

"How did you know?" said Julie, giving Doc a quizzical look. "Oh, Beth filled you in. Of course." They both laughed at once, realizing they probably knew more about each other than they thought.

"So what do you think of Malibu?" asked Doc.

"It's really incredible. I can't believe I'm working here," said Julie enthusiastically.

"She's the new head table waitress," said Chris, interjecting himself into the conversation.

"Really? That's great!" Doc replied. "A very prestigious job I might add."

"Thank you." Julie beamed. "I understand that you've worked here for two summers. How lucky. I think this is the most beautiful place I've ever seen," she added, her big blue eyes fixed on Doc's.

"Well, I think you're the most beautiful lady I've ever seen," Doc confessed, his words as sincere as ever.

"Thank you." Julie blushed, feeling very flattered. "You're not so bad-looking yourself," she said, trying to keep the conversation playful.

Chris, who had been listening to this exchange, began to feel awkward and even embarrassed by what he was hearing. Realizing this, Doc quickly changed the subject. "So are you two going up to the mixers?"

"Yes, and you?" Julie answered.

"No, I can't. I've got some work to finish up."

"Do you need some help?" Chris asked Doc, relieved that he finally had something to say.

"No, it's okay. You should go to the mixers. But when they're done, come down and meet me in the harbormaster shack. We need to take out the garbage."

"The garbage? How do we do that?" Chris asked with a puzzled look.

"We use the Seinskiff. You're not afraid of bears, are you?"

"Bears!" yelled Chris and Julie in unison.

"Well, just one. He's a big ol' brown bear. I call him Yogi. Real original, huh? I've never really shook paws with him. I definitely keep my distance, but I've been feeding him now for two summers. He shows up every evening when we dump the garbage."

"Where?" Julie asked.

"Right up around that bend." Doc pointed down to the right side of the inlet. "There's a small cove over there. Between Yogi, the seagulls, the fish, and the swirling current, it all disappears overnight, kind of like a giant garbage disposal."

"That's amazing," Julie said as she looked down the inlet toward the cove.

"It's one of Vic's many ingenious ideas. What the heck, it works." Then changing the subject, Doc said, "You know, Julie, you should really go on the inlet trip tomorrow morning. I know you'd enjoy it. Chris is going."

Chris immediately turned back toward Doc. "I am? But what about checking out the boats?"

"Don't worry, I'll have one of the counselors cover for us. I need to teach you how to pilot the *Nefertiti* and how to run the inlet tour."

"Cool," said Chris, excited by the new opportunity.

Doc turned to Julie. "So, are you coming? I'm sure your work crew boss will let you go."

"Okay, it's a date," said Julie, with a hint of flirtation.

"A date? That's even better." Doc winked at her.

"You know what I mean," said Julie, a tad embarrassed. "Ten o'clock, right?"

"Ten o'clock. I'll see you then." Doc gave her a quick wave goodbye as she and Chris headed up the wide stone stairs next to Big Squawka. Doc watched as she quickly climbed the stairs. When she was no longer in sight, he turned and made his way back down to the floating dock.

An hour or so later, Chris entered the harbor master shack where Doc was busy painting some oars. He spotted Doc hand-brushing white paint along a freshly sanded wooden oar.

"Hey, Doc!"

"Hi, Chris. How were the mixers?" he asked with interest.

"Too much! You should have seen my friend Rusty. He was in 'pass the bod.' It was really funny." Chris laughed just thinking about it.

"It's a great way to break the ice and meet new people," Doc commented. "Was his counselor participating?"

"Oh yes. He seems like a really cool guy."

"Who is it?"

"I think his name is Bob Ferguson."

"Fergie's one of the best. This is his second year at Malibu as a counselor."

Chris gave Doc a concerned look. "Well, I hope he can do something with Rusty. I'm worried about him."

"Why is that?" Doc was intrigued.

"Some of the stuff he says, and does, concerns me."

"Like what?"

"Well, he's been in some trouble. To be honest, we both have. But I think I've changed and matured a lot this past year since going to Young Life Club."

"And becoming a Christian?" asked Doc.

"Exactly," Chris answered proudly. "I just feel like I have more meaning and direction in my life. You know, purpose."

"I bet your attitude's better now, isn't it?" Doc placed his hand on Chris's shoulder and looked straight into his eyes.

"Yeah, definitely," Chris said with certain pride. "But Rusty's got his same old bad attitude, a chip on the shoulder, trying to be the big shot, impress the girls—in all the wrong ways. No respect for anyone. Hanging out with the wrong crowd."

"Sounds like he doesn't have any respect for himself," Doc speculated, "and doesn't even know it."

"I think you're right, Doc. That's exactly right. He has no self-esteem."

"Well, let's hope, let's pray, that he listens to the Word this week at camp. It could change his life," Doc said with confidence.

"I hear that," Chris agreed.

"Well, we'd better get that garbage dumped before club starts," Doc said as he headed for the door.

A few minutes later, the Seinskiff was slowly moving up Princess Louisa Inlet in the direction of Chatterbox Falls. The Seinskiff was a navy-gray, open, twenty-four-foot workboat with a powerful diesel engine, designed originally to close large fishing nets used by ocean-going trawlers. It had been converted by Malibu into a camp work-boat to tow large amounts of freight and other material. Tonight, however, the hefty boat was not towing, but in fact pushing a big blue wooden box full of disgusting, smelly garbage. The twenty-by-eight-foot container mounted on two large logs was attached to the bow of the Seinskiff and was being pushed through the water at about ten knots. Doc was at the wheel while Chris stood alongside, studying his every move.

"See that small cove over there?" Doc asked as he gestured off the starboard side, pointing directly at a diminutive bay almost hidden along the shoreline of the massive mountain. "That's where we're headed."

"So, when does Yogi the Bear show?" Chris asked.

"I'm sure he's already aware of our presence. He should be down by the shore any second now."

"How close do we get?" Chris said with a hint of apprehension. The thought of a wild bear, or any bear for that matter, made him a bit nervous.

"Pretty close. But not close enough for him to grab the box. Vic designed this thing with a hinged bottom. Once we're near the shore, we'll go astern, unlatch the bottom, and the garbage will be forced out. The current will do the rest. All that junk will float right over to Yogi. Speaking of Yogi, there he is."

A large brown bear appeared on all fours, slowly moving toward the cove's shoreline. He growled and sniffed as he made his way to the water's edge. His head was down as he moved, but it was obvious that he was looking over at Doc and Chris.

"It's suppertime, Yogi!" Doc yelled, without even the tiniest amount of fear in his voice. He wasn't at all worried about the large grizzly approaching the boat.

"You didn't tell me how big he was," Chris exclaimed. "That's a monster bear, wow!"

"It's all that good Malibu cooking. You'll have to compliment Popeye when you see him," he said. "Okay, here we go." Doc slowly moved the boat and barge near the shore by Yogi. He quickly reversed gears and gave the boat some gas. "Now! Pull the latch, Chris!"

Chris, who was somewhat anxious trying to do his task well, unsnapped the bottom door latch. The workboat was moving astern at a speedy pace; and the garbage, just as Doc said it would, floated to the surface and began moving toward the shore and Yogi. The husky brown bear, with his big claws, reached out and grabbed some food waste. Doc slowed, changed gears, and slowly moved until they were about twenty yards from shore.

"You're not going in any closer, are you?" Chris nervously asked Doc.

"No. I think we're close enough. I just want Yogi to eat the garbage, not us!" Doc yelled over to the bear as he devoured more waste, "Enjoy the dinner, Yogi. We'll see you tomorrow!" Just then, Yogi looked up, opened his monstrous mouth, and roared loudly at Doc and Chris, almost as if he was thanking them for the meal! Doc turned the wheel and headed out the cove back toward the camp. Chris was obvioulsy still amazed that he had just fed a grizzly bear.

"Take the wheel, Chris," Doc instructed him, talking over the engine noise. "You might as well learn how to drive her since you're going to be here for four weeks."

"That's fine with me!" Chris said happily as he quickly moved into position at the helm.

"Just keep her steady and head directly toward Malibu." Doc sat down on the engine cover facing the bow. "So, Chris," Doc said over his shoulder, "a little geographical question: do you know why they named this inlet the Princess Louisa?"

Chris shook his head no in response.

"See that mountain on the far side of Malibu, on the other side of Jervis Inlet?"

Chris looked ahead carefully and nodded his head.

Pointing at the mountain, Doc continued, "The princess is lying down on the very top. Now, if you start from the right, see her hair and forehead . . . and nose? Move on to the left. That's her neck, and on down is her . . . well, you know."

"Oh, I get it. Wow! She's a pretty healthy girl, huh?" They both grinned at each other.

"That she is." Then changing the subject, Doc said, "Tell me about your friend Julie. How well do you know her?"

"She's terrific. We're good friends. Quite the foxy lady, huh? Everyone had a crush on her at Frontier. She's pretty amazing for someone who's so attractive! You know, the way she handles herself."

"What do you mean?" Doc asked with a somewhat puzzled look on his face.

"Well, you know, she's not at all stuck on herself or conceited. She's really a nice person, and a lot of fun too. She loves to laugh."

"Really?" Doc was delighted. "Well, that's a good thing, right?"

"Right. You should have seen her when you were being the camp doctor. She was in hysterics."

"She didn't think it was stupid or silly?" Doc asked uneasily.

"Not at all. She really liked it."

"How old is she? Do you know?"

"Yes, she's your age. Eighteen," Chris answered. "She graduated this year."

Doc couldn't wipe the grin off his face. He was thrilled to hear she was his age.

The sunlight was fading into dusk as they began to approach the camp. Even though the boat and barge was noisily chugging along, Doc and Chris could hear faint singing coming from the night's Young Life Club assembly, which had begun in Big Squawka, the resort's largest building. It was about fifty feet wide and one hundred feet long. Doc looked at Chris, who was standing at the helm with his eyes and attention focused on the task of piloting the workboat.

"Sounds like you're going to be a little late for club, but that's okay," Doc assured him.

Inside Big Squawka, over two hundred campers, counselors, work crew, and staffers were sitting on colorful long-cushioned mats that had been placed on the hardwood floor. The adult guests were sitting comfortably on padded folding chairs in the back of the room along the windows. Singing filled the room as Jake conducted everyone from a stage, which was built against the back wall. There were no windows along this wall because on the other side there was a separate room called Little Squawka. It was a smaller space that had two Ping-Pong tables where campers would compete with each other. Occasionally it was a meeting space for smaller groups.

Inside Big Squawka, the wide rock fireplace was burning mild and cozy. There was a large black bear rug mounted on the wall on the right side. On the far end of the room was a string of windows and a door that led to a large deck, which overlooked the inner dock and Princess Louisa Inlet.

When the singing ended, Jake reached for the microphone and dragged it and its long cord out to center stage.

"Hey! That was great for your first night," he said to the crowd. "And now, our camp manager, Chet Raley." Chet bounded up on to the platform as Jake handed him the microphone and exited the stage.

"Thanks, Jake. That was some terrific singing, gang. I can tell that many of you have been to club before? So, did you all have a good time here at Malibu today?"

Every one of the teens sitting on the floor below Chet cheered, whistled, and clapped. It was clear they all had had a wonderful first day. "Well, we're just getting started," Chet continued. "You're going to meet some of the neatest kids your age here this week. Believe me, we're very proud of our work crew and staff. And the whole purpose, the reason we're here, is to show you the greatest week of your life. An essential part of that is to give you an honest look at the Christian faith. We want you to not only have a chance to have a fun time, but for you to get to know yourselves and to get to know the One who made all of this." He gestured out the side windows toward the inlet and mountains. "That's the key. That living life on this amazing planet without knowing Christ—our Savior, our God, and our Creator—is incomplete. The kids who work here, they don't get paid. They're here to make sure that you have a wonderful time so that you'll take time to consider the Christian faith! And also that you too can get in on the good thing that we call the Good News. And the Good News is that God loves us so much, that He gave us 'free will'. We're free to live our lives without puppet strings attached to our Creator. Freedom of choice, and that He sacrificed His own son for us for the good of humankind so that we would have everlasting life, and that the mere existence of life itself is a miracle! And for all of this, we feel blessed and give thanks! Amen."

Many in the room were quick to respond aloud with an "amen!" It was obvious by Chet's smile that he was encouraged that this week's groups of campers and work crew were already responding in a positive way to the glorious message of Jesus Christ.

CHAPTER 3

Magnificent Chatterbox Falls

The inner dock area was quiet and peaceful when Doc and Chris met in the harbormaster's shack early the next morning. Scattered fog was thinly spread far down Jervis Inlet just above the waterline, and disappeared where the narrow waterway turned into Princess Royal Reach. There was no wind, and even the normally noisy seagulls were quiet. The sun had burned the fog off Princess Louisa Inlet, and it too was quiet and calm.

"It's so calm and tranquil this morning, it almost feels eerie," observed Chris.

"Yes, it's really peaceful, isn't it?" Doc answered. "After a while, you'll get used to it though. The entire camp seems to be sleeping in this morning. Pretty typical after all the excitement of the first day."

They fell quiet as they began to organize their equipment for the upcoming day's activites, sorting life jackets and arranging oars into matching sets.

As Chris was finishing the work at the harbor, the campers were having breakfast in the dining room, where they were entertained once again by the comical antics of the Malibu band. Jake had introduced the plan of the day while everyone ate. He went over all the activites and recreational sports, making sure the campers knew all the options they had for the day. One of the tours he mentioned was a two-hour cruise to the end of Princess Louisa Inlet to see Chatterbox Falls.

A few hours later, Doc, Chris, Julie, Rusty, Diane, and twenty-two other campers were inside the larger workboat, *Nefertiti*, as it sliced through the deep blue waters of Princess Louisa on its way to Chatterbox Falls.

Doc was at the helm of the makeshift tour boat, barefoot as usual. He smiled as he took in the view, which included Julie, who was standing near the bow with her friends, oohing and aahing over all the magnificent beauty that surrounded them. She wore a yellow two-piece swimsuit with a short white cover-up, and white tennis shoes, and she frequently turned to look and smile at Doc. She was making it difficult for him to concentrate on piloting the boat. Meanwhile, several girls were talking to Chris, trying to win his attention. A few of the kids were taking pictures, with their Brownie cameras, of the remarkable suroundings.

"If you look up the mountain off our port or left side, you'll see the huge granite face that the Sechelt Indians named One Eye," Doc called out to his passengers over the engine noise. "We're at sea level, and the glaciers above One Eye are over eight thousand feet high, making this mountain one of the tallest mountains for its height!" Julie gave him a sarcastic look, which was followed by a smile.

Chris immediately spoke up to state his own observation. "And I suppose Hamilton Island, which we just cruised by, is a rare island because it's completely surrounded by water?"

Doc smiled at Chris. "Hey! I like that! You're hired!" Now all the voyagers were laughing. Doc steered the tour boat into the end of the inlet, which opened up to a large protected bay. As the *Nefertiti* completed its turn and came closer to the bay, Chatterbox Falls came into full view. Everyone aboard the tour boat was astonished.

"As you can see, we're almost to Chatterbox Falls," Doc continued. "The lower falls you see there are 120 feet high. There's a trail that leads up to the top of those falls. The upper falls are hidden by the mountainside hundreds of feet higher."

"Can we hike up there?" Rusty interrupted.

"You can go to the top of the lower falls. But let me caution you. You'll see the warning sign on top. Don't cross the fence and climb out on the flat rocks above the falls. It's extremely dangerous! We must obey the safety rules up there." Doc spoke with unwavering intensity to get the gravity of what he was saying across to the group. By the looks on the faces of the campers, it appeared he succeeded.

Doc steered the *Nefertiti* near the base of the enormous waterfall, which had a forty-foot wide stream of freshwater flowing into the inlet from the furious pool of water directly below its base. From a distance, the blue *Nefertiti* looked like a tiny toy boat against the massive, roaring waterfall. Everyone in the boat felt the wet, heavy spray of water on their faces while they listened to the thundering sounds of the fall's mighty power.

Minutes later, Doc changed course and turned the boat away from the mist toward the dock located at the very end of the inlet. There were three private yachts tied to the dock, two of which were expensive sailboats, the third an exquisite motor yacht. Moored to the far end of the dock was a modest, forty-foot houseboat. Doc slipped the *Nefertiti* into a space between the two moored sailboats. As soon as he was alongside, Chris took the bowline and jumped on to the floating dock. He secured the line to a cleat as Doc hitched the stern line.

The teens disembarked and walked past Vic Hookums and James "Mac" McDonald, who were sitting Indian style on the planked dock playing chess. Doc and Julie locked eyes when he helped her out of the boat.

Spotting Vic playing chess out of the corner of his eye, Doc finally peeled his gaze off Julie. "Vic! Mac! Who's winning?" he called.

Vic was quick to answer. "Won't know for a while, mate," he said in his deep voice. "He's giving me a tough time today." Mac was a white-haired man in his late sixties with incredibly dark, weathered skin, an indication of how much time he spent in the sun. He was wearing only white shorts and white tennis shoes.

Mac looked up and smiled at Doc. "Hello, Doc. New group of campers?"

"Yes, it is. Hey, everyone!" Doc spoke loudly to his passengers. "This is Vic and Mac. Vic is Malibu's caretaker and my boss, and Mac lives down here at Chatterbox during the summer." They all waved and greeted each other from a distance.

Julie turned to Doc and said quietly, "He lives in that little houseboat?"

"Yes, and during the winter, he lives in Acapulco, Mexico," Doc said softly. "We keep his houseboat at Malibu during that season. Come with me, Julie, I'd like you to meet him. He's a legend in these parts."

When Doc took her hand and started walking down the dock, Julie was obviously pleased.

"Chris! Come on with us. Hey, Fergie! Would you mind taking the group on up the trail? Chris and Julie will catch up to you in a minute."

"Aren't you hiking with us?" Julie asked.

"I've been up there a dozen times. But if you insist."

"I insist!" grinned Julie.

Doc smiled, then led the two of them over to Vic and Mac, who were still playing their game of chess with the intensity of professionals.

"Gentlemen!" Doc proclaimed. "I'd like for you to meet Julie, our new work crew girl. And Mac, this is Chris." Vic and Mac nodded their heads, as if to say, "Nice to meet you," but remained focused on their chess game.

"Where are you from, Julie?" asked Vic without looking up.

"Spokane, Washington," she replied. "I've never been there, what's it like?" Vic responded.

"I think it's beautiful. There's a spectacular river and falls that runs through our downtown. And there's lots of tall trees surrounding our small city. I think it's a great place to grow up." Julie then scanned the magnificent bay. "But not like this. This is amazing!"

Doc spoke up. "Hey, Mac. Would you mind if I showed Julie and Chris the inside of *Seaholm*?"

"Not at all. Go right ahead."

"I'm going to wait here," said Chris. "My dad and I play a lot of chess together. Maybe I can pick up a few pointers."

"Okay," said Doc as he nodded to Julie to follow him over to the houseboat. After climbing aboard, they soon found themselves inside the living quarters of the floating home.

Outside, Vic looked up at Chris, who was watching the progress of the game. "Let me see your knife. Are you keeping it nice and sharp?"

"Yes, sir, I am," answered Chris.

"Good for you." Vic carefully checked the blade and peered up at Chris. "I understand your dad's a famous film actor and comedian. Tell us about him."

"My dad?" Chris asked, puzzled. "You mean you've never heard of my dad?"

"No disrespect, Chris, but you must remember, there are no televisions up here nor are there movie theaters," explained Vic with a grin.

"Oh, that's right. It's just so weird. Everyone knows who my dad is. I've never met anyone who doesn't know who he is."

Mac spoke up. "Well, now you have. Tell us about him, son."

"He has his own hit television comedy series, *The Dick Van Heuson Show*. And he's been in a few movies. In fact, he just completed a Disney film that takes place in England around the turn of the century."

"England?" Vic repeated with interest.

"Yes, he plays a chimney sweep!" As Chris continued to explain his father's new role in his latest film, which had been filmed on location in England, Doc and Julie were busy checking out Mac's houseboat.

The *Seaholm* was clean inside, but still somewhat cluttered due to the diminutive size of the living space. Both the galley and stateroom were small. A number of Indian artifacts and nautical and Mexican collectibles decorated the living room. On one wall, a half dozen photographs, of visiting yachtsmen Mac had taken over the years, were hung. There were windows, along with one porthole on each side of the living space, but because they were little, they only allowed a diminutive amount of light to filter into the cabin. Fortunately, the barge had a built-in generator, so there were several lights mounted on the overhead and bulkheads, which helped to illuminate the quarters.

"Isn't this cool?" Doc asked Julie as he looked around the space.

"It sure is, look at some of the stuff he's collected." Julie was looking at all the funky objects mounted on the cabin's bulkhead.

"Why is he considered a legend?" Julie asked.

"He bought this land in the late twenties and had a log cabin built on it. Then, after he got married in 1940, he brought his bride down the inlet to their new home here at Chatterbox. And as they were rounding the bend out there, they discovered the house was on fire. It burnt to the ground, and they lost everything."

"Oh! How awful!"

"Yes, it was some kind of generator problem. It was so devastating that it caused her to have a nervous breakdown. She got really sick . . . so sick she almost died. They ended up in a divorce."

"How tragic," Julie said sadly. "I hate divorces."

"Me too. It's just so hard on people when they split up," said Doc with a heavy heart.

"I agree. And it's especially difficult when they have children." A look of concern crossed Julie's face. "Our neighbors in Spokane divorced recently. They have two little girls. It was really awful!"

Seeing that the conversation was making Julie upset, Doc decided to quickly steer it back to Mac. "Anyway, in '53, Mac donated this land to the yachtsmen of the Northwest, and needless to say, he won the hearts of hundreds of boaters."

"What a story," Julie said solemnly. Doc reached out and took both her hands and slowly pulled her close to him.

"Speaking of hearts, mine's pounding faster than a hummingbird's wings!"

"Mine too," said Julie. They both looked intensely at each other and began to lean in for a kiss.

"Hey, Doc!" Vic shouted from outside. "You'd better get going. You've got a schedule to keep." Doc's and Julie's lips hadn't yet touched. They paused for a brief moment and looked deep into each other's eyes.

Doc, who was clearly disappointed by the interruption, shouted back to Vic. "Coming, Vic!"

He turned back to Julie and whispered, "I guess we'd better go." Julie nodded her agreement.

60

A few minutes later, after Doc and Julie had departed the *Seaholm*, the pair joined Chris and began hiking up the narrow dirt path, which wound through the thick forest toward the top of the waterfall. The dense vegetation obscured much of the bright sunlight. Chris was in awe of the towering trees and their innumerable shades of green. A small stream of water tumbled down some jagged rocks and fallen logs next to the hiking trail. The sound of the running water was masked by the noisy roar of Chatterbox Falls close by.

The narrow dirt path included a few short wooden bridges built over several small streams. Each bridge curved around the mountainside as it paralled the waters of the main falls. Even though the falls was not visible from the trail, the crash of the massive amount of water against the enormous granite boulders resonated through the forest. Cold, wet mist blanketed the trio as they climbed the sloped trail. The sound of the falls was even louder under the lush canopy of the forest, making conversation difficult. One had to holler over the thunderous noise to be heard. Chris spoke first, almost yelling at Doc and Julie.

"I can't believe Vic and Mac had never heard of my dad! What about you, Doc? You've never asked me about him. What do you think about my dad?"

A little out of breath from trekking up the rocky path, Doc paused to collect himself before answering. "To tell you the truth, he's one of my heroes. One of my idols. I think he's the funniest guy on television."

Chris was taken aback by Doc's response. "Are you serious?" he asked, a little stunned. "How come you've never asked me about him?"

"Because, putting myself in your shoes, you probably get kind of tired of people always asking and talking about your dad. Am I right?"

"Yes, that's absolutely true," said Chris, without skipping a beat. "In fact, to be honest, Julie and I have talked about this. Sometimes I don't know who my real friends are. Do they like me for me or because I'm Dick Van Heuson's son? It really bugs me!"

"I'm sure it does," said Doc sympathetically, "but it goes with the territory. Having a famous, popular dad. But this is who you are, right? The main thing is that you're aware of it, so all you can do is know that the possibility exists and deal with it. You certainly don't blame your dad, do you?"

"Oh, not at all. I'm proud of my dad. And I admire him a lot. It's just difficult to be his son sometimes."

"I'm sure it is," Doc agreed, "but life's a challenge, Chris. The important thing is that you know who you are. Have faith in yourself and in God, and the rest will fall in place."

Julie chimed in, "Doc is right, Chris. You've got a lot going for yourself as an individual. You don't need your dad's popularity to be liked."

Chris looked relieved as he took in a deep breath. "Yeah, I understand. Thanks. I hope you guys don't mind, but I think I'm going to run ahead and catch up to the rest of the gang."

"Sure, go ahead," said Doc. "We'll see you up there."

Chris moved more quickly up the path, leaving Doc and Julie hiking the trail together alone.

Julie smiled warmly at Doc. "That was really nice what you said to him."

"Well, as cool as it would be to be Dick Van Heuson's son, I'm sure it's tough sometimes to really know who your friends are."

"It would be. He had a really hard time at Frontier, but he seems to be dealing with it a lot better now."

"That's good," Doc said, focusing on the passing ground below him. "It's amazing how everyone has their own problems to deal with. Life's just not always that simple or easy."

The pair continued the climb up the mountain, with Julie slightly behind Doc. When a few minutes had passed, Julie touched Doc's right forearm to get his attention. He stopped and turned toward her. "I understand this hasn't been an easy year for you." She spoke caringly, but directly. "Beth told me about your dad passing away last October. I'm really sorry."

"It's okay, really," said Doc, positively. "I've had a lot of support from friends. I don't know if Beth mentioned it, but I'm living with my Young Life leader and his family for now."

They began walking again, but still close enough so they could talk over the roar of the falls off to their left.

"Your mom's been gone for some time, is that right?"

"Yes," Doc answered, stopping and lowering his gaze to the trail as if deep in thought. "I really never knew her. She drowned in a boating accident when I was less than a year old. My aunt helped my dad raise me until I was sixteen. She's back east now." The pair continued walking, at a slow pace, up the mountain. At times, Doc would swipe his hand through the occasional spiderweb that crossed the path so Julie could pass easily.

"Maybe this sounds weird, but I sometimes think about how awful it must have been for my dad losing my mom in such a tragic accident. I'm sure her sudden death was hard on him. Plus I was just a baby. That couldn't have been easy for him."

"That doesn't sound weird to me at all," Julie said to him in a kind voice. "In fact, I think you're being really sweet and sensitive to have those kind of feelings."

"Thanks. I do appreciate that. I can't help but think what it must have been like for my dad. Not only did he have to deal with me, a young child, but I'm sure he felt a lot of frustration, and pain, thinking about my mom not getting to raise me and watch me grow up. Does that make sense to you?"

"Sure it does. I'm sure your dad had many moments over the years of wishing your mom could have shared in all the memories of your childhood and the three of you as a family."

Julie took his right hand, hoping he could feel her compassion. "Were you close to your dad?" she asked.

"Yes and no. There was certainly love there, but we were very different. He was a gunsmith who was into hunting and fishing, and I was more into the arts. Don't get me wrong, I enjoy the outdoors, skiing and stuff, but I wasn't really into shooting or hunting, which, I think, disappointed my dad. It just wasn't my thing. I'll never forget how my dad reacted to that difference between the two of us. I played football my first couple of years in high school, and I was a pretty decent player. I quit the team at the beginning of my senior year because I wanted to pursue drama and be in some school plays. I couldn't do both. I chose drama over football because that's what I was hoping to do as a career. I wanted to become an actor or an entertainer. Anyway, my dad went ballistic. He was really upset and angry with me. For whatever reason, he seemed to hate acting. He just couldn't understand why I would stop playing football to be in a couple of 'stupid' plays! It's like he thought I was some kind of sissy or something, which, of course, really hurt my feelings and consequently damaged our relationship."

Julie could hear the hurt in Doc's voice.

Doc continued sharing his story as they both hiked the dampen trail, with Julie still holding on to his hand. "Then when I started going to Young Life Club meetings, and confessed to him about my faith and wanting to attend chuch, he began distancing himself from me. He never had interest in being religious or spiritual. He died a short time after that," Doc continued. "And I've always felt like we never really resolved that issue. It's lousy." He rubbed Julie's hand with his thumb, surprised by how comfortable he felt divulging his unhappy past to her.

Julie studied his face and found tenderness in his eyes. "Sounds like you both just had different interests and hobbies, and there's nothing wrong with that," she said, looking to comfort him. "I don't think kids always need to be just like their mom or dad. We're all individuals with our own likes and dislikes. You're obviously creative and have talent in drama and that stuff. And what's more, you really enjoy it. Your dad obviously liked macho, outdoor sports—like hunting and football."

"I like sports too, especially football," Doc answered. "I really did enjoy playing the game, it was fun and challenging and kept me healthy. In fact, my dad and I went to many Oakland Raider games together, which was very cool. That was something we really enjoyed and had in common." Realizing he was domonating the conversation, and ready to move on from his history, Doc was eager to hear about Julie's. He turned toward her. "Enough about me. Tell me about your family." By now the trail was becoming narrower and steeper.

Still talking over the loud sounds of the falls, Julie answerd Doc. "Well, as far as religion is concerned, my parents are quite the opposite. They both have been Christians for years and are active in our community church. Young Life was a natural fit for me since I belonged to our church's youth group."

A couple of steps in front of Julie, Doc again turned his head back toward her and said, "That's fantastic. What does your dad do?"

Julie smiled and let go of Doc's hand. With an open gesture, she answered, "He's a drama professor at the University of Spokane."

"You're kidding!" Doc responded, clearly surprised. "That's quite a coincidence, wouldn't you say? Wow! That's neat, I'd like to meet him some day. How about your mom, what's she like?"

"Oh, she's super. We're really close. She's into music—plays the piano and the violin, and she also teaches music. She's really pretty too."

"I can believe that!" Doc said flirtatiously. But then his expression became more sober. "Listen, Julie, I owe you an apology for my behavior back there on the *Seaholm*."

"It's okay, really," Julie said sincerely.

"But I hardly know you. I mean, we just met," Doc confessed, trying to make sense of the strong feelings he felt for her. "This is going to sound really corny, but I've never been so attracted so quickly to someone in my life. I don't know what it is, but there's something about you that I just . . ."

"That you just can't put your finger on," Julie said, finishing his sentence. "There's a kind of weird closeness between us, almost like we've been together before?"

"Exactly!" Doc quickly replied. "So you feel it too?"

"Yes, I feel it, and it scares me a little. I don't understand it, do you? To be very honest with you, Doc, I can't keep my eyes off of you either," she admitted. "I can't even stop thinking about you."

The spray from the waterfall kept Doc's face cool and moist, which he appreciated because if it weren't for the mist, his face would have been blushing with delight at Julie's admission. He quickly looked around to make sure the two of them were alone before gently taking Julie's hands and pulling her closer to him. He gazed into her eyes.

"I know I shouldn't do this, but I really can't help it." He embraced her for just a few seconds, and when he pulled away, they were looking deeply into each other's eyes as if trying to understand each other's thoughts. Doc reached up with both hands and began stroking her long blond hair. Then he reached up to her face and, with both hands, gently pulled his fingers through her bangs, combing them behind her ears. He held the back of her head and moved in to kiss her, but stopped just short of her mouth and released her. Doc took a deep breath in an attempt to regain control over his feelings, but they both remained locked on each other, sharing an obvious mutual attraction.

A few moments later, Doc took Julie's hand. "I think we'd better catch up to the others."

"You're right," Julie said reluctantly. "We'd better get going. How much farther is the top?"

"Not that far," said Doc. "Only about another ten or fifteen minutes." He took the lead, still holding her hand, and they started back up the wet steep mountain, this time at a much faster pace, eager to reach the top of the falls.

On top of Chatterbox Falls, Fergie, Chris, Rusty, and the others were gathered at the end of the trail, looking out in silence over the violent glacier water crashing down the mountain near them. The roar of the rushing water was almost deafening. Only by shouting could they express their excitement and share observations. It was exhilarating to be so high and be able to see out over the inlet below. Finally, Doc and Julie emerged from the dense, damp forest.

"There you are," Chris yelled as they emerged from behind a large tree.

Doc, who had let go of Julie's hand just before reaching the top, greeted the other hikers. "So, what do you think?" he shouted, hoping to be heard over the thrashing of Chatterbox. "Amazing, huh? Can you believe this view and the incredible falls?"

Rusty called out a question to Doc. "So why can't we cross over the fence and get closer? I know, the warning sign. But it doesn't look that dangerous! Nobody's going to know."

It was clear Doc's talk before the hike hadn't been enough to deter everyone. Doc motioned for everyone to gather close to him so they could hear him talk. "As I said earlier," he began, pointing over at the permanently afixed warning sign, "it is too dangerous to go beyond this spot."

He turned to Rusty and gave him and the entire group a stern look. He knew he had to impress upon them the danger if he wanted his message to be heeded. "If you cross over this fence and try and get closer to the falls, you'll end up slipping and being pulled into the rushing water, which will drag you over the cliff, and you will die. It's that simple." At this, everyone leaned in even farther; they were hanging on Doc's every word. "Here's the problem, gang. Once you get out on that flat rock, you're in trouble," he continued as he turned and pointed at the rock. "I know it looks fairly safe, but it isn't. These falls have been flowing for thousands of years now, and those rocks are as slippery as glass. Think about it, the water's been rushing over them now and has turned that granite into slippery, dooms-day boulders! And that moss out there? Attached to the rock? You can't grab on to it. It's too wet and slippery. Once you start sliding, there's simply nothing to grab hold of. The other problem is, the falls doesn't drop directly into the inlet. The water dumps into a large deep hole before it empties into a stream, and then into the inlet. That hole is full of jagged rocks and crevices. So believe me when I say that you don't want to be slipping off these falls! As the sign says, six people have dared to climb out there, and every last one of them fell to their deaths." The teens looked horrified.

"The sign isn't lying, people! Let me tell you all a quick story before we have to head back down." He knelt down and gestured the group to come even closer. "I was harbormaster at Malibu when the sixth person fell to his death down these violent falls. That was last year, and the boy was only eleven years old. He was a Canadian Sea Scout. His troop came up to Chatterbox on a training exercise from the Sunshine Coast. There were about twenty-five of them on an eighty-five-foot vessel, learning seamanship skills for five days. Like us, the group hiked right up to where we are now so they could see the breathtaking view. A young boy, Danny, waited until the leaders were distracted and climbed over the fence. Once on the other side, he quickly walked over to that flat rock by the edge of the falls."

Doc turned and pointed again at the rock to reinforce his point. "By the time someone noticed him out by the falls, he had already slipped and fell on his butt. He was terrified and screamed for help, frantically grabbing at the moss. But either the moss simply broke away or his hands just slipped right through because it was too wet. He was gone in a flash. Over the falls he went! It happened just that quick!" The assembled teenagers were shocked.

"His body was recovered by the Canadian Rescue Coastguard later that afternoon. Vic and I escorted them by boat from Malibu after they landed their large seaplane by the outer dock on Jervis Inlet. The plane was too big to land in Chatterbox Bay. Vic and I also helped them carry Danny's body to the *Neffertiti* from the bottom of the falls. It's a memory I wish I could erase."

Doc looked away, the thought of what happened obviously was painful. "You can imagine how all his friends felt about his death, which happened simply because he didn't follow the rules. The Sea Scout leaders were devastated. Bottom line, everyone, we need to respect these falls. Same with the hike up to Inspiration Point if any of you choose to make that hike later in the week."

Doc pushed himself up off the wet grassy area. After everyone was standing, Doc nodded to Fergie. "We'd better head back down the trail," he said. "It's time we motor back to Malibu."

With that, everyone began to head toward the trail that would lead them back down the mountain and their waiting boat. A few took a moment to glance out at the now infamous wet rocks one more time, thinking about the poor young boy losing his life. Shaking their heads with sadness, they turned back and caught up to the others who were disappearing into the thick forest in a single line, headed for the boat and Malibu.

CHAPTER 4

Regatta: Be Entertained

The next morning, Doc and Chris were once again up early and down at the inner dock area accomplishing their tasks. That day was even more challenging than normal since it was the morning of the regatta, one of Malibu's best weekly events. The harbormaster and his fresh assistant were high up on ladders attaching colorful, nautical broad-flags to tall wooden poles, which were temporally lashed to the four corners of the upper deck. The freshly painted white wooden rowboats were strategically lined up along the floating dock ready to be used by assigned teams. As a cool breeze made its way across the inlet waters and into the small Malibu harbor, the vivid, lively flags began to wave dramatically. Kyle and Dale, the ski instructor and lifeguard, arrived and pitched in by hosing off the upper deck and lower dock and by securing three foot Canadian flags to the stern of a half dozen ski boats moored along the outside of the floating dock. The several campers who were walking by were intrigued by the preparations and transformation of the harbor area. Little did they know that in less than two hours, the whole inner dock area would be occupied and packed with the entire population of the camp. Hundreds of screaming teenagers would be cheering on their perspective teams as they competed in a fun and hilarious maritime contest.

An hour or so later, after breakfast had been served and coed teams had been assigned by cabins—and after the participants had been given detailed rules and instructions during a twenty-minute humorous chalk talk in Big Squawka—the teams of teenagers and their counselors headed down to the inner dock area to prepare for the regatta competition. As they all found their designated team area in the harbor's upper dock and ramp area to cheer for their teams, the uniformed Malibu Band was lining up down on the floating dock, near the rowboats. Each of the band members had their instruments in hand, ready to respond to Jake's commands. As they formed a straight line along the short T-section of the dock, which jutted out to the left of the main floating dock, they each were facing the crowd of teens. Jake then stepped out from the middle of the assembly and raised his large blue megaphone with his right hand up to his mouth.

In a loud voice, which is amplified considerably by the handheld broadcast instrument, he announced with great enthusiasm, "As part of our opening ceremonies for the famous Malibu Ya'chette Regatta and to recognize those of you participating today from the USA, the New Ashmolian Marching Society and Student's Conservatory Marching Unit Band will perform for you several difficult and intricate movements, forming the first letter of the most famous and renowned universities of the great nation of America."

Edna blew her whistle and began pumping her toilet plunger baton in the air as the band began playing a popular university marching song. Immediately, the band members started marching erratically and individually around the immediate area of the dock, turning circles and bumping into one another as they played. Soon they wound up on the main floating dock and lined up in a straight line, one behind the other, with Jake in the front facing the teams of smiling campers and their counselors. The scores of competitors and spectators were above the band, along the upper dock railings and along the long wooden ramp, which was built on massive cement stilts, and led up to the camper boys' lodging dormitory, Sitka.

Jake again spoke loudly into the megaphone. "The University of Indiana!" Edna again blew her whistle, and the band members repeated the marching around and back into the same straight line. "The University of Idaho!" Jake proudly blurted out. Immediately the band once again marched erratically along the dock, continuing to bump into one another until they were back into their straight-line position, one behind the other. "The University of Illinois!"

Jake announced through the megaphone. Everyone was howling with laughter, including Julie, Diane, and their friends, as they were among the scores of spectators lined up along the Sitka wooden walkway. Near them were Rusty, his friends, and his counselor, Fergi. Doc was, of course, in the band, standing directly behind Jake and Edna, making his usual funny face.

The regatta officially started when Jake lifted his right hand up high into the air and pulled the trigger of his black starter-pistol. *BANG!* The loud blare of the blank gun signified that it is time for a dozen members of each team to decorate their assigned rowboat for which their chosen king and queen would proudly ride aboard during the Parade of the Regatta Royalty! Some of the decorators ran out to the golf course to gather foliage and greenery while others installed and hung vivid colorful banners on their boats, displaying the creative team name of which they were proud to introduce to the entire camp. Inspired by Malibu's surroundings, the teenagers were quick to cleverly place an identity to their squad. The week's lineup included Totem Warriors, Seaweed Surfers, One-Eyed Jacks, Malibu Marauders, and the Nautical Navels. When the ornamental schemes were finished, the parade of boats began the short journey along the length of the floating dock and shoreline, slowly moving through the mirrored surface of the dark inlet waters, in single-line formation. While two guys from each team paddled their respective boats, moving them forward, the adorned king and queen aboard each boat were honored, as they smiled and waved to the crowd, who were clapping, chanting, or cheering for their own majestic couple. As the six floats circled the inner harbor, they one by one returned to the dock, and the occupants disembarked. Team members immediately removed the signage and sprays of leaves and branches, which were attached inside each boat. The greenery were swiftly tossed out into the inlet at the far end of the dock and was quickly moved outwardly as it was consumed along the surface of the water by the outgoing tide.

The competition had been under way now for a while as the five rowboats, with four team members each, were racing out and around a bright-yellow buoy anchored seventy-five feet from the dock. The scores of kids were cheering for their perspective teams. The excitement was building as Chris and Kyle were on the dock preparing for another upcoming regatta race. Still in his band uniform, Jake was using his megaphone to announce the event. Doc was in a ski boat drifting next to the race area with Turtle aboard. Doc and Julie made eye contact and waved to each other.

Soon the In and Out Race was taking place. Using their hands as paddles, the team contestants were not only racing around the buoy, but when Jake blew his whistle, they had to jump out of the boat, and then get back in. It is one thing to jump out of a rowboat into the chilly waters of the Princess Louisa Inlet, but it is an entirely different challenge to have to climb back in! When you grab the side of the boat, not only does it want to rock toward you, taking away the stability of pulling yourself into the craft, but you need hardy strength to haul your body weight up, out of the water, and back into the boat. It is not an easy task. That is why the experienced councilors chose the slim and the strong from among their troop of campers. The two-boy and two-girl teams were once again cheered on by their excited cluster of friends hollering from up above.

Once the In and Out Race was over, the last race of this wet, nautical event was about to start. Probably the most fun occurrence of the entire regatta was the famous Swamp Race. The six rowboats were positioned in the center of the inlet, between the dock and the shore, with each of their bows pointed in toward one another. Doc, who was carefully crawling to the point of the ski boat bow, had a steel twelve-inch diameter, half-inch-thick ring in his hand and, with skillful success, tied each rowboat to the ring with their bowlines. Turtle was able to expertly and slowly guide the fourteen-foot fiberglass ski boat in among the rowboats. Each boat contained four guy teammates in bathing suits, wearing their team-color bandana's around their foreheads, ready for action. Each equipped with a #10 can, the participants were holding their *weapons of destruction* close to the waterline, ready to fill and engage. As soon as Jake blew his whistle into the powered-on megaphone, the cold wet saltwater began to fly! Within seconds, the twenty-four brave combatants were drenched from head to toe. As the boats began to take on water, the "water warriors" were laughing so loudly, they often swallowed large amounts of the pungent inlet water. The object of the race, of course, was to swamp your opponents' boats, with the contestants aboard. Two of the experienced counselors had coached their swamp teams to have only three guys throw the seawater into the challenging boats, and one teammate to use his tin can to bale out their own boat. The battle of this hilarious water war continued for almost ten minutes until one of the contending rowboats was sinking like the *Titanic*. As it rapidly took on water, the four-man team, showing defeat, stood as tall as they possibly could, and with an honorable navy salute, they showed their disappointment with frowning faces. A couple of minutes later, there was a winner, as the remaining two boats slid under the water, submerging the eight challengers. The winning team, "The Nautical Navals", who were partially beneath the surface of the water themselves, were standing up in their water-logged vessel, arms raised high, each with a proud grin, mocking the losers who were swimming their way toward the floating dock.

After about an hour and a half of regatta games, the competition ended, and the contestants either headed over to the pool for some swimming and sunbathing time, or they headed off to their room to change into dry clothes. The entire camp dispersed into different areas of the resort. The day was once again filled with numerous activities. Some of the campers elected to water-ski, hike to Inspiration Point (located six hundred feet above Malibu), or simply hang out on Main Street and talk to friends. Doc and Chris were busy down on the harbor cleaning up after the regatta, sweeping off the dock and removing the many flags and banners from around the upper dock area and those attached to the stern of the ski boats. Once the inner dock area was in shipshape, Chris started organizing the sign-up sheets in the harbormaster shack so that the use of the boats and the water ski program could begin. Doc took a few minutes to run an errand, as he headed up the long sloped wooden walkway toward Main Street. He walked up the narrow alley toward the kitchen back door and near the short-cement ramp that led to the food storage locker. Just as he was reaching for the kitchen screen door handle to pull it outward, Julie appeared from the inside, and not seeing Doc, she pushed open the door, banging the metal frame into Doc's hand. He immediately reacted with a resounding, "Whoa!"

"Oh! I am so sorry, Doc!" Julie, looking embarrassed, responded. "I didn't see you there. I didn't hurt your hand, did I?"

"Oh, no! It's fine. Don't worry," Doc assured her as he shook it off.

"I was just heading up to the food locker," Julie responded. "I need to grab a couple of things. What are you up to?"

As they both stepped away from the door and into the alley, Doc answers. "I just came up to play some music for the camp," Doc answered with a prolonged smile, suddenly stopping Julie by seizing her hand. "How are you? It was good seeing you enjoying the regatta. Pretty fun stuff, huh?"

"Oh yea! It was definitely a challenging and hilarious contest. What a great way to kick off the team competition."

"Well, you've been to Frontier Ranch, Julie, so you know how important camp activities and the program is to connect with the campers. Not to mention, we want to show them a great time and teach them that being a Christian doesn't mean you can't have fun, right?"

"Right!" Julie quickly responded. "And it's such a wonderful feeling for them to be included as part of a team. I thought the Swamp Race was the best!"

"Yea, everyone loves that one! How often do you get the chance to purposely sink someone's boat with them aboard? Vic thought that one up!"

"Fun, funny stuff," Julie continued, with a cunning glance at Doc.

"Aha! I saw that look. You enjoyed seeing the defeated 'going down with the ship,' huh? And the glorious amusement of the winners indulging in their success—ha ha! Oh, we're going to get along great, and with Vic too!"

"Gosh! Am I that bad?" Julie asked with a cute grin as she gently slapped Doc on the arm.

"Well, yea! Look at you, you're already beating up on me again!"

"Stop it!" she laughingly ordered him.

"Okay, okay, as long as you stop hitting on me!"

"Hitting on you? Oh, and now you're suggesting that I'm hitting on you, is that it?" Julie said to him with a sly, mischievous tone in her voice.

"No, that would be me," Doc replied in almost a whisper, as he moved his face closer to hers and slowly and carefully pulled her closer to him. It is a good thing that they were alone in the alleyway since they were once again almost embracing. Doc looked deeply into her eyes as he continued to softly speak to her, "Yes, I guess I'm hitting on you . . . sorry again, blond one!"

Julie slowly moved her eyes across his face and paused to focus directly into his dark pupils, then she softly said, "We'll see about that, dock boy."

Just then, Beth pushed the screen door open into the alley and noticed Doc and Julie standing there together, as they promptly split apart. "Oh, hi, Doc," Beth exclaimed. "What's up?"

"Not much. Just here to play some music," he quickly answered as he regained his composure.

"He was just explaining to me about the music, weren't you, Doc?" Julie said to Beth convincingly, even though as she turned to look back at Doc, she winked at him with a calculating, secret expression.

"So, Julie," Beth obliviously changed the conversation. "Do you need some help?"

"Oh, no, I'm fine. I just need to grab a large jar of olives out of the locker. I'll be right in."

"Okay," Beth responded, as she headed back into the kitchen, once again leaving Julie and Doc alone in the alleyway.

Julie said to Doc, "Yikes! That was a little too close, if you know what I mean?" Doc agreed by nodding his head and widening his eyes. Then, as if to purposely and quickly change the subject, Julie inquisitively asked Doc, "What do you mean you're here to play some music?"

"Oh, have you noticed the music playing around camp? Kind of . . . almost in the background of things?"

"Yea, actually I have. It sounds great, and I like the selection. So you're the one that . . . ?"

"Yep, that's me," Doc interrupted. "I've been doing the daytime music for Malibu for two summers now."

"Really? That's cool. So . . . I mean, how do you do it? How does it work? It seems like I hear it everywhere during free time."

"Well, the way it works is that we have a reel-to-reel, quarter-inch, four-track Sony player installed in the kitchen, near the pull-cord for the air horn. It'll play for about two hours before someone has to flip it over and start a new track. I only come up to change the reels since I'm the one who recorded them at home during the winter months."

"You're kidding me! You recorded all this awesome music I keep hearing? Wow!"

"Oh, thanks! Well, as I'm sure you've noticed, I try and mix it up with some oldies from the late fifties and early sixties, plus some Beach Boys, Beatles, and the Four Seasons—they're my favorites. We've actually got over a half dozen speakers mounted around camp. A few are inside some of the buildings, like the dining room, kitchen, and Big Squawka. I've got one down in the dock area, and there's one here on Main Street too."

"That is so 'out of sight'!" Julie replied with fascination in her voice. (*Out of sight* was a word used often in the midsixties by teenagers. Its meaning was "terrific," "great.") Enthralled, she continued, "I didn't know that you were so into music."

"Oh, big time."

"I mean, I know you play the trumpet, duh, but I didn't realize that you liked the rock and roll stuff that much. I guess I'm not that surprised though."

"I actually like pretty much all kinds of music. Except maybe opera. I'm not sure about that."

"Yea, me too. I'm not a big fan of opera either. Well, gee, I'm impressed, Doc. You're just a guy with many talents, aren't you?"

"I don't know about that. But as far as the music stuff goes, I think my favorite is getting to help with the spiritual song selections for our club meetings here at Malibu and at home. There's just something about how uplifting those new or old gospel and hymns can be. I'm always amazed at how the new campers seem to thrive at learning and singing them. Praise God. Gosh! I'd better get back to work before I get fired," he said to her with a teasing voice. "Sorry to hang you up so long. Although, if you've got just a minute . . . and after you grab your olives, come and find me in the far right back corner of the kitchen, and I'll show you our magic music machine, and you can behold the music master at work!" he proudly proclaimed.

"If you insist. But don't get too cocky with me, Mister Music Man," she countered with a grin, exposing her charming dimples. "You're not that special!"

"I'm not?" Doc asked with a frown.

"Well, not just yet. We'll give it some time, okay?" Just then, Beth called out to Julie from inside the kitchen. "I'll be there in a minute!" Julie yelled to Beth as she and Doc simultaneously winked at each other while they turned and headed off in different directions.

Late that evening, after dinner and club had occurred, most of the camps' inhabitants were gathered in Big Squawka to enjoy and experience an hour of entertainment; one of the highlights of the week. The many talented staff personnel, along with some councilors and work crew, share their musical ability and humorous skits and sketches. During the final ten minutes of the program, the short theatrical comedy routine that all the personnel of Malibu refer to as the Movie Skit was performed. The entire room was dark, as the stage lights slowly illuminated the platform, but not with too much brilliancy. The raised stage was supposed to simulate the seating area of a movie theater. There were about twenty-five metal folding chairs set up facing the audience of campers, who were seated on the large wooden floor on their cushioned mats, along with several dozen others standing and leaning along the three walls of the room. The chairs were placed in four rows across the stage with a single aisle simulating an actual movie theater. The seats were supposedly facing the movie screen. In the middle row of chairs, Ken was sitting on the left aisle staring straight ahead, focused intensely just above the audience. He was in normal street clothes. In the same row, three seats to his left was Edna, wearing an older style hat and dress, and looking some-what nervous. From the pitch-black darkness of the backstage, sud-denly Doc appeared and began walking slowly down the aisle, also in normal street attire, holding a large bag of popcorn, a cup of soda, and a chocolate ice cream cone. He was squinting as he pretended to be in a dark theater, searching for a seat. Even though there were many empty seats, he chose to enter the row where Ken was seated in the aisle. Still acting as if it was almost pitch black inside the cinema, he touched Ken's face and lap, and then awkwardly climbed over Ken and took the seat next to Edna. When he clumsily passed over Ken, face-to-face, he accidentally smashed his ice cream in Ken's face. As the cold dessert was dripping off Ken's nose, Ken continued to stare straight ahead, as if it never happened. Once Doc was seated and glanced over at Ken, with chocolate ice cream covering a portion of his nose and face, Doc gave him a double take. The audience was now in hysterics, laughing profusely. After Doc placed his popcorn on the floor at his feet, and with his Coca-Cola drink cup in his left hand, Edna suddenly asked him if he knew the time. Turning his left hand over to read his watch, the entire contents of the soda spilled into his lap! The campers and everyone continued to laugh aloud.

Sitting in the dampness of his sticky, cold, liquid soda soaked into his lap, Doc continued looking at the invisible movie screen above the heads of the audience.

Again, from the darkness of the backstage, Jake appeared at the top of the aisle.

"Ruth, Ruth!" Jake murmured, not so softly. "Where are you, Ruth?" he asked as he slowly walked down the aisle, stopping at the row Edna was in. Turning and looking carefully down the aisle, he stuck his head in front of Ken as he spotted Edna sitting on the far side of Doc. "RUTH!" he shouted in a booming voice. Doc, who was eating his popcorn, was so startled, that he jumped high in his seat and the popcorn went everywhere, as hundreds of salted, yellow kernels were flying up into the air and landed all over the place! Once again, the viewers were extremely amused. Julie was sitting on the floor, near the back, with some work crew friends, almost in tears with laughter. She had a distinctive laugh, which Doc could hear over the entire laughter of the audience. With pleased thoughts from inside, he was careful not to smile and show his happy thoughts of Julie enjoying his performance.

Jake again leaned down in front of Ken's face, and looking down the aisle, he hollered at Edna, "You've got two minutes, Ruth, two minutes! You hear me? You'd better be in the lobby. I'll be waiting for you, Ruth. Now, hurry up!" He turned and headed back up the center aisle and disappeared into the darkness. Edna soon began to cry.

"I don't know what to do," she said in a blubbering voice. "I'm so afraid. I just want to be alone," she said as she began to cry some more. Doc, who was looking at her with passionate concern and anxiety, started to cry himself. Soon he was sobbing loudly as he tried to comfort Edna. He then reached into his front T-shirt pocket and pulled out a white handkerchief. Just as he brought the hankie up to his nose and began to blow hard, Edna, in the blink of an eye, swiftly reached over and pulled the cotton handkerchief out of Doc's hand for her own use. He blew his nose into his bare hands. Ken was still showing no emotion of any type, as he was focused strictly on the movie screen. Big Squawka's entire audience, including the adult guests, continued to laugh aloud.

Jake entered the scene again, as he quickly walked down the center aisle, stopping once again beside Ken. Obviously, more angry than before, he hollered over to Edna. "Aren't you listening to me, Ruth? I said two minutes, and you're still sitting there in the dark. You come right now," he paused for a moment, "or I'll—oh wait, I get it," he interrupted himself with a livid expression. "You're with this clown." He pointed at Doc. Knowing that this guy was extremely upset, Doc quickly tried to defuse the situation by rapidly moving his head back and forth, indicating the word *no*.

"That's right!" Edna said to Jake, as she grabbed Doc's arm and pulled him close to her. "I'm with him. What of it?" she responded with defiance.

"I'll take care of that!" Jake blurted out with disgust in his voice. He promptly leaped over Ken, who was still staring straight ahead as if nothing was happening around him. Jake grabbed Doc out of his chair, picked him up, and threw him to the floor. He then reached down inside Doc's outer long-sleeve striped shirt and pulled at Doc's white cutaway undershirt beneath, ripping it off him in seconds and throwing the garment ruins back down on top of Doc, who was lying in between the row of metal chairs. Jake then turned and scrambled back over Ken and immediately stormed up the aisle out of the imagined theater. Doc slowly pulled himself off the floor and back into his seat, moaning and weeping. He gradually turned to Edna and said with a quivering, wimpy voice, "Boy, lady, your husband sure is a grouch."

With anger in her voice, Edna responded, "My husband a grouch? Well, I never!" She reached down and grabbed her large heavy bag off the floor and began beating Doc with it until, once again, he was down on the floor between the seats. Edna hastily climbed over him in disgust, slithered by Ken, and promptly walked up the main aisle and out of the make-believe movie theater.

Doc, who was once again moaning and shaking his head in disbelief, gradually took his seat. He looked over at Ken, who was still staring straight ahead, and obviously hoping for some sympathy, he said to him with a frown, "Can you believe those people? I was just sitting here, watching the movie and minding my own business and—"

Breaking his constant stare and silence, Ken at once stood up, looked at Doc, and shouted loudly, "Would you shut up!" Doc instantly turned his head toward the audience and, with wide eyes, had a stunned and bewildered facial expression. The stage lights instantly went out, resulting with the room in total darkness. The audience was roaring with complete laughter, and then began to holler and clap with much enthusiasm!

Soon after everyone had exited Big Squawka, Chris and Rusty bumped into each other on the crowded Main Street and stopped to talk. "I don't know about you, Rus, but my stomach still aches from laughing so hard at that movie skit!" Chris said with a grin.

"I hear you," Rusty agreed with a giggle. "That guy Doc is hilarious. He's almost as funny as your dad, no disrespect."

"None taken," Chris assured him.

"I have to admit, Chris, this camp is a lot more fun than I thought it would be. Honestly, I expected it to be sort of boring with a bunch of religious stuff shoved down my throat. You know, the fire-and-brimstone preachy junk."

Chris gently grabbed Rusty's upper left shoulder, and with a serious tone in his voice, said, "I'm glad you're enjoying yourself here at camp, Rusty. I knew you would like this place, that's why I wanted you to come this week."

"So, Chris," Rusty interrupted with an unexpected request. "Do you think I could talk to Doc, just to thank him for being so funny and making me laugh so hard?"

"You mean right now, right this second?" Chris asked with a somewhat puzzled look.

"Yeah, right now. If that's okay?"

Chris thought for a few seconds, thinking that maybe this would be a good opportunity for Doc to have some one-on-one talk with Rusty. "I don't know why not. Sure, let's go say hi. He's in Little Squawka, the doors right over there behind you." As the two of them entered the smaller building, at a quick glance, Rusty realized that the space was like a back stage area for the performers using the main stage in Big Squawka. Two pool tables and one ping-pong table were also located in this spacious single room, along with two comfy couches. As the two friends descended a few stairs inside the building, Chris spotted Doc, who had already changed out of his soda-soaked shirt. "Hey, Doc!" Chris called out to him.

"Oh, hey, Chris, what are you two up to?" He immediately took notice of Rusty's presence.

When they walked over to Doc, who was near the steps that led up to the stage, Chris said to him with a slight wink, "Rusty was hoping to talk to you for a minute."

With a broad smile, Doc asked Rusty, "What's up, buddy?"

"I just wanted to tell you how funny you were in the Movie Skit. You just totally cracked me up. So I just wanted to say thanks in person for making this such a fun night."

"That's really nice of you, Rusty. I'm glad you enjoyed it. I'll pass your thanks and compliments on to our small cast of performers. As you know, it was definitely a team effort." Doc was hoping to instill some teamwork into Rusty's thoughts. "Are you having a good time here at Malibu, Rusty?"

"Oh yeah, a fantastic time! Did you know that our team won the regatta this morning? The Nautical Navals. They can thank me, since I was the one who mostly swamped the last boat, and down it went!"

Chris was embarrassed and jumped into the conversation. "It's not all about you, Rus."

Quickly trying to defuse the situation, Doc interrupted, "I think what Chris is trying to say, Rusty, is that team building is just that. It's not all about one person, it's about working together and having trust and faith in your teammates to accomplish a goal together, not as one individual. It also allows everyone on a team to feel important and to be proud that they were a part of something greater than just themselves. Does that make sense?"

Rusty nodded his head, yes, as he continued to carefully listen to Doc. It was obvious that he had respect for him and trusted his advice.

Doc motioned them to take a seat on one of the couches, as he sat at one end, with Rusty in the middle. "Anyway, it's like a football team. Oh sure, the quarterback gets most of the glory, but if it weren't for his other ten teammates on the field, the play wouldn't be successful. This applies to everything in life. Having a good healthy relationship with your peers builds camaraderie and friendship. Connecting well with people, Rusty—and this is for you too, Chris." Doc glanced briefly at his assistant harbormaster. "Connecting well establishes not only trust, but communication as well. Let me give you an example. Believe it or not, this camp is not just for fun and games. Are the activities and sports important? Of course they are. We want, we expect, everyone to have a superfun week here at Malibu. But everything we do here has a purpose. There's a subtle message behind our actions and our relationships here." Rusty looked somewhat confused and puzzled. "In other words, there's a kind of delicate plan taking place here, a faint balance between our program and our message of Christianity. It's like one big team or one big family. There has to be an honest, sincere, connection between all of you campers, the work crew, the staff, counselors, and the management. It's the engine that only works when all the necessary parts are in sync."

"Gosh, Doc. That's a lot to process and understand," Chris said, a little worried that Rusty was perhaps feeling overwhelmed with Doc's words.

"Yes, you're probably right, Chris. Maybe I have shared a little too much insight on our mission plan here at camp. But I have a strong feeling that you, Rusty"—Doc reached out and briefly grabbed one of Rusty's upper arms with his left hand—"are a smart guy with leadership qualities. And I wouldn't have opened up with you about all of this, except I have trust in you and feel that you are strong enough, in both mind and body, to understand and grasp what I have just shared with you." He let go of Rusty's arm and turned to Chris and said, "You too, Chris. Now, one last thing, Rusty."

"Sure. What's that, Doc?" Rusty asked with genuine interest.

"We're friends now, right?"

"Yeah, sure," Rusty answered with commitment in his voice.

"I want you to do me a favor," said Doc with conviction. "When you go to the evening club meetings, I want you to listen to what Chet has to say. I mean, really listen carefully. Allow his message to really penetrate your brain and thoughts. Promise me that you will try and understand and consider what he talks about, okay?"

"Okay, I will. I promise," Rusty spoke up quickly, hoping that Doc would truly trust him.

"With that said, I'm sure it's almost cabin time, and soon, bedtime. So, off you go. Chris, I'll see you at the shack in the morning. Rusty, thanks for stopping by. I appreciate it." With that, they said their quick goodnight to each other and went their own way.

CHAPTER 5

The Rain Dance

The weather at Malibu can certainly fluctuate during the course of the summer. If you attend camp in June, then you are more likely to experience some rain and cool breezes moving through the region. At times (though rare) the wind and freezing rain can be so violent that the entire camp inhabitants escape the wet, cold onslaught of damp, brutal weather by retreating to any nearby shelter the resort has to offer. Fortunately, these conditions do not occur often in June, since it can literally dampen the outdoor activities at the camp, something teenagers can certainly be frustrated and disappointed about. If there is an advantage to attending Malibu as a camper in June, it would have to be the fact that the beauty of the area during the beginning of the summer is enhanced by the amount of snow that is still present along the high peaks, such as One Eye and Sun Mountain. As the sun reflects off the white crystalline flakes covering the high elevations of the mountaintops, it becomes the icing on the cake with regard to beautiful scenery. The massive elevated earth creating this narrow inlet of sea, along with the snowcapped mountains, formulate this fiord, the Princess Louisa Inlet, into the most beautiful inlet in the world, as described by a travel writer in the 1960s. Whether or not high school teenagers consciously appreciate this unique beauty is debatable to some. One would like to think that they are aware of this exceptional design of creation. Perhaps not to the degree of adulthood, but that they do admire their different and distinctive surroundings. Regardless, summer is where it is at when it comes to playful conditions.

Winter in the northwest inlets of Canada is another story, with harsh cold for weeks on end. Even though Malibu's peninsula is at sea level, snowfall is not uncommon. August is, of course, the warmest time of the year, with temperatures reaching into the eighties, sometimes even the nineties. It is the best bet for warmer temperatures. Although, by then, the elegant, glistening snow will have all melted off the peaks that can be viewed from Malibu, as the frozen flakes liquefy and swiftly stream down the mountainsides, creating glorious, magnificent waterfalls for all to enjoy. July is generally the perfect month for consistent pastime, outdoor, recreational conditions. However, on this particular day, the camp was not experiencing typical July-like weather. The peak temperatures had risen into the upper eighties by the midafternoon hour. No wonder there were scores of campers gathered inside and outside the Totem Inn. Since one of teenagers' favorite pastimes, and cravings, was eating ice cream, it was not a great surprise that on an unusually hot day, these young people would be indulging, with comfort and bliss, this tasteful, creamy, frosty, delicious dessert. Offering a variety of flavors, the small inn was known for its homemade churned ice cream. Crammed and seated around one of several larger four-foot diameter, round, wooden green tables was Chris, Rusty, Fergie, Vic, Ken, and two of Rusty's Portland roommates. Lunch was recently served around the pool area, and the leisure time activities were not scheduled for a half an hour, thus allowing Chris a break from his harbor duties. When work crew and staff have an opportunity to visit and mingle with the campers, it is a favorable and serviceable experience encouraged by camp management. The underlying purpose and mission of Young Life is to promote and present the Christian faith, so what better way to express that than to show witness and friendship by forming relationships of interest with their young visitors. Sometimes, this can even be achieved by engaging in practical jokes! Who would be better to perform such undertaking than the prank-master himself—Englishman, Vic Hookums.

Vic had the "soot windmill" and handed it to Chris as he carefully winked at him, sending him the sign to play along. Just then,

Doc walked up from the dock area and dragged a chair behind Vic and Ken.

"Hey, guys," he said, as he sat down, already knowing what was about to happen.

Chris was examining the little black box, as if he had never seen it before, turning it over and reading what was printed on it. Vic spoke up, "Since you don't smoke, Chris, you should be able to really crank up the rpms on this baby." Chris was careful to place the "safe" blowhole in his mouth, as he started blowing hard. The windmill turned at a rapid pace. Rusty was watching with intense interest.

"Here, Rus," Chris said to him, "you're a smoker, see what you can do." He immediately pushed the windmill toward Rusty's face but, quickly and carefully, flipped it around so that the soot end was in position. No one noticed the "flip switch," including Rusty, who was eagerly ready to try it. "You'd better blow really hard," Chris continued. Vic, Doc, and Ken were all waiting with anticipation. Rusty took a deep breath and blew as hard as he could. The soot was instantly released and blackened his entire face, especially his eye sockets. Everyone was in hysterics. Rusty, somewhat stunned, was trying to look around at all the onlookers laughing at him, some even bent over in laughter. He spotted Fergie howling with laughter, which caused him to immediately start smiling and laughing himself as he tried to wipe the soot from his eyes with his shirt.

"Sorry, ol' buddy. I couldn't resist," Chris confessed, patting Rusty on the back.

"I gotta admit, you really got me," Rusty blurted out.

Handing Rusty some napkins from the table, Vic said to him, "Yea, hook, line, and sinker. That's the way we like it."

Julie and Beth appeared from the alleyway between the dining room kitchen and the Totem Inn. "What happened to you?" Julie asked Rusty as she noticed him wiping off the soot from his face.

"Here, blow into this," Rusty said to her as he shoved the windmill toward her mouth. Doc quickly grabbed the black box from Rusty's hand and said, "No way. You need to pass on this one, Julie."

Julie, with a curious look, said, "What is that thing?"

Handing the soot windmill back to Vic, Doc said to Julie, "I'll show you later."

With a confused look, she said, "Well, okay." Then changing the subject, she continued speaking, "So, Doc, that was a funny skit you performed last night. I see you've changed your lovely shirt."

"Yep," Doc answered with a smile as he checked out Julie in her amazing two-piece light-green swimsuit. "Why don't you ladies grab an ice cream or soda and join us?" he said with encouragement.

"Yea, I could use something cold to drink," Julie acknowledged.

"Julie, you should try that new Bear Tracks fudge flavor. It's amazing!" Beth eagerly suggested.

As the girls hurried through the open doors of the inn, Rusty said to Vic and Doc, "You two sure enjoy your mischievous pranks, don't you? And you're good at them, right, guys?" Everyone in close range of the question responded by either nodding their heads yes or by verbally blurting out, "Oh yea!"

"We'll take that as a 'practical joke professional' compliment, right, Doc? Ken?" Vic proudly engaged his deep accented voice, finishing with a broad smile and a twinkle in his left eye. Doc instantly agreed with a right-hand thumb raised at eye level.

Curious Rusty once again spoke up. "So, what other prankish stuff have you guys pulled here at Malibu?" Vic, Doc, and Ken (better known as Malibu's Three Amigos) looked at one another with quick deep thought.

Ken jerked his natural-wood chair forward closer to Vic and Doc and said, "Maybe we should tell them about Ron Hartland, last year in August . . . the drought."

"Oh yea!" Doc agreed. "That's a good one. What do you say, Vic?"

With his booming voice, Vic scanned the group of eager listeners and began the story. "It was the driest August we had ever experienced here at Malibu, at least during the four years Edna and I have been here. And yes, we were definitely in an unwanted drought. The area hadn't seen rain in almost four weeks." Julie and Beth returned and walked over to the group with ice cream and soda in hand. Doc turned to them and offered his chair to Julie while Ken did the same for Beth. The ladies immediately sat down, thanking the two gentlemen.

"What's going on?" Beth asked.

"Oh, Vic is telling a story about something that happened last summer," Doc explained as he politely moved Julie's chair closer to the table and Vic. "Listen up, you'll enjoy this." Doc placed his hands on the top back of Julie's chair and leaned his head down and over close to the back of her right shoulder, looking straight at Vic. Ken was standing up straight, like a soldier, with his arms folded across his chest. His most frequent stance.

Vic continued, "It wasn't that the lack of rainwater was affecting our ability to provide fresh water for the camp. That unlimited source comes from a steady waterfall located about fifty yards past the outer dock, along the Jervis Inlet. We pipe it over to camp. But normally we anticipate enough precipitation to fall during August to at least keep our golf course green and other vegetation watered around the resort. As I said, last August was much drier than normal, and it was the talk, and worry, of the camp . . . watching our fairways turn brown!"

Once again, Rusty popped up with a question. "Doesn't the golf course have a built-in sprinkler system?"

"No. When it was originally built in the forties—and by the way, the dirt and sand was shipped by barge from the Gold Coast south of us, to create the course. That entire side of the mountain was primarily granite and thick plant life, along with a forest of cedar trees. Anyway, Hamilton, the owner, opted not to install a sprinkler system, figuring that it wouldn't be a necessity, as Mother Nature would do her part. Not so last August!" Vic paused for a moment as he positioned his head down closer to Julie and then slowly moved his upper body around those sitting closest to him around the table, making sure that everyone around him was directing their full attention toward him. As he began to converse again in his crisp, low-pitched voice, his right eye at times closed partway, suggesting a sign of cunning behavior. Once again, he gave the impression of a pirate about to share his havoc plans of destruction against the crew of an unaware sailing vessel.

"Our intended, direct target, mates, was the camp manager, Tom Olson, who for days had been asking our staff and work crew to pray for much-needed rain. Ken, Doc, and I decided that the best way to create rain is by using the service of a professional rainmaker. In these here parts, that would be, of course, an Indian rain-dancer. Enter Ron Hartland, a full-blooded Cherokee Indian. Ron was on work crew and Doc's assistant that month. Listen up now, mates." He once again scanned the group, who had now moved in closer to him as they finished eating their ice cream cones and quietly slurped down their remaining ounces of soda. "When you pull a prank, you go all the way, and you do it right. There is no such thing as *halfway* or *try*, only *do* and *do right*, understand?"

Everyone again nodded their heads yes, or they spoke up with a positive "Right!" No one in their right mind would want to disagree with Vic, who, with his commanding voice and committed attitude, is slightly intimidating. He continued as the dozen, or so, listeners were focused and quiet, yearning to here the rest of the story.

"Our goal was not only to achieve the element of surprise, but to end with an astonishing, spectacular, unexpected finish. So here's what we did."

Julie turned her head around and glanced at Doc with a pleased, delightful smile. As he looked down at her and winked, she turned back around in earnest anticipation of Vic's tale of the rain dance.

"After Ron agreed to participate in our little plan, the first thing we had to do was provide him with the proper, authentic Indian attire."

"This wasn't a problem," Doc interrupted, "because we have access to some Sechelt outfits and artifacts that Mac has given Malibu over the years, including a full chief headdress and costume, right down to the deerskin moccasins."

"Yea, that's right," Ken dropped his folded arms and jumped into the conversation. "That was simple and easy. It was the *mechanics* of the prank that was a challenge for us, right, Vic?"

"That's exactly right," Vic answered with assurance and enthusiasm to continue sharing the story. "It's one thing to surprise Tom Olson, the camp manager, on the dining room stage, with an Indian rain dancer, but it's an entirely different objective to accomplish the task of the perfect practical joke. Are you following me?" Once again, most of the inn's audience signified with a yes—nodding their heads up and down or simply spoke out loud, "Yes!" "We had a difficult obstacle facing us," Vic continued. "Actually, before I explain that, let me first take you back and describe how it all went down—the event in real time."

"Again, listen carefully, everybody," Doc inserted a word of advice. "Go ahead, Vic."

"The camp had just finished lunch in the dining room, and Tom walked on to the stage and up to the microphone and once again made mention of the steadfast hot August weather, and just as we predicted, he pointed out the windows to the clear blue skies with no clouds in sight. Just then, from behind his back, Ron entered the room from the kitchen, outfitted in his full-dress Indian ward-robe, with a small leather-laced tan drum and stick in one hand. He slowly shuffled his way toward the stage. Everyone in the dining room, including staff and work crew, were taken by surprise by this unplanned, unusual circumstance happening." Vic's audience was intensely listening. "Not recognizing the Indian chief as Ron Hartland and not having a clue as to what was going on, campers began to stand, point, and giggle." Vic began to display his recollection of this humorous event with a broad smile of satisfaction, as did Doc and Ken. With some devious laughter in his voice, he continued to describe the scene from August past.

"Tom doesn't have any idea what's going on behind him until Ron reaches the back of the stage, stepped up on the platform, and joined the camp manager." Vic, along with several others in the group, started to laugh openly, no longer concealing their amusement. Making eye contact with those smirking and smiling, Vic said, "When Tom turned and looked at Ron, he was completely startled and bewildered. Ron immediately crossed his chest with his empty arm and announced out loud in a booming voice." Vic stood straight up from the table with perfect posture to further the dramatic moment of Ron's statement. "Me—skilled Indian rain dancer!' Tom then dropped to his knees in laughter. When he finally stood back up, he was so out of breath from laughing that he could hardly speak into the mic. He finally said, 'Did you hear that, gang? We have a rain-dancer to our rescue. Our prayers have been answered!' With an immense smile, he looked back at Ron and asked, 'I suppose you want me to beat this drum so you can perform your dance, right?' Ron stood there with perfect stilted posture, answering with a nod of his head, up and down, signifying a yes."

"I immediately placed a kitchen chair up on the stage from the back," Doc butted in, as everyone looked over at him.

"Tom then quickly sat down as Ron handed him the drum and drumstick," Vic jumped back into the story. "At once Tom started beating the drum with a fairly slow, methodical beat, as if he had practiced before time." Still standing, Vic certainly had the attention of all ears near him. "Understand, everybody, that Tom is quick to ad lib and play into the candid circumstance. He's a good sport, mates. Anyway, Ron began his rain dance—lifting his feet and bowing some as he turned his body around, chanting and moving his head slowly up and down, as we've all typically seen in the movies. Right, Doc?"

Without hesitation, Doc recognized Vic's hint and quickly began to dance the rain dance, imitating his friend Ron Hartland. Everyone howled with laughter. Julie turned in her chair toward Doc as she impulsively blurted out her distinctive, charming laugh. Doc continued his dance as Vic loudly announced, "And then—and here's the kicker, folks—without warning, and from straight over Tom's head, while Ron continued to beat the drum, a shower of water begins to spray, or rain down on him with alarming, immense force and promptly soaked him, as if he were taking a shower in his cabin!" Vic's audience was in almost disbelief and was now in major fits of laughter.

Rusty had to ask, "Water from over the stage? How did you do that?"

"We'll get to that in a minute," Vic said to him as he sat back down. Doc stopped dancing and moved back over above Julie, re-placing his hands on top of her chair. Vic started up again, "Because Tom knows how to gracefully play along with a practical joke, he purposely remained seated, looking straight out at everyone, with a blank stare, as if he were the comedian, Jack Benny . . . or as Ken here did last night in the Movie Skit! He continued to allow the wet water to engulf his clothing and body, as it streamed down his face, into his lap, and began forming a puddle on the stage floor. Then the water suddenly stopped, as did Ron's dancing. Tom stood up—his clothing dripping wet, and his face and hair soaked with cool fresh water. He stepped back to the microphone, which was front stage, away from the small puddle of water, and with confidence announced, 'We have rain!' He then turned toward Ron, bowing to him with hands flat together in front of his chest—like a Japanese citizen would honor a friend—thanking him for his assistance and expertise and creating rain. Everyone present began clapping and cheering," Vic said in a proud, pleased tone. "Am I right, gents?" he turned and asked Doc and Ken.

"Oh yea, and you should have seen the amused expressions on the faces of the staff, work crew, and counselors," Doc interjected. "It was priceless!"

One of the Portland boys spoke up, "I don't get it . . . how did you create the rainwater?"

"We had to plumb it," Vic quickly answered with obvious satisfaction.

"Plumb it?" Julie questioned with confusion.

"Yep!" Doc said to Julie, as she looked up at him. Ken and Vic spent an hour in the dining room installing a small plastic—"

"Synthetic neoprene," Ken quickly corrected Doc with his mechanical knowledge.

"Oh yea, neoprene pipe, that ran all the way from inside the kitchen, out and over the stage."

Vic spoke again. "We installed a showerhead, and once Ron began to dance, Doc signaled Ken, who was standing just inside the kitchen, watching him through the glass window in the door, who—in turn—signaled me to turn on the newly installed faucet, which was connected to our infamous water source mounted over the stage, and over the camp manager. Voila! Instant rainwater," Vic said, as he deeply laughed with the devious glance of a young schoolboy plotting to steal sweets out of the family cookie jar.

Ken moved closer to Vic's captured audience and added, "From planning to execution, it took us several hours to make it all happen."

Chris engaged his voice and asked the question, "You all spent that much time and work for only seconds of gratification and reward for your efforts?"

"Again, Chris," Vic was pleased to answer. "Here's the deal: if you're going to pull off the perfect stunt, you need to be willing to put some thought and energy into it. You don't just hastily make an unworthy attempt. You need to be eager to exert some time into the scheme."

Ken spoke up again, "In other words, be dedicated, don't do anything half—well, you know what I mean."

"Half-ass?" Rusty extensively shouted out. Once again, everyone suddenly broke into resounding laughter, including Ken, Doc, and even Vic.

Fergie jabbed Rusty with his left elbow. "Rusty!" he hollered out for everyone to hear.

"Oh, sorry," Rusty sheepishly replied, as he turned to his friends and enthusiastically proclaimed to his new buddies, "I can't wait for us to make some practical joke plans."

"No, you don't!" Chris grabbed Rusty's arm.

Many of the outside Totem Inn group were giggling, as Beth softly said to Julie, "Oh no."

"That's right, Rusty, do not participate or share in pranks here at Malibu. Leave that to all us crazed, professional, staff personnel," Vic instructed him with a commanding voice and his right index finger raised and waving at him, as if Vic was scolding a young child. Promptly changing the subject, he then turned to Doc, Ken, and Chris. "Well, men, we had better get back to work so that these young, fine people can have a fun, active day." With that, Chris immediately stood up out of his chair and looked at Doc.

Julie started to carefully pull her chair back, making sure she did not bang into Doc standing directly behind her. Standing, she said to Beth, "Yea, we'd better get going too."

"So, where are you girls off to?" asked Doc.

"We're heading over to the Totem Trader," Beth answered.

"Oh, that's right," Doc seemed to recall.

As everyone began to disburse the area in front of the inn, Julie turned to Doc and sweetly, but somewhat craftily, asked him, "Doc, would you tell me what this Totem Trader thing is all about? I'm sure you know."

"Can't. It's a secret. You'll find out soon enough." With her hands on her hips, she gave Doc a frustrated look of betrayal. Then she promptly smiled and winked at him as she turned and headed down Main Street with Beth. Doc, who at first could not pull his eyes away from Julie's lovely backside, finally gained his composure and walked over to Chris, who was engaged in conversation with Rusty and his friends.

"So, Chris, don't you have to meet over at the Totem Trader too?" Doc questioned him.

"Yea, I do. So come on, Doc, you can tell me what this is all about, right? What are we—"

"You'll find out," Doc interrupted him with a smile. "Go enjoy, and good luck." A bit reluctant, Chris said goodbye to everyone. "Later, guys. You too, Doc." He headed down the boardwalk, as Doc and the others left as well.

After the third evening of club in Big Squawka, friendships and personal bonding began to materialize. There was something about sitting on the colorful floor pads with new friends from your cabin and team. The teens were singing Young Life songs, laughing together at the humorous program director and his small group of staff comics, and finally having the opportunity to listen seriously to Chet talk about the life teachings of Jesus Christ. It was definitely a spiritual experience that was best shared with new friends. After the club meeting, campers were beginning to gather and form a cluster of teenagers on Main Street outside the Totem Trader's two large display windows. Obviously, something inside the windows had caught their attention. As they were looking up through the large sheets of clear glass, installed on both sides of the open front door (which provided the main entrance), the onlookers were talking, giggling, pointing, and aahing at what they saw. Just then, Doc and Ken entered the scene and politely squeezed their way through the dozens of kids.

They moved toward the window located left of the elevated door, which had two steps to allow entry. Wanting to get a glimpse of the scenery inside, they repeatedly tapped shoulders and politely said, "Excuse me!" "Sorry!" "Coming through!"

Soon they were close enough to the window, and they allowed several girls who were shorter to stand next to the glass so they too could view and enjoy the unusual exhibit inside. A grin formed on Doc's face as he quickly observed his assistant standing in the display window like a statue. A mannequin would be a more accurate description. Chris was modeling Malibu's latest fashion of Canadian clothing. He was wearing a colorful red-and-white sweater with a design of maple leaves sewn into the fabric worn across the chest and along one arm sleeve. Chris was definitely poised for ridicule from his peers. His heavy wool pants were solid bright red, as he sported black leather footwear and a white beanie-style wool cap. He was stiff as a board, with his left arm raised at arm's length. His index finger was pointing out the window at an imaginary object in the far distance. In his right hand was a pair of binoculars that he was holding down by his side. Behind him, from floor to ceiling, was a creative, beautiful, lifelike painted mural, depicting a scene of the Canadian outdoors, with snow-covered jagged mountaintops and tall high-elevation trees cloaking the landscape. There was also a painted alpine lake in the far distance of the colorful picture. The bright blue sky at the top, along with a few puffy clouds, certainly added to the scene. Chris remained steady and focused. Beside Doc and Ken, Rusty had pressed his way through the crowd—not so politely—anxious and determined to disrupt Chris's concentration of portraying the perfect anatomical model. Passing in front of, and then through the petite gals, he positioned himself next to the popular, entertaining window. He began waving and shouting, "Chris! Hey, Chris!" His plan didn't work. Chris remained in character, not even blinking an eye. Frustrated, Rusty slapped the window hard with his left open hand.

Ken instantly grabbed Rusty's left shoulder and sternly said to him, "Hey, cool it, Rusty, you could break the window. Not smart, pal!"

Wanting to defuse the incident, Doc said to Chris, "Notch it down, Rus, Ken's right."

Rusty withdrew his hand, but again turned toward the window, waved both arms over his head, as if he were signaling a rescue plane from a deserted island, and yelled, "Your mom wears combat boots, and I'm dating your little sister!" The crowd near the window broke into laughter. Ken and Doc looked at each other and shook their heads in frustration, but could not help but crack a faint smile themselves. To everyone's surprise, Chris still did not flinch. His arm and finger were still pointing, as if he were wearing some kind of brace to keep it stiff. There were not even signs of him breathing, since his chest did not appear to be moving, even in the slightest. He was performing his task well. Everyone was amazed. Doc was proud of him.

He and Ken began to move through the crowd of teens again, past the front entrance of the Trader, and over to the second large window on the right side. The crowd of kids was as much interested in who was occupying this display as they were with Chris and his spectacle. Doc and Ken again excused their rite of passage (common respect given to staff) to allow them to again gain access to be adjacent to the next presentation. Not surprised, Doc quickly inspected the contents of the window display and behold, there she was. Julie was standing alone inside the decorated space, as if she too were a mannequin. She was also modeling fashionable clothing available for purchase in the store. Wearing white shorts, white tennis shoes, and a multicolor short-sleeve top, she (like Chris) was staring out the window, as if focused on a unique, rare bird. With a camera in hand by her side, she sported a delightful smile as her long alluring blond hair was dancing in the breeze, cleverly created by a hidden portable fan mounted on the floor near her. The scene was enhanced and intensified by a background painted mural depicting a large flower-covered meadow with rolling green pastureland, beyond the grassland. A bright sun and the all-blue sky was drawn skillfully and shown above and to the left of Julie. Doc was intensely fixed on her. Gazing at her remarkable beauty, as she continued to stand absolutely still, wanting to achieve her goal of convincing her onlookers that she was, indeed, a mannequin—not of flesh and blood—but almost the replica of a wax human figure. But the truth be known, along with the crowd, Doc knew that this attractive young lady was alive and genuine. With a continued mesmerized expression on his face, it was fairly obvious that Doc was definitely infatuated with her. Ken glanced over at Doc and instinctively snapped his right fingers in front of Doc's face.

"Hello, Doc. This is planet Earth, come in." As if he was standing alone, without scores of campers surrounding him, gawking at Julie from outside the window, Doc almost seemed hypnotized. He spoke in a somewhat monotone voice. "She is so righteous." (*Righteous* was another word used often by teens in the midsixties to mean "perfect" or "awesome.")

"Well, I have to agree. She, without a doubt, is a fine-looking lady," Ken whispered back. "So what's your point, Doc?"

Gaining control of his feelings, he started to quietly explain his thoughts to Ken, "She's more than that." Just then, from inside the store, two work crew guys popped open one side of the canvas mural and stepped up into the window display. They carefully began picking Julie up, one wrapping his arms and hands around her legs and lifting her while the other muscular bulky gent held her from the back. She tried to stay as rigid as possible, wanting to continue to simulate a store mannequin. As they turned and began to move her away from the window, she made eye contact with Doc and winked at him. He impulsively winked back with a pleased smile.

"I saw that," Ken whispered directly into Doc's left ear. "What was that all about?" he said with obvious concern and suspicion written all over his face. As the two of them began carefully forcing their way back through, and away, from the crowd of teens, they headed down the granite steps next to Little Squawka toward the inner dock area. Only a step behind Doc, Ken gently grabbed Doc's right shoulder, causing him to stop. Doc turned around to Ken, who said, "Well?"

"I'm in trouble, Ken."

"Don't tell me . . . another Suzanne?"

"Worse. I'm really falling for her . . . she's perfect." Doc glanced around the area, making sure no one was within earshot. He even looked up at the Big Squawka deck above them to secure his worries of a possible eavesdropper in the vicinity. Then he softly placed his hand on top of Ken's shoulder, and with a beyond-serious, unmistakable expression of thought, he said to him, "Look at me, Ken. She's the princess I've been looking for. I know it."

Ken dropped his head down and, after just a few seconds, raised it back up and placed his hand on Doc's shoulder and said in a concerning voice, "Cool your jets and take a deep breath, buddy. You hardly know this girl."

"That's just it. I hardly know her, and yet, I know she's the one. There's something in my gut that draws me close to her. Not just because she is exceptionally good-looking, but I feel like we have a special bond. It's a mystery, Ken. I can't explain it." They both dropped their arms down off each other's shoulders as Ken rubbed and scratched his chin in a nervous, fidgety manner. Doc paused a moment and then, in an important, sober voice, asked Ken, "Would you secretly deliver a note to her from me? Please. I'd really appreciate it, pal."

"Oh, man, here we go again," Ken reluctantly responded. "I'm warning you, Doc, you'd better be cool about this. You know the consequences." He put his head down again and started shaking his head slowly back and forth, indicating his personal, honest feelings of uneasiness and concern.

"I know, I know," Doc reassured him with reluctant confidence. "I promise to be supercareful."

With a serious tone, Ken responded to Doc, "Besides being supercareful, perhaps you should look to the Lord and have a chat with Him about all of this. If you feel this passionate about this girl, Doc, then I think it would be wise to pray about it. Only the Lord can truly guide your heart."

"You're right, Ken," Doc said to him. "That's exactly what I'm going to do." And with that said, they continued over to the upper deck and then scrambled down the gangplank, Doc in front, as they both headed for the floating harbormaster shack, securely attached to the end of the long main dock.

CHAPTER 6

A Teenager's Challenge of Manhood

Joe Sheldon (Doc) was not always a "good guy." Before he entered high school, he had a short history of being in some considerable amount of trouble, which of course did not please his dad or his aunt (who was helping to raise him with her brother). When he was thirteen, attending junior high school, he met two brothers who had recently moved in down the street from his house in Oakland. Originally from Sacramento, Kevin and Steve Rogers's father was a California Highway Patrolman. He trained as a CHP officer at a facility near the state's capital. While in the city of Oakland, he rode a bulky Harley Davidson motorcycle on the job and worked the swing shift. Sometimes he would give his sons rides around the neighborhood, and a couple of times he even allowed Joe to sit behind him on the loud two-wheeled vehicle as they sped along the black paved roads near their homes. He was a good and honest man, a divorced father raising his two sons alone. Unfortunately, his two boys had a devilish demeanor about them. Kevin was the oldest and attended ninth grade while his brother, Steve, was a year behind him, the same grade as Joe. The young Doc was six months older than Steve, which classified him as a midtermer—proving to be a positive factor later on when he began playing high school football. It was not long after Joe's relationship with his newfound friends that he joined them in a number of mischievous events. First there was the smoking of cigarettes during his year one as a teenager. Joe quickly learned how to carefully steal them—a few at a time—from his dad's carton of Marlboros, something the brothers had been doing with their dad since they were twelve and thirteen. There was an old abandoned house up the block from Joe's house that the three buddies would often hang out in and puff on the tobacco, trying to look cool and feel older. Sometimes they would play poker as well.

A few months went by, and following Kevin's lead, the three boys began stealing some food at the neighborhood market, near the junior high school, located three miles from Joseph's community of modest homes. The items they stole, with capable, proficient skill, were low-valued articles, such as packages of cheese and baloney. Something three young hungry teenage boys could munch on during their frequent visits to their makeshift hideaway, at the old abandoned structure on the dirt lot nearby their homes. Nevertheless, it was still stealing, certainly a moral infraction that Joe was taught never to do by his dad and aunt. It was even one of the Ten Commandments, for heaven's sake. Kevin's ingenious plan as to how to carefully steal the tasty goods without being caught was to have one of the three juveniles distract the old Chinese man behind the cash register by simply talking to him or by purchasing some cheap candy. Then the other two bandits would raid the cold cuts cooler in the back of the store, stuffing packages of sliced meat and cheese down their shirts and back pockets hidden beneath their shirttails. Successful thieves for about two months, repeating their grocery store distraction routine, and by rotating the distracter, Joe gained enough confidence to move it up a notch and steal something of a little more value.

One warm Saturday afternoon during the summer, before starting eighth grade, he was in downtown Oakland and stopped by the 5 & 10 Cent Store with his aunt, who was shopping for 'ladies' undergarments, something Joe certainly did not want to be part of. Perusing through the Top Forty record department, he came across a number of 45 rpm singles that he really wanted, but was not willing to part with his meager cash for them. Even though he had a paper route, delivering the daily *Oakland Tribune* near Lake Merit, the money he earned for that low-wage job, he put into a savings account so that someday he could buy a car, his dream in life. Although that day, the temptation was too much for him. The song hits were among his all-time favorites, including "Rock Around the Clock" by Bill Hailey and the Comets, "Lil Darlin'" by the Diamonds, "At the Hop" by Danny and the Juniors, "Chain Gang" by Sam Cooke, "Splish Splash" by Bobby Darin, and "Don't Be Cruel" by Elvis Presley. Alone, and a tiny bit scared, he had just enough confidence and courage to be up for the challenge of swiping a half dozen 45 rpm records. His aunt had left him in the store to shop next door for other items she was looking for.

"So, why not?" he asked himself silently. "I can pull it off. I don't need the Rogers brothers to back me up." He waited until the store aisle of the hit recorded songs was bare of shoppers and onlookers. It was time to make his move. He rapidly pulled out the six, individually wrapped, 45 vinyl circular records, the ones he had already previously gathered together and placed them all in one slot in a section closest to the isle, ready for removal. This way all he had to accomplish was to shift them from the metal display holder in to the front of his underwear, the perfect hiding spot. Soon it was mission accomplished! Joe had successfully snatched the goods and placed them securely down his front pants and inserted all six into his white undershorts. Now it was time to gracefully escape the scene, but not too fast, as that could possibly cause suspicion by the store clerks working in the vicinity. He walked normally along the row of 45 rpm records and dozens of LPs (long-playing twelve-inch vinyl records) stacked upright in alphabetical order for sale and then sauntered over to the center aisle of the store, which led to the main front doors. Showing some nervousness, his heart started beating rapidly, and his face became flush with a reddish illumination. The last twenty-five feet of the floor, before reaching the outside sidewalk of freedom, seemed like the length of a football field. Now his eyes were fixed on the two wide metal-framed doors. All he had to do was to push one open and cross the threshold. But moments later, just as he was exiting the doorway, and taking an enormous sigh of relief, suddenly and without warning, a hulking hand grabbed his right shoulder, stopping him in his tracks. At first Joe was tempted to try and pull away and run, but then he thought that perhaps he was being detained for a different reason than stealing. Besides, how would anyone know he had lifted the records, since he was extremely careful and watchful, making sure that no one was observing him pillage the 45s? As the towering, broad man in a security guard uniform spun him around, Joe realized he was facing a sizeable person, who was not about to let him run. He immediately focused on two things: (1) the guard's bright shiny silver badge and (2) the displeasured expression on his weathered face looking down on him. As the middle-aged officer forced him back inside the store, he pulled Joe aside and said to him sternly, "You can either voluntarily pull those 45s out of the front of your shorts, or I'll reach in and grab them out myself. Which way do you prefer it?" Without hesitation, Joseph pulled up his shirttails, held up the top of his pants with one hand, and reached down inside his underwear with his other, retrieving the half dozen records.

"But, how did you know?" he quickly asked the guard with a baffled look.

"Do you see that gadget up on the ceiling over there?" pointing at an instrument mounted near the ceiling, in a corner of the store. "That's a camera! And behind that dark small window up there, in the back, is our security room—with a bird's-eye view of our entire sales floor." Spotting both the camera and the window, Joe guiltily dropped his head down, knowing that he had been caught redhanded. While being escorted and marched through the store with dozens of shoppers and sales personnel staring at him in disgrace, he already began thinking about the consequences. *What will Dad and Aunt think? What will they do to punish me? What about the store . . . the law? What's going to happen to me? Am I going to jail?* He silently asked himself. As the guard was holding on to his upper left arm, guiding him up the wooden circular stairway, which led to the second-floor security room, Joe's thoughts suddenly shifted to feeling so stupid and for convincing himself to be so overconfident and cocky. He knew he could not turn back the clock. He was truly in trouble!

While climbing the stairs with the detective, all he could hear was the echoing sounds of the guard's handcuffs clanking against each other. Noticing the tall man's holstered revolver, Joe could not help but think, *I'm sure glad he didn't shoot me as I was walking out the front door!* After being questioned by the officer, regarding his name, address, age, school, and grade he attended—and his parents' names—Joe was left sitting alone to ponder his horrible situation. With two other guards in the small dimly lit room, he noticed the arresting officer talking on the phone, across the way. He was too far away from the security guard to clearly hear the conversation, as several minutes passed by.

Is the security guard already talking with local police about having me transferred to Juvenile Detention Hall? Joe thought. At least twenty minutes had passed, and no one had said another word to him, not even the guy who caught him. In fact, that guard who arrested him had been off the phone now for almost that same amount of time.

I wonder what's going on, Joe was thinking. Suddenly, from the steps that he had earlier entered the room from, in walked his dad and his aunt. As they both quickly looked over and glared at Joe, the hulky officer walked over and greeted them both with a handshake. It was not long after, perhaps fifteen minutes, that Joe found himself in his father's car, as they were driving back to the family home. His aunt was in her car following them. As it turned out, the security guard who arrested Joe and placed him in custody knew Joe's dad, James Sheldon, from the gun store that James owned in town. He had recently purchased his revolver from James, which is why he called him on the phone. He figured out that Joe was James's son. Joe knew that he had dodged a bullet because the officer allowed him to go free as a favor to James. Although Joe's dad agreed with the guard that if his son was to ever get picked up again for shoplifting, he would make sure that he was sent to Juvenile Hall.

While Joe's dad was furiously lecturing him in the car, Joe awkwardly asked him, "Why didn't I just ride with Aunt Lois? Don't you have to go back to the shop?"

"No. I'm done for the day. Roy is taking care of things," his dad said to him with an angry tone. "We have some business to attend to once we get home, son." Joe sat quietly during the rest of the short journey home. He knew he was in big trouble with his dad and aunt. When they arrived, he was told to sit at the kitchen table. As his aunt started preparing some food for dinner, James sat down next to Joe and placed a brown, closed paper bag in front of his son.

"Open it," he said with a stern tone. Joe reached into the bag and pulled out the short stack of six 45 rpm records that he had stolen.

"He let you keep the records?" Joe asked his father.

"Of course he did. I paid for them. That was part of the deal." James then got up from the table, reached into a kitchen drawer, and pulled out a steel hammer. He handed it to Joe and said to him, "Now, stick those back in the bag, and then you know what you need to do, right?"

"You want me to use this hammer to smash the records? You're kidding me, right, Dad?"

"Do I look like I'm kidding you?" his dad said with another stern look.

"But, Dad . . . these are brand-new . . . great records . . . top forty singles. That would be such a waste, right? I'll pay you for them."

"I am not going to ask you again. Use the hammer. Now!"

Slowly shaking his head in disbelief, Joe shoved the records into the bag, raised the hammer over the container, and as soon as he closed his eyes, his arm came down with a quick blow, striking the bag and smashing the records inside. It was a loud bang as the hammer crunched the vinyl 45s and then hit the sturdy wooden table.

"Are you happy now?" Joe said as he turned to his dad.

"Don't be a smart-mouth with me, son. You're the one who is responsible for this outcome. Now, after you put this bag of shattered records in the trash, I want you to sit back down here. We're not done." When Joe sat back down as instructed, his dad continued, "Now, we're going to discuss your punishment for this act of misbehaving . . . this embarrassing and disgusting action of theft!" Joe sat there knowing that whatever his dad had planned for him, it was not going to be pleasant. His aunt was surely listening to her brother, even though she was trying to look busy and distracted as she prepared the upcoming meal.

"Do you remember last week when I discovered that the breaker in the basement popped off and shut down the freezer for days?" James asked Joe.

"Yeah, I remember."

"Well, as you know, all the frozen food I had stored in there was spoiled, including pounds of venison from my last hunt. Plus, all the other food-stuff that was stocked up in there. It all thawed, and I wasn't aware of it. Now it's a big smelly mess that needs to be cleaned up. That's where you come in, my son. You are going to go down there and remove all that gross, ghastly, rotten meat and stuff from the freezer." Joseph was again slowly shaking his head and looked like he was going to vomit. His aunt was hiding her pleased smile from him, as she obviously was happy with her brother's disciplinary action.

"Then, after you've disposed of all that sickening junk, you're going to clean all the freezer compartments out with hot, soapy water and disinfectant. I mean a major scrub inside and out. It needs to be pristine when you're finished, got it? I want to be able to use that freezer again in the future." Joe was still sitting there with his head down and with his hands covering his face.

He looked up and said, "Is that it? Can I go now?"

"No. We're still not done."

Joe was thinking, *Oh great! Now what?* His dad started up again, as his sister continued to listen as well.

"This is actually good timing since I was about to talk to you regarding another issue that I have recently uncovered." Joe started squirming in his chair, wondering what it is that his dad could possibly be talking about. "I have come to realize, with your aunt's help, that you have decided to become a smoker, am I right?" Lois turned from the kitchen counter and looked directly at her nephew.

Figuring at this stage that he had better not lie, Joe answered his dad with a simple, "Yes."

"Well, I'm not surprised, since I've discovered that some of my cigarettes have been missing from my Marlboro pack. So you want to be a smoker, huh? You think it makes you feel older, do you? And your aunt's been smelling smoke on your clothes for a while now. You want to be a tough guy, is that it?" Joe was once again too embarrassed to look straight at his dad's face. "Well, I would like to see how you look as a smoker. It turns out that I still have seven cigarettes left in this pack. So, here's the deal. Since you like smoking so much, you're going to sit here in front of me, and your aunt, and smoke all seven smokes. Got it?" A short while later, Joe was on his fifth cigarette and was obviously not feeling so well. "Come on, son, I know you can drag 'em down quicker than that. Be a man. Suck those things harder. I want to see how cool you can look." Joe was coughing and hacking as he sucked and blew the smoke into the air. The kitchen was beginning to look like a fogbank, hovering over the Golden Gate Bridge. Even James and Lois were having a hard time not being affected by the thick smolder of fire and smoke. After Joe finished the seventh cigarette, he was holding his stomach, as if to prevent a possible sickness from exiting his mouth.

James turned around to his sister and, with a grin, looked back at Joe and said, "Oh, we're not done. Since you want to be such a big shot, I think you should advance your game and enjoy a nice big fat cigar! What do you think?"

Having difficulty talking, Joe looked at him and dreadfully asked, "Are you kidding me, Dad?"

"Oh, no. I'm not kidding. I'm going to share with you one of my prized cigars given to me by a friend who happens to be a police-man—a CHP to be precise." Joe knew he was speaking of Kevin and Steve's dad and wasn't about to tell his dad that it was his two friends who had got him started smoking. No way was he going to be a snitch and get his buddies in trouble. James reached in a kitchen drawer and pulled out a sizeable, long cigar wrapped in clear plastic. He then told his son to unwrap it, bite off the end, and stick it in his mouth. Reluctantly, Joe did as he was told, as his dad removed a match from the same box he was using to light the cigarettes. James struck the stick match and ignited the end of the stout cigar. Joe immediately started hacking with a violent cough as large amounts of heavy, dark smoke filled the room.

"Oh, come on, son. Inhale that, bad boy! Don't just suck on it like a baby!" James said to Joe with a smirk.

It took twenty minutes for Joe to finish smoking the large black smelly cigar. His face was a shade of green, as he finally could not stop himself from vomiting all over the table and into his lap. Lois had already vacated the area since the smoke was too much for her to deal with. James handed his son a couple of kitchen towels and told him to clean everything up and then take a shower and lie down. He went on to say to him that he could wash and clean the freezer tomorrow after he attended church with his aunt, something James does not engage in since he does not think he believes in God.

The next day, Joe spent his entire afternoon scrubbing and cleaning the putrid freezer. Several times, he almost (once again) vomited as he removed and washed the storage unit. His only savior was wearing a bandana with Vaseline smeared on the part of it covering his nose. At least that helped to cut down the awful smell. One would think that this experience of punishment and embarrassment would cure Joe of misbehaving, but to his family's surprise, he wasn't done.

One Saturday afternoon in the fall, while his dad was on a hunting trip with a friend, Joe, along with his pals Kevin and Steve, made another poor decision. Joe's aunt Lois was enjoying some time with a friend, attending a play in San Francisco. The three boys were bored and wanted some excitement in their lives, so Kevin came up with the not-so-brilliant idea of, "Hey! Let's borrow your aunt's car and go for a joyride."

"You mean, steal my aunt's car? You can't be serious, Kevin," Joe quickly responded.

"Sure, why not? What's the big deal? I'm sure I can drive it just fine."

"You're only fifteen. Are you kidding me? Have you ever driven a car?" Joe asked him with serious concerns.

"Of course I have. Well, actually, it wasn't a car. It was my uncle's tractor on his ranch in Livermore, but it's basically the same thing."

"Really? Hmm! I'm not sure about this," Joe said to Kevin with hesitation.

"Oh, come on, Joe. It'll be fun! I know my brother can handle your aunt's sedan—no problem," Steve said with complete confidence and enthusiasm.

Kevin slapped Joe on the back. "Come on, buddy. We'll have a blast!"

Fifteen minutes later, Kevin was behind the wheel of the black Chevy as he backed the car out of the driveway. Joe was sitting in the front passenger seat, while Steve had the entire backseat to himself. To Joe's surprise, Kevin actually drove the car fairly well and safe, although there were times that he definitely was driving over the speed limit. They drove out of their neighborhood and around Lake Merit, located only a couple of miles from their homes. Sticking their heads out the window, Joe and Steve were hollering at pedestrians and girls who were walking along the lake path, nearby the road they were traveling on. After about an hour, they safely returned to Joe's home, where Kevin pulled the car back into the garage, behind the house. The three friends certainly chalked up the occurrence as one of the best times ever.

The next evening, when James returned home from his short hunting trip, his sister pulled him aside in the living room while Joe was upstairs in his bedroom. Soon thereafter, James hollered up to Joe to come downstairs. Once again, sitting at the infamous kitchen table, where Joe had smoked for over forty-five minutes in a sickening, smoke-filled environment, James told his son to sit down. Also sitting at the table was his aunt Lois, with her arms crossed, as if there was a problem involved.

"I'm going to ask you a question, Joe, and I want the honest truth. Don't lie to me!"

Joe, once again, fidgeting in his chair, was wondering what this was all about and simply answered, "Okay."

"Did you take your aunt's car for a drive yesterday while she was in San Francisco? Be careful. I wouldn't be asking if we weren't suspicious or we didn't have proof."

Joe, biting his bottom lip and looking around the room, finally spoke up. "Yes, we did."

"We did? Who's *we*?" his aunt asked with anger in her voice.

"Oh, well . . . my friends . . . Kevin, Steve, and me, we just took a short little drive around the neighborhood."

"Really?" James responded. "So let me get this straight. You and your pals, Kevin and Steve, stole your aunt's car. Is that correct?"

"Well, we just . . . kind of . . . borrowed it."

"No, you stole it and drove it without my permission. And you're only fourteen!" Lois said loudly to her nephew, as she promptly stood up from her chrome kitchen chair.

"But Kevin's fifteen . . . he drove."

"So now you're telling me that you allowed your crime buddy, Kevin, to drive your aunt's car? Are you kidding me! He doesn't know how to drive. And he doesn't have a license!"

"He drove fine! We didn't crash or get pulled over or nothing. We just took a short drive, that's all."

"So you don't think anything's wrong with you boys doing that?" his dad asked.

"Well, I wouldn't say that . . . yeah, I guess we were wrong to take her car, but . . . it was just an innocent ride. We didn't pick up any other friends."

James slapped his hands on the table. "You're lucky you didn't get pulled over. Do you know what could have happened? Not to mention if Kevin had hit another car or ran some pedestrian over. Did you ever think about that?"

"No, I guess not. I'm confused though. I mean . . . how did you figure it out? We were careful to put the car back in the garage, where it was parked."

"When your aunt went to church this morning, she noticed that the emergency brake wasn't engaged. She always pulls the brake handle up in the garage. She also found a candy wrapper in the back seat. And she noticed the mileage was more than what she had written down on Friday, the last time she drove the car. She's been keeping track to check her gas mileage. There was an additional twenty-three miles clocked on the speedometer."

Joe, dropping his head back down toward his lap, straightaway covered his face with his hands and, in a whisper, said, "Crap!"

"Well, I guess you know what this means. More punishment! Lois, it's your car. Do you want to do the honors?"

"Absolutely," she answered without hesitation.

"Great. I suppose you're going to ground me for a week," Joe said to his aunt, shaking his head in displeasure.

"Oh, no! I wouldn't do that." Immediately, Joe had a relieved look on his face.

"Well?" James asked his sister. "What's the penalty these days for stealing a family car?"

"Oh, that's easy. Joe is going to be my best friend for a week. He is going to do everything I do. Whether it's cleaning the house or watching my TV shows or washing and ironing all our clothes, helping me cook, and doing the dishes, he's going to do it with me. Oh, we're going to have lots of fun together, trust me!"

Joe had dropped his head in disbelief, with his hands flat across each side of his face. Looking back up, he addressed his aunt, "You're not serious, are you?"

"Of course I am—dead serious. And I'm not finished. As a little added chore, you and I are going to wash and wipe clean every window in our house. Inside and out! You're going to be on a ladder, outside, while I'm cleaning the same window inside, making sure you're doing a perfect job. What do you think about that?"

Joe looked pathetically over at his dad, who had a grin from ear to ear. All Joe could blurt out was, "Ahhh!"

The seventh, and final, day of the week of being his aunt's best friend, helping her tackle scores of chores, they were now working hard on washing the house windows. James was at the shop working, and just like Lois had told Joe, he would be working outside while she was cleaning the same window so as to make sure he was cleaning every little spot on the outside of the framed glass. Maybe because he had much respect for his aunt and because they were quite close during his years of growing up—or perhaps it was sinking in that she was an amazing, dedicated aunt, helping her brother to raise his son after the tragedy of his wife (Joe's mother) dying from a drowning boat accident—Joseph somehow was forgetting the punishment part of his task to clean the windows, and even the intense labor of washing every pane of glass in the entire house. While they both were working on an upstairs window, and Joe was carefully balancing himself on a ladder, he started making funny faces at his aunt. She immediately responded by laughing and poking her thumbs in her ears while at the same time sticking her tongue out at him and crossing her eyes. Joe at once crossed his eyes and licked the window with his tongue. The two of them were laughing so loud, Lois started to worry about Joe falling off the ladder, so she stopped and just waved and smiled at him. Joe, smiling back, then kissed the window and said loudly, "That's for you, my tyrant aunt!" She smiled as she quickly blew her nephew, whom she adored, a kiss.

That was a major breakthrough for the two of them as it was the beginning of Joe showing his caring love and admiration for his aunt. Their relationship had grown and improved. Joe was starting to mature.

Six months later, he would face an important turning point in his life. One Saturday evening, after dinner, Joe approached his dad, who was sitting on the couch watching television. He said to him that he had just gotten off the phone with Kevin and was wondering if he could go for a ride with him and his brother. Kevin had recently attained his California driver's license and got permission from his dad to borrow the car to go to a friend's house for a while.

It did not take long for James to tell his son, "No. I don't want you going out this late. Besides, I'm still not comfortable with you driving around with Kevin and Steve. Sorry, but I'm just not convinced that they're trustworthy to hang out with. Especially Kevin driving around the neighborhood."

"But, Dad, we're just driving a short way to Matt's house. We're just going to play some records and stuff."

"My answer is no, and that's final. Do you understand?"

"I guess so, whatever." Joe, obviously disappointed, headed for the wall phone in the kitchen to telephone his friend that he could not go. It was not so much that James didn't trust his son, but that he truly was still concerned about Kevin and Steve's intentions. Were they really just driving over to a friend's house nearby? Or were their real plans to drive down to Lake Merritt, to the popular drive-in hamburger place, near the lake. The young attractive waitresses were on roller skates as they serviced their parked customers. The featured item on the menu was a normal-size delicious hamburger for only nineteen cents! Were they hoping to hook up with a crowd of bored teens on a Saturday night? *Or perhaps hooking up with the wrong crowd?* he thought.

As it all turned out, no was an absolute blessing and a correct decision that his dad made for Joe that evening! Kevin and Steve, without their pal Joe, took the drive anyway that night. But they did not go to Matt's house, as they had told their dad. Instead, Kevin decided to test his driving on the long curvy road located on top of the Montclair hills, a distance above their neighborhood. This ten-mile stretch of dangerous road snaked among the tall pine trees of the secluded ridge of land, owned and occupied mostly by city and state parks. A few miles down the road heading south, Kevin picked up speed, wanting to prove to his brother that he was an outstanding driver, with his vision to someday become a race car driver. The car started skidding as it entered some of the tight turns that Kevin was trying to navigate. Admitting later that evening that he had frightened Steve with his erratic, amateur driving skills, he eventually had driven into a turn too fast. It was a tight, hairpin turn, which he could not handle with his lack of driving experience. His dad's Ford sedan speedily slid off the road and down the side of a steep cliff, crashing into the trunk of a solid redwood tree. Kevin suffered a broken leg, some bruised ribs, and a severe laceration on his head. His brother, Steve, died in the horrible, pointless crash.

When Joe, James, and Lois heard about the awful tragedy the next morning, they were so thankful that Joe had not taken the ride with them and that his dad had firmly told him that he did not have permission to join his friends. Joe broke down in tears as he embraced his dad with grateful feelings, something the two of them rarely did since James was not particularly an emotional, hugging-type person. After that terrible incident, Joe stayed away from associating with Kevin.

Over the past several years, going further back in time—from when Joe was in his last year of grammar school—he had never had a problem meeting and establishing relationships with girls. Considering his handsome appearance and his sociable personality, he had already had a number of girlfriends and young, uncomplicated relationships, none of which had been too serious. The only risky and momentous sexual occurrence that he encountered was with a girl in the tenth grade of high school, when he was fifteen. Her name was Bonnie O'Brien, and they had been going steady for several months when she coaxed him into the little hay barn, where she boarded her horse, on the local private ranch near the school campus. Her horse, Beauty, was a gift from her prosperous parents, who resided in the Montclair District of the Oakland hills, which was a wealthy residential neighborhood, with spectacular views of the San Francisco Bay Area. The horse was a nice-looking, brown-and-white paint. Bonnie was a cute petite redhead who was an amorous flirt, and continued for the longest time to engage in her physical desire with her boyfriend, Joe.

That particular cool afternoon in late November, Joe did not show up for football practice, and the ranch manager assumed Bonnie was not able to ride that day. Sneaking through some broken boards of the whitewashed, five-foot wood fence (which surrounded the twenty-seven acres of the horse ranch), the two young teenagers quietly entered the property from behind the barn. Knowing exactly where the side door was located, Bonnie grabbed Joe's hand, and without delay, the two quickly ran over and entered the sheet metal building. Like a classic scene in a Western movie, they were both giggling with muffled sound as Bonnie impatiently pushed Joe into a stall of fresh piled hay. As he landed on his backside into the fresh-cut crop of golden strands of hay, he glanced up at the inside wall of the barn and spotted a large pitchfork secured to the wall of the simple structure. Happy that no such piercing tool was hidden beneath the large pile of hay he lay in, he welcomed Bonnie as she leaped upon him. They quickly and savagely embraced, rolling in the hay, as so often described in romantic Western novels. It was not too long before Bonnie had lip-locked Joe, and they began passionately kissing, as they smothered each other with clasping arms. Still giggling, Bonnie stopped and pulled her powder-blue sweater up and over her head, tossing the garment to the side, like a baby would discard a pacifier. Without hesitation, Joe reacted by pulling off his long-sleeve dark-blue cotton shirt. Now, with his bare chest exposed, he gently embraced Bonnie, and as she kissed the side of his neck, he at once became physically aroused as his young male hormones ignited. She grabbed his right hand and guided it around her back to her bra-strap, obviously hinting for him to unlatch the white cotton brassiere, which would expose her young breasts for him to caress. He started to fumble with the delicate latch fastening the tight bra-strap in place, when suddenly his conscience got the better of him.

In an instant, he could hear a voice in his head warning him and angrily scolding him with expressions of guilt-causing conscious-ness. The voice he heard was his aunt Lois: "Be smart, don't be stu-pid!" He could hear her saying to him, "Don't let your emotions dic-tate and control your life! Don't let bad judgment ruin your future! Remember, Joe, there are consequences in life! And don't let some girl allow you to get her pregnant! You'll regret it forever!"

In a flash, Joe could hear these words resonating in his mind. Suddenly, without warning, he dropped his hand and pulled away from Bonnie. For a moment, he stared at her. He still could not help but notice her alluring, seductive body with his eyes, but then with-out further hesitation, he said to her in a lucid voice, "I am so sorry, Bonnie, but I can't do this."

With a disappointed gaze, she responded to him, "Why not? Don't I excite you?"

"Of course you do, but I just can't do this . . . not now," Joe said convincingly and with confidence as he reached for his shirt. Perplexed and upset, Bonnie promptly pulled on her sweater and quickly dashed out the side door of the barn. Joe sat in the pile of hay for several minutes, pondering what had just happened and why he was so quick to end such a satisfying and arousing moment in his young life.

In the end, he had no regrets. During Bonnie's senior year, she got pregnant, but not by him. Rumor had it that the baby was con-ceived in the little hay barn. Joe never told a soul about his encounter with Bonnie that day. He had too much respect for her as a young, playful fun girl who required a great amount of physical attention. He also had respect for himself and embraced his privacy.

When Joe was a sophomore in high school, he met a new friend in his gym class; his name was Ricky Riggins. He was a really nice kid who had an exceptionally pleasant, loving family. Ricky and Joe hit it off right away since they both were interested in sports and soon played on the school football team together. They spent many weekends hanging out since James and Lois were impressed with Ricky's good behavior and polite manners. Either Lois would drop Joe over at Ricky's house, or Ricky's older brother, Bobby, would take his younger brother to Joe's house for the day, or sometimes for an overnight. It wasn't long before Joe became a friend of Bobby's as well, who was in his first year of college. Bobby treated Joe with respect and interest, and as time went on, Bobby took him under his wing, as if he were like another younger brother. Later that spring, Bobby took his brother and Joe waterskiing for a weekend to a nearby lake, not far from the Bay Area. Joe had already learned to ski when he was only eleven because his dad had a boat, and they would spend ten days camping and skiing every summer at Shasta Lake, in upper Northern California. Bobby was quite impressed with how well Joe could ski. In fact, Joe could even "trick-ski," which of course surprised Ricky as well. Neither Bob nor Ricky had ever seen anyone ski backward before on one ski. They were absolutely amazed at Joe's skill on the water. His boating ability was remarkable as well. At a young age, Joe was lucky, because one summer at Shasta Lake, a neighbor camper happened to be a professional skier at a popular water park in Vallejo, California (in the north bay), and that week he taught Joe some skiing tricks, including how to ski backward out of the water. Joe not only enjoyed many sports, but was fortunate to be a natural athlete.

Before the school year was out, Bobby had talked his brother, Ricky, and Joe, into attending a club that he belonged to for a couple of years called Young Life Club. Bobby became a volunteer leader after attending the club his senior year. Ricky had heard about it, but wasn't that interested until one day Joe said to him, "Hey! Let's check it out. If your brother, Bobby, likes it, I'm sure it's a cool thing, right?

Besides, I understand from others at our school that a lot of girls go to Young Life. It might be a good place to meet some ladies and hang out. Your brother says it's really lots of fun." So Ricky and Joe started attending Young Life Club with Bobby, who was their ride to the meetings. Bobby was right, it was loads of fun, and indeed, Joe and Ricky did meet some nice, fun girls at the club and Young Life activities. But beyond all the fun and games, the two friends soon realized that there was a deeper message Young Life shared, the message of the Christian faith and how it was possible for everyone to have a relationship with our Savior, Jesus Christ. This did take awhile for Joe and Ricky to grasp, but after hearing the many messages spoken at the club meetings by the head leader, they began to seriously listen and consider the historical life of Jesus, His teachings and who He really was, as they shared from the gospels of the New Testament in the Bible. The club leader had a special gift of explaining and sharing this crucial information with humor, but with conviction. His personal strong belief in the Christian faith and this ability to communicate with teenagers soon had an effect on Joe and his personal thoughts and feelings toward the meaning of life and how he interpreted his own faith. The results of these significant and enlightening club messages, along with witnessing the joy and unshakable belief of his fellow peers, was enough for him to pray and ask the Lord into his heart. In time, he knew the Holy Spirit would fill his heart with great love, and it was so.

Although it took Joe's friend Ricky a longer time to accept Jesus as his Savior, in time, this would become his reality as well, which overjoyed his big brother, Bobby.

While attending the Young Life Club meetings, Joe and Ricky also learned of the many camps that Young Life owned and operated during the summer. One day Bobby approached Joe and shared his personal experiences working for two summers at one of the unique Young Life camps, which was located in British Columbia, Canada. As it turns out, Bobby was Malibu's water ski instructor. He told Joe that this coming summer he was not going to be able to work at Malibu because he was traveling to Australia with a friend for the entire summer and had some work lined up there. He suggested to

Joe that perhaps he should apply for the water ski instructor position at Malibu. He certainly had the skills and knowledge to be a successful trainer. Bobby went on to say that he would gladly write a letter of recommendation to the property manager, who is also responsible for hiring staff to operate the resort.

Joe was extremely excited about the possibility of landing this prestigious position at Young Life's Malibu Club in Canada. He approached his dad and aunt about it, and they were open to the idea, having respect for Bobby and being pleased that Joe was interested in working at a Young Life Camp. Being a Christian-based organization that reaches out to high school–aged teens, Joe's dad, and mostly his aunt, felt this could be a good opportunity for Joe. Even though James was still confused about his thoughts of God, he knew that this group of kids and leaders would have standards of good conduct, and be a safe environment for his son. It wasn't long before Joe received his answer in the mail from Canada. With the help of Bobby's letter and positive recommendation from his Young Life local leader, Joe was accepted for the position of Malibu's new water ski instructor, during the upcoming summer, before his senior year. His dad and aunt had never seen him so excited and happy to be chosen for this exclusive position, working at a secluded, self-contained resort in a foreign country.

What they did not realize was that for Joe, not only was he thrilled about teaching waterskiing, at a dream-come-true resort, but spiritually he knew that working and participating with other Christians would be fulfilling and rewarding. Plus being able to witness his own faith daily while working and interacting with campers would allow him to express his love for the Lord and how wonderful it is to be a Christian. Sadly, he could not share this enthusiasm and feeling with his dad, but in time, he was able to have an open and honest conversation with his aunt. She respectfully listened to her nephew's views of Christianity and his perspective and personal belief in Christ Jesus. This really pleased Joe and even gave him hope that someday his aunt, and even his dad, would accept Jesus as their Savior.

After being Malibu's water ski instructor during the month of June, in 1965, he was promoted to the harbormaster position. This was because the current harbormaster had to abruptly return to the States due to a family crisis, and could not come back that summer. The harbormaster job had more responsibility since the duties included having a harbor assistant, supervising the new water ski instructor and current pool lifeguard. The Malibu Club would change Joe's life forever.

CHAPTER 7

Cold Feet and Warm Hands

A couple of days have passed at Malibu, and Ken had successfully passed on a note to Julie from Doc. The note simply read,

> *Hi Julie!*
>
> *I thought it might be better to use a messenger to give you this note. I just wanted to let you know that I've been thinking about you a lot. I think you're beautiful, and sweet. And would really like to get to know you better. I have to admit, I already have strong feelings for you . . . if you know what I mean?!*
>
> *If you would like . . . and if you can . . . how 'bout meeting me after Club & Cabin time? Down at the end of dock, next to my Harbor Shack would be perfect. But only if you can. Don't take a risk of getting in trouble, okay? I will be there. If you don't show-up, I'll assume you couldn't cautiously break-away from your room.*
>
> *Doc*

Late that evening, Doc was by himself at the doorway of his harbor office. Extended far out from the gangplank, the end of the floating dock was dark and quiet. Doc could hear the slight waves breaking along the bottom of the floats and against the half dozen ski boats tied up along the inside of his shack and the dock. The temperature was pleasant, in the midsixties, so Doc only had on a pull-over long-sleeve black shirt. Wearing his normal Levi's, he of course was still barefoot. As he was in anticipation of Julie's, hopeful, arrival, he was sitting on the dock, facing the upper deck and Big Squawka. It was quite picturesque, as Malibu stood there, illuminated by the many tiny lights, powered by the enormous diesel generator located in a granite crevice near the laundry building, so named the Laundry Nook. Soon he could hear some footsteps along the gangplank, as he spotted the outline of a figure approaching him. As he stood up, sure enough, it was Julie.

"Hey, you made it," Doc said to her in a whisper, as she came into view with a smile.

"Yea, I hope you haven't been waiting too long, I had to wait to kind of sneak out of my room," Julie told him in a whisper as well, standing close to him, with their eyes completely locked on each other. "I'm sure everything is cool, my roommates were fast asleep."

"Well, I'm glad you didn't take any chances. I really don't want to do anything that will get us . . . *you* mainly . . . in trouble, understand?"

"Yes, I do . . . thanks. I don't want you getting in trouble either though. This 'no frat' rule is kind of a pain, huh?"

"Yea, it is," Doc agreed, as Julie turned back and looked at the striking scene of Malibu dimly lit, with shadows of tree branches reflecting against the buildings and the wooden walkways lighted faintly for safety.

"Golly, that is amazing. What a peaceful sight. Malibu is so incredible, isn't it? I still can't believe I'm working here."

"It really is a unique place. Take a look straight up," Doc said to her as she spun around and gazed up at the magnificent dark sky, displaying massive amounts of bright, twinkling stars.

The two of them were looking up together now, as Julie softly and slowly said, "Wow! The heavens are right above us. It's just all so incredible, this whole creation of the universe, isn't it?"

"Yea, that's for sure," Doc spoke softly, as he gently put his right hand on Julie's waist. "So, you want to sit on the end of the dock here and tangle our feet in the water?

"Okay . . . but isn't it kind of cold?"

"Oh, a little . . . but you'll get used to it really quick, trust me." Doc immediately reached down and pulled up his pant legs and then sat down at the edge of the dock, dropping his bare feet into the inlet. Julie removed her white tennis shoes, rolled up her blue cotton pants, and joined him promptly, as she sat next to him on his right.

"Oh yea, that's not so bad. A little cold, but actually, it feels really refreshing." She playfully knocked her left foot into Doc's feet, splashing some of the saltwater up on to his knees.

"Are you playing footsie with me, girl?" Doc questioned her with a big grin.

"Yep. Is that okay?" she said back with a smile, once again revealing her cute dimples. "So, Doc . . . by the way, thanks for the note. I hope Ken wasn't too concerned about delivering it to me. He seemed really embarrassed and uneasy. His face turned a bright red when he handed it to me. I'm glad he spotted me out by the golf course, I was watering some hanging flower baskets, and there wasn't anyone else around. We didn't talk much. He just said it was from you."

"Oh yea, he's just really paranoid about this 'no frat' thing. And I understand. Young Life is just trying to eliminate distraction among the staff and work crew. They want us to be completely focused on the campers . . . no relationships. Ken is obviously worried about me getting too close to you. He knows that I like you a lot and have been thinking about you. I hope my note was okay and didn't freak you out."

"Oh, gosh no. It didn't freak me out at all. It was very sweet, and I'm really glad that you like me and have been thinking about me. I've been thinking about you too, trust me. I think you're wonderful."

"Well, I have to admit, you've certainly got my attention, beautiful. And not just your good looks, but you seem like such a great person, with a caring heart. To be honest with you, I wish I could just embrace you right now and hold you close to me. That's how I feel about you, Julie. I want to be close to you. There is definitely a physical attraction I have for you. But I don't dare hold you in my arms out here because I can't be sure who may be watching, right?"

"Yea, I agree. And yes, I feel the same about you. I would love for you to hold me close, but I guess we'll have to settle with just holding hands for now. Does that work for you?" Julie said with kindness and compassion as she reached for Doc's right hand and clasped his hand with hers, fingers intertwined, providing pleasure and warmth. Several minutes go by as they learn a little more about each other. Asking simple, trivial questions like "Do you have a favorite recording artist, or group?"

Doc answered, "I guess it'd have to be the Beach Boys," and Julie said, "I really like the Beatles and 'Simon and Garfunkel' . . . but the Four Seasons are a favorite too . . . it's hard to choose."

"I like them too," Doc admitted. "Did you know that recently Frankie Valli, their lead singer, was interviewed about what he thought of the British Invasion, and he said that the English boys were actually helping his career. And the same was true with the Beach Boys, and that new sound . . . Motown. They're all having more success since the Beatles arrived on the music scene. Kind of a surprise, don't you think?"

"Yes, I do. So, what about movies . . . what's your favorite?" she then asked.

"Gee, that's a hard one. How 'bout my favorite two films?"

"Sure, why not," Julie quickly answered.

"Well, I would say *Ben Hur*, with Charlton Heston, and *Spartacus*, with Kirk Douglas and Tony Curtis."

"Really? Two movies about the Roman Empire."

"Oh yea, I didn't even think of that. I guess, because I really enjoy that period of history, and I love epic, spectacular films on the big screen. What about you? What are your two favorite movies?"

"Hmmm . . . I would have to say, *The Sound of Music*, with Julie Andrews, and *Doctor Zhivago*, with Julie Christie."

"Hey! Three Julies . . . how did that happen?" Doc responded with a quiet laugh.

"Golly! I never thought about that. You're right . . . two Julies, and me!" She quietly laughed as well.

"Well, I'm not surprised about the musical *Sound of Music*, since you're so into music, playing violin and piano. Actually, I like musicals too, which my dad thought was stupid and feminine." Doc had a disappointed look on his face, but then promptly let it go and smiled at Julie. "Did you ever see *West Side Story*? That was a good one. I enjoyed the dancing too."

"Yea, I did. You're right, that was a great film . . . music production."

"And you're right about *Doctor Zhivago*, I saw it last year when it premiered. It was amazing . . . with Omar Sharif. Speaking of Omar Sharif . . . do you have a favorite actor, actress, that you admire most?"

Julie took a few seconds to think about that question, as she rolled her eyes, and then answered Doc.

"I really admire Audrey Hepburn. And as far as an actor . . . hmmm, I'd have to say Gregory Peck and Paul Newman."

"Two handsome men, right?" Doc said with a broad smile.

"Oh yea! But that's not why I picked them. I think they are really talented actors, do you?"

"Yes, absolutely! You're right. My picks would have to be . . . as far as my favorites on the big screen . . . Steve McQueen, Kirk Douglas, and Burt Lancaster."

"Hey! That's three!" Julie gently hit his shoulder.

"Oops! You're right . . . sorry!"

"Oh, I'm just teasing you. Those are all three really good actors too. Do you have a favorite comedian?" Julie asked Doc, still trying to whisper.

"Well, you know that I'm really into comedy . . . so that's really a tough one . . . there's so many. I've always liked Red Skelton, Jerry Lewis, Danny Thomas, and Bob Hope. But some of the new guys are good too . . . like Bob Newhart, Jonathan Winters, and—of course—Chris's dad, Dick Van Heuson. How about you?"

"Wow! You enjoy a lot of different comedians, huh? Yea, I like a lot of those guys too. There's some funny ladies out there too, right? Like Lucille Ball and that new gal Carol Burnett. Have you seen her yet?"

"Oh yea. She's funnier than heck! Good choices. Did you ever see the movie *The Long, Long, Trailer*, with Lucille Ball and Desi Arnaz? That was so funny!" Doc started laughing again.

"I did see that with my mom and dad. We all really laughed over that one!" Julie immediately joined Doc in quiet laughter.

Not purposely changing the subject, Julie popped up with a personal question on her mind for Doc. "So, dock boy, I've been meaning to ask you this. Why are you always barefoot? Do you ever wear shoes. I noticed that on our hike up to the top of the lower falls of Chatterbox, you were still barefoot, and didn't seem to have a problem with it. You must have really calloused skin on the bottom of your feet!"

"Yea, I do. They're really hardened. I can actually run around any area of Malibu, and it doesn't bother me or hurt me . . . weird, huh? I don't know exactly how it got started, but last year I just started going barefoot in June, it seemed easier to not wear shoes, or boots, when it rained, and eventually my feet just got tough enough to not worry about it. I kind of like the feel of it too. No, I never wear shoes while at Malibu. I go for three and a half months bare-foot. That's why they're so tan too. It was really strange last summer when I finally had to put shoes on, when we got to Vancouver, and I was heading home to California. It felt odd . . . but I got used to it. I started out with only tennis shoes, because they were softer, lighter, and more flexible. Anyway, I guess, because I'm always barefoot, it's become my trademark here at Malibu."

"I think it's cool . . . and yea, it's a great trademark," Julie said, as she grinned with approval.

Just then, they both heard some footsteps heading their way. Startled, Julie quickly asked Doc, "Who's that?"

"I'm not sure."

They both turned and pulled their feet and legs out of the water, then shifted around, facing toward the gangplank to see the silhouette of a person in the dark approaching them. Into the light emerged an old, hunched over, skinny, medium-height man with a white, scraggily, long beard, wearing some old green pants and a red hooded Malibu sweatshirt. For a sudden moment, Julie was briefly frightened and shrieked!

"It's okay," Doc whispered. "Trust me." Now, with normal volume, he said to the old man, "Hi, Steve. Everything all right?"

"Yep!" Steve answered him in a high-pitched voice.

As Julie was looking puzzled, Doc continued, "Hey, I see you're wearing one of the new red Malibu sweatshirts."

"Yep!"

"Did you ever get that yellow one you wanted?"

Steve immediately reached down to the bottom of his red shirt and began peeling back other shirts. First a green color, then blue, then orange, and then yellow.

"Yep! Got it!" he answered Doc with a little proud smile.

"Great!" Doc smiled back at him with a pleased look. "Oh, Steve . . . this is Julie."

"Howdy, miss." She waved a simple hi from her waist. A slight breeze suddenly came off the water. "Gonna rain tomorrow in the morning . . . eleven o'clock. Only a couple of hours though." He unexpectedly turned around and began walking back up the dock toward the gangplank. "See ya, Doc. Good to meet you, Julie," he blurted out.

"Going fish'n?" Doc asked him, raising his voice a bit so that Steve can hear him.

"Yep!" Steve didn't turn around, but continued walking.

Julie whispered to Doc, "Fishing? At nighttime?"

"Yea. He's an incredible fisherman. He catches huge salmon over by Forbidden Island."

"Who is he? I haven't seen him around."

"He's Old Steve," Doc answered, as they both turned toward each other and scooting closer. As Julie looked at Doc with curiosity, he continued, "Old Steve, the hermit. Don't worry, he's harmless. He lives just across the narrows near our lumber mill. He helps Vic with the mill and also finds golf balls up on the golf course and turns them in for cash so he can buy stuff at the Totem Trader and Totem Inn. Could you believe that bit about the different colored sweatshirts he was wearing?" Doc laughed quietly, as Julie joined in.

"That was bizarre. Was he serious about the rain?"

"Oh yea. He's amazing. He has a knack for predicting the weather in these parts. Steve's lived in this inlet for over fifty years. His parents brought him and his sister to the Princess Lousia Inlet when they were just kids, and he's been here ever since. He never went to school and was married to a Sechelt Indian years ago—she died. Anyway, I don't know how he predicts the weather the way he does, but he's usually right on. I guess because he's lived here for so long. In fact, he once told me that it got so cold here one winter, years ago, that during slack-tide, the Princess Inlet froze, and he was able to walk across the narrows to this side. But I'm not sure if I believe him, sorry to say . . . he can stretch the truth sometimes. I'm so sorry he scared you."

"It's okay, really. I'm just glad I was with you. So you say he lives across from Malibu, across the narrows?"

"Yea. His little shack is somewhat hidden, facing the Jervis Inlet. You have to kind of know where to look for it. Sometimes you can see his stovepipe smoke, if he's cooking. It's really close to the lumber mill."

"You said he helps Vic. Isn't he too old and skinny to be much help? He looks pretty weak to me."

"Oh, no. You'd be amazed. He can move boards—two-by-fours, and so on, faster, and with ease . . . simpler and easier than any young work crew guy I've witnessed, even if the high school kid is a football player. I'm serious. He's been handling lumber for so long now, he knows precisely how to handle long, heavy boards. He taught me some. It's all in the leverage. That's the key. Knowing how to balance each board when you're handling it, while you're either moving it, tossing it, or stacking it. Anyway, he's pretty amazing, considering, like you said, how skinny and old he is! He also does most of the stripping . . . removing the bark from the logs."

"Wow, that is amazing. What an interesting character," Julie said with a serious, curious voice.

"Yes, he is a colorful Malibu personality, that's for sure! There was this other guy who lived in the inlet before Old Steve. His name was Herman Casper, and he used to own all this property, before

Malibu was built. He sold it—get this—for only five hundred dollars to Tom Hamilton, who later started building Malibu in 1940. I'll tell you more about Hamilton later. That's another fascinating story. Anyway, Herman Casper lived in a little cottage with his twenty-something cats, and helped build Malibu. He left about the time Malibu first opened for business, catering to the rich and famous . . . mostly Hollywood celebrities. I guess Herman didn't want anything to do with the well-known folks! I'll have to tell you more about those well-known people too . . . later. But . . . darn, I hate to end this super evening out here with you, doll, but I guess you'd better get back before someone comes looking for you. Besides, it's almost time for me to turn the lights out."

"Turn the lights out? What do you mean?"

"Oh! I guess you don't know. One of my responsibilities is starting and stopping Malibu's main generator, which powers all our electricity. I'm sure you've heard it running. It's quite loud, so that's why it was positioned down in a crevasse. At least that helps with the noise a little."

Julie responded, "Yea, I've heard it. It's down near the Linen Nook, right?"

"Yea, exactly. I'll have to take you down there some time. It's really interesting. And also super loud when it's operating . . . and a bit smelly too. Oh! And the diesel room is also really warm . . . almost hot! In fact, the Diesel Shack is where we dry our custom-made water skis. It's perfect, because it takes a lot of heat to properly dry the type of glue we use, to bend the front of the ski."

"That does sound interesting. I would like to check it out sometime," Julie interjected with obvious sincerity. "I didn't even know that you made your own skis. That's awesome!"

"Julie, you can't believe how dark it can get here at Malibu once I shut down the generator. It's eerie and kind of spooky. Especially when there's no moon out. You can't see six inches in front of your face. I'm not kidding!"

"Really? I never thought about that."

"Yea, that's why it's mandatory that everyone in camp, individually, must have a flashlight with them near their bed at all times. It's for safety reasons. If we had a fire in the middle of the night—God forbid—at least it would help everyone to escape. Of course, it also allows you to use the bathroom in the night, right?" Doc started laughing again quietly.

Julie shook her head with a smile. "That's true. A flashlight is a necessary tool here at Malibu."

Doc continued, "One night, I was about to turn off the camp power, and I had placed my lit flashlight up on the top of our smaller, backup diesel. After I had completely shut down the main generator, I reached up for my light and accidentally knocked it off, and when it hit the cement floor, it broke. We keep a spare flashlight in the Diesel Shack, but it was so pitch-black, I couldn't find it. It was so dark outside, I couldn't begin to find my way back to Andy's Shanty, to go to bed. So, I just hung out inside the shack, trying to sleep, when Ken found me. He wondered why I didn't show up back at the shack, so he grabbed his large, aluminum, bright flashlight and came looking for me. I was very thankful that he checked the Diesel Shack. Of course, doing the big brother thing, he had to lecture me some, but at least he never told Vic about it. Vic would have been unhappy with me. Although knowing him, he probably would have laughed about it behind my back, thinking it was funny to think of me being stuck in the smelly shack." Again, Doc and Julie chuckled some more. "Oh, and again, when I first left the shack to try and head back up the ramped boardwalk—but realized it was way too dark to continue—I stood there for a while, gazing up at the black, star-filled sky. I can't even begin to describe how massive the amount of stars there were. I could totally see the Milky Way. It was astonishing! The most stars I had ever seen in my life-time!"

"Golly! That really must have been amazing!" Julie looked up again at the star-studded sky above them.

"So, not to change the subject, but before you go, I wanted to share an idea with you," Doc said to her.

With a curious look, Julie again grabbed on to Doc's hand and asked, "What's that?"

"I have an idea as to how we can be alone together . . . I mean, really alone. Would you like that?"

"Of course I would, but how?" Julie quickly responded.

"Tomorrow night is Mac Night. He comes for dinner, and then in the evening, just before club, he does a talk about the Sechelt Indians and the spirits of the inlet . . . you'll see. Anyway, Vic usually picks him up at Chatterbox in the late afternoon, and I take him back before dark. I was thinking that since you're off work by then, maybe you could ride down with me to take Mac home. Then we'd have some private time on the way back. Wouldn't that be great?" Doc squeezed Julie's hand with anticipation.

"It sure would. I'd like that," July responded with enthusiasm. "We wouldn't have to worry about anyone spying on us. But wouldn't you have to check with Vic about it? Do you think it'd be a problem?"

"No, I don't think so. For one thing . . . he really likes you."

"He does? How do you know?" Julie seemed somewhat surprised.

"Let's just say he knows a good thing when he sees it. He mentioned you one time to me, and it had nothing to do with *us*. He just thought you seem sweet, genuine, and special . . . and you are."

"Thank you." Julie was pleased.

"And don't forget. It's okay for us to be friends and to even show how we care about each other . . . even our fondness for one another. We just have to be careful not to cross the line and reveal any desires of affection that we have between us. Does that make sense?"

"Yes, I understand."

"The other thing, good-looking, is that I'll plan to mention to Vic that you're quite fascinated by Mac and would truly like to get to know him better. And would like to have a chance to ask him some questions about his life, and so on. And that wouldn't be lying, right? You did seem to have a sense of curiosity about him when we were in *Seaholm*, correct?"

"Without a doubt," Julie answered Doc with a tone of conviction. "You're right. I think he's so interesting and captivating. I would love to learn more about his past and spiritual thoughts . . . ideas."

"Well, I'll talk to Vic first thing in the morning. Darn! I guess you'd better get going. I've really enjoyed this time with you."

"Me too. I wish we could just stay out here all night together . . . talking and sharing our thoughts, in such a peaceful surrounding."

"I know," Doc agreed. "The more we talk and share our lives, the more I want to be with you. But it's best we be smart, and say goodnight." Doc whispered to her, "Sweet dreams, princess," while he was now tenderly holding both of her hands, with his face only inches from hers.

"Princess. I like that." Julie smiled adoringly, with a squeeze of her hands, along with a slow wink. She then reluctantly let go of her hands, turned, and walked speedily toward the gangplank. Doc watched her silhouette disappear into the darkness once she reached the upper deck. The sound of her steps have now faded into silence.

Standing there alone at the end of the dock, he once again looked up at the magnificent sky of stars. With eyes wide open, he whispered to himself, "Thank You, Lord."

The next morning, after breakfast and cleanup, Julie and Beth were in their room, which overlooked Forbidden Island. Their other two roommates were out watering the dozens of hanging flower baskets, located along the numerous wooden ramps and walkways. The moderately small room had two sets of bunk beds for the girls to sleep in. The bedspreads were vivid colorful native wool blankets, with Malibu Club embroidered in large script letters across the center. The rustic structure was built with rough cedar walls and a small bathroom with a shower. There were four small dressers, each with a narrow mirror on top. In one corner was a desk to encourage the girls to write letters home. Between the dressers, on the wall, were paintings of Canadian scenery. Julie was sitting at the desk writing a letter. Beth was folding some laundry on her bed and looking out the window at the charming, quaint Forbidden Island and the Jervis Inlet waterway.

She spoke aloud and revealed to Julie, "Darn! It's starting to rain outside."

"It is?" Julie asked promptly, as she turned toward Beth. "What time is it? Are you wearing your watch, Beth?"

"Yea. Its a few minutes after eleven. Why?"

"Oh, I was just curious." She turned back around, and as she looked back down at her letter, she said to herself, under her breath, "Old Steve, he was right...hmm. Wow!"

Beth walked over to Julie. "Hey! If you want that letter to go out today with Mr. Campbell, you'd better finish it up pronto. He usually flies out to Vancouver about 11:30 a.m. Who are you writing to?"

"Oh, just to my mom and family. I'm anxious to let her know how I'm doing and what's been going on here. Just stuff in general."

"So, Julie . . . did you write her about Doc?" Beth said shadily.

Julie spun in her chair and looked up at Beth. With a hint of embarrassment, she answered, "Doc? Why would I do that?"

Beth folded her arms and lightheartedly said, "Come on, Julie. You don't think I haven't noticed?"

"Noticed what?" Julie asked, as her face began to turn a slight shade of red.

"You and Doc, you know. Julie, it's me," Beth replied without any threat in her voice.

"Is it that obvious?"

"No, not really," Beth assured Julie. "It's just that I'm overly nosy. Hey, it's okay. Listen, don't worry. Nobody else knows to my knowledge. You just need to be really careful, because of the 'no frat' rule, right? Listen, I like both of you so much. You know I'll do what I can to help. You can trust me. Gosh, you guys make the cutest couple."

"You really think so?" Julie asked, as her face began to lose its redness.

"Absolutely. I already told you that I think Doc is totally boss.[1]

"Thanks, Beth. I can't tell you how happy that makes me. And how relieved I am that you're okay with it . . . and understand. Neither one of us planned for this to happen, of course. We're just really attracted to each other, we can't help it!"

"Have you guys kissed?" Beth asked with a cringed expression of curiosity. "Sorry, I just had to ask."

---

[1]   A 1960s popular word, expression, used primarily by teenagers, meaning "fantastic" or "special."

"Honestly . . . no, we haven't. We're both really trying to be good and not cross the line . . . since we're here at Malibu, working. I've got to tell you though . . . it's hard."

"Yea, I bet! Well, good for you two. That can't be easy when you feel passion for each other."

"Trust me, it's not." Julie shook her head with certainty.

Beth walked over to Julie and placed her right hand on Julie's left shoulder, and with a solemn voice, she said to her, "This might be easy for me to say, but maybe this is a good time to place this in God's hands."

"I already have," Julie answered. "I've been praying about this ever since I knew that I had feelings for Doc. I know as a Christian I need to have faith in sharing it with God. I know He will give me the answers I need."

"Good for you, Julie," Beth answered as she dropped her head to the side. "You're doing the right thing and the smart thing. He will answer your prayers." With an apologetic look, Beth said to Julie, "Well, I apologize for being so personal. It's just my brutal honest approach to most everything. It's an inherited trait that I got from my mom."

As Beth cringed with some embarrassment, Julie slightly laughed and said, "Oh gosh! It's okay . . . believe me. I'm glad that we can be honest and confide in each other. It makes me realize that our friendship is real, and growing. I'm a little uncomfortable and feel funny that you know about me and Doc. But it's kind of nice to know that I can talk to you about it."

"Honestly, I like you, Julie. I'm glad you're my friend and my roommate. And I truly hope that things work out for you and Doc."

"Yea, he's a great guy . . . and handsome too!"

"No argument there!" Beth said with a smile, as she began folding her laundry again.

With a serious expression, Julie asked, "So, Beth, since you talked to me about something personal, and kind of private, would you mind if I asked you a personal question?"

With a quick, questionable look, Beth put down on her bed a blouse that she was about to fold and stepped closer to Julie.

"Of course not. What did you want to ask me?"

"A while back, when we first met, you mentioned to me, when we were talking about our families, that you're an identical twin."

"Yea, I am."

"And I think that is really cool, but I was wondering . . . I know, this is kind of a silly question, but I'm just curious . . . do you and your sister, Carol, have the same fingerprints?"

"Actually, that's funny you ask, because Carol and I, when we were younger, wondered about that too. The answer is . . . no, we don't. It's interesting, because we share the same DNA, but our fingerprints are definitely different."

With obvious curiosity and interest, Julie quickly commented, "Hmm! I always wondered about that. I do think that identical twins are intriguing. In fact, even fraternal twins are fascinating to me. I've always wondered what it would be like to be a twin."

"Well, I have to tell you . . . first of all, I don't know what it would be like not to be an identical twin and the same with Carol, since that's all we know. But I can tell you that we've had some magical, mysterious moments together over the years."

"Like what? What do you mean?"

"Well, I think we share a special connection . . . more than just being sisters. It's really weird. For example, one time we purchased the exact same pair of pants, in the same color, on the same day, at the same retail chain. I was in a different town visiting a friend, and later that day, Carol and I talked on the phone and discovered this uncanny coincidence, which we don't think was a coincidence at all!"

"Wow. That is weird."

"And one time, when we were in grade school, Carol got in trouble for faking a report card, and when she got spanked, I totally remember feeling the physical pain as well."

"That is amazing," Julie expressed with curious interest. "Do you think you have some kind of ESP between you . . . like you know what the other one is thinking?"

"I do. I remember one time when we were little, my parents took us to Sea World. We were shopping in the gift store, and we got split up. My mom took me with her when we left the store to buy a soda. She assumed Carol was with my dad, and he thought she was with me and my mom. Carol got confused too and left the store to look for us. So she was alone and lost from all of us momentarily, and of course was upset and freaking out. My dad soon found her, and we all eventually were together again. But here's the weird thing, Julie, or odd thing that happened. During those few minutes when Carol was alone and lost, I was feeling agitated and out of sorts, telling my mom that we need to go back and find Carol. Of course my mom thought my sister was with my dad. We all later discovered what actually happen when we were together again. And that's when I realized why I was feeling agitated. Carol and I knew it was because we were identical twins."

"Gosh! That is a fascinating story. Does it happen very often?"

"No, not very often, but it does happen. I think it kind of depends on the circumstances . . . the situation."

"Well, I think it's all very cool. And you should be extremely proud to be a twin, an identical twin at that!" Julie said with a smile.

"Thank you. I am proud to be a twin. I'm glad you asked me about it," Beth said to Julie, as she went back to folding clothes. Julie turned back around and continued to write her letter.

Beth suddenly glanced out the window as she scanned the rainy sky, hearing the sound of an airplane overhead. "Hey! You'd better run your letter down to the office or you'll miss Mr. Campbell's mail pickup."

"Oh yeah! Thanks for reminding me," Julie said to Beth with a smile. She quickly signed her letter, stuffed it in an envelope, and out the door she went.

CHAPTER 8

Did someone say, 'FIRE DANCE'?

Mac had been in camp now for a couple of hours and had already enjoyed the delicious beef stew served in the dining room for dinner. Vic had picked him up in the late afternoon, using Malibu's fastest boat, the *Skookum*, a classic 1950s sixteen-foot teakwood Chris-Craft. The *Skookum* was the only boat at Malibu stored in a boathouse, protecting it from the elements.

A half an hour after the camp had taken pleasure in another wonderful meal prepared by the kitchen staff, the air horn sounded, and everyone gathered in Big Squawka. The campers were clueless as to why they had assembled early in the large room prior to the normal club time. Once everyone had secured their seats and were settled in, counselors began to close all the drapes covering the windows. With the lights already off, this made the room quite dark. Immediately, there was chatter and laughter among the large group of teens, until a spotlight from the back suddenly brightly lit one of the side doors leading out to the side deck. Suddenly, the sounds of an Indian drum could be heard, as the door flung open, and Mac entered the room wearing a chief headdress, deerskin pants, and was shirtless. As he slowly walked towards the stage, he carefully slithered through the kids sitting on the floor. Doc also entered the room from behind Mac. He too was wearing Indian attire, war paint on his face, and brandishing a single eagle feather behind his head, attached to a thin red scarf. As Doc continued to arithmetically beat the authentic animal skin-covered drum, he followed Mac up on to the stage and sat behind him on the floor, next to the back black curtain. Other than the sounds of the drum, the room was totally silent as Mac took center stage, with the spotlight focused firmly on just him. The dramatic scene had certainly got the attention of everybody in the room. As Doc softened the sounds of the drum, Mac raised his right hand up to his face and extended his fingers as he placed his hand above his eyes, as if he were searching the horizon from a mountain bluff. With a solemn look, he glanced around the room, slowly and dramatically turning his head from left to right. He then dropped his hand down to his waist and began to speak to his silent audience.

"My presence here this evening is to share some tribal history of the Sechelt Indians," Mac projected loudly to his listeners, with confidence and commitment. "I speak of tribesmen who were native to Jervis Inlet, Nelson Island, and the Sunshine Coast." The large group of teens in the darken room appeared to be magically mesmerized by Mac as he continued.

"They lived in communal settlements where members lived together in a longhouse, a large, open building constructed with logs from the large cedar trees, so common along our coastline. The women would spend much of their time weaving cedar baskets. The men were great fishermen and hunters. They were also skillful and capable warriors, when it was necessary to protect the tribes." The silence in the room was almost deafening, as Mac moved across the stage to his right and pointed his left hand in the direction of the Princess Louisa Inlet. His boosting voice again engaged. "Even today, we can see and discover pictographs—rock paintings—still visible among the granite rock formations lining the sides of the inlet. And here at Malibu, the many totem poles were all carved by authentic tribesmen of British Columbia, each telling its own story. The Sechelt Indians had respect for the afterlife and spirits becoming part of nature. They also believed in good and evil . . . and spirits to represent each. However, in these mythologies . . . the concepts were not quite so black-and-white. Many times a spirit that was considered to be evil was actually necessary to keep the balance." Mac paused, as he slowly moved across the stage again, allowing the spotlight handler to follow his movement. He then turned, placed his hands on his hips, and looked straight out over the tops of the crowd of kids with a thought-provoking expression, as if he were posing for a native portrait.

"The Sechelt of the Northwest had a fear of ghosts, which was evident in the places they chose for burial. There were many Sechelt who believed that the spirit of someone who was not buried properly, or whose grave had been desecrated, would be doomed to walk the earth, unable to rest. Generally, it was believed that a spirit who was at peace when they passed went on to the next plane of spirituality. A spirit who was not, or whose rest was disturbed, would stay earthbound."

Now Mac turned stage left as he pointed out the other end of the darken room, toward the direction of Jervis Inlet. "The reason the small island near the entrance to the narrows is named Forbidden Island is that it is a particularly significant little island to the Sechelt Indians. This island is where they bury their chiefs. The chosen few, along with their medicine man, performs the sacred ritual, with the body of the chief wrapped in animal hide and placed on a woven bed of cut branches. Then his supported body is lashed on seven-foot stilts, which lifts the deceased chief up into the air, and away from earthly evil spirits. Once the brief ceremony is completed, the body is abandoned and left there for seven days, at which time the body is then lowered by two tribesmen, and immediately taken out to the center of the inlet in a uniquely painted canoe. After speaking a few customary and sacramental words, the men carefully slip the covered body into the waters of the inlet. Once they return to their people in the canoe, they at once torch the small boat and send it adrift off shore, as the tribe lay witness to this significant ceremonial event. As the flames rise from inlet waters, all the tribesmen fall to their knees and place their heads into their laps, showing respect for their fallen and dead chief. So now you know why the small island just off Malibu, across the other side there"—Mac again pointed out the left side toward the Totem Trader—"is forbidden. No white man is allowed to ever place a foot on this sacred and holy piece of land. Oh! And one other piece of worthy information I would like to share."

Mac now has a rather sly, devious look on his face. Doc strengthened the sound of the drum from behind him. "Regarding the part where the chief's body is placed on the stilts, up off the ground . . . because of the awful smell of his rotting body filling the air, not only do the ants crawl up the stilts and make their way in and through the animal hide to eat the flesh, but the seagulls and buzzards also quickly smell the scent and fly to the scene." Doc began to beat his drum with a faster pace. "They frantically pick at the body with their pointed, sharp beaks, which soon penetrates the hide so that they too can ravage and digest the rotting human tissue." Doc stopped the drumbeat as the majority of the teens listening to this horrific description of the dark side of Mother Nature immediately reacted with vocal expressions of disgust and displeasure. There were a few young men who blurted out comments of amusement and delight at Mac's ghastly description, and naturally Rusty was one of them. Obviously, this was the response Mac was hoping for. In the back of the room, Vic and Ken, who were leaning up against the back wall in the dark, were grinning with contented pleasure.

Once the muttering in the room calmed down, Mac continued his presentation. "Before I perform for you the sacred fire dance of the Sechelt Indian Warriors, I first would like to share a short story for you of Sechelt folklore." Murmurs of "**Fire dance?**" suddenly engulfed the room as Mac kept talking. "This is a story that happened just last year among the modern-day Sechelt. The Sechelt Indians who still populate Nelson Island asked their chief in autumn if the winter was going to be cold or not. The chief, not really knowing the answer, but wanting to show confidence in his great power and leadership, replied that the winter was going to be cold and that the members of the village were to collect wood to be prepared." Again, Mac had the attention of his crowd, as they quickly were absorbed into the tale. With his arms crossed, Indian-style, he said, "Being a good leader, and after a week or so, the chief then went to the nearest telephone booth and called the National Weather Service and asked, 'Is this winter going to be cold?'

"The man on the phone responded, 'Yes, this winter is going to be quite cold indeed.'"

Big Squawka was filled with laughter, and, soon after, with applause. Doc could easily hear Julie's distinctive laughter among the rest as she joined her friends Beth and Diane in amused delight.

"So the chief went back to speed up his people, telling them to collect even more wood to be prepared. A week later, he called the National Weather Service again, 'Is it going to be a very cold winter?' 'Yes,' the man replied, 'it's going to be a very cold winter.' So the chief went back to his people and ordered them to go and find every scrap of wood they can find. Two weeks later, he called the National Weather Service again and asked, 'Are you absolutely sure that the winter is going to be very cold?' 'Absolutely,' the man replied, 'the Sechelt Indians are collecting wood like crazy!'" With that, the room was roaring with laughter. Even Vic and Ken, who have heard this story many times, were in the back of the room laughing aloud. And once again, Doc could hear Julie's laugh, as she was amused, displaying her pleasure from the last row of those sitting on the floor. The crowd of kids and adults then clapped, expressing their genuine enjoyment of Mac's Sechelt weather story.

Once the clapping ceased, Doc began to softly beat his drum again. As his methodically slow thump on the drum hide captured the audience's attention, Mac explained his next demonstration.

"As I earlier mentioned, it is time now for me to skillfully and expertly demonstrate and reveal the famous Sechelt fire dance—performed by warriors in celebration of defeating an enemy. Dangerous and daring, be not afraid, as I have successfully performed this thrilling dance dozens of times. For your safety, however, I ask that those of you seated close to the stage, please scoot back a couple of feet." With that said, those up front heeded Mac's warning and pushed themselves back away from the stage. Mac turned around and walked over to where Doc was sitting. On the floor, next to Mac's drummer, were three Indian wooden-torch-clubs, which Mac at once reached for. The spotlight instantly went out, which left the room in total darkness. Some of the young boys seated on the floor reacted by making haunting sounds, as if a ghost was about to appear on stage. Just then, the three clubs held by Mac, hollow and filled with alcohol-soaked material, were lit on fire by Doc, which instantly lit up the stage area with bright white, yellow, and red flame. When Mac turned toward his audience, without delay, he began to juggle the three flaming clubs, as well as lift his feet up and down in a simple methodic Indian dance. This spectacular act had certainly gotten the attention of those in the room. Especially those teens who were seated on the floor, directly in front of the stage. If the darkness did not conceal their faces, one would have seen their wide-eyed expressions of awe.

As the clubs were tossed in the air, not only did they display a multitude of flickering light and shadow around the platform area and beyond, but the sound of hot flames and wooden clubs being twirled and falling through the air were curious and almost spooky. The brightness of the fire also illuminated Mac, causing his white hair to glow at times, and his brown tan upper torso to be easily revealed, even without the spotlight turned on. After about two minutes of juggling these dramatic flaming torches, and chanting sounds of authentic Sechelt language, Mac extinguished one of the clubs by sticking it into a nearby metal bucket on stage, which was half full of water. The steam and smoke erupted, as the hot fire was submerged inside the bucket.

Suddenly, to all the first-timers' surprise, Mac, without warning, took one of the two flaming torches he was holding and quickly passed the lighted club across his forearms, which caused a flash of flame on his arms. At once, Mac loudly hollered-out, "Umqua Hah!" The full house in Big Squawka was stunned and expressed fright and concern. Doc was hitting the drum harder with two tom-toms now, as he sped up his constant beat. Mac responded with vocal sounds of pain and courage. After extinguishing his arms by quickly rubbing them with his bare hands, he then—to everyone's amazement—took both flaming clubs and ran them across his chest, instantly igniting his upper torso. His chest was literally on fire! Although this event was awkwardly entertaining to his audience—who were now breathless—the outward sound of concern was unanimous, and perhaps justifiable. Within a few seconds, Mac again used his one bare hand to smother and extinguish his flaming chest, while the other hand was holding the two clubs, still ablaze. Once he had completely wiped out the fire on his torso, he yelled out, "Umqua Hah!", again, signifying the end of his fire ritual. Doc directly quit his drumbeat, as Mac stood tall like a statue, with the flaming two wooden clubs raised up in the air above his head.

For maybe three seconds at most, the room was silent with disbelief. Then suddenly, Mac's audience exploded into cheers and clapping. The houselights came on as Mac bowed to his spectators and then extinguished the remaining torches in the bucket. All the teens seated on the floor mats promptly rose, as did the others in the room from folding chairs in the back, giving Mac a standing ovation. With a pleased and appreciative expression of gratitude, Mac again bowed to his audience and simply said, "Thank you, my friends, and good evening!"

While everyone was exiting Big Squawka through the main double doors, Vic and Ken slipped out by themselves through the single door in the back. As they were walking down the stairs off the deck, and with a snicker, Ken said to Vic, "Rubbing alcohol applied to the arms and chest can sure make a difference in a fire dance."

Vic quickly chimed in, "Better to burn off the alcohol than to actually roast your skin! It's a great trick, mate, and the kids loved it!"

CHAPTER 9

The Kiss . . . or Not?

The camp had an hour of free time after Mac's exhilarating performance, before they all headed back into Big Squawka for club, for a chance to gather together again to sing songs and listen to the camp manager deliver a short message of the Christian faith. Many of the campers headed to Main Street to the Totem Inn so they could indulge in the many wonderful homemade desserts available for them to purchase, satisfying their hunger for ice cream, candy, or soda. Others took a moment to shop at the Totem Trader for souvenirs, books, or clothing items.

Aboard the *Skookum* were Julie and Mac, as Doc steered the sleek, eye-catching boat, away from the inner dock area, with a heading of Chatterbox Falls and Mac's houseboat. Mac was seated in the front with Doc while Julie was comfortably seated in the middle of the back seat, just behind the two guys. Sporting a pink short-sleeve blouse and white short shorts, Julie certainly caught Doc's attention, as he was having a hard time not to continuously twist his head around to catch a glance of her beauty. Fifty yards out in front of them was the Seinskiff pushing the large blue garbage box. Chris was at the wheel, and Chuck was aboard to help him empty the stinky container. As a few seagulls swooped down over the smelly wooden box, Doc and his passengers soon caught up to the Seinskiff, slowing down, as he navigated the Chris-Craft next to their port side.

"Hey, gronk brother!" Doc shouted out over the Seinskiff's noisy diesel engine. "Taking Yogi his dinner I see!"

"Yea, he and I are pretty good pals now, although I still keep my distance," Chris shouted back, as everyone listened. "Hey, Mac! I sure enjoyed your stories, and the fire dance was far-out! Hi, Julie!" They all waved to each other as Doc engaged the throttle, and at once the *Skookum* sped up, slicing through the dark inlet water. Julie's long, striking, blond hair was blowing in the wind, while Doc and Mac were protected by the boat's windshield.

"Far-out?" Mac asked, as he had to shout over the boat's motor.

"It means *really great*," Doc explained, sporting a smile.

"Gronk brother?" Julie shouted to Doc with a puzzled look.

"Garbage buddies," Doc shouted the answer, with an even broader smile now.

Looking at Doc, Julie continued to speak loudly, "Okay, you guys are sick!" She gave Doc a quick smile and then turned to Mac. "Say, Mac, can you tell me anything about totem poles? I think they're so fascinating."

As Doc pulled the throttle back some, in order to lower the engine noise, Mac turned his head and body to the right, trying to face Julie the best he could.

"Totem poles always tell a story, Julie, but what I think is fascinating is, if you look at the reflections of the steep granite walls over there"—he pointed toward the shore to his right—"see how they're mirrored in the glossy surface of the water? Now, if you turn your eyes to observe the horizontal picture of the shoreline of these reflections, in a vertical formation, it almost looks like a totem pole. Get it?" Julie had turned her head toward the granite slabs of rock wall and was cocking her head to try and understand what Mac was describing to her. Thinking she got it, she nodded her head yes. Mac continued, "Many of the intricate geometric designs the Indians use in their artwork on blankets and beads come from sources like this. Personally, I think there's a strong spiritual connection between the totem poles, the water, the mountains, and the sky. I believe that true life has to have a spiritual dimension to it. What do you think, Julie?"

"Well, I know that in the book of John, it says, 'God is Spirit, and those who worship Him must worship in spirit and truth.' So yes, I agree."

As Mac nodded his head in approval at Julie, Doc engaged the throttle forward, and the streamline craft quickly picked up speed. In less than ten minutes, they were at the Chatterbox dock, tying the *Skookum* with only the bowline to the closest cleat near *Seaholm*, Mac's low-profile houseboat. As Mac disembarked, Julie handed him a plastic bag containing a few of his personal items. They said their quick goodbyes, as Doc untied the bowline and shoved off. As Julie jumped into the left front seat where Mac had been sitting, she turned back around to wave to Mac; he smiled with a wave back, extending his arm up high and showing his bright-white teeth, in contrast to his dark tan face. Soon the *Skookum* was up to speed, and Doc and Julie were skimming across the water in the fast boat, their hair blowing frantically, as the wind easily filtered in from around the protective windshield.

Within five minutes, Doc had pulled back the throttle, slowing the boat down quickly, as he maneuvered the craft into a small cove on the mainland side of Hamilton Island, a round island about three times larger than Forbidden Island. This placed them about halfway between Malibu and Chatterbox Falls. As Doc disengaged the throttle to neutral, he turned the key off, and the engine suddenly was quiet. The boat was now just drifting leisurely in the mirrored dark water of the inlet. The warmth of the sun was still shining on the faces of Doc and Julie, adding to their pleasant float near the island and the land.

As Julie scanned the area, she looked over at Doc next to her and said, "Gosh! This is so pretty in here. It's like our own private little spot here in this cove."

"Yea, it is nice here, huh? And the best thing is that we're here alone. There isn't anyone around." Doc looked directly at Julie and smiled. "Oh, except maybe some wildlife."

"Speaking of 'wildlife', Julie chimed in—, did you ever go to Wyldlife before you started going to Young Life Club?"

"No, I missed out on that. I didn't start attending Young Life until my junior year in high school. What about you?"

With an excited smile, Julie answered with, "Oh yea. Wyldlife was awesome. That's where I met two of my best friends. Our councilors were so cool and hilarious."

"That's great. So what do you think of Mac and his stories and stuff? He's pretty articulate, isn't he?"

"Oh my gosh! I thought he was amazing and so interesting. I loved all the Indian history. It's so fascinating. I bet you didn't know it, but I'm part Cherokee—just a little bit."

Doc responded with an intrigued comment, "Really? I've got Cherokee blood in me too, just a small portion as well. My mom was part Cherokee, at least that's what my aunt told me."

"Well, that's a coincidence—mine's from my mom's side of the family also. Cool! Oh, by the way, I thought you played the drums well for Mac, and I liked your outfit."

"That's an authentic Sechelt costume. It was mounted on the wall in Big Squawka when Hamilton owned Malibu."

"So tell me more about Mr. Hamilton." Julie carefully stood up in the boat and pointed over at the island next to them. "You said this is Hamilton Island, right?"

"Yea, in fact, this is where he wanted Malibu to be built—on this island." Doc then stood up as well; keeping his balance, he slowly swung around and pointed at the large, open flat area behind him on the main body of land nearby. "Part of the resort was also going to be built over in that open area, overlooking the island."

"What happened? How come he didn't build it here?"

"His wife liked the land and area where it's at now. I think she liked the whole peninsula idea, along with the rapids. And looking out at Jervis Inlet and Forbidden Island."

"She must have been a really strongheaded woman, if she was able to convince her husband to build it there instead of here. Good for her." Julie giggled.

With a subdued laugh, Doc agreed, "Yea, maybe she wore the pants in the family. Ha ha!" They both openly laughed, as they returned to sitting down in the front seat of the floating craft.

"Tell me more about him—Tom Hamilton. Remember, you promised me you would. So, why did he build Malibu in the first place, and when?" Julie asked with honest curiosity.

"Well, he was a rich developer, and he built Malibu to attract the Hollywood celebrities of the time, and politicians . . . along with others who had money . . . movie producers and such. In fact, that's partially why he named it Malibu, after Malibu, California. And his one-hundred-foot yacht was named *Malibu*. There's been some famous people who have stayed at Malibu. William Holden honeymooned there. Remember him in *Bridge Over the River Kwai*?"

"I didn't see that movie, but my dad said it was really good. Who else has been to Malibu?"

"Yea, that film was incredible. I saw it . . . and a true story too. Well, let's see," Doc rolled his eyes while he thought for a second. "Oh yea, Bob Hope and his wife . . . John Kennedy and Jackie. Let's see . . . ahh, Walt Disney and Art Linkletter, John Denver, and Ann Margret. Oh, and John Wayne was here just last year. We shot our cannon at him off the point as he sailed out of the Princess Inlet, through the narrows. It was so great! He couldn't believe it! We totally caught him off guard and shocked the heck out of him. It was so funny!"

"That is so cool. Did he stop?"

"No, he just kept going. Too funny. We got the best of tough guy John Wayne!"

"So how did Hamilton make all his money?"

"Well, he was a successful businessman, but his big money came from when he bought the patent for the variable pitch propeller. Do you know what that is?"

"No, I haven't a clue. What is it?" Julie asked with a confused look.

"Well, it's when a pilot is landing an aircraft, he can hit a switch, and the prop blades actually change their pitch so that it helps slow down the plane. Does that make sense?"

Julie, obviously still a little confused, said, "Yea, I think so."

"It made him millions, because almost all the planes in the world use that type of propeller now."

"Hmm. So, how did Young Life get the property?"

"Actually—you met Mr. Campbell, right? Our hostess's husband with the airplane . . . the Cessna . . . he takes out our mail sometimes."

"Yes, I met him the first night in the dining room. He seems like a really nice man. I like his gray hair. He looks so distinguished."

"Well, he was the guy that flew Jim Rayburn, the president and founder of Young Life, to look at Malibu. It was for sale, because World War Two kind of shut Malibu down for a time. Plus, the Hollywood people didn't come like Hamilton thought they would, since it was so far to get here, in those days. Hamilton bailed. All of a sudden, one day, he was done and told all his staff to pack up and leave on the seaplanes and boats he provided. He even left dirty dishes in the sinks. And unmade beds and everything. He just left. That's the kind of guy he was."

"Well, that's strange," Julie added, shaking her head.

"So Young Life ended up buying it for a song . . . dirt cheap for what it was worth. I think God had something to do with it."

"Yea, for sure, I agree. He definitely had a plan for Malibu, and it wasn't for the rich and famous."

"So when I was telling you about William Holden honeymooning at Malibu, I forgot to tell you that the little cabin he and his bride stayed in, facing the Princess Louisa Inlet, Hamilton decided to name it the Honeymoon Cottage. Isn't that neat?"

"That's very sweet," Julie smiled and intensely looked at Doc.

"So I bet they kissed a lot in that cabin, what do you think?" Doc reached out and slowly clasped his hands with Julie's.

"Oh, I'm sure they did," she answered Doc, as he scooted closer to her and gradually moved his face closer to hers.

"I think we've talked enough about Malibu's history. I think it's time we talk about us," Doc said to her softly and calmly, even though his heart was beating overtime.

"Us?" Julie asked him with a whisper. "Is there an us?"

"Yes, I believe we're an us," Doc whispered back, gently holding her hands, and now only a few inches from their lips about to touch.

"I believe that we are one hundred percent attracted to each other, don't you?"

"Oh yea, I do," Julie calmly answered him with a serious gaze, scanning his face with her bright blue eyes.

"I think it's our turn to kiss. What do you think?"

"I would like that," Julie softly said, now totally focused on his eyes.

Doc, now intensely staring in her eyes, and little by little was moving his face even closer to hers, whispered again, "I have to tell you, Julie . . . when I kiss you, it'll be forever." Their faces were so close now, they could hear and feel each other breathing. Doc continued, "There's no turning back."

Julie responded with a quiet whisper, "My eyes adore you." And then with a lump in her throat, she slowly started to close her eyes, as if to encourage Doc to place his lips on hers. Suddenly, and without warning, there was a noticeable splash in the water right next to the port side of the boat, only a few feet away. Both startled, Julie instinctively pulled away from Doc and turned her head down to the water to see what caused the sudden disturbance. Doc too instantly pulled his head back and quickly stood up. Staring at the two of them from the cold inlet water was a young black seal. With water dripping from the seal's long whiskers, he looked at Doc and Julie, as if they were long-lost pals. He did not seem to be afraid of them at all, and even gave the impression that he wanted to be their friend.

With the seal's head still popped up out of the water, Julie quickly blurted out, "Oh! Isn't he cute?"

"Yea, I have to admit . . . he is. His timing isn't exactly great, but he is adorable. There are lots of seals in this inlet." Just then, the playful seal started splashing around the boat, as if to put on a private show for Doc and Julie. As they followed with their eyes and heed his movements, his swimming about the floating craft, Julie, who was obviously enchanted by the little fellow, said to Doc, "I always forget that this is seawater. It just seems so much like a lake!"

"I know. Kids get confused all the time about this being an inlet, saltwater, from the Pacific Ocean, even though there are a lot of freshwater streams flowing into it. Just like Chatterbox Falls." The little seal was still splashing near the boat, diving under the water, and then popping back out again, as it appeared to be putting on a water show for the two humans in the cove. Turning toward Julie, Doc explained, "We even get killer whales in this inlet from time to time. Bet you didn't know that?"

"Golly! No, I didn't know that. Really?"

"Oh yea. They show up in the spring sometimes, even in early summer . . . June. I remember one time I was down on my dock, pumping the bilge out of the Seinskiff—this was a year ago, June—I had just become the harbormaster—Vic came running down from the upper deck, hollering for me and Kyle to get the skiers out of the water because he spotted a pod of orcas heading for the narrows from Jervis."

"Oh my gosh! You're kidding me?"

"No, I'm not. It just so happened that the *Skookum*, this baby right here"—he opened his arms toward the boat's interior—"was tied alongside the dock, so I hopped in and hauled as fast as I could to warn all the boat drivers pulling skiers. By the time I got out to the last boat, the killer whales were swimming alongside us. It was wild . . . and a bit scary!"

"Wow! I bet it was. Did anybody get hurt?"

"No . . . fortunately. But one skier—a gal—was still in the water when one of the larger whales passed by her only a few feet away. She freaked! But the driver, with the help of the spotter, was able to pull her in quickly and safely. I'll never forget that day, nor will she, I'm sure!"

"What happened to the whales?"

"Oh, they swam around for a while. Mac said he saw them near the falls. But they were gone—back out the narrows—by evening. The entire camp watched them with amazement. It was so cool when they swam back out the rapids and past Forbidden Island. Edna took a few pictures from Flag Point with her camera."

"So, speaking of Edna. And talking about how articulate Mac is . . ." Engaging in conversation again, Doc and Julie sat back down in the comfortable cushioned leather seats, in front near the helm and bow.

Julie continued, "I was talking to Edna this morning, and she told me about when she became a Christian a couple of summers ago here at Malibu. She said it started when she witnessed the power of the love between the work crew, staff, and councilors. She said she watched it flow between them like an electric current. Isn't that neat?

"That is neat."

"And then she said, one night—after listening and reading about the Christian faith for weeks—she'd given up trying to reason things out, and in one living moment, she was engulfed in clarity. She believed and accepted Him. She said it was like a strong tide that rushed in on a quiet bay and washed it clean. She said it was the beginning of a joyful awareness of Christ in her life. Is that beautiful or what?"

"Yea, it sure is. I remember that time. She hasn't stopped glowing ever since!" Doc said with a broad smile. As the Chris-Craft continued to float quietly in the cove, Doc shifted his body once again closer to Julie. He gently held his hand up to the side of her face and hair. Softly fondling her hair, he slid his fingers down the strands to her shoulders and said, "You are incredibly beautiful, did you know that? I love your eyes and your hair and your nose." Julie reacted with a faint smile. Doc then said, "I don't want to let go of you, my princess."

"I don't want you to. Please hold me closer."

They embraced with a hug for a few seconds, and when they let go and faced each other again, with intimacy in his voice, Doc looked straight into her vibrant eyes and said, "I think I'm in love with you, Julie."

In silence, a few seconds went by, and then Julie, with a slight tear in her eye, said softly to Doc, "Me too."

Doc, trying to be sensitive and sweet, responded to her by quietly saying, "You're in love with you too?"

Breaking into a giggle, Julie quickly, but tenderly, struck Doc on the arm with her left hand. "No, silly. You know what I mean."

"I have something for you."

"You do?" Julie wiped her tear and then asked, "What?"

Doc stood up in the boat so that he could easily reach down into his front right jean pocket and pulled out a small old blue jewelry case. He sat back down, and as he held it up near Julie's face, he opened it to reveal a delicate ruby cross necklace. Julie had an astonished look on her face.

"This was my mother's," Doc explained, as he carefully lifted it out of the hinged-top little case. Setting the container next to him on the seat, he gently held the necklace up from its delicate silver chain, as the ruby cross hung and swung in front of Julie's surprised face. "It's the only personal thing I have of hers. I want you to have it."

With a dumbfounded look, Julie immediately said to him while slowly shaking her head sideways, "Doc . . . I couldn't possibly—"

"It's important to me," Doc interrupted her. "I want you to wear it. Nobody here's ever seen it, so they won't know that I gave it to you."

"But, why would you give this to me . . . we're just getting to know each other," Julie said with obvious uneasiness and embarrassment.

"I'm serious, Julie . . . I really am falling for you. I already feel in my heart a special love for you, beyond just being a friend."

"You are so sweet and kind, Doc. I feel that same extraordinary love for you too. Remember that special connection we talked about at Chatterbox, on the hike? How we both feel like there's a weird common closeness between us . . . as if we've been together before? You know, when you tried to kiss me, you bad boy!" She giggled.

"Yes, I do, of course. Well, anyway, my dear pretty lady, I absolutely—one hundred percent—want you to have, and wear, my mother's necklace, as a token of my love for you."

"Gosh! It's so beautiful. I love that it's a Christian cross."

"Beautiful enough to be worn by a princess—my princess."

Julie, stunned—but happily and proudly pleased—told Doc, as he slowly placed the necklace over her head and into place around her neck, "I will cherish it forever. I promise."

As she bent her head in a downward position and looked at the tangling, attractive necklace, Doc gently held her hands and said to her, "Julie, there is something I would like for you to do for me."

Quickly looking up at Doc, she responded, "What's that? Anything."

"When we're together . . . alone. Don't call me Doc. Please call me Joseph, okay?"

"I don't understand . . . why?"

"Because I just think it's more personal . . . does that make sense? My real name is Joseph, and so I just prefer you to call me by my real name. According to my dad, my mother loved the name *Joseph*. In fact, she named me."

"Okay, Joseph," she sweetly said to him, as she gently squeezed his hands. "I love the name *Joseph*, and it's a very biblical name as well."

As Doc squeezed her hand back, he said to her, "So, speaking of kissing, a bit ago. I think we need to resume with our inevitable kiss. Don't you?"

"I've already kissed you in my dreams . . . but if you insist."

Doc shifted himself over closer to Julie, when all of a sudden, Julie quickly cocked her head slightly, her eyes looking curious; she uttered to Doc, "What's that noise?"

Doc spun around in his seat, causing the boat to sway some-what, as Julie grabbed a hold of the top back of her chair. Just as Doc stood up, keeping his balance by grabbing on to the back of his seat, a white, thirty-five-foot sailboat entered the cove from the backside of the island. With its sails down off the mast, the craft chugged swiftly into the small body of inlet water, powered by its diesel engine, below deck. Immediately, Doc and Julie could see a few folks aboard, as the skipper angled the boat toward the *Skookum*. Although somewhat frustrated, the duo looked at each other with a startled look, obviously disappointed that their first kiss got inter-rupted again. Soon the nice-looking sailboat was by their side, as it slowed down to anchor in the cove. The middle-aged man behind the wheel, wearing all white, waved his hand toward Doc and Julie as he hollered out, "Ahoy!"

"Hi there!" Doc hollered back as Julie waved. "Going to hang out here for a while, are you?"

"Yes, we are. I'm Robert Dingerman, and this is my wife and son. We're from the Seattle area." They all greeted one another with smiles and waves. "I think we'll plan to anchor here overnight. We're not infringing on the two of you, are we?"

"Oh, gosh no! In fact, we were just getting ready to head back to Malibu, the resort you passed by as you came through the narrows. We both work there. I'm the camp's harbormaster, and Julie works in the dining room."

Instructing his thirteen-year-old boy to man the anchor up on the bow, Robert then turned back and responded to Doc, "Well, it was a pleasure meeting you both. That's quite a spot you've got there at the Jervis Inlet—magnificent."

"You should stop by on your way out of the Princess Inlet. We have a hostess that would gladly give you all a quick tour of Malibu. Are you going to head down to Chatterbox Falls tomorrow? You should," Doc exclaimed, with conviction in his voice. "The falls are amazing."

"Yes, we plan to do that. We'll hope to see you in a couple of days," Robert answered, with his grayish hair blowing slightly in the breeze.

Doc started up the *Skookum* as Julie took her seat. Soon the Chris-Craft was slicing once again through the dark water that now had a little ripple to it. As the Malibu's fancy ski boat moved away from the anchoring sailboat, Julie and Doc noticed the name on the stern, which read, *Splish Splash.* They both giggled, as they assumed the name was taken from the popular rock-and-roll song recorded by Bobby Darin in 1958.

Smiling at each other, and before engaging the throttle to a faster pace, Doc said to Julie, with discontent in his voice, "Well, so much for our first kiss. I think someone's trying to tell us something."

Looking discouraged herself, Julie reached out and placed her hand on Doc's arm, which was rested on the seat, while his other arm and hand was steering the boat. "Gee, maybe you're right." The boat had now moved around the island and was about to enter the main inlet. "You could pull back the throttle and kiss me here, right? I'm good with that, my dear Joseph."

"Yea, that is so tempting, huh? I don't know. Now I'm thinking we need to wait, for some reason. It's weird. It's like, why do we keep getting interrupted? Is someone trying to tell us something? God perhaps? I mean, it's driving me crazy, princess. I have such a desire to kiss you . . . but now I'm thinking . . ."

"You're thinking what?" Julie slipped her hand down his arm, to his hand, and held it tight. "Have you changed you mind about your feelings for me?" she asked him, with concern in her voice.

"Oh, gosh no, Julie! I just want to do what's right. Maybe—for whatever reason—we're not supposed to get physical with each other quite yet. I don't know." Doc had a confused, troubled, look on his face as he looked directly into Julie's eyes.

"It's okay, Joseph . . . really. We can both be patient and kiss when we think it's right. I'm good with that. Well, kind of. I want you to kiss me, and me you. But let's just wait a while, until we figure all this out, okay? I care enough about you that I can wait for physical intimacy."

Squeezing Julie's hand, still steering the boat with his other hand, Doc calmly said to her, "I agree. But please just know that I truly feel love for you, understand?"

"Absolutely. I feel the same. I know we can wait, okay?"

"Okay." Doc grinned at her as he let go of her hand and turned his head toward the front of the bow. He then placed his left hand on the wheel, as he used his right hand to engage the throttle forward. Speeding swiftly through the inlet waters of the Princess Louisa, Doc aimed the craft toward Malibu. Doc and Julie both relaxed back into their seats, enjoying the bouncy ride across the wind-driven waves of the spectacular inlet. The sun was beginning to set, as the resort began to appear only as a silhouette against the radiant sky.

CHAPTER 10

The Past Can Certainly Reveal A Persons Character

Before living in Spokane, Julie grew up in Eastern Idaho as a young girl. Located near the Henry's Fork of the Snake River, St. Anthony was a small, windy town, established just north of Idaho Falls and west of the famous Teton Mountains of Idaho and Wyoming. Surrounded by dozens of farms and ranches, the town was also known for its juvenile detention center. In those days, the population of St. Anthony was only about 1,300. Winters were cold, with a few feet of snow and cold howling winds, but summer was hot, mostly in the nineties.

Julie's young parents were struggling to pay their bills, so they lived in a humble, single-story, older house near St. Anthony's two-block downtown district. Her dad, Jack, was a schoolteacher at the little redbrick high school nearby, teaching tenth grade and drama. He was also studying for his master's in theater and creative arts at Idaho State University in Pocatello, which was ninety miles away from St. Anthony. He commuted twice a week round-trip. Her mom, Mary Jo, taught private piano and violin lessons out of their home. Even though it was difficult for them to financially make ends meet each month, the small northwestern town was ideal to raise children in a safe, healthy environment in the 1950s. The detention center was well managed and guarded, so it was not an issue, regarding the security of the town. There was little crime, and the people were pleasant, courteous, and respectful. Julie's parents were well-liked in town and were members of the historic Presbyterian

Church on Main Street. Her mom volunteered to play the piano for the congregation each Sunday, and her dad was a trustee. Many of her music students attended the church. Julie was in the children's choir and a member of the Brownies, an organization for younger girls before entering Girl Scouts. Not only was she a pretty little girl, but her kindness and sweet demeanor made her the Pollyanna of the town. Everyone, including the church minister, always talked about how special and caring little Julie was. (*Pollyanna* is in reference to the popular 1960s film about a young orphan of that name who believes life's most difficult problems can always be surmounted by a positive attitude and pragmatism.)

One of Julie's mom's favorite stories about her young daughter was when Julie was about three years old, she was terrible about going to bed. Mary Jo, or Jack, would tuck her in bed, read her a story, and turn out the lights. Only minutes later, when her parents were either watching television in the living room, or preparing music or school assignments in the study, they would look up from their activity to discover that Julie had slowly walked into the room.

"Can I have a drink of milk?" she would sheepishly ask. Or "I have to use the bathroom." Her little mind had every excuse in the book to allow her to not have to return to her bed. Sometimes her parents would allow her to stay up for a while longer, but usually they insisted that she go back to bed, as they escorted her into her bedroom and into bed again. When Julie was approaching four, and this behavior could not continue, her mom was tucking her into bed for the third time one night. She sat next to her on the bed and told her that she had to stop getting up from bed. She said to Julie with a soft, but serious voice, "Did you know that it's my job to put you to bed and make sure that you go right to sleep?" As Julie curiously listened, her mom continued, "God told me and assigned me to this job—this task of making sure you get your sleep. Do you know why it's my job?"

"No!" Julie simply answered with her sweet small voice.

"Because I'm your mommy, and God made it my job to make sure you sleep well at night so that in the morning when you wake up, you'll be rested and will have the necessary energy to eat your breakfast, play, and enjoy your day. So, you don't want God mad at me for not properly doing my job, right?"

Again, her mom heard a simple, soft, "No," from her three-year-old, who had her head on her pillow and blankets covering her little body.

To her parents' surprise that night, their young daughter did not get out of bed again, but did as she was told, and soon fell asleep for the night. The next morning, before her dad had to leave the house for work, Julie's mom was serving her some Cheerios cereal with some orange juice for breakfast, and she asked Julie if she had sweet dreams last night. As her dad was also listening nearby for her answer, Julie looked up from the table at her mom and calmly said, "I think so . . . but before I fell asleep, I talked to God and asked Him if he would please fire you from your job."

As her mom quickly turned away from Julie and glanced at Jack, she had difficulty not to burst into laughter. Her dad had to immediately turn away as well as he tried to hold back his amusement. As hard as it is sometimes for young parents to keep self-control when their child suddenly says something enormously funny, there are moments that cannot be easily dealt with. This was certainly one of those moments. But surprisingly enough, Julie's parents did not break into laughter in the presence of their innocent young child, Julie. Why? Because together they made a sudden break for the living room, where they could share in muffled laughter as they faced each other with astonished expressions. They decided that this moment is one of the wonderful reasons of having children. And besides getting to enjoy this humorous incident over and over through the years, the really good news that morning was that from that day forward, Julie never got out of bed after being tucked in and lights off. Perhaps, in her young mind, she just assumed that God would not okay her prayer request. She probably decided that He would not fire her mom from her job of making sure she stayed in bed and went to sleep. "God was the boss, and that was that!"

When Julie was twelve, and would soon be entering middle school, her dad received his master's degree in creative arts and was offered a position at a college in Spokane, Washington. He couldn't pass it up, because the pay was significantly higher than his current teaching job in St. Anthony. So they soon packed up and moved to the heart of the Inland Northwest. The city of Spokane was a major change for them, since the population was close to 125,000 people. They soon settled into this outdoors-lovers paradise and enjoyed the beauty of Washington State. The Spokane River runs through the downtown with spectacular falls on the western end of the city core. There was plenty of shopping available, along with entertainment and cultural events. With much less wind than St. Anthony, the hiking trails and lakes nearby were particularly inviting, which Julie's parents soon took advantage of, sharing their adventures with young Julie and her little sister, Robin. Jack was not only a professor at the university in Spokane, in charge of the drama department, but he also was the head of the popular Spokane Performing Arts Theater, which certainly boosted his income, and he also became well-liked in the performance community. Living in a much nicer two-story home, located in one of the older influential established neighborhoods, the Copelands were comfortable and content. Julie's mother was once again teaching private piano and violin lessons in their home music room, adjacent to the study and library. With the help of Jack's contacts, she had a full schedule of students, along with a waiting list of children who were hoping to become part of her music program. Soon after moving to Spokane, the family joined the First Presbyterian Church, located near the center of town and established in the 1930s. The tall white bell tower steeple played a prominent role in the town's landscape and could be seen from almost anywhere near the city. The congregation was large, and when she had the time, Julie was involved in the successful youth program that the church offered.

Julie was quite happy in the middle school she was attending and was an honor student her first year. She was extremely popular with her classmates and was active in the music program and cheerleading for the basketball and football teams. For a short while, she got involved in Girl Scouts, but then a close friend introduced her to Job's Daughters. She was quick to enjoy all the activities that the international organization offered, including swimming parties, dances, family picnics, slumber parties, miniature golf, and marching in the Spokane parade on the Fourth of July. She also enjoyed and appreciated the service projects, helping the less fortunate in the community and supporting the Hearing-Impaired Kids Endowment (HIKE). With a rich heritage, Job's Daughters was a wonderful young women's organization that taught Julie leadership skills, helping others, and commitment to quality friendship and moral principles. She enjoyed wearing the Grecian robes, provided by the Bethel, and respected the solemn initiations and meaningful ceremonies presented by the Bethel officers. There were many adult volunteers, with whom she became close to. Being a member of the Job's Daughters, she learned skills that would help her throughout her life.

Another pastime that Julie enjoyed was being a volunteer storyteller at the main library downtown, reading stories to young children every Wednesday evening. She loved little kids and had a talent of teaching and working with children. They loved her too and flocked to her like bees to honey. At an early age, Julie had an amazing gift of patience. She also had the ability to communicate well with the young. Her sweetness and determination helped her to be successful with her childhood audience. Even the adults in the room, the parents of these young children, were impressed with Julie's flair for storytelling. Sitting in a big, ornate chair and wearing clothes that would enhance her presentation, she always had the attention of all the kids, who were sitting on the floor. As she read the story, she would dramatically bring it to life, along with sharing the illustrations in the books. She would often stand up and move about the front area, which allowed her to interact closely with her audience. Julie started at the library when she was in eighth grade, and she continued her storytelling on through her high school years.

Julie was an amazing big sister. She adored her younger sibling, Robin, who over the years always wanted to emulate her. The fact that they were six years apart in age did not diminish their closeness. From the day Robin was born, Julie began bonding with her and never stopped. She sincerely enjoyed spending time with her. When Robin was young, Julie read to her and attended her tea parties. When she was old enough, Julie began teaching her how to play the violin. Whenever it was possible, they were inseparable. The two of them enjoyed every minute they could spend together. Julie was always patient and accommodating with her little sister. Her love for her was unconditional and enduring. And when she could, she protected her and shielded her from feelings of disappointment and frustration. There were times when she took the blame for something Robin had done to protect her from the consequences. As Julie got older and more mature, she realized that, as a Christian, she knew it was her responsibility to help teach Robin the value of proper morals—such as honesty, kindness, and decency. Her parents had certainly instilled these values upon their youngest daughter, just as they did with her. However, as Robin's older sister, Julie felt that she could impress upon her these values through personal example, knowing how much Robin looked up to her.

One day at home, when Robin was ten years old, Julie was teaching her a new song on the violin in the music room. Robin asked to take a break so that she could get a glass of milk. Placed on top of the refrigerator was an antique glass cookie jar, which had been given to Jack in years past by his grandmother. Passed down from several generations, the screw-top jar was a family heirloom. Whoever was last to replace the container atop the large appliance did not push it far enough back to properly secure it safely. Over time, and after many door openings and closings, the jar had evidently shifted toward the front and top edge of the door. When Robin opened the refrigerator to retrieve the milk carton, the cookie jar came crashing down! It barely missed the top of her head, as the cylindrical container struck the floor and completely shattered. Tiny pieces of glass went flying in every direction of the kitchen floor and beyond. The loud noise of the impact was instantly heard by Julie, who was still in the music room nearby. She swiftly ran into the kitchen to investigate the disturbance, and soon discovered Robin standing completely still next to the open refrigerator door. Her sister's "deer in the headlights" expression was a clear indicator that an accident had just occurred, along with the signs of broken glass distributed throughout most of the kitchen floor. Julie instinctively blurted out, "Are you okay?"

Robin slowly turned her head toward her big sister and sheepishly answered, "I think so."

Carefully navigating through the shattered glass, Julie quickly moved over to Robin and began looking her over carefully. "What happened?" she asked, as she continued to inspect her sister's well-being.

"I don't know! I just opened the refrigerator door, and the cookie jar suddenly fell off the top!" Robin answered with an anxious voice.

"Well, that's strange," Julie responded, as she looked up at the refrigerator for a short moment and then glanced down at the scattered pieces of glass and broken cookies on the floor.

Suddenly Robin had a worried thought and immediately shared it with Julie. "You don't think I was trying to reach the cookie jar, do you?"

Without hesitation, Julie said, "No, of course not." But then after a brief pause, she added, "You weren't, were you?"

"No, I swear, Julie! Honest! You believe me, don't you?"

"Yes, of course I do. Besides, I don't see a chair nearby, and you couldn't have reached it without one. It was an accident. I'm just glad you're all right."

"But, Julie, the cookie jar! Dad's going to be mad at me."

"No, he's not. It wasn't your fault. Somehow that jar must have caught the edge of the door, and when you opened it, it fell. It could have been anyone of us opening the door causing it to fall."

"But can you just tell Dad that you opened the door, and it fell?"

"Robin, listen to me. As I said, it was strictly an accident. He will be glad that you're okay too and that you didn't get hurt. And no, I'm not going to lie and tell Dad it was me who opened the door."

"But that was his grandma's cookie jar . . . and now it's broken in a thousand pieces. And I broke it!" Robin began to whimper. Julie reached out and gave Robin a hug. Her worried little sister looked up at her and said, "It was also our great-grandmother's cookie jar."

"I know, and it's unfortunate, but it's just a thing. It's just a material object, and it can be replaced. Unlike more important things, like your head!" They both slightly giggled, as Julie placed her hand on top of her little sister's hair. "And besides, Robin, when we choose to use something, like this cookie jar, then we have to expect that it's possible for it to accidently get broken. We're lucky that it's been part of our family's history for such a long period and that we got to use it and enjoy it for as long as we did. You agree with me, right?"

"Yea, I guess so. I just feel bad for Dad. I'm sure he'll be upset when he finds out."

"He'll feel bad about it, you're right. But he's not going to be mad at you—at all. Dad will be happy that you didn't get hurt, I'll guarantee you! Now, with that, we had better clean up this mess. Don't move, stay right here. I'm going to get the broom and dustpan." Julie had such a loving, comforting way with her younger sister, Robin. It was a relationship that continued to grow strong as time went by.

Julie wasn't allowed to date until she was sixteen, and even then, she was always chaperoned until her seventeenth birthday. From the time she was in upper grade school, she was well-liked and popular with the majority of her peers, and even with some in the grade ahead of her. Her moral beliefs, established by her parental upbringing, along with her church and Job's Daughters' affiliation, helped her to make wise decisions regarding her behavior and choosing friends during her adolescent years. The only time that she may have slightly drifted outside those boundaries was a recent relationship with a boy in her senior year, just before the summer and working at Malibu. The young man in question was her age and a member of the football team. He was good-looking and quite popular with his classmates. Being a star athlete at high school certainly made him recognizable and accepted as one of the well-known seniors. But after dating him a few months, Julie came to understand that she had made a mistake. Life was all about him, and in the end, he was not the boyfriend she wanted to be with. In fact (as it turned out), it was not just because he always had to come first and had to make all the decisions, but he really was not a nice person. Over time she began to see how he treated people with little respect, sometimes even degrading them and treading on their feelings. She concluded that he was conceited and uncaring. He always had an agenda, and if it did not benefit him, then he was an unhappy person. During the beginning of summer, in early June, she broke up with him. He took the news hard and was basically in denial that Julie no longer wanted to be his girlfriend. Fortunately, her trip to Malibu quickly emerged, and therefore, she soon left town to work in British Columbia.

Julie became active in the local Young Life Club when she started high school, because some of her friends in middle school invited her to participate in Wyld Life, a younger-aged organization, which is affiliated with Young Life. Wyld Life was so much fun that it was only natural for her to attend Young Life in her sophomore year. During the summer, before starting her senior year of high school, she signed up for camp at Frontier Ranch in Colorado, one of Young Life's original camps, which started operating in the early 1950s. She had such a great time that week as a camper, the following school year she immediately talked to her Young Life leader about applying for work crew at camp. He suggested that she apply to the Malibu Club, in Canada, a shorter distance from Spokane. And it would be an entirely different experience than returning to the ranch in Colorado. Since Julie had been to a Young Life camp, and because she was growing spiritually with her Christian faith, she was chosen to work at Malibu in July of 1966.

CHAPTER 11

A Letter from Camp

When Mary Jo heard the front door open, she hollered out from the kitchen.

"Is that you, Jack?"

"Yes, it's me, sweetheart," Jack quickly answered, as he opened one of the heavy oak front double doors, with an etched-half-round glass on the top end. When he entered the entryway into their beautiful two-story colonial-style home, he hollered back, "I'll be right there. I just need to drop off this briefcase in the study." While walking along the hardwood floors, and passing the attractive staircase on his left, which displayed a massive banister, he entered the study to his right. Jack was a handsome, tall, slender man in his early fifties. He was wearing a light-blue suit, dark-blue tie, and sporting a Vandyke-style goatee.

While Jack was dropping his work off in the walnut-paneled spacious study and home library, Mary Jo shouted out to him again.

"We got a letter from Julie today."

"Great!" Jack hollered back, as he exited the study, heading for the kitchen. "What did she have to say?" he asked, while walking from his home office to the well-lit, mostly white kitchen, located in the back corner of the house. The large rectangle windows on the upper corners, along with a skylight installed in the center of the nine-foot ceiling, allowed plenty of sunlight into the sizeable room. The modern kitchen, with upgraded appliances and a big built-in handcrafted walnut table, was spotless and well decorated. It had a country flavor to it, with several beautiful flowering plants adding color to the room. There was a wide ornate-metal baker's rack along one section of an inside wall. When Jack entered the room, he found Mary Jo at the half butcher block, half-white counter island, which had two heavy oak barstools on one end. Mary Jo was chopping carrots as she prepared dinner. She was an attractive woman in her late forties, with few wrinkles and smooth light-tan skin. With stylish medium-length blond hair, she was wearing a powder-blue country summer dress (which matched her eyes) and a long white apron, which was tied in a bow in the back of her slim waist. Jack entered the kitchen with his jacket removed, ready for his wife to answer his question about Julie.

Mary Jo looked up as she stopped using the kitchen knife and said, "She's having a fantastic time. The letter is right over there." She pointed with the knife toward a small built-in desk, located at the end of a long counter. Jack quickly walked over to her and leaned down to her five-foot-three stature and placed a quick kiss directly on her lips. As he turned and headed for the desk, she spoke again. "Go ahead and read it . . . she met a boy."

"What do you mean she met a boy?" Jack responded with puzzlement in his voice.

"He's her age, and on summer staff. He's the camp's harbormaster."

"Are they just friends or what?" Jack asked with a degree of suspicion.

"Relax, Jack." Mary Jo smiled at him and slightly shook her head. "No. I think they're more than just friends. Read the letter."

"What about Richard?"

"What about Richard?" Mary Jo repeated the question back, as if she didn't understand the question or the relevance.

"I thought she and Richard were a steady thing?" Jack said back, again looking somewhat baffled.

"Not really. I mean, they were, but she's been trying to break up with him for over a month now. You know, Jack, he really doesn't treat her very well. I think his parents' wealth has spoiled him too much."

"Well, that may be true. The family business has made a ton of money. I always thought he was a little cocky and seemed a bit too nice to me. You know what I mean? I'm not happy to hear that he's been treating her badly. That I don't like, so I'm glad to hear she's breaking up with him. So what's with that? What do you mean she's been trying to break up with him for over a month? Doesn't he get it?"

"No, I don't think he does. He's really stubborn and in denial," answered Mary Jo with a concerned look and voice.

"Maybe I need to talk to him," Jack quickly reacted.

"No. Not just yet, Jack. Let them work it out. She's hoping that being up in Canada for a month, he'll forget about her and start dating someone else."

As Jack glanced down at the handwritten letter in his left hand, he continued to talk. "Well, whatever. I just hope that she's not getting out of line with this new guy at camp. My understanding is that the work crew are not supposed to have steady relationships between each other."

"I'm sure she's being cautious about the whole thing. Read the letter, honey . . . he's into drama."

"Oh, he is . . . really?" Jack continued to read Julie's letter. With a more positive expression, he continued his conversation. "Well, then he must be okay if he likes acting and performing." He looked up and made eye contact with Mary Jo, winking at her and smiling, as she smiled back.

"He's also been involved in Young Life now for a number of years, and if you read on, Julie writes that this is his second year working at Malibu, and that he's really dedicated to his Christian faith." Her husband continued to listen to her as he read the letter. "That's the other thing too, Jack . . . Julie told me once that Richard has no spiritual feelings or, for that matter, doesn't even believe in God. In fact, he evidently has verbally attacked Julie about her Christian beliefs and for attending church. He even tried to get her to stop going to Young Life Club."

Jack looked up and said to her, "Well, now I see why she wanted to break off their relationship and why she's interested in this new guy, Doc----that's his nickname, I guess?"

"Oh!" Mary Jo interrupted. "I don't know if you've read this yet, but camp management made her the waitress for the head table, which is where the camp manager and adult guests sit. Isn't that great?" Mary Jo exclaimed, with pride in her voice.

"Yea, that's wonderful," Jack agreed, still reading the letter. Looking up again, he asked, "By the way, where's Robin?"

"Oh, she's upstairs. I think she's drawing a picture for Julie for when we write her back. She sure misses her big sister."

"Oh, I'm sure she does. So do I . . . and I know you do too. But this is great experience for her, and I'm sure she's having fun!" As Mary Jo nodded her head yes in agreement, Jack returned to reading the letter and, without looking up, said, "Well, our little Robin still has over three weeks to go before her big sister's return. She'll be okay though." He spoke with assurance.

CHAPTER 12

Howdy, Partner

At the end of another fun-filled day of activities at Malibu, the campers were surprised to learn that the daily Young Life Club meeting in Big Squawka was scheduled for early evening, before dinner. Everyone had gathered under the roof of the jam-packed structure, centrally located just below Main Street in Malibu Village. Accompanied by two acoustic guitarists, Jake was on stage conducting the singing as the volume projected from his audience was loud, but cheerful. With everyone in the room participating in a joyful way, Jake knew that the campers, counselors, adult guests, work crew, and staff were all enjoying this time of letting their hearts sing out in fun and praise. The tiny songbooks distributed and used by everyone was a helpful guide to remember the words of happy songs, ballads, and hymns, sung each evening during the club meeting.

When Jake finished directing the songs, he was quickly replaced on stage by the camp manager, Chet, who wasted no time continuing his message about the *greatest story ever told*, the historical life of Jesus Christ. On the previous night, as he continued to reference the Phillips version of the New Testament, he shared with his audience some of the important teachings and miracles that Jesus had taught and performed during His early adult years. Chet's verbal communication with his young audience this evening would be centered on Christ's brutal beatings and crucifixion on the cross. He told his young listeners the sad truth of His false judgment, tortured punishment, and the final barbaric act of God in the flesh being nailed to timbers of wooden planks, atop a hill above the city. Then he described how the Roman soldiers dropped the base of the heavy cross into a hole, whereby Jesus would be on display and suffer and die, as the sun beat down upon Him. Chet's detailed description of this horrible day certainly got the attention of all the young campers sitting on the floor in front of him. Many of those inside the room were wide-eyed and tearful. He continued to talk to his audience more about the intense pain and agony that Christ suffered, but soon went on to explain that God was willing to sacrifice His only son for the sake, and sins, of mankind. He then continued on to concisely explain what occurred on the third day following Jesus's crucifixion. Chet described the significance and importance of His resurrection and the historical facts of the guarded tomb that had been discovered empty the next morning, the huge granite stone mysteriously rolled away from the entryway. Again, reading scriptures from his Bible, he spoke about the many people that Christ came in contact with after His resurrection and before His ascension into heaven.

There was no doubt that Chet had a gift for clearly speaking and communicating to young people, and this club meeting was no exception. He had undoubtedly connected with his audience this evening to a point of them almost being mesmerized by his gift of reaching out to them verbally and emotionally with this crucial knowledge and information that could ultimately change their lives forever. After his closing prayer, Chet asked that everyone immediately proceed from Big Squawka to their living spaces in camp to participate in their evening cabin time. (Cabin time was an opportunity for small groups of roommates, along with their councilor, to discuss the *message* that Chet had just delivered in the club meeting. A chance to weigh in on the dialogue and conversation about what the camp manager had just been speaking to them about. Open discussion with friends and your councilor was a good way to dissect and converse one's thoughts and feelings regarding what was taught and said by Chet.) So when everyone began to exit the building, there was a great deal of chatter among the hundreds of kids, most of whom were tossing their little songbooks into the available bins nearby the doorways. The talk was mostly related to Chet's words, and continued as the groups of individuals began to split apart as they headed for their respective cabins.

To mark the end of cabin time, a loud blast from the camp's air horn was heard throughout the resort. As the camp guests were mostly filtering into the center of Malibu Village, many right away spotted a curious scene on Main Street. The word got out quickly, and everyone maneuvered themselves around the outskirts of the main boardwalk so that they could see what was about to happen there. What they soon learned was that the staff and work crew had transformed the center of Malibu into a scene from the Old West. With simple sets as a backdrop to depict an old dusty Western town of the late 1800s, about two dozen cast members entertained their young audience and adult guests with a gun-blazing bank robbery and shoot-out! Among the participants were Doc, Julie, Vic, Ken, Jake, Chet, and Chris. At the end of the wild, rowdy, five-minute event, the town sheriff (Vic) shot the bank robber (Doc) with his quick-draw trusty Colt .45 (blank) revolver. *BANG!* Doc fell to the ground, dropping his revolver and bag of cash. As the (fake) paper money spilled out onto the boardwalk, the Western bystanders (in character) gawked at the incident. At that moment, all the actors in the entire scene, except for Vic, froze, as if time had stopped! Shouting loudly up into the air, and turning a full three hundred and sixty degrees, allowing everyone to hear his boosting deep voice, he hollered out, "Ladies and gentlemen. In forty-five minutes' time, come to the Grand Hotel for dinner, drinks, and fun—on the house. Everyone, come!" He then pulled his revolver out of its brown leather holster, cocked the hammer, and fired another blank into the air. *BANG!* The shinny, blue-steel gun was smoking! Rusty and his friends, who were on the deck just above Vic, suffered the loud blast of noise from the revolver.

With excited shouts of yahoos, everyone, including the performers, began moving around and greeting one another. Doc quickly jumped up from the boardwalk and glanced down the boardwalk looking for Julie. As soon as they made eye contact, she smiled at him, and he nodded at her. Those around him were laughing or reaching out to him with a handshake of "Job well done, partner!"

The entire camp had a fun time at the Grand Hotel (Malibu's dining room). The food and drinks were delicious and refreshing, as was the enjoyment of everyone participating in Western attire and singing a few old favorite Western tunes such as "Home On the Range" and "Red River Valley." The meal consisted of Cowboy Stew, with plenty of bread and butter, and root beer served in glass mugs. Dessert was cherry pie with two scoops of vanilla ice cream.

After the pleasurable time in the dining room, the campers and everyone gathered down in the inner dock area for some more fun and entertainment. Several bales of hay, used for scenery in the short Western scene before dinner, were up on a small stage near the gangplank. Julie was on the stage playing her fiddle, and was still wearing the long yellow Western church dress from the earlier boardwalk scene, but without her bonnet. Her beautiful flowing straight blond hair was dancing in the breeze as it blended nicely with her gown. Also on the raised platform with her was Chet, playing a gutbucket bass, which consisted of a large metal bucket turned upside down with a long narrow four-foot stick mounted into the bottom, and a bass string drawn taught against it. Popeye, the cook, was standing next to them playing rhythm guitar. The trio, performing acoustical, could be heard well by their listeners. Many of the campers and councilors were surrounding the front of the stage, or they were out in front of the performers on the large open deck. The adult guests were standing against the wooden railing on Big Squawka's back deck, high up above the teenagers and musicians. Jake too was on the stage with his megaphone, hollering out the dance steps to the tune "Oh Johnny Oh," as scores of teens were square dancing, partially dressed in Western clothing. Many of the guys had simple straw cowboy hats on as well, which were loaned to them by their counselors. A dozen or so of the gals were wearing country bonnets, which had also been borrowed from their leaders. There was a lot of hooting and hollering going on, as everyone was having a good ol' time, enjoying the music and kicking up their heels!

Doc, Ken, Chris, Vic, and Edna were standing to the right side of the stage enjoying the wonderful live music, along with the delight of watching the campers square dancing and laughing aloud. They found the dancing quite amusing, as many of the teens would often miss a step, since it was their first time to ever try this style of dance. The five of them were still in their "boardwalk scene," Western costumes as well. Doc was facing the stage, clapping his hands, as he was completely focused on Julie performing the song. When there was a break in the music, he quickly moved to the foot of the stage and complimented all the musicians on how great they sounded. He then turned directly to Julie and said to her over the noise of the crowd, "You can sure saw that fiddle, Julie. That was fantastic. Wow!"

"Yea, wasn't that something?" Chet agreed with Doc.

"Thanks," Julie expressed her sincere appreciation for the compliments. "I really do enjoy playing. And I think you guys are terrific! Great job, Jake, calling out the steps. I think the campers danced really well, don't you?"

"Yes, they did," Jake answered her. "There's nothing like live music to get your legs moving. It's sure a lot better than using records. You're going to spoil us, young lady. Say, do you know 'Cotton Eye Joe'?"

"Sure," Julie said to him with a big smile, once again exposing her cute dimples.

Doc looked at Julie with adoration as Jake turned to his trio and said, "Well, let's get stompin'!"

Julie straightaway started bowing her fiddle, and Chet began plucking his gutbucket again. Popeye jumped in with his guitar, as Jake grabbed his megaphone and began shouting out instructions to the teen dancers out on the large deck. The time was about 8:00 p.m. (Malibu time), and it was still light outside with a temperature at sixty-eight degrees. The sun would not set for another hour and forty-five minutes. Rusty and Diane, smiling and enjoying the fun, joined the scores of kids who were once again on the makeshift dance floor kicking up their heels. Doc returned back to Ken and the others. Standing close to Ken, he whispered in his ear, "Isn't she amazing?"

"Calm yourself, cowboy," Ken whispered back to him.

"I had no idea she was so talented," Doc whispered again, with a tone in his voice of true infatuation. "I wonder if she fiddles around," he said with humor. Ken gave him a concerned look, as Doc started clapping again to the music, sporting a broad smile.

CHAPTER 13

Oh No! Some Must Say Goodbye to Malibu

The next day, Malibu was once again in full swing. All the activities were up and running, including the swimming pool, waterskiing, Four Square, basketball, fishing, golfing, reading, hiking, and boating. At the pool, the diving board was quite popular, along with the slide at the other end, as teens were lined up to glide down the blue plastic curvy chute into the fresh cool water. Sunbathing was another enjoyable activity, along with talking and visiting with old and new friends. Atop one of the large granite boulders above the unique pool, and next to a large colorful totem pole, was a counselor having—what appeared to be—a serious talk with one of his cabin kids. In the far corner of the dining room balcony, overlooking the pool and all its activities was Chris and Rusty leaning against the round wooden railing. They were engaged in conversation, as a large white motor yacht—surely bound for Chatterbox Falls—sailed through the fast running rapids of the narrows and into the Princess Louisa Inlet.

"Gosh, the week went so fast," Rusty said to Chris, as they were watching the yacht pass behind the massive granite rock above the pool.

"I know, it seems like we just got here," Chris commented back to Rusty.

"You're so lucky you get to stay. Listen, Chris . . . this has been, without a doubt, the best week of my life, and I have you to thank for it, because I never would have come if you—"

"Hey, forget it," Chris quickly interrupted him. "I'm really happy you came and had a good time."

"I had more than just a good time, trust me. This place is magic. The people are so friendly and nice. They're just so real. Everyone takes off their masks, if you know what I mean? You can just unwind and be yourself. My counselor was a gas. He kept me in stitches the whole time. I could talk to him about stuff, anything!" (The word *gas* was another adjective frequently used by teenagers; its meaning is "fun.")

Placing his hand up on Rusty's shoulder, Chris seriously said to him, "You've changed, Rus. You're different than when you first got here, and I'm glad."

"Yea, I was such a jerk. Especially to you. I'm really sorry, man. I don't know, Malibu has just really opened my eyes to a lot of things, you know?"

"Yea, the beauty here is definitely a gift from God. But I think what truly stands out are the people. Like you said, they're real. And I think it's because they're focused on a common belief, their faith. That God's love for us is pure and unconditional. And that He has a plan for our lives. Sorry, I don't mean to sound all preachy, and so on, but I really believe that being a Christian is important in life. Oh, and not just because it happens to be my namesake!" Chris laughed.

Laughing as well, Rusty agreed with Chris, "I think you're right, Christian."

That evening, in Malibu's dining room, everyone was just finishing dessert. Julie was busy serving coffee to the adults in the far corner of the large room, just inside where Chris and Rusty had their conversation earlier in the day. The Malibu band had already entered the room in the normal "march through," around the tables that one and all were seated at. The band had played their theme song as everyone in the room was once again laughing at their humorous uniforms and expressions. After Jake rang the brass bell behind him, mounted on the stout cedar beam, he stepped up to the microphone and began speaking.

"And now it is with great pleasure that on this suspicious occasion, on the eve of your return back to civilization, that we honor this week's winning team." Ken started a drumroll. "Feast your eyes on this magnificent perpetual *tropy*." (Jake purposely mispronounced the word *trophy* in order to produce further laughs from his audience.) He uncovered the trophy that had been placed on a chair on the stage, covered with a folded red-checkered tablecloth. The *tropy*, as he called it, was tarnished, dented, and flat-out ugly. "This gorgeous, valuable *tropy* is to be presented to the captain and queen of their conquering crew. The team, who had to endure and overcome the magnitude of leaps, of courage and strength. The team that—"

"Get on with it!" shouted Edna (the majorette), who playfully slapped the back shoulder of Jake.

Jake immediately continued speaking. "This week's winner for the big race to the roses, by an ignominious decision, is the Nautical Navals!" In the middle of the lower level of the dining room, several tables of campers and counselors erupted with enthusiasm. They were genuinely overwhelmed with excitement. Cheers and boasting were heard throughout the large room, as were boos and gestures of thumbs-down. "Will King and Team Captain 'Mr. Enthusiasm' Rusty Johnson join us on stage along with the Queen for a Week, Ms. Diane Grimston."

The band right away began playing their theme song, "The Mickey Mouse Club Song," as Rusty and Diane proudly walked up and on to the stage. Everyone was hootin' and hollerin'! Rusty gave Diane a big hug, as Jake handed the unsightly trophy to them. Rusty then took hold of the tarnished award and lifted it up over his head, moving it from side to side so that everyone in the dining room can get a good look at it. The room exploded in laughter; everyone was clapping and eventually standing in praise for the winning captain and queen, and team. Rusty started chanting into the microphone, "Nautical Navals rule! Nautical Navals rule!"

A few minutes later when everyone was exiting the dining room, Rusty's councilor, Fergie, pulled him aside to talk to him privately.

"I'm proud of you, Rusty. No wonder our team voted you in as their team captain. You have great leadership skills and lots of enthusiasm! You and Beth both did a great job of keeping our team's spirit high and encouraging everyone to focus on the task, but to have fun doing it."

With a proud smile, Rusty said to his counselor, "Thanks, Fergie, it was definitely some great teamwork, but without Beth and your advice along the way, I'm not sure if I could have kept up my confidence in everyone. But in the end, we prevailed and beat all the other teams. Pretty cool, huh?"

"Absolutely, Rus! Job well done, buddy!" Fergie grabbed Rusty's right shoulder with his hand, in a gesture of pride. Then he moved slightly closer to him to talk more personally. "So, Rusty, I hope you're enjoying our Young Life clubs in Big Squawka in the evenings. I've noticed that during the last couple of cabin times, you've been showing interest in Chet's talks. In fact, you've even been willing to share and add some of your own thoughts and ideas about what he's had to say about God and Jesus, and other spiritual views and facts regarding Christianity. I just want you to know that it's encouraging to me to know that you are interested in more than just the fun things and activities that Malibu has to offer. That you're allowing yourself to ponder your thoughts about serious, life-changing issues and ideas. I also want you to know that if you ever want to talk *one-on-one* about this stuff, or if you have any questions related to what Chet and others have talked about, then I would be more than happy to be here for you, understand?"

Rusty somewhat reluctantly responded to Fergie, "I really appreciate that. I mean, you and I have already talked about some stuff, but I have to admit, if I want to be honest and open about it, I do find that the things Chet talks about in club are interesting and fascinating, and he definitely has my attention. I guess just processing it all, and believing and understanding, is the hard part. But I promise, Fergie, if I have any questions or want to talk more about it, you will certainly be the person I will come to. Thanks again for the offer. You're a terrific counselor."

Fergie smiled and simply said, "Anytime, Rus. Hey, I'll let you go and be with your friends. Again, great job as team captain! I'm truly proud of you, pal." Rusty scurried off down the dining room boardwalk to find his friends, while Fergie stood with his hands on the wooden railing, above the swimming pool. Standing there by himself, he closed his eyes in silent prayer.

After their final dinner, the campers enjoyed an hour and a half of free time before the last Young Life Club meeting of the week would begin. Some of the activities were still available, including golf, the craft shop, and shooting pool in Little Squawka. Many of the kids were shopping at the Totem Inn, purchasing last-minute items to take home, such as Malibu souvenirs, books, and clothing. Other campers, and perhaps their councilors, were sitting in small groups talking or walking around camp enjoying the breathtaking views. Some were hiking out by the outer dock and golf course, while others were just hanging around camp either on the boardwalk, down in the inner dock area, or out by the swimming pool. There were a few campers and adult guests who were in their cabins already packing and preparing for the journey home the next day.

When everyone heard the blast of the loud camp air horn, they knew that the club meeting would start in a half hour. Soon the sounds of blissful singing were heard, as the voices penetrated the large cedar structure in the center of Malibu Village. After at least a half dozen songs were sung, Chet once again took to the stage in front of the closed black curtains. He started out with a quick overview of the week. Their first day in camp, all the fun activities, the many humorous skits and entertainment by Jake and his program staff, the Chatterbox tours down the Princess Louisa Inlet, the organized team competition, and then a quick review of his club messages each night.

His last message to this group of campers, and others in the room, is about salvation and God's unconditional love for all of us. "God is love. God created love. Sometimes we hear people say, 'Love is God.' But that's incorrect, because God came first. He is our creator, and He also created Love, not the other way around." Chet read several quotes of scripture referencing God's great love, and why this is true. He talked about our own personal lives and how God has a plan for all of us. He sympathized with the difficulty of being a teenager, and he recognized how hard it is at times for young people to deal with the world around them: school, parents, siblings, friends, politics, sports, stress. He explained to them that if they accept Christ for who He truly is, they too can have a personal relationship with Him. They can let go of trying to control, and run, their own lives. That allowing Christ into their heart, they can know and trust that He will guide their everyday needs and decisions. "You are not alone, gang. The Lord is always ready to take control of your lives if you're willing to give Him that chance. Jesus is alive and well. He is the living God. You only need to reach out to Him with sincere love and belief and allow Him into your life."

The sun was beginning to hide behind one of the high western peaks overlooking the inlets and Malibu. The silence in Big Squawka was almost deafening, since everyone inside was holding on to every word that Chet spoke. "Jesus is knocking on your door, but you have to open it and invite Him in! I'm telling you, everyone, it's so simple to accept Christ into your heart and into your life. But you need to pray and sincerely give thanks to Him for His sacrifice and for your salvation. Believe in Him with your heart and soul, and ask for forgiveness. Tell Him that you're willing to embrace His love and that you need Jesus to be in the center of your life. I'm not saying it will be effortless to surrender your life to Christ, as there will be challenges, and you will falter from time to time, as all of us human beings do. But the reward is so worth it. Your life will never be the same. So much of our daily burdens will be carried by the Lord, and He will pick you up when you fail or derail from your amazing life's journey. When you wander off the path of Jesus, or take a wrong trail, I'll guarantee you: He will guide you back to where you belong."

A few minutes later, Chet had finished speaking and asked everyone to bow their heads while he said a short prayer. After he closed his prayer with an amen, and with a broad eager smile, he introduced the entire work crew to come join him on stage. They had been gathering quietly backstage in Little Squawa. The floor-to-ceiling curtains were drawn open, as dozens of work crew boys and girls

179

began to filter out on to the risers of varied heights. As they emerged one by one from the wings, many of the campers, seated on the floor, either whistled at them or hollered out their names with admiration and recognition. Bob Rawlings, the boys' crew boss, and Leslie Morrison, the girls' crew boss, were standing at opposite ends. Once they were all lined up in three rows, Chet stepped back out in front to speak briefly about them as a terrific group of young people and work crew. He praised them for all their hard work and dedication to the camp and guests of this incredible teen resort. He reminded everyone that they all were strictly volunteers and that none of them were paid, except for their room and board. He continued to say that they were there to serve Malibu's guests and to serve the Lord. "All these individuals on work crew are Christians," Chet said with pride in his voice. "They proudly serve you and this camp. And now, they have a song they would like to sing for you." With that, Leslie stepped forward off the first-row riser, turned to the body of work crew, and directed the start of the singing. Soon it became apparent that the song they had chosen was the familiar and beautiful hymn "How Great Thou Art." The work crew kids had obviously rehearsed this exquisite, lovely, hymn often, since their voices blended superbly. The tune resonated with many in the room, since they all frequently sang this song under the direction of Jake during the club meetings. Many of the campers sitting on the floor were silently mouthing the words, while the work crew sang.

When the hymn was over, the work crew received a loud applause from the audience. Chet stepped back out in front to speak again. "During every last club meeting of the week, it is a Malibu tradition to introduce to you a couple of individuals who want to share their personal testimony of their Christian faith. I would first like to introduce to you a young lady who joined our work crew the beginning of this week. Many of you met her on the *Malibu Princess* on the way up here from Vancouver, or know her now as the adult-guest waitress and our camp's fine fiddle player. Julie Copeland, please step forward." Doc, who was present in the room, leaning against the side wall near the back door and deck, intensely watched Julie as she stepped down off the riser on to the stage.

She received a warm applause and then began to speak. "Thank you. I would first like to share with all of you that my parents are both Christians, so I basically grew up in a Christian home. We attended church weekly, and my mom was even a Sunday school teacher. In fact, she also played the piano during our services. I was involved in our church youth group, and then when I became a sophomore in high school, in Spokane, Washington, I started attending Young Life Club. The summer after my junior year, I went to Frontier Ranch in Colorado. It too is an awesome Young Life camp, especially if you like horses, and I do." One of the girl campers in the room hollered out a positive "Yahoo!" Julie smiled and then continued speaking. "I always kind of thought that I was a Christian. I guess because I went to church and my parents were Christians, so that meant that I was automatically a Christian. I really didn't get it until I was older, when I was in high school and attending Young Life Club. Learning and understanding that you can actually have a personal relationship with Jesus, that was new to me, until our club speaker was explaining it to us campers at Frontier. He was a fantastic speaker, similar to Chet." She turned and gave him a dimpled smile, as he clasped his hands and slightly bowed, with gratitude. "It was when Tom, our speaker at Frontier, was talking to us about Jesus and how much He loved children that he really got my attention. He read several scriptures to us from the New Testament, referencing Jesus's interaction with children and His disciples. And he also told us about the gospel referring to us as *children of God*, that the Lord thinks of us and accepts us as His children. But then, he went on to tell us a true story about something that happened with his wife and young child, which is what really hit home with me. He said that one day he was at a football game to support his Young Life kids, who were playing, and his wife was home with their two young kids. She was carrying the two-year-old in her arms down the flight of stairs inside the house, when she accidently tripped and fell. While she was falling forward, she instinctively tried to lay her child down safely, and gently, on the stairs in front of her, which she did. But while doing so, she sacrificed herself, as she did a face-plant, and also ended up breaking her ankle. But her little girl was fine. She was willing to forfeit her own self to protect her daughter. The fact that there are so many Bible stories about Jesus loving children and how important they are to Him and that we are all His children really resonated with me. In life and love, you put your children first. You sacrifice for them. And this is exactly what this mom did. I thought it was such a great example of the power of love, and how God loves us so much, and how He profoundly considers us as His children. Hearing this story that evening at Frontier Ranch really affected me. I believe that's when I truly understood what Tom was trying to teach us about God. I finally could visualize the big picture of the Lord's great love for us. Later that same evening, I asked Jesus into my life. Since that day, my life has been so much better and happier. Listening to Tom speak that evening at camp, telling us the story of his wife and her sacrifice through love for her daughter, it all became clear to me why God sacrificed so much for us. Because we are His children. He was willing to sacrifice His own Son, the Christ, through love—for me, and all of you." Julie opened her hands out over the crowd of campers sitting on the floor and, with a broad smile, finished by saying, "Thank you for listening to my story." As she stepped back on to the riser, everyone in the room applauded her.

Chet moved back out to center stage, and after he politely thanked Julie for her wonderful testimony, he began to introduce another camp worker. "Normally, I would have two work crew kids give their testimonies, a girl and a boy, but tonight I have decided to switch it up a bit by allowing one of our staff members to come up and witness before you. I have chosen someone with whom you all know. Not only do you know him as the trumpet player in Malibu's fabulous band, and someone who's often involved in program, but he's also our camp's harbormaster. Doc, come on up."

Doc began weaving his way through the scores of teens on the floor while most everyone in the room either applauded, whistled, or hollered with gusto. Once he's up on stage, he glanced over his audience with a posture of confidence and immediately began to speak. "Gosh, thank you all for such a warm welcome. Well, to start with, unlike Julie, I was not brought up in a total Christian family. I was raised by my dad and my aunt, and my dad was not a believer, nor did he ever attend church. My aunt went once in a while, but I rarely did because my dad didn't want me to. That's not to say he didn't believe that there is a God, but they certainly rarely prayed. When I too was a sophomore in high school, in Oakland, California, the older brother of a friend of mine started taking us to Young Life Club meetings. Of course, my original interest in going was to meet girls." Many of the boys in Big Squawka whistled aloud while others, including girls, smiled and laughed. "Well, I'm just being honest," Doc said with a big grin. Standing behind him on a riser was Julie, showing her dimples again, as she smiled. "Anyway, I was going to club almost every week, and eventually, I was fortunate to come here to Malibu after my junior year, not as a camper, but as the new water ski instructor. I had a lot of experience in boats and skiing, so it was a perfect fit. I was lucky to have gone to a couple of weekend Young Life camps at Mt. Hermon, in the Santa Cruz Mountains, so I was already quite familiar with being a camper and attending club for two years. Believe me, I was thrilled to have been chosen for the position to teach waterskiing here and, later, becoming the harbormaster. But honestly, looking back, and even though I really was interested in hearing stories about Christianity, Jesus, and His life, I really didn't get, or understand, the personal relationship part of it. Not until I heard an awesome speaker here at the beginning of last summer did I discover and figure out what it means to truly turn your life over to Jesus. To allow Him in and to surrender yourself to Him. It was the last night of the first camp in early June, when the speaker, Ryan was his name, was talking about how we, as human beings, naturally want to control our own lives. We want to make all our own decisions and take charge. He said that we want to be the captain of our ship. Which, obviously I could totally relate to that analogy, being a boat captain and such. But then he went on to talk about how difficult it is trying to run our own lives when life itself, and the world around us, is so complicated and grueling. Not only is life in general complex, but it can be extremely challenging at time. And to go it alone is not the answer. Especially when the Lord is willing and able to step in and take charge. Ryan said that Jesus as your captain will lead you along the correct heading, the right path. And He will guide you through the storms of life. Life's many setbacks, problems, times of sadness, frustration, anger, confusion. God knows the way. He knows the best course. He can keep us from wandering down the wrong trail. If you allow Him to be your skipper and captain of your ship, He will keep you in still waters. He has a plan for all of us. I am convinced that it was part of God's plan for me to come to Malibu, and not just to be the water ski instructor here and harbormaster, but He knew that this is where I would meet Him truly for the first time. This is where I would begin my personal relationship with Him. This message really clicked with me, and it opened my eyes to a better understanding of what Ryan was trying to tell us and teach us. That same night, just like Julie, I privately asked Jesus into my life. I prayed and asked Him to be the captain of my ship, my life. And He did. Somehow, I felt a huge weight, a massive concern, about trying to control everything around me being lifted off my shoulders. With God totally in charge, with Jesus as my captain, I now feel free from the troubled burdens of the world and things that were out of my control. That doesn't mean to say that I don't still have responsibilities and consequences. I do. Just because Jesus is at the helm of my life, at the wheel steering me into calm waters, there's other duties that have to be done aboard my ship, my life. Tasks and chores below decks and above are important. As His first mate, I need to do my part in helping the ship to operate and sail properly and correctly. But with Jesus in charge, I have peace of mind knowing that my creator, the Lord who loves us unconditionally, will always be here for me, and He certainly knows better than me the best way to live my life. I deal with fewer storms now and don't worry about running aground or sailing into an island. With Jesus as the captain of my ship, it's easier for me now to stay the course and avoid hazardous waters. And just like Julie, my life is happier now, and it makes more sense. I don't want to be blind to an iceberg out there somewhere, and sink my ship, and get eaten by a great white shark! Yikes!" Doc widened his eyes and opened his mouth wide, simulating the fear of such a scary thought. The room is suddenly filled with laughter. Doc paused for a moment and then finished his testimony. "Thanks, everybody, for listening to my story, my life-changing decision to put

God first, asking Him to be the captain of my ship. My prayer for all of you is that you will seriously consider allowing Christ into your lives. As Chet said earlier, He's knocking. You just need to open the door and invite Him in. Thanks again." Doc stepped off the stage, and as he again weaved his way through kids on the floor, heading for the back side wall, everyone in the room applauded him.

When Chet returned to center stage, he immediately announced that there was one other tradition that was done on the last night. "I would now like all of you, not just campers, but everyone—work crew, staff, counselors, adult guests, even me—to exit Big Squawka quietly and without talking to anyone. This is what I want us to do. I want you to find a place in Malibu Village, a comfortable spot, where you can have some private time with yourself, and perhaps with God, as well. You may want to just think about your week here at Malibu or about what I have been talking about, along with what's been said in cabin time. And perhaps even some thoughts about what Julie and Doc just spoke to you about. This is your time. I think it's important that we all have our private moments to reflect and ponder our thoughts and feelings. To maybe even pray and talk to God. And then, in about fifteen minutes, you will hear our air horn blast, and you'll know that our quiet time is over. After that is free time for everyone, and the Totem Inn and Trader will be open for business. Okay, let's exit, everyone." The large body of people in the room began to quietly exit Big Squawka, just as Chet asked. The mood was fairly somber and somewhat eerie. Every person left the building and disbursed themselves around camp. The sounds of footsteps along the many cedar boardwalks were the only noise heard, as individuals walked to their destination. Once everyone had chosen where they wanted to be, total silence blanketed Malibu. The only sounds that could be heard was the flow of moving water from the tide rushing in, and perhaps a fish momentarily leaping out of the inlet waters. Even the birds were silent in the darkness of the night. Depending upon where someone was at determined the view of camp and its surroundings. If you were outside, like almost everyone was, then you saw the many bright lights illuminating Malibu Village. Chris had made his way down by the harbormaster shack, while Ken was leaning against the doorway to his shop. Beth was outside her cabin on the Sitka deck, staring out at Forbidden Island. Rusty was down by the end of the lighted swimming pool, sitting on a wooden bench, as the roar of the narrows was loudly heard nearby. Julie was standing on the deck outside the dining room in the corner where she could view either the pool or Forbidden Island. She heard a splash in the inlet just below her and quickly spotted a small seal swimming nearby the large boulders along the shore. It made her think of the time she was with Doc alone, near Hamilton Island, when they had spotted the baby seal playing in the waters near the boat. She looked up and asked God in silent prayer, "Is this a sign, Lord? Do you purposely want me to focus my thoughts on Joseph?"

At that exact moment, Doc was standing in the middle of the gangplank that led from the upper large deck below Big Squawka, down to the floating inner dock. He was staring at the inlet waters and at some of the debris floating into the area from the moving incoming tide. His thoughts were on Julie and her earlier testimony. Silently, he prayed to God about her and asked for His forgiveness regarding his deep desires to spend time with her and how he even felt love for her. Praying simultaneously, Julie and Doc thanked their Lord for the opportunity to bear witness to all those present at the club meeting earlier by sharing their testimonies of their faith. When Julie was finished praying, she looked over and noticed Rusty sitting alone on the bench at the far end of the pool. As he was looking up toward the sky, she thought she could see his mouth opening, as if he was talking to someone. She hoped that he was reaching out to God in prayer, but she could not be sure of that. Suddenly, the loud air horn blew a short blast, and one and all knew that the private time was over. Everyone began to move about again and started to engage in conversation. Many of the campers headed back to Main Street to meet up with their friends. The Totem Inn was soon crowded with customers, along with shoppers in the Totem Trader. The camp was once again buzzing with evening activity. Some folks had even decided to go swimming in the lighted pool, while others were playing pool in Little Squawka. The only area of Malibu that was off-limits was the golf course and outer dock. Assigned councilors stood by the boardwalk leading out to that section of camp, to stop campers from wandering out to those grounds. The management wanted to keep all the campers in the Malibu Village vicinity in order to keep them safe and because it would soon be time for bed.

The next day, in the early afternoon, the *Malibu Princess* was tied to the outer dock on the Jervis Inlet. It was a pleasant, bright morning, without a cloud in the sky. The small ship's cargo of new guests had already hiked the short trail over to Malibu Village. The campers and guests, who were leaving to go home, had almost all boarded the ship. Chris, Rusty, Diane, and Julie were standing together near the bottom of the dock's steel staircase leading up to the ship. At one end of the dock, Doc was supervising the work crew boys while they were unloading the freight from the vessel.

"I can't believe it's over," Diane said to her friends, with tears in her eyes.

"I'm glad you had such a good time, Diane," Julie sympathetically said to her. "Hey . . . when I get back, we'll have a Malibu photo party, okay?"

Trying to control her emotions, Diane responded, "Okay. Thanks again for inviting me to Young Life Club. Otherwise, I never would have known about Malibu."

Chris turned to Rusty and said, "Well, this is it, buddy. I know it's a bummer. Sorry you got to go. Gosh, it seems like we just got here. Maybe next summer you could come back on work crew."

"Hey! I gotta come back, dude. I love this place." Just then, Rusty grabbed Chris's upper right arm and whispered to him, "Hey! I need to tell you something. Something that's personal."

Chris looked at him and quietly said, "Sure. Come over here for a minute." He pulled him over to a corner of the dock, off to the side, where they could have a quick and private conversation. "What's up, Rus, what do you want to tell me?"

"Chris, I feel like I have to share this with somebody, and you're the first person I thought of."

"Well, good! I appreciate that." Chris gave him a smile of encouragement. "Go on."

"Last night, during the quiet time we all had after the club meeting, you know, after Julie and Doc talked. Well, I was down by the pool, and I . . ." He paused for a moment and looked around, as campers were boarding the ship.

"Yea, go ahead, Rusty, tell me what happened."

"I looked up at the star-filled sky and prayed to God. I told Him that I really wanted to be a Christian and that I felt I wasn't doing a very good job running my life. I said to Him that I was proud of our team winning the competition for the week and that I hoped He was happy with my part as the team captain. But, I know when it comes to my own personal life, I'm really a lousy captain of my ship. And I said to Him that I'm honestly not very confident, and I don't believe I always make the right choices. In fact, a lot of my decisions are terribly wrong, so I need His help."

Listening intently, Chris asked him, "Okay, what did you say to God after that?"

"Well, I think I sort of made a deal with Him by praying that if he would take charge of my life, and be my boss, I would commit myself to Him and read and learn more about Christianity, and so on."

"Wow! That's fantastic, Rusty. I think you really made a good decision asking Christ into your life."

"But how do I know that He accepted me? It wasn't like I saw some big fancy bright message in the sky telling me all's good with Him and me and that He'll take charge from now on."

"That's not how it works, Rus. You're not going to see a big sign in the sky. Trust me, He accepted you. Just know that He loves you and will always be there for you. That's what we call faith. You do your part, He'll do His, I'll guarantee you. Continue to read the New Testament, attend Young Life Club, and keep praying, okay?" Chris grabbed Rusty's shoulder and suddenly said, "You'd better get going, you need to board the *Princess*, buddy."

"Okay, thanks, Chris. Enjoy the rest of the month, man." Rusty then turned toward the far end of the dock and hollered loudly, "Doc! Take care, huh?"

"You too, Rusty," Doc shouted back. "Keep going to club, and keep the faith, pal! I hope we see you here next year!"

Rusty, with thumbs up, hollered back to Doc, "You got it, man!"

The four of them turned to one another, standing at the bottom of the stairs; they said their goodbyes, as Rusty and Diane headed up the sturdy steel stairs to board the *Malibu Princess*. Minutes later, the ship was underway, about thirty yards from the dock. Several of the work crew guys were in the *Nefertiti* organizing the load. Doc was standing on the wharf talking to Julie alone.

"That's a week neither one of them will ever forget," he said with confidence.

"That's for sure," Julie quickly agreed. They both were looking out at the ship, as it was slowly beginning to shrink in size, moving away from the outer dock. Julie tapped Doc on the shoulder and inquisitively asked, "Say, Joseph. I keep meaning to ask you something. When is your birthday?" Just as Doc was about to answer her, the *Malibu Princess*'s loud horn blows for several seconds, disrupting any possible conversation on the dock, since its thunderous blast penetrates the air. As soon as the blaring sound ended, the work crew kid Chuck shouted, "Doc! We're ready to go here!"

Since being interrupted, Doc forgot to answer Julie's simple question, as he answered Chuck, "Okay, Chuck, I'll be right there!" Standing close to Julie, he right away and quietly said to her, "I guess I'd better head back to the inner dock. Do you want a ride?"

"I'd better not. I'd be too tempted to want to hold your hand," she said to him with a flirty smile.

"Hey, that sounds like a Beatles song to me . . . 'I want to hold your hand,'" Doc said to her as he laughed. Julie instinctively joined in, exposing her cute, unique laugh.

"Besides, the walk will be nice," she told Doc. "I promise to daydream about you all the way back to camp." With that, she smiled and winked at him and headed toward the massive gangplank that led up to the upper wooden walkway. Doc watched her step onto the thirty-degree angled ramp, rigged seven feet in the air above the large boulders, and beyond the shore and dock.

Alone on the large floating dock, he glanced up to the sky and said a quick prayer, "Lord Jesus, please, Father, help me to understand and believe that the loving thoughts that I have for Julie are real and that You bless the feelings I have for her. And I too pray for Julie as well, knowing how much she loves You and would want Your blessings for her too. Thank You, Lord. Amen."

CHAPTER 14

Some Surprises in Life Can Be Overwhelming

Back in Spokane, Washington, Julie's mother, Mary Jo, was sitting at an antique rolltop desk in their home office and library, set in the center of the house on the main floor. Above the desk were numerous professionally framed photographs that were placed upon several walnut shelves, which stretched the length of the entire west-side wall of the cozy room. Many of the family photos were of Mary Jo and Julie playing music together. Some were of the two of them performing twin fiddles, and others were of Julie standing next to the black grand piano playing her violin, while her mom, Mary Jo, was at the keyboard. They were both smiling at the camera as they performed one of the many songs they enjoy playing together. There were also many framed photographs of the entire family, or some with just Julie and Robin. Family and friends were also part of the display, as were several framed awards that Jack had been given regarding plays that he had directed.

The fine-looking, refinished oak desk was quite organized with envelopes and paperwork placed neatly in the many slots above the desktop. All the office supplies were placed in the back area of the desk so that the writing surface was clear of unwanted materials. Mary Jo, wearing a simple dark-blue housedress, was holding a letter in her right hand and was on the telephone. The listening-hand device was in her hand, which was attached by a cord to the main body of the heavy circle-faced black desk phone. She had placed it against her left ear as she spoke to Jack, who was at the campus in his office.

"Oh yea, she's still having a wonderful time, Jack," she said positively to her husband. "But listen, Jack, the boy she wrote us about . . . the one that she likes . . . Doc, well, his real name is Joseph, and he grew up in Oakland!"

"So . . . what are you trying to say, dear? I'm not sure if I understand," Jack spoke to her with confusion in his voice.

"What I'm trying to say, Jack, is . . . oh, Jack, you must know what I'm thinking. I can't help it."

"I don't think you should go there, my darling wife." Jack seemed to know what her thoughts were, and he obviously was concerned.

"I can't help it, honey. I know there has to be lots of Josephs living in Oakland, but it just gives me goose bumps thinking about it. What if . . ."

Quickly interrupting her, Jack said, "I think you're putting the cart before the horse, sweetheart. You're talking about a needle in a haystack, Jo."

Surrendering to Jack's practical advice, Mary Jo said to him with disappointment in her voice, "I guess you're right. The chance of him being my Joseph is one in a million. I'll try not to think about it, at least until I learn more about him."

"I think it's best to not get your hopes up. It would be like winning the big jackpot at the slots in Las Vegas, Nevada. Your chances are mighty slim, dear. I just wouldn't even go there. Listen, I'll see you later, honey, I've got to get to the theater for rehearsal. I love you."

"I love you too, honey. And I know you're probably right about this, Jack. I'll see you when you get home. Bye." Mary Jo slowly hung up the phone, as she looked up at the photographs with a blank stare on her face.

Several days later at Malibu, the new week was underway. The new campers were already taking tours to Chatterbox Falls with Doc or

Chris. Hikers were challenged by the difficult, but rewarding, hike up to Inspirational Point, located up on the cliff directly above Malibu. The view from the large flat rock that stuck out at the open area of the end of the hike was amazing. Hundreds of feet above the camp, the bluff allowed everyone to view the entire Malibu peninsula, or just enjoy looking down the Jervis and Princess Louisa inlets. Still, the point above the camp was only a fraction of the nine-thousand-foot mountain above. The hikers looking down at the unique camp could see that the inner dock area was busy with visiting yachts being tied to the float, water-skiers being pulled by a half dozen ski boats, swimmers and sunbathers enjoying the pool at the tip of the peninsula. What they could not see were Julie and Beth setting their respective tables in the dining room with silver utensils, white shiny plates, and tall glasses for milk or juice. They also could not see Ken, in his dimly lit shop—located below Big Squawka—working at fixing a badly broken thirty-five-horse Johnson outboard motor. As well, they could not see the dozen or so campers and counselors playing golf under the canopy of trees far below them, to their right. Nor could they see the advanced water-skiers taking rides off the outer dock, even farther to their right. Regardless, the camp was once again busy with the day's activities.

Later that evening, when everyone was in Big Squawka for the first Club Entertainment Night, the window drapes were closed, and soon the stage curtains opened wide. The stage lights were on, and two bright spotlights from the back lit the entire platform. On the stage were Doc, Chris, and Jake—all wearing red acrobatic tights. There was a cloth white sign hung on the black backdrop that read, The Far-Flung Flying Garbanzo Brothers. In the middle of the stage was a five gallon empty metal ice cream container, lying on its side, with a long, thin board, over the top of it, forming a seesaw. The three acrobats were doing simple tumbles, and then would bounce up on to their feet, facing the audience, with hands up in the air for applause. The campers and everyone inside the large dark room were laughing and cheering the boys on. Chris then positioned himself at the end of the board, which was touching the stage. Doc was now on the opposite side standing next to the other end of the board, which was up in the air. Jake stepped up on a metal chair and climbed up and stood on Doc's shoulders. Doc held Jake's legs at the ankles. The three all turned their heads and looked at the crowd, who were mostly sitting on the floor in the dark. They smiled and turned their heads back, when Jake suddenly leaped, feetfirst, on to the end of the raised board, to propel Chris up into the air. *CRACK!* The plank broke in half, leaving them standing there with a failed act. The three of them looked out at the silent audience with a frown, as the stage lights and spots were promptly turned off. The audience suddenly broke into hysterical laughter. With all of the kids laughing and enjoying the show, Doc was thrilled to see and feel the comradery of the kids. His hearing also picked-up the sounds of Julie's distinctive laugh, which resulted in a broad smile.

As the sun arose over the high mountaintops the next morning, it rapidly shined brightly on all the Malibu buildings. All of which were made from rough-hewn cedar logs, or siding, and cedar shakes. All the large decks were supported by cedar poles. The many authentic totem poles began to brighten up the camp, as the sun enhanced their variety of colors. Malibu in some ways was rugged, yet it had a unique serene beauty about it. It was not long before the camp became alive once again with campers and counselors beginning to roam the boardwalks, talking, reading, or just enjoying the incredible scenery. Some were sipping hot chocolate, coffee, or tea, provided by the kitchen crew, who set up tables just outside the dining room's main doors on the wide boardwalk. Large containers, to keep the ingredients hot, were available, along with porcelain cups for self-serve.

After a delicious hot breakfast was served, the new campers began their day with the famous Malibu Regatta. Once again, everyone was enjoying the fun and competition of this amusing and amazing event. Later that afternoon, during free time for the campers, all the activities were fired up once more. There were teens in Little Squawka playing Ping-Pong, and pool, while others were happy eating the Totem Inn's homemade ice cream.

Later in the afternoon, the campers and counselors were all gathered at the swimming pool for their next event. Leaning against the base of the stout totem pole, installed on top of the granite stone that slightly jutted above the pool, was a wide blue temporary sign that read in white letters: malibu water olympics. Above the sign, and attached to the totem, were five Hula-Hoops placed to resemble the Olympic Rings, each painted the appropriate bright color of the universal symbol. While the five teams, stationed around the pool area, were preparing for a series of competitive water events, they suddenly looked up to see Doc entering the scene from the dining room area, up above. He quickly ran down the massive Smoker's Rock toward them. Wearing ancient Greek Olympian–style clothing, with a grape-leaf wreath on his head, he approached the crowd. They all began cheering him on, as Jake was standing on the diving board announcing his arrival with his megaphone. Doc was carrying a lit Olympic-style flaming torch, and as he approached the pool, all those near him parted the way, allowing him to reach the pool's edge. Just before he ran over to Jake, who was along the side of the pool, he did a comedic slip and fell into the pool's deep end, near the diving board. The torch was at once extinguished! The crowd around the pool was laughing loudly, most knowing that his falling into the pool was not an accident. As Doc surfaced, with his wreath still on his head and holding the unlit torch up out of the water, Jake continued announcing Doc's Olympian momentous arrival, as if the water accident had never happened. Julie, watching all of this unfold from outside the dining room, above the pool on the narrow wooden walkway, was shaking her head and laughing profusely.

After club and Entertainment Night that same evening, Doc and Julie privately met on Maliburger Point. A small, low-lying bluff that extended out over the Jervis Inlet, this spot was located at the foot of one of Malibu's eighteen holes of pitch-and-putt golf. Close to the dirt path leading out to the outer dock, the grassy round-shaped area was used only once during the week, when the camp enjoyed a barbeque lunch after the Olympic competition on the golf course. The large redbrick barbeque, built back in the Hamilton era, worked perfectly for grilling dozens of hamburgers and hotdogs at once.

The moon was full that night, as its brilliant light danced across the inlet waters, making for a picturesque and romantic sight. Doc and Julie were sitting at one of the several redwood picnic tables positioned near the tip of the tiny peninsula. As far as they knew, no one else was around, but they agreed they would be careful not to embrace with romantic desire—just in case. They had arranged to meet prior that morning, after they had ran into each other and spoke briefly, near the Linen Nook. The two of them were now in conversation, as they sat at a table that was only about thirty yards from a blinking navigational warning beacon, located in the entranceway to the narrows. Doc was explaining to Julie about the bright rotating beacon.

"Next time you pass by here, or look over from Nootka during low tide, you'll see how many rocks and boulders protrude into the area of that warning beacon. Yacht folks can see it when the water's down, but at high tide—which is the best time to enter the narrows—that's when these rocks can be extremely dangerous, especially at night, of course!"

"Yea, I can imagine," Julie agreed with understanding.

"Early fall, last year, a guy piloting a gorgeous fifty-three-foot motor yacht didn't heed the warning late in the afternoon. He was going between the beacon and the shore here. He rammed his yacht onto these huge rocks right there." Doc pointed in the direction of the flashing light. "He couldn't go astern to release the boat from the rocks, and the tide was going out. So the boat ended up beached on the jagged boulders, and eventually the yacht literally broke in half, because of the weight distribution. It totally destroyed it! Can you imagine?"

"Oh my gosh! Are you serious!"

"Oh yes, I'm serious. In fact, Ken and I had to rescue them off their yacht with the Seinskiff, it was a bit tricky. There were six people aboard, including his dad, a senior citizen, and two young children. But the worst part was when the skipper, the owner, could only watch the tide go out and witness his expensive craft being destroyed!"

"Gosh! That's terrible!"

"At least no one got hurt. If the tide was coming in, he would have been okay. Because then he could have just waited until the tide raised the yacht up and above the rocks. The tides up here in these inlets are so amazing, so extreme."

"I know," Julie agreed with interest. "I just can't believe how the current runs so rapidly through the narrows when it's coming in, then becomes completely slack, or smooth. And then soon after, it starts rushing back out the other way. It is remarkable! Have you ever had a problem driving one of your boats through the narrows when the current is running heavy?"

"Oh yea!" Doc answered with an expression of eagerness to explain. "Last summer, before Malibu purchased the *Nefertiti*, we were using a large wooden raft that the work crew built under the supervision of Vic. It was large enough to tow all the luggage in one trip to the inner dock. And then all the food crates and stuff on a second trip."

"A raft?" Julie asked, as if she were somewhat confused as to the design.

"Yep! Just like you see in the movies. It was just a large cedar-planked flat raft, with no siding. We used blocks of Styrofoam for buoyancy, which were attached underneath."

"Gosh! Wasn't that a little dangerous towing it through the water, and through the waves?"

"Well, it was, but it was the best we could come up with to move the luggage and freight, until we could afford a bigger freight boat this past spring. The Seinskiff just wasn't big enough. However, she was the workboat we used to tow the raft. Well, anyway . . . this one week, after welcoming a new camp, the work crew guys had placed and stacked all the weeks' luggage on to the raft, and I was starting to tow it through the narrows. The problem was, the tide was coming in, and it was a max tide, so the water was at its peak speed, in the middle of its cycle, rushing through the narrows."

"But you were going *with* the tide, right? Isn't that better than going against it?" Julie asked with curiosity.

"You would think so, but actually, no, it isn't. The problem when you're going with the tide is that you have to make sure your traveling at a speed faster than the current itself. Plus, since I was towing a raft, using a heavy rope, not only did the Seinskiff have to be going faster than the water, but so did the raft. The rope had to be completely taught to drag the raft through the current. Otherwise the violent water action could take control of the raft and force it to crash into the rocks!"

"Wow! So what happened?"

"Well, my speed wasn't the problem. I was going faster than the water rushing in through the narrows, and my rope was taught, with the raft perfectly being towed directly behind me without a hitch. But because the waves were so violent due to the swiftness of the water rushing through that narrow area, it caused the rope to twist and snap! It broke! I was right in the middle of the narrows, and my line snapped right between the boat and the raft!"

"Oh my gosh! What did you do?" Julie frantically asked, as if she was witness to the actual event.

"Well, first of all, I knew that there were many new campers who were checking out the swimming pool, and now they were watching this whole situation evolve, concerned about their suitcases, along with staffers too. Even Vic and Ken were monitoring the tow through the rapids, since they both knew it was more dangerous than usual. Fortunately, Vic and I had earlier discussions about these kinds of scenarios, and what would be the best solution to avoid disaster! At that moment, I recalled that he had discussed, and told me, that if my line had ever broken during a tow, and especially inside the narrow rapids, that I should just continue forward, not trying to turn and reattach a line to the raft. He explained to me that that would be way too dangerous and could wind up causing more havoc than if I just back off and let the raft deal with the situation on its own merits."

"Really? So, is that what you did?" Julie asked with elated inquisitiveness.

"That's exactly what I did. I just continued on in the Seinskiff, piloting her into the Princess Louisa, and into smoother waters, all the while turning and watching the raft inside these violent, rushing, churning waters. The entire camp's luggage was at stake, riding on the top of this flat raft, as it began to slowly spin in circles and bobbing up and down like a rubber raft in a fierce river! Everyone on shore watching was startled and dismayed, including Vic and Ken. I thought for sure the raft was going to catch an edge and flip over, tossing all the suitcases into the moving waters of the inlet."

"Well?" Julie gently slapped Doc's upper left arm, as she was anxiously awaiting the outcome of the story.

"Much to my surprise, and just as Vic predicted—had this ever occurred—which obviously, it did, the raft continued to spin around a half dozen times. But it did not tip over, as I feared it would. Within a minute or so, the raft exited the narrows, as the waters began to calm down and smooth out. The raft stopped spinning, and soon started slowing down and flattening out. The probable calamity was avoided. I was so relieved."

"So then what did you do?"

"Once the raft was definitely in safe, smooth, slow water, I immediately drove the Seinskiff back over to it and tied another, shorter line on. Then I just slowly towed her over to the inner dock, where Vic and Ken, and several others, were there to greet me with praises of 'Job well done!' I didn't want praise. I was just glad that it all turned out well. It was Vic's earlier instruction, and advice, that allowed me to make the right decision. I was just so happy that we saved all the luggage. That would have been a mess if it had all gone into the drink!"

"Boy, that's for sure. What a guy! You're just such a great harbor-master, Joseph!" Julie clasped his face with both her hands, as if she was praising a small child for eating his vegetables.

"Oh! You need to hear this story real quick," said Doc, as another thought came to mind. "A few weeks later, during another max tide, my assistant and I we were taking the camp's luggage out to the outer dock, to the *Princess*—for the camp that was leaving, and I had another incident happen in the rapids."

"Oh no! What this time?" Julie quickly asked with anticipation.

"Just as we got in the middle of the narrows, as we were pulling the raft against the fast incoming current, I realized that the Seinskiff didn't have enough power to move us forward. I was at full throttle, and we weren't gaining any ground—or I should say water! The rope was taut as a tightrope, dragging the loaded raft through the white-water waves. But we were stuck! Not moving an inch."

"You're kidding! What the heck did you do?"

"Well, after about ten minutes, I could notice that we were beginning to gain about a foot every minute or so, but that wasn't enough. Good thing I had a half tank of diesel fuel aboard. Anyway, by then, Vic had gotten wind of our dilemma. Turtle, who was cleaning the pool, spotted us and ran over and told Vic, who was working on some firehoses by the Linen Nook. So, Vic grabbed Ken and took the *Atom Skier* out to rescue us."

"The *Atom Skier?*" Julie asked.

"Yea. It's got a Chevy V8 engine in it, so it has lots of power and torque. We don't use her much, because she's such a gas guzzler. Anyway, they knew that Moondoggie and I—he was my assistant at the time, an American Indian kid from Oklahoma. They knew that we could not just back off or try and turn around in the narrows. It was too dangerous. Plus, if we slowed down, the rope would go slack, and the raft would start spinning out of control like before. We couldn't let that happen—too risky."

"So was Vic and Ken able to—" Julie promptly asked, as Doc interrupted her with the answer to her obvious question.

"Yea, they were. But it was tricky, because first they had to get around us without the churning waves bouncing them into us, which would have been disastrous! Once they slowly, and carefully, got past us, Vic—who was at the wheel of the powerful ski boat—positioned his boat directly in front of us, as Ken threw Moondoggie the nylon ski towline. The first toss into the Seinskiff was a good one. As I was steering our workboat straight ahead, behind the *Atom Skier,* Doggie carefully crawled up on the wide flat bow and tied the rope securely to our bow cleat. Once he was safely back inside the boat, Vic began to push the throttle forward on the V8. Sure enough, it worked. By then, with dozens of campers and work crew looking on, the loud, powerful ski boat began to pull us forward, along with the raft and luggage, through the fast incoming tide, and out near Forbidden Island—into smoother, less swift-moving water."

"That must have been a relief," Julie said, with a sigh in her voice.

"It was, trust me! And now we are so thankful to have the *Nefertiti*. She's got plenty of diesel power and loads of room inside her for the luggage, or the freight."

"And also for the Chatterbox Falls tours in midweek," Julie added with a wink and a cute dimpled smile.

"Okay. Enough about my stories here at Malibu. I want to hear more about you, missy. We've talked a lot about your music and all of that . . . and your folks, what else can you tell me about you? It's once again sharing time, princess!" Doc gave her a wink and a broad smile back.

"All right. Well, speaking of sharing. I don't think I've told you that for three years now—during the school year—I read, and share stories, to young children at the main library in Spokane. What do you think of that?" she proudly said, waiting for Doc's reaction.

"Really? That's cool! I had no clue," he answered with a pleased expression. "So tell me more about it. How often and when do you do that?"

"Well, first of all, I do get paid . . . some . . . not a lot, but that's okay. I really enjoy it. It's every Wednesday evening, from 6:45 p.m. until 7:30. I get to pick the stories myself from an array of children's books and short stories, fairytales, and so on . . . available, of course, in the library. The little kids all sit on the floor in the main lobby area, near the check-out counters. I sit in a big, fancy—kind of ornate—multicolor chair, with long carved curvy armrests."

"Wow! How fun," Doc broke in with a positive, quick comment.

"Oh! And I dress, depending on the story."

"What do you mean?" asked Doc with interest.

"I try to dress like one of the main characters in the book—usually female, of course. Or if the story takes place during a certain period in time, I'll dress in appropriate costume for that century, or whatever."

"Does the library provide the outfits, the dresses, for you?"

"No, actually my mom makes them for me. She's quite the talented seamstress and really enjoys the challenge of designing and sewing these garments," Julie explained with obvious pride in her voice.

"Golly! You must have dozens of these costumes . . . outfits," Doc said with amazement.

"Well, not dozens, but quite a few. Some of them are fairly simple, and others are quite fancy and detailed."

"How many kids usually attend these readings?"

"It varies, but anywhere from twenty to fifty. It's usually a great turnout."

"With you there reading the stories, I can certainly see why," Doc squeezed her hand.

"You're so sweet. Oh, and by the way, I don't just stay seated in my fancy chair, I do get up at times and move around in front—just to be more animated and keep the kids, especially the younger ones, from getting too bored or distracted. That's part of the fun of it, to challenge myself in keeping each and every child focused on me as I gesture and read the story in an exciting and meaningful way."

"Do you try to change your voice some for the different characters in the book?" Doc questioned her with interest in her sharing.

"I most certainly do. That's a challenge within itself. But I've gotten pretty good at it," she proudly assured him.

"Well, that is so awesome. I can totally see you doing that. Are you ever a princess, princess? As in, perhaps a Disney princess?"

"Actually, yes, I am. I have done some Disney stories. I can look the part of Sleeping Beauty pretty well, once I put some wave in my hair with the help of my mom."

"I'm sure you can . . . and *pretty* and *beauty* are the perfect words." Doc reached up to the left side of Julie's face, and with his right hand, slowly and softly, he ran his fingers down through her shiny golden locks. The strains of her straight hair glistened in the moonlight, as Doc let it go at her waist. He paused for just a moment and then adjusted his legs to move closer to Julie. "Okay, good-looking." He reached over and grabbed Julie's left hand. "Let's talk about us?"

"Really? So, what about us?" Julie asked with a bit of flirting in her voice. "Is there truly an *us*?"

"Well, to be honest with you, blond girl, let me just say this. You've become the light in my life, kind of like that moonlight out there. Soft, warm, glowing, and cool!" He reached down below the picnic table bench and pulled out a bouquet of wild flowers, tied at the stems by a rubber band, and handed them to Julie.

"Really, Doc? You are so sweet! So, where did you—"

"Oh, that's a secret," Doc quickly interrupted her. "No, not really . . . I picked them on the golf course on the way over here to meet you, ha ha!" he said proudly.

"Well, they're absolutely beautiful! What a sweet thing to do," Julie softly said to him as she took a moment to smell the aroma of the colorful wildflowers. Doc looked deeply into her eyes, and she said to him, "I love how your eyes smile at me."

"You're right. My eyes are smiling at you. I must tell you, princess, you're the first thought on my mind when I wake up in the morning and my last thought before I fall asleep at bedtime!"

"Really? How lovable you are, Joseph. You really think about me that often, handsome guy?" Julie was obviously happy to hear Doc admit that. "Okay, it's my turn." She squeezed his hand and, with her dazzling blue eyes, scanned his entire face and said to him in a whisper, "I already have such a strong feeling of affection for you, and I can't believe it myself."

"I have a strong desire to kiss you right now, Julie, but I'll be good and restrain myself and save that moment for another time, okay?"

"Yea, I guess," she answered him with disappointment, but also with clear understanding of them waiting when the time was right to physically interact. At that moment, they both knew she had better head back to her room for the night. So they both said their temporary good-byes and left Maliburger Point separately. Julie walked the trail back to Malibu Village while Doc left moments later for Andy's Shanty, the close-by little shack that he and Ken shared. Next to Haida, and near Flag Point, the small cabin was cozy and comfortable for the two of them to live in during their four-month stay. Before going to bed, Doc waited another forty-five minutes when it was time for him to walk the short distance, with his flashlight, to the

Diesel Shack. Soon thereafter, the noisy sound of the massive engine was shut down, and Doc returned to the Shanty in the moonlit night.

Julie's mom, Mary Jo, was in the kitchen of her appealing colonial home, as she began to prepare dinner, when suddenly the doorbell rang. The pleasant chimes could be heard throughout the house, as they echoed from the entryway. When she opened the heavy oak front door, Julie's friend Diane was standing there with a smile, fresh from returning from Malibu.

"Oh, hi, Diane!" Mary Jo said with a smile back, anxious to hear how her trip was. "Did you have a good time at Malibu? Come on in."

"I had a fabulous time, Mrs. Copeland. Gee, I really can't come in. I have to get back to babysit my little brother. I just wanted to drop this off." She handed Mary Jo an envelope with a letter inside. "I promised Julie that I'd hand-deliver it to you—definitely faster than the mail."

"Yes, for sure. That's great." Mary Jo was pleased, knowing that it was a letter from Julie. "Well, I wish we could talk. I want to hear all about your adventures at Malibu and what Julie's been up to."

"I'll try and come over in a couple of days, okay?" Diane explained, anxiously wanting to share some stories with Julie's mom. "There's a lot to tell."

"I bet. Thanks again, Diane."

"Oh, you're welcome, Mrs. Copeland. See you later." She turned and quickly stepped down the several white wooden stairs exiting the porch and walked down the narrow cement path to the city sidewalk, surrounded by beautifully groomed lawn and landscaping. The red and yellow flowers planted and blooming in the front of the house, along the entire length of the white porch, were especially lovely.

Minutes later, Mary Jo was sitting at the kitchen table reading the letter from Julie. All of a sudden, she had a stunned look on her face. She anxiously reached up and grabbed the white kitchen wall phone and started dialing a memorized number.

"Jack, it's him!" she said in a frenzied tone.

Jack immediately asked, "Who? What are you talking about?"

"Joseph! My Joseph. It has to be," she answered in a frantic voice.

"Calm down, honey. Take a deep breath. Now, explain to me what you're talking about," Jack said to her patiently.

"I just got a letter from Julie, and she wrote that his dad was a gunsmith."

"I assume you're talking about Julie's new friend, the harbormaster . . . correct?"

"Yes, I am."

"What do you mean, his dad *was* a gunsmith?" Jack was somewhat confused.

"*Was* . . . he passed away last year of a heart attack. Bless his soul. But, anyway . . . she goes on to write that his mother drowned and that he was raised by his dad and aunt. Jack, it has to be him!" Mary Jo's voice was trembling.

"Sweetheart . . . again, you need to calm down, okay?" Now Jack was worried that she was truly jumping to conclusions.

"I can't calm down. There are too many coincidences. This is my son I'm talking about. I just know it, Jack," she said with confidence in her voice.

After a brief pause, Jack responded, "Okay. Let's just say it is Joseph . . . what are you feeling? What do you want to do?" Jack was obviously beginning to agree with her, or at least starting to give her the benefit of the doubt.

"I have to see him. I have to go up there . . . to Canada," Mary Jo said with assurance.

"Are you sure about this, Jo? Maybe we should wait."

"I can't wait, honey. I want to see him now. Jack, think about this. If he is my son—and my heart tells me he is—he's having a romantic relationship with his sister, and vice versa! It has to be stopped now. Don't you agree?"

After another short pause, Jack's thought process immediately responded. "Oh my, you're right!"

"Look . . . in a while, I'll call Julie's friend Diane. She's the one that dropped the letter off a few minutes ago, and just see, if by chance, she knows his last name. If she does, that will certainly clinch it, right?"

"Yea, there's no doubt about that," Jack quickly answered in agreement.

"Jack . . . can you come home? We really need to discuss this. Honey, I need you right now," she said with tearful emotion in her voice.

"Certainly. I'll immediately wrap stuff up here and have someone fill in my last class for me, not a problem. I'll be home as soon as I can, I promise."

"Thank you, honey. I know this is shocking news to you too," Mary Jo said to him with concern and anxiety. She slowly hung up the phone and began to cry, placing her hands over her eyes.

It had only been about forty-five minutes when Jack walked through the front door of their family home. When he pulled into the wide driveway, leading to the two-car garage in the back, he promptly parked the car next to the lawn and dashed across the gray, round, stepping stones placed in front of the row of colorful flower beds. Once he entered the house, he instantaneously walked into the kitchen, where he could hear his wife sobbing. As soon as he entered the brightly lit room, Mary Jo ran over to him, reaching out for a hug. As he hastily embraced her, he asked her, "Did you talk to Diane again?'"

Taking a moment to gather herself together, but still in tears with her head buried into Jack's chest, she answered him, "Yes, I did. It's him, Jack . . . it's him!"

With a bewildered expression, Jack carefully pulled her away from his body a few inches so that he could look down at her and ask, "Are you sure?"

"Yes, I'm sure. Diane said she remembered someone mentioning that his last name is Sheldon. It's him. It has to be him!" she answered Jack while wiping the tears from her face.

"Oh my gosh!" Jack responded in disbelief. "Should we call up there?"

Still standing alongside her husband in the middle of the kitchen, Mary Jo answered him with some perplexity. "Malibu doesn't have any telephones, remember? Only a ship-to-shore radio, which I understand doesn't work very well, half the time. And besides, Jack, I don't want to talk to him on a telephone. I want to see and talk to him in person, face-to-face. He thinks I'm dead, Jack. It breaks my heart!"

"I understand. You're right. Let's get on the phone right now and make some arrangements to fly up there."

"When?" Mary Jo looked up at him for an eager answer.

"Tomorrow morning, my love. There's no reason to wait," he promptly assured her. "I'll call Edgar at the university right now. It'll be okay."

"Are you sure?"

"Absolutely! We'll figure this out."

Mary Jo started weeping again as she embraced her husband with gratitude. "I love you, Jack. I know this isn't easy for you. And I know you're worried about what you're going to have to tell Julie. Jack, you are her father. Maybe you're not her biological, blood father, but you are her father, in every way that's important. You understand me, right?" Jack let go of his embrace as he cupped his hands around the back of his wife's head. Looking directly into her blue eyes, he just simply shook his head slowly up and down, indicating that his answer was yes. "You've raised her. She loves you very much. I know it'll be a shock to her, but it won't change things between the two of you. I believe that in my heart and know it to be true."

Now with tears in his eyes, Jack softly said to her, "I know. It'll be all right. It's time she knows the truth anyway." The two of them embraced again as Mary Jo began weeping once more.

CHAPTER 15

Alone Again at Last . . .
How Sweet It Is

The waterskiing and boating program at Malibu was over for the day. Chris and Doc had tied all the rowboats and sailboats securely to the inside cleats of the lower floating dock. Kyle, the water-skier instructor, had made sure all the ski boats were tied correctly alongside the remaining dock space as well. The inner dock was buttoned up for the evening, as everything was in shipshape order. Near the harbormaster's office, at the end of the floating dock, were several camper girls still in their bathing suits, each holding a #10 tin can. While Chris leaned up against the shack watching, the three young ladies were dipping their cans into the main inlet side of the dock, and once their cans were full of seawater, they quickly walked over to the other side of the dock, facing the shore, and dumped out the water. Julie, who was up on the main deck above the gangplank looking down, spotted this curious scene, while the girls were repeating the process over and over. Somewhat suspicious, and wanting to figure out what exactly was going on, Julie hurried down the wooden gangplank and approached Chris.

"Hey, Chris. So where's Doc?" she asked with inquisitiveness in her voice.

"He's at the Shanty changing for dinner," Chris quickly responded.

Speaking in a whisper, she leaned into Chris's face and asked, "What are those girls doing?"

"Oh, them," Chris said in a guilty tone. "They're leveling the dock for me. You see, Julie, after the tide has come in, you always have to level the dock so that it's not tilted one way or the other."

"And they believed you?" Julie answered, now speaking with normal volume. "You are a big tease. You've been around Vic and Doc too much. Hey, girls!" She immediately walked toward the three campers who were still filling and emptying their shining cans of inlet water.

As she began to talk to them, Chris called over to her, "Julie, wait!" He started to run over to her while the young girls swiftly approached him halfway.

One of them blurted out, "Why, you brat!" She and the other two campers began tossing the cold saltwater from their cans at Chris, who was taken by surprise. They were all laughing, including Julie, as they enjoyed the revenge. Deciding to be a good sport, Chris just stood there on the dock, soaking wet, as he wiped the water from his face with his long flannel sleeves. He too began laughing and shaking his head in defeat.

Later that evening on Flag Point, another small peninsula, which jutted out about seventy-five feet from the dirt path in front of Haida and Andy's Shanty, were Julie and Doc sitting on a brown, weathered, wooden bench at the very tip of the grass-covered bluff. This protrusion of land was wider and longer than Malibuger Point and was much closer to Malibu Village. Its location was only sixty yards from Nootka (the girls' dorm) and straight across from Forbidden Island. The bench was planted in the long grass, a few feet in front of the two tall flagpoles flying two different Canadian flags. Both of the six-inch-diameter steel poles extended up into the air, thirty-five feet. One flag was the traditional red-and-white National Flag of Canada, bearing the maple leaf, with wide red strips on each end. The other was the British Columbia flag, topped by a Union Jack, with a bright-yellow sun at the bottom, which represented the glory of the province, along with wavy blue lines. The bright-blue lines represented the Pacific Ocean and the province's position on the western coastline of Canada. The two flags were making a constant swishing and snapping sound, as they were waving in the wind.

As the sun began to set over the western mountains, across Jervis Inlet, a cool breeze blew along the waters on to shore. It had rained earlier in the day and was beginning to look like wet weather may return. Doc was wearing his Levi's jacket, and Julie was bundled up in her blue fleece. They were sitting fairly close to each other, but not too close, as not to suggest to anyone who might see them together that they were being in any way romantic. Since Nooka was just across the way, some of the campers, and perhaps some work crew girls, could possibly notice them sitting together. So they purposely were careful not to scoot too close to each other.

"I can't believe the prank that Chris pulled on those innocent camper girls," Julie continued her story to Doc about Chris having several young girls "leveling the inside dock" for him. "At least they got revenge and soaked him good with cold inlet water! I know that he's learning to engage in these pranks, thanks to you, Ken, and Vic mentoring him, right? Bad boys!"

"You're absolutely right, beautiful! And I'm proud to be a part of these harmless mischievous practices," Doc smugly said to her.

"So, do I dare ask what other pranks you've pulled in the inner dock area, Mister Harbormaster?"

"Well, let's see." Doc paused briefly. "Oh! I think what we had Woody, my last assistant, do last month was quite amusing."

"Yea, and what was that?"

"We're just so clever." Doc laughed, as Julie gave him a look of slight disgust. "Ken and I had Woody pretend to drop his knife in the inlet toward the end of the dock. There were a dozen or so campers around, and when they weren't paying attention, Woody dropped an old engine part into the water. When it made a splash, he immediately hollered out, 'Oh no, my knife! Vic and Doc are going to kill me!' With that, he right away jumped in the water after it."

"I don't get it. So what happened?" Julie asked Doc with a confused expression.

"Well, here's the deal. When Woody went under the water, he directly went underneath the dock where there were air pockets in the spaces between the large Styrofoam sections, the pieces that keep the dock afloat. Anyway, he raised his head up into one of those air pockets so that he could breathe."

"Are you serious? Are you telling me that he stayed under there for a while, making the kids up on the dock worrying that he was drowning?" Julie was somewhat shocked that they would do such a thing.

"Well, yea. That was the whole idea. He stayed under there for several minutes, while Ken and I were hanging out on the upper deck enjoying the perfect prank."

"Doc, you can't be serious! Didn't any of the campers begin to panic and yell out, or jump in the water to save him?"

"I think they were so shocked that he was still under the water, they didn't know what to think, or do. Just as someone finally yelled over to Kyle, who was instructing a skier, Woody, with perfect timing, popped his head up out of the water alongside the dock with his knife in hand. He proudly announced that he had found, and grabbed his knife, in the cloudy water before it sank to the bottom of the inlet."

Julie, with her head shaking with some disbelief and semidisgust, but who was also obviously enjoying the story of this crazy, bold practical joke, said to Doc, "You guys are too much. So, I have to ask you, have you ever tried to pull one of your pranks, and it either backfired or something went wrong?"

"I don't remember any of our pranks backfiring on us, but there was a prank that went horribly wrong, and could have been disastrous!" Doc shifted his body slightly closer to Julie and looked at her with an alarming expression.

Julie grabbed a hold of his arm and, with concern in her voice, asked him, "Tell me, what happened?"

"This was one of Vic's creations. The plan was for us to pretend that we were moving a refrigerator down on to the inner dock to load into the Seinskiff. We were to take it to the logging camp across Jervis." Doc turned his head and pointed across the wide inlet to a sprinkle of small structures near the shore, on the other side. Since the sun had dropped farther behind the mountains, and the light was dissipating, Julie could barely see the small camp that Doc was referring to. No matter. She knew precisely what he was pointing at, since they had talked about the logging work taking place on the mountain, when they were together on Maliburger Point. Doc turned his head back around and continued with the story. "This was an old, upright refrigerator that had broken, and we actually just wanted to get rid of it. Like many other items around camp that we wanted to dispose of, we just simply sank it off the end of the inner dock, near my harbormaster shack. It's hundreds of feet deep there."

"Really? That can't be good for the environment, right?" Julie asked with surprise and disappointment.

"Yea, you're right. This was last summer, and since then, there's been discussion about this practice. We don't do it anymore. Now we haul old stuff like that on to the *Princess* and take it back to Vancouver to dispose of it."

"Oh, good. Well, anyway, continue, what happened? What went wrong? And what exactly was the prank?" Julie asked with interest shown through her striking blue eyes.

"Everything was going as planned. Ken and I, with the help of a furniture dolly, had successfully moved the large heavy appliance down the gangplank and over to my workboat. Vic was leaning against the wooden railing on the upper deck watching the prank unfold. What Ken and I wanted to do was to begin loading the refrigerator up and over the stern of the Seinskiff, sliding it aboard. The plan was to purposely let it slip out of our hands and into the drink, which, of course, it would quickly sink down into the inlet. Then he and I would act really upset about allowing the refrigerator to slip away from us and be swallowed up into the deep water. We planned to say something aloud like, 'Oh my gosh! I can't believe that just happened! Vic is going to kill us!' The dock was busy with free-time activities, skiing and boating, so it was the perfect time to pull it off. There were lots of campers and counselors around. Then Vic was going to run down the gangplank and on down the dock to us and chew us out about losing the refrigerator. And about it being promised to the loggers across the Jervis!"

"And? So, go on, what happened?" asked Julie again, with curiosity.

"I made a bad judgment," Doc admitted, with a look of embarrassment.

"Huh?" Julie looked at him with puzzlement.

"At the very last second, just as the fridge was slipping out of our hands, I fell into the water on purpose. I decided to pretend to fall in, and *splash!* I went into the inlet with it!"

"You did? Why?"

"You know how I'm always pretending to fall into the water, either with the band or other stuff. Like when I purposely fell in at the pool during the Olympic competition, remember? Well, I just thought it'd be funny if I tumbled into the water as well."

"You said something went terribly wrong. I'm almost afraid to ask, handsome. What happened?" Julie had a look of concern, but knew that whatever happened, it must have all turned out okay, since Doc was sitting there with her, telling the story.

"It was a freak accident, but truthfully, I could have easily drowned."

Julie, with a horrified expression, instantly placed both her hands over her face, but soon grabbed Doc's upper arms and said to him, "Oh no! Again, what happened, Joseph?"

"As I entered the water with the refrigerator, somehow one of my belt loops slipped on to the pointed, open end of the pull-out door handle, I was hooked to the heavy, sinking appliance!" Julie instantly put both her hands over her mouth, showing a sign of fright. "Thank God I had my knife attached to my belt, so I instinctively grabbed for it, as I was being pulled swiftly down into the dark waters of the inlet. I forcefully pulled it out of the sheath and somehow was able to quickly cut my belt loop away from the door handle, so I escaped from being taken down to the bottom of the inlet. Believe me, it was close to a miracle!"

"Oh! My God!" Julie exclaimed, as she could not help but place her head on Doc's left shoulder and chest.

"*My God* is right. To this day, I believe God had something to do with this close encounter with death. I guess He decided it wasn't my time." Doc momentarily embraced Julie, and then, as they pulled away from each other, he continued, "To this day, I'm not sure just how I was able to find my belt loop so quickly, or how I was so quick to cut myself loose. And how I was able to hold my breath and find my way to the surface in that dark, murky, inlet water. It really was a minimiracle in my book!"

"Ken must have freaked!"

"Oh yea! Vic freaked too. He evidentially came running down in a panic, because he knew I should have popped up out of the water much sooner. Fortunately, by the time he got to Ken and the Seinskiff, I had already surfaced and was gasping for air."

"Gosh! I bet he and Ken were mighty thankful when you broke the surface of the water. But, I bet the two of them were upset with you too, right?" Julie gave him a confident look of correctness.

"After they both helped to pull me out of the water, Vic instructed me to follow him into my harbor shack. Ken joined us, and I got a tongue-lashing of sorts. I mean, Vic was thankful that I survived, but was mad at me for going in the water that close to the refrigerator. Once he was finished scolding me, and done with warning me of the dangers of unplanned acts, then we all three had a quick group hug, said a short prayer of thanks, and then that scary incident . . . we put behind us, thank goodness!"

"Well, I'm just happy that you're alive and here with me now and that I can look at how handsome you are and how wonderful you are. You be careful, dock boy!" Julie commanded him, as she gave him a flirty wink. "I'm so thankful you had that knife on you."

Doc reached down and carefully pulled his knife out of its sheath, which was attached to the right side of his belt. When he held it in the air in front of Julie's face, and safely turned it around for her to examine, he said to her, "Me too, trust me! It really is an important tool to have when you're working around water, and with boats."

"Chris showed me the one you guys gave him."

"Loaned him. I know he'd love to keep it, but as we told him at the time, it's strictly a loan. We pass that buck knife on to our current assistant harbormaster. Oh! That reminds me, I should tell you about Ken and his knife accident. But you have to promise me that you won't mention it to him. He would be so humiliated if he knew I told you this story."

"Why? What happened?" Julie was once again intrigued by Doc's upcoming tale.

As dusk set in, lights began to appear in several windows of the two-story ladies dormitory, Nootka. A number of standing, wooden pole lamps began to illuminate on a few of the wooden boardwalks, in view of Doc and Julie. The temperature was slowly dropping, as the sunlight was almost gone, and low clouds had made their way down Jervis Inlet, closer to Malibu.

"One evening after dinner, this was late last summer, Ken was sitting right here on this bench. He was using his knife to whittle a piece of driftwood that he had found washed up near the Shanty, just behind us, over there." Doc momentarily twisted around and pointed over his shoulder toward the shore, to Andy's Shanty and Haida. Julie turned her head sharply, but briefly, to look in the direction Doc was pointing. "He was carving it into the shape of a fish, a salmon, to be precise. It was about fifteen inches long and oval in shape. Anyway, it was about half done and was looking really cool. He had it on his lap and was working on shaping and sculpting the fish's gill. He was holding the tail end of the wooden fish with his left hand and had a tight grip of the knife handle. He was forcing the sharp, pointed end of the knife into the soft wood. The mistake he made was that he was cutting toward himself, instead of outward, away from his body."

"Uh-oh! What happened?" Julie quickly questioned Doc.

"Well, he was forcing the blade down hard to cut the wood, and oops! The knife slipped, and he stabbed himself right in the stomach, just below his navel!" Doc described the incident to Julie by showing her Ken's movement with his own hands.

"Oh my gosh! How far did the knife go in?" Julie was shocked and troubled by the past incident.

"It went in about two inches. Blood began squirting out profusely!" Doc illustrated the frightful scene.

"Oh no!"

"Once he pulled the knife out, he immediately put pressure on the gash by holding his hand over the wound and came running toward the Shanty. When he got to the path out in front, he yelled at me to come help him. He knew I was inside reading a book, so once I realized what had happened, I grabbed a towel from our bathroom and ran out to him. We right away placed the towel over the wound, and with us both holding it tight against his stomach, we hurried along the boardwalk toward camp and straight to the Medicine Man. Fortunately, the doctor was there taking care of a camper who had an earache or something. Anyway, once the doc got the bleeding stopped, he bandaged him up, and that was that."

"Well, I can see why you wouldn't want me to mention it to him. What did Vic say about the whole thing?"

"He was surprised it happened because he thought Ken was smarter than that when it came to using a knife. Obviously, he lectured him—actually both of us—about never using a knife with the blade pointed at you. Always point the blade away from your body. That way, if it slips, it'll move away from you. Anyway, it was really embarrassing to Ken that he allowed this to happen. But accidents do happen. So you learn, and continue on, right?"

"Yea, that's true," Julie agreed. "Life is a constant learning experience."

"So from then on—even till today—in private company, Vic and I will tease Ken by telling him that he's the only person we know that can say he has two navels, two belly buttons!" Doc chuckled, as Julie joined in. Then she stopped and quickly, but softly, hit Doc's left shoulder with her open hand.

"That's mean of you guys! You shouldn't tease him like that. It was just an accident."

"Oh, trust me, he can take some teasing from us. He always joins in with us and laughs at himself," Doc assured her.

"Well, that's a good attitude. Good for him." She gladly accepted Doc's statement.

Just then, a strong, cold wind struck them as it swooped up from down the inlet. The clouds had thickened, and drops of heavy wet rain began plundering their faces and clothing.

They both promptly stood up from the bench, as Doc blurted out, "I think our little party's over! We'd better wrap this up and get out of this storm moving in. I'm sure it's only going to get worse, sooner than later." Julie agreed, as she gave Doc a sad look of not wanting to end their private visit, but knew that they needed to run for cover before they both got drenched. With a sudden thought, Doc said to her in a soft voice, "Do you think you could meet me in about forty-five minutes? Then we could continue our private personal time together."

"Yea, sure. But where?" Julie asked with perplexity in her voice.

Doc grabbed her arm and gently turned her around and pointed over toward Nootka. "See that room, or cabin, that's attached to the left bottom of Nootka? The one with the new, fresh, cedar siding and the lighter-colored wood?"

"Oh yea. I see it. I never even knew that was there. I guess I just never paid attention," she answers, surprised.

They turned and began to hustle toward the Shanty and the wooden boardwalk that led to Malibu Village. "That's Toad Hall," Doc told Julie in a louder voice, as they were trotting side by side, trying to escape the rain.

"Toad Hall? What's it for? Who stays there?" she hollered back to him.

"Nobody. We use it for storage. There's a ton of stuff in there. Furniture, supplies, you name it. We also store some of our old props and stuff for some of our skits and theme competition events. I'm sure you can find your way to it. Just look for the stairs off to the right from Nootka's first-floor deck. And there's a small sign over the door that reads, Toad Hall. Forty-five minutes, okay?"

"Okay!" Julie answered in agreement, as the two of them split ways from each other. Doc headed directly straight toward the Shanty, as Julie jogged over to the boardwalk toward the center of camp. Doc truly would have loved to have invited Julie into his temporary camp home, Andy's Shanty, but he knew that there was a hard rule about not having those of the opposite sex in your personal living space. Besides, his close neighbors were Vic and Edna, in Haida, so he wasn't about to take a chance of one of them seeing her enter, or exit, his cabin.

A half hour passed, and Doc was already inside the cluttered, dusty Toad Hall, awaiting Julie's presence. The thirty-five-foot-wide by twenty-five-foot-deep room, with an unusual seven-foot-low ceiling, was dark and cold. Just as he had told Julie earlier, there was an assortment of items stored in this out-of-the-way place. Dust-covered furniture such as couches, lamps, chairs, tables, mirrors, and a couple of oak desks were among the items. There was even a variety of kitchen appliances and equipment stacked over in one far corner. The room was rarely occupied and only had two small horizontal windows that were covered with heavy drapes. In the farthest and darkest corner of the room, Doc was sitting on an old tattered couch, partially covered by a faded painter's drop cloth. On a sturdy, cardboard box on the floor in front of him was a flickering candle mounted in a small antique tarnished silver holder. The candle barely gave off enough light to illuminate Doc's upper body. It was not long before Doc heard footsteps approaching from outside, on the narrow wooden deck. Assuming it was Julie, he left the candle burning. The door slowly opened, and Julie peeked her head around, looking into the gloomy room. When Doc saw her blond locks and her eye-catching face, he called out with a heavy whisper, "Julie, over here!"

Julie was squinting, trying to adjust her eyes to the darkness. She then quietly entered the room and gently closed the door behind her. As she carefully and slowly made her way between all the large cluttered items toward Doc, her pupils began to dilate. She was beginning to see objects better than when she first entered. Soon, beside the flicker and smell of fire, she could make out the silhouette of Doc, and then finally his facial features.

"I'm so glad you made it," Doc whispered to her, as she slipped in behind the box supporting the candle and sat next to Joseph on the couch. "Did you find it okay?"

"Oh yea. Just as you said." Scanning the room with her now adjusted eyes, she glanced around the entire space. "Gosh. You're right. This place has a collection of everything. What a bunch of stuff. Is this all discarded, or do they ever use any of this junk—for lack of a better word, sorry."

"Truthfully, a lot of this stuff *is* junk and will never be used again. On the other hand, sometimes the furniture is reused, and of course the props we use often. That's why they're stored closer to the door. Well, enough about that. I'm so glad you're here, princess."

"Me too," Julie said to him with a smile, as she scooted closer to him. "But I can't stay very long, because our work crew boss wants us girls to gather later for a short meeting and cabin time." She voluntarily positioned her hand and arm around Doc's waist, as she nudged even closer to him. With a pleased smile, Doc reacted to her by clasping her hand and clinching her fingers tightly between his.

"I understand. We'll make the most of it, okay?" With his other hand, he reached over and gently touched her face in a gesture of fondness. He softly said to her, "I'm glad you're wearing that jacket, it's not exactly warm in here, is it?"

"Yea, I noticed. But I'm glad we can at least hug up next to each other. That certainly helps and feels good." Julie slowly laid her head down upon his shoulder and neck, obviously wanting to be as close to him as possible.

"I'll keep you warm, I promise. It's so nice to finally get to snuggle with you, doll."

"I agree. Okay, I have to ask you, Joseph." She lifted her head away from Doc's body and was face-to-face with him when she asked him a question.

Before she could speak, Doc quickly interrupted her, as he was gazing at her remarkable, pretty face, "You are so beautiful, Julie, do you know that?"

"Thank you, Joseph. You are so sweet to me," Julie responded with a pleased cute grin. "Did you notice what I'm wearing? I know the lighting in here is really dim." With her right hand, she reached up to her neck and carefully pulled out the ruby cross necklace that Doc had given her a week or so earlier.

With a proud smile, Doc said to her, "It makes me so happy to see you wearing my mother's necklace. Thank you."

"Oh, no. Thank you," Julie responded, gently placing it back underneath her blouse. "It's so lovely. Believe me, I'm proud to wear it." She then looked back up at Doc and was again face-to-face with him. "Okay, now I have a question for you."

"Shoot! What's on your mind, princess?" Doc asked her, ready to give her an answer.

"You seem really familiar with this spot, even perhaps this couch. Are you sure you've never met another girl down here in Toad Hall?" There was a short pause, and Julie added, "Now be honest with me."

"No, I swear . . . I . . . . ah, well . . . oh, man . . . gee, I can't lie to you. I won't do that. You need to hear the truth." Julie gave Doc an expression of concern. After another short pause, Doc spoke with guilt and embarrassment in his voice, "Yes, I have."

"Joseph!" Julie said to him with quick discontent; she instantly let go of his hand and gave him a punch in his upper arm.

"Ouch!" Doc responded.

"Oh, that didn't hurt. Don't be a baby. Besides, you deserve it!" she said to him in a loud whisper. "You sat right here with another girl?" She turned her head forward and immediately folded her arms in disgust and dissatisfaction.

"Well, it wasn't exactly right here. We were somewhere over there." Doc pointed toward the far corner of the dark room. "And I swear, it wasn't this particular couch." He scrambled to defuse the situation. "And listen, it was a mistake, really! We didn't do anything, honest." Julie turned her head and looked straight at him again with an expression of doubt, her arms still folded tightly against her chest. "Well, we kissed a couple of times, but that was all." Doc admitted, sheepishly.

"You kissed?" Julie dropped her arms down. "Are you serious? *We* haven't even kissed once."

"I know, I know . . . and I'm not sure how to explain this, but, gosh, I don't know . . . with you, I feel so different."

"Oh! You don't want to kiss me?" Again, Julie abruptly folded her arms in front of her in a huff.

"No! That's not it. Of course I do. I've been dying to kiss you. You're beautiful, and amazing, but I don't want to mess this up, or ruin it!"

"What do you mean, 'mess this up'? And what exactly is *it*? You're confusing me, Joseph," Julie said to him with insecurity.

"Well, it's just that . . . with—oh, shoot, I shouldn't mention her name."

"Why? Who was she? Never mind. I don't want to know. Were you in love with her?"

"No, I wasn't," Doc quickly admitted, trying to convince Julie. "And that's the point. I wasn't in love with her. I liked her a lot, and we were attracted to each other . . . but—"

"But what?" Julie interrupted Doc, with her arms still folded.

"But I knew that I wasn't honestly in love with her. We were young, and we both got caught up in the whole 'need for physical affection' thing. It never should have happened. But trust me, we only kissed a couple of times, that's it."

"Do you still think about her?" Julie slowly lowered her arms.

"No, I don't. I really don't. All I think about these days is *you!*" Doc reached over and gently grabbed both her hands and gave them an affectionate squeeze. "She's in the past. I didn't even know that you existed when she and I were superficially attracted to each other."

"But why haven't you kissed me, Joseph?" Julie whispered as she looked directly into his eyes.

"Again, this is hard to explain, but I guess it's because I care about you so much. I respect you so much, that I don't want to over-step my bounds or make it all about physical attraction, and kissing, or touching. Does that make sense? Besides, if we got caught, I don't want to even think about that, especially getting you in trouble. We both know the frat rules, so even what we're doing now, we're taking a chance. But if someone saw us kissing, yikes! We'd really be up a creek in a chickenwire canoe! Agree?"

Julie giggled about the canoe depiction and said to Doc, "Yea, I'm sure you're right about that."

"Well, anyway . . . going back to the 'mystery girl' from my past . . . please believe me, we were just good friends, and we took it a little too far. That's the truth."

Julie squeezed Doc's hands and asked, "So, you think you love me? You did say that."

"No, I *know* I love you, my princess." Doc squeezed her hands again, as he moved his head to the side of hers and gently kissed her cheek. "There, now I've kissed you," he whispered to her with a loving smile.

"Well, I guess that'll have to do for now. But one of these days I want to taste your lips. Is that okay with you?"

"Of course. And as I told you before, once I kiss you on the lips, there's no going back, agreed?"

"Agreed!" Julie winked at him, and then continued with a somber tone in her voice, "I love you too, Joseph. I know I do. And I feel safely hidden in here with you. In fact, I kind of feel like we're in that dance scene in *Westside Story*, when Tony and Maria lay eyes on each other in the gymnasium. They slowly walk toward each other in perfect focus, but everyone around them at the dance are blurred. It's like the two of them are protected and are the only ones in the room. You saw that movie, right?"

"Yes, I did. We talked about it before. Regardless, I did a scene from that musical in drama class last year. I love that film," Doc said to her, pondering his pleasant memories.

"But, Joseph, even though we're in this room, sitting here alone and in each other's arms, I also know that we can't hide from God. I feel like He must be angry and disappointed with us. Doesn't that bother you?"

Doc slowly let go of her hands and gently pulled her, once again, closer to him, placing her head into his left shoulder and neck, allowing her to snuggle with him. While she relaxed against his upper body, he slipped his left hand around her back and down around her waist and tenderly said to her, "Julie, listen to me. We're not doing anything wrong. We're not even kissing each other, just hugs and embraces. I mean, I know we're breaking the Young Life frat rule, but two people falling in love isn't evil or sinful. Love is a beautiful thing. The Lord created this extraordinary place out of love for us. He even said that the greatest thing in the world is love. Like Chet said in club the other night, 'God is love.' And it's only natural for two people who are attracted to each other—physically, emotionally, and spiritually—to be in love and need to be together. Maybe the timing isn't the best for us right now, but it's not like we're going to do anything that we'll regret."

"Like what?" Julie asked as she looked up at him.

"Well, you know what I mean. If I'm . . . if *we're* willing to refrain from kissing on the lips for now, then we're certainly not going to allow ourselves to go too far, at least for now. Not that I don't want to, mind you. You understand, right?"

"Yes, I do. It's awfully tempting, isn't it? It's almost kind of like driving too close to the edge of a cliff though. Why would you do it? You might get too close and fall into a canyon and ruin everything. It's better to just stay safe. Don't take a chance of destroying every-thing. Besides, it helps us to feel a whole lot less guilty, don't you think?"

"Yea, it does," Doc agreed.

"You are so sweet and kind, Joseph." She lowered her head for a moment in thought, and then looked back up to Doc, who looked down at her with a slight smile of care. Then Julie once again spoke in a whisper, "What are we going to do about the future, Joseph?"

"What do you mean?" asked Doc, with a bewildered expression.

"I mean, this real living dream of ours . . . this paradise, Malibu. It's going to end in a couple of weeks when I have to go back to Spokane. And then after the summer is over, you'll be going back to Oakland, back to California."

"I know." Doc shook his head in concern and puzzlement. "We have to figure something out. We need to be together. Maybe you could go to college in the San Francisco Bay Area."

"Or maybe you could move to Spokane," Julie quickly sug-gested, again looking up at Doc. "The State University is a really good college. And my dad could instruct you in drama. Wouldn't that be cool? He's going to love you. So is my mom."

"Just pray that I don't get drafted to Vietnam. To be honest, I really don't want to get stuck in a foxhole over there. Although, on the other hand, I'm kind of tempted to enlist. I know our military needs riverboat skippers, and I could certainly—"

Julie right away covered Doc's mouth with her hand to stop him from finishing his sentence and sternly said to him, "Don't say it! I would die if you got shipped off to that awful war. Young men are being killed over there every day. And I'm not sure, or convinced, that we should even be there."

Just as Doc was about to engage in conversation with Julie about the war, they both heard footsteps on the boardwalk just outside Toad Hall. Doc immediately said to Julie, "Go hide!" Julie jumped up from the couch and slithered away into a dark corner while Doc blew out the candle, stood up, and moved behind the old couch. Just then, the door opened, and someone entered the room.

"Is anyone in here?" The person hollered out into the room. A bright light of a flashlight appeared as it was scanning the interior of the storage hall. Doc, at once, recognized the voice and moved out from behind the couch, answering, "Ken! Over here!" Doc reached into his pocket and pulled out a box of matches as Ken engulfed him with light from his powerful flashlight. Doc striked a match and relit the candle directly in front of him. As the flickering flame began to illuminate the area of the couch, Ken moved toward Doc, dodging the obstacles in his path.

"What the heck are you doing in here, Doc?" Ken asked with certain concern and perplexity.

"Hey! I can ask the same question of you . . . what are you doing here?" Doc challenged Ken in defense, knowing that he had been caught.

"I'm here because I just ran into a lady councilor who stopped me on Main Street to tell me she thought she smelled some smoke in her room, which is right above us. So, what's with the candle?"

"Oops! I guess the smoke was making its way up through the floorboards above us, sorry." Doc sheepishly admitted.

Ken, who was now standing next to Doc, asked, "Who's *us*?"

Doc turned his head around in the direction of the far dark corner and called out in a heavy whisper, "Come on out, Julie, it's okay."

Julie slowly emerged from behind an old walnut bookshelf and walked toward the two guys standing within the flickering candlelight as Ken whispered firmly to Doc, "No, it's not okay. What are you doing, Doc? Do you want to get kicked out of here? And what about Julie?" Ken looked over at her as she awkwardly walked over and stood next to Doc. "If you guys get caught, they'll send her home too. Is that what you want?"

"Of course not, Ken," Doc promptly answered Ken's unwanted question. "Look, first of all, we honestly weren't doing anything wrong. I mean, I know we're not supposed to be fraternizing, but I swear to you on a Bible that we were just talking and enjoying our private company, that's all. No kissing, nothing like that, seriously."

"He's right. We weren't kissing, or anything, honest!" Julie interjected in their defense.

"Well, I'm not a Malibu policeman, you guys know that. And I would never say anything to anyone. I just care about you both and don't want to see you get in trouble, that's all. You understand, right?" Ken placed his hand on Doc's shoulder and looked at both of them with a caring expression.

"Hey, I know that, pal. Of course you wouldn't turn us in. I'm just glad that it was you standing inside the door, and not someone else, like Chet or Jake . . . or one of the head councilors."

"Well, look, you two better beat it out of here. And do me a favor: don't come back here, okay?" Ken looked for a sign of agreement.

"We won't. I promise," Doc said to him in a serious tone.

"Maybe the three of us should leave separately, a few minutes apart, okay?" Ken suggested as he nodded to Julie. "Just to be on the safe side."

Julie gave Doc a quick simple smile, turned, and headed toward the door. Ken shined the light in her direction, illuminating her path of exiting the dark room. When she quietly slipped out the door, Ken shined the light on Doc's face and said, "Look, Doc, I'm sorry this happened, but I'm telling you, you'd better cool it, or this is going to blow up in your face, right?"

"Well, yes, I agree, but I'm telling you right now, there's no way that I'm going to stop caring about that amazing lady. I'm in love with her, Ken, seriously. I feel her in my heart. I've never felt so sure about anything in my life." Doc looked at Ken with an expression of positive thought.

"That's fine, I get it, but just do me a favor and be supercareful and conscious of your acts of togetherness. I care about you, buddy, I don't want you to be sent home, got it?"

"I got it. Thanks, Ken. Okay, I'm out of here." Ken once again shined the light for Doc, as Joseph carefully and skillfully headed toward the door. After he waved back to his friend and roommate, he too quietly exited and disappeared up the wooden steps toward the lighted Main Street of Malibu. Seconds later, Ken extinguished the glistening candle and, using his flashlight, safely exited Toad Hall and disappeared into the dark.

CHAPTER 16

Several Unexpected Guests Visit Malibu—Surprise!

The sun was shining once again at Malibu. It was a beautiful warm afternoon, and Julie was on her way back from the winding dirt path along the golf course and rocky shores of the spectacular Jervis Inlet. She was walking directly in front of Haida, toward Malibu Village, from her "watering the hanging plants" duty. Approaching from camp, Vic was walking toward her, as he was heading home for a while. When they began to cross paths, they greeted each other with smiles.

"Hello, Ms. Julie," Vic said to her in his booming, deep voice. "How are you today?"

"Hi, Vic. Oh, I'm wonderful," she answered him, as they both stopped to talk. "How can one not be wonderful in this magic place of beauty? And how are you doing?"

"Couldn't be better," he expressed his joyful mood. "So, Julie, I've been meaning to ask you something. Since you're from Spokane, do you know the Brewers? They own a large, successful, lumber mill just outside of Spokane."

Somewhat startled, Julie's face quickly turned a slight red, showing signs of embarrassment. "Yea, actually, I do know them. I mean, I know who they are. Do you know them?" she asked Vic with obvious interest and concern as well.

"Yes, I do know them. Mr. Brewer is responsible for our fuel here at Malibu. He donates it to us, thank goodness. It sure saves Young Life a great deal of money. He is a very generous, kind man."

"Gee, I didn't know that about the fuel." Julie's uncomfortable reaction, and face, had fortunately began to calm itself down.

"Well, to be honest, it's kind of twofold. You see, his family has a small fleet of yachts they moor in Seattle, and they like to come up here once a summer and anchor down at Chatterbox Falls for a week, or so. They need a place to refuel, and since we don't sell any gas, or diesel, here at Malibu to yachtsmen . . . well, the fact that he gives us our fuel for free, I'm sure you get the picture, right?"

"Oh, sure. That totally makes sense," Julie agreed.

Vic continued, "The reason I brought this up with you, just now, is that they're due to arrive here with their boats this afternoon. I just thought you might know the family, since you all live in Spokane."

With some dismay in her voice, Julie said to Vic, "Yea . . . hmm? Well, thanks for telling me, Vic. I'll certainly keep an eye out for them and say hello if I should see them in camp."

Reading the signs of uneasiness, Vic decided to ask her, "Are you all right, Julie?"

"Oh yea. I'm fine. I guess I'm just a little tired today, that's all. Bye, Vic," she said to him, as she stepped up on to the boardwalk and swiftly walked in the direction of the village. Vic, seemingly not convinced at Julie's explanation of being tired, turned and walked up the short path toward Haida.

Minutes later, Julie was in her cabin talking to Beth. Their other two roommates were busy working at the Linen Nook. "What am I going to do, Beth?" Julie asked her anxiously, standing by one of the windows and looking out at Forbidden Island and Jervis Inlet. "What if Richard's with them? He never told me that he'd been to the Princess Louisa Inlet with his family. I can't believe this is happening."

Beth, trying to calm her new friend down, asked her, "But you told me that you broke up with him before coming to Malibu."

"Well, not exactly. I mean, I did. I broke up with him. But you don't know Richard. He's very controlling and doesn't easily take *no* for an answer. He still thinks we're a couple, believe me." Julie turned around and faced Beth, with a worried expression.

"That's silly. Didn't you give him back his ring?" Beth folded her arms in front of her, somewhat confused.

"Yes, I did. But somehow, he just won't accept it. He won't accept the fact that I broke up with him. It's kind of like that Ricky Nelson song, 'I believe you're going steady with nobody else but me!' That's how he thinks. In his mind, he can't allow me to *not* be his girlfriend. Does that make sense?"

Beth dropped her arms down by her side and answered, "No, that does not make sense, at least to me it doesn't!"

Still trying to convince her of Richard's "thought process," she told Beth, "You have to understand something, he's always had everything he wants, and he *wants* me. But I'm not in love with him. I'm in love with Doc." Julie turned back around and stared out the window again, obviously upset.

"What are you going to do?" Beth asked her with hesitation.

Julie turned and slowly walked over to her bed and sat down. Facing Beth, she answered her in a soft voice, "I'm not sure what I'm going to do, Beth. I guess if Richard shows up, I'll have to corner him and make it very clear that we're not going steady anymore. I just hope he listens to me, and gets it. And I pray that Doc doesn't find out about any of this. If he does, I know it'll really upset him. It's already upsetting me!" she said, as she placed her hands over her face and dropped her head into her lap.

Beth walked over to her and sat down next to her on the bed. She sweetly placed her arm around Julie and whispered to her, "It's going to be all right. I'm sure if you carefully explain to Richard your true feelings about him, he'll back off."

With tears in her eyes, Julie looked up at Beth and said to her, "I sure hope you're right. I'm really worried about this. Thank you, Beth, for being such a good, caring friend." She then hugged Beth briefly. A moment later, Beth stood up and slowly walked to the window, feeling bad for Julie.

While looking out the window, she suddenly said to Julie, "Julie, come here! Could this be them?"

Julie hurriedly stood up and ran over to the window, next to Beth. When she looked through the glass, she frantically shouted out, "Oh my gosh! I bet that's them!" The two girls were both looking down at the inlet with their eyes focused on a small fleet of fancy blue-and-white motor yachts. The second yacht in line was towing a competitive-style, sixteen-foot blue ski boat. As the three luxurious boats passed in front of Forbidden Island, Julie continued, "That is them. See the guy driving the last boat? That's Richard. Beth, what am I going to do?"

They faced each other, as Beth answered her, "Okay, take a deep breath. Listen to me, Julie." She grabbed Julie's hands, "If it were me, I'd hurry down there right now, down to the inner dock. And, assuming they stop for fuel, I would at once straighten out things with Richard. I really think that's what you should do. Nip it in the bud, before it all goes haywire for you and Doc. Don't you think?" Beth's question was of care and concern.

Not really wanting to face her worst fear of having to deal with this distressing issue, she answered Beth, "Yea, you're right. That's what I have to do."

It was not long before Julie had made her way down to the inner dock area. While she was walking across the wide upper deck, there was a lot of activity going on in the floating dock area of the inlet, including the water ski program, boating, and some fishing. Immediately, Julie spotted two of the three Chris-Craft yachts heading down the Princess Louisa Inlet, approximately a thousand feet away from Malibu, starting to make the slight right turn toward Chatterbox Falls. When she approached the top of the gangplank, she stood by the wooden railing and looked down, and at once saw the third, smaller, blue-and-white motor yacht tying up alongside the outward section of the long floating dock. With the bow of the stubby, thirty-two-foot boat pointing toward the far end of the dock, the lines had already been thrown out, and Doc and Chris were scrambling to secure the boat to the cleats mounted into the wood planking. Richard Brewer, an older blond teen sporting a crew cut, was standing behind the wheel of the controls and was shouting out commands to another teenage boy, who, seconds before, had already tossed out the bowline to Chris. A younger girl was standing near the helm next to the shouting "skipper," who had now turned off the craft's powerful diesel engine. Sitting at a small white fiberglass table in the back of the boat was an older man, smoking a fat cigar, which was disgustingly dangling from his mouth. The dense white smoke was blowing out into the open clean air. He had just sat down, after hurling the stern line successfully to Doc. The name of the boat was painted on the wide stern in bold gold letters and read, RICH BREW! It included some artwork of a green dollar sign and a mug of beer. Richard, a moderately handsome young man, was just short of six foot and was wearing expensive yachtsmen-style blue-and-white clothing. Leaving the helm, he hurried over to the port side of his yacht, as his craft was floating against the dock. With an unpleasant tone to his voice, he yelled down to Doc, who had already secured the stern safely and correctly to the heavy steel cleat, "Hey! Can't you pull me in tighter? I don't want your ski boat waves ramming her into the dock."

Doc quickly gave Chris a glance of annoyance but politely answered Richard, "Yea, no problem. Welcome back to Malibu." With that, Doc immediately untied the line, slightly pulled the boat closer to the dock, and then retied the white rope once again to the cleat.

Richard, without delay, jumped down off the boat on to the dock. Chris was walking over toward him and Doc as Richard looked back up to his crew and guests aboard and said to them, "Stay aboard, everybody. This won't take long." He then turned to Doc and said to him, "I met you here last year, right? You've got that weird name, what is it? Duck?"

"No, it's Doc," Joseph corrected him, again glancing at Chris with a nauseating look on his face. "You're Rich, right? Mr. Brewer's son?"

Doc extended his hand, but instead of Richard following through with a gentleman's shake, he slapped Doc on the right shoulder and answered, "Oh yea! I'm Rich!" he proudly responded with a smirk and glanced at his expensive yacht. "Hey, pal! I need some fuel for my ski boat," he demanded. He then turned up at his boat and hollered to the other teen boy his age, "Freddie! Grab me those two five-gallon tanks from the storage bin." When he turned back to face Doc, he continued, "Listen, do you know a girl who works here? Her name is Julie. Julie Copeland?"

Again, Doc quickly glanced at Chris with an expression of surprise. "Yea, I know her." After quickly giving it some thought, he said to Richard, "Oh, that's right. You're from Spokane too. So I guess you know her, huh?"

Richard was amused and was quick to laugh aloud, once again slapping Doc on his shoulder. "Know her? She's my babe! Good-lookin' chick, huh?"

Doc was trying to remain calm, wondering if he had possibly misunderstood what Richard had just stated and asked him, "Your babe?"

"Yep! We've been going steady for about three months now." Doc was standing there with a stunned look on his face, as was Chris, who was overhearing this entire conversation. "Do you know where she might be right now? Man, is she going to be surprised to see me."

Doc couldn't help but say to himself aloud, but softly, "I bet."

Julie, who had backed away from the railing, out of sight of this whole scene, was standing in the middle of the upper deck, trying to gather her thoughts. Beth, wanting to support her friend during this unexpected, disturbing situation, had decided to follow Julie down to the inside dock area. Spotting her standing alone in the center of the upper deck, she at once ran over to her.

Julie turned to her and, in a frantic voice, said, "Oh no! Beth, this can't be happening. What am I going to do?"

"Calm down, Julie," Beth counseled her. "What's going on?"

"He's here! Richard's on the dock, talking to Joseph!"

"Okay. Listen to me. Gather your composure. Again, take a deep breath." Beth placed both her hands on Julie's upper arms and forced her to look straight at her. "Julie, look at me. We don't know exactly what they're talking about down there, but I think you need to assume that Richard could be asking about you, right?"

"Yea, I'm sure he is. He's probably asking Doc, right this second, where he can find me!" she answered Beth with a rattled voice.

"Well, that's why you need to go down there now, and face the music. You need to try and resolve this without any hesitation, before it blows up in your face, Julie! I would just let Richard know your honest feelings, again. Remind him that you are no longer a couple, period! Say it right in front of Doc, if he's still standing there. Whatever you do though, don't say anything about you and Doc, that wouldn't be good for now." She let go of her arms, then encouraged her some more, "Listen to me, Julie! Go now, don't wait!"

Julie slowly turned away from Beth and walked toward the gangplank. Seconds later, Beth briskly followed in her steps until she reached the railing where Julie had stood earlier. She leaned against the wooden white rail while she watched Julie carefully walk down the slanted planked narrow bridge toward the lower dock.

Sure enough, Richard, who was facing in her direction, spotted her and called to her, with his arms extended out. "Julie baby! Surprise! Aren't I great? You didn't know that I knew about this place, did you? I've been keeping it a secret from you. Get down here and give your boyfriend a hug, darlin'!"

Doc had his back to Richard and Julie, since he was talking to Chris. He instantaneously turned a hundred and eighty degrees around, looking at the two of them, and gave Julie a discomforted, puzzled look. Julie casually approached Richard and reluctantly gave him a simple hug. She then looked directly at Doc with uneasiness. Just then, and without warning, Richard suddenly lifted her up into the air by her waist and spun her completely around in a circle motion.

"I've missed you, kid," he said to her, as he put her back down on the dock.

"What are you doing here, Richard?" Julie questioned him at once.

Discreetly, shaking his head, Doc turned around and started walking down the floating dock, past Chris, towards his office.

Richard proudly announced to Julie, "I told you, babe, I wanted to surprise you. My dad vacations up here at Chatterbox Falls every summer. I was here last year." Pausing for a moment before he continued, he hollered at Doc, "Hey, buddy! Don't forget my gas. I need it right away for my ski boat. Pronto!"

Doc, who was still walking away from them, barely turned his head around toward Richard and Julie and shouted back, "Yea, sure. Hey, Chris, bring me those two gas cans, will ya?"

"Still giving orders, I see," Julie, embarrassed, scolded Richard. Folding her arms, she continued, "You shouldn't have come. I told you, it's over between us. I'm sorry, Richard, but I'm not your girlfriend anymore. Why can't you get that?"

"Oh, come on, Julie. I don't want to hear that, especially not now. Look, everything's going to be fine. Just you wait and see. Listen, I want you to come down to Chatterbox with me right now, okay?" he commanded her, as if he was still giving orders to his guests aboard his yacht. "My parents really want to see you." Turning toward his elaborate yacht, he bragged to her, "Look at my boat, isn't it fine?"

"Yes, it's very nice. Richard, I need to talk to you. I have something important to tell you." In her mind, Julie was already considering telling Richard that she had met someone.

"Okay, that's fine. We'll talk down at the falls," he instructed her, which was his way of defusing and controlling the situation.

"I can't go with you down to the—"

"Give me a break!" Richard interrupted her with some anger in his voice, obviously irritated. "I came all the way up here to see you. The truth is, I could be in Hawaii right now, if I wanted to. I had the choice. The least you can do Julie is—"

Julie grabbed his left arm, hoping to calm him down in front of onlookers, including a few campers and counselors. She quietly asked him, "Will you promise me that you'll hear me out? As I said, I have something important to tell you. And, I have to be back to prepare my table for dinner. That's only in a couple of hours. Do you understand that?"

"Hey, no problem." Richard was quick to agree, since he felt he had won the argument and he was getting what he wanted. "Whatever you say, sweet cheeks."

"Don't call me that!" she irritably said to him in a loud whisper. "You know I don't like that, Richard." She then turned around and looked up at the top of the gangplank, sensing that Beth would be standing there looking down on them, which she was. "Hey, Beth!" she called up to her. "Would you please let Leslie know that I'll be back in time to set up and serve."

"No problem, Julie," Beth shouted back down at her with a look of uncertainty and confusion. Not being able to hear their personal conversation from up top, Beth was feeling somewhat uncomfortable about what exactly was going on.

Julie then said firmly to Richard, "Stay right here. I'll be right back." She hurried along the dock toward the harbormaster shack, attached near the end.

Richard hollered at her, once again in a commanding voice, "Hey, jewels, tell that guy I'll get the fuel tomorrow! He's too damn slow. I want to get going!"

Julie ran up to Chris, who was standing near the far end of the floating dock, just outside the shack. "Where's Doc?" she asked him with anxiety in her voice.

With a disappointed, baffled look, Chris casually pointed over toward the gas dock. "He's in the Seinskiff, almost to the fuel station and boathouse near shore. He's on his way to the gas dock to fill up those cans for your boyfriend," Chris answered her, shaking his head in a negative manner.

"He is not my boyfriend. He was, but he's not now. Please believe me, Chris. You have to give a message to Doc for me, okay? Tell him that I'll explain everything about Richard to him when I get back from Chatterbox Falls."

"You're going to Chatterbox Falls with that guy?" Chris asked her with concern in his voice.

"I have to, I need to fix this. Richard is stubborn, and he needs to listen to me. Please, just tell Doc to trust me. Tell him I'm sorry . . . and, Chris, tell him—Chris, are you listening to me?"

Chris looked straight at her and answered, "Yea, I'm listening. Tell him what?"

"Tell him that I love him," Julie said with a somber tone and solemn look.

"You love Doc?" Chris asked her with obvious mystification.

"Shhh!" Julie quickly shushed him by placing her finger over her lips. "Don't say anything to anyone. Do you understand? This needs to be kept a secret. No one, Chris, don't tell anyone, please."

"I won't, I promise. I understand," Chris assured her.

"Thank you. You're a good friend, to both of us. Listen, I'll be back before dinner. We'll talk later." Julie hurried back down the dock toward Richard's boat. He was already aboard, and the lines were untied. The vessel was floating against the dock with the diesel engine idling. Soon, Julie was alongside the yacht looking up at Richard and the other guests aboard.

"Help her aboard, Fred," Richard barked out orders again to his friend who was acting as first mate. As soon as Julie was on board the extravagant motor yacht, Richard wasted no time before he engaged the throttles of the twin-screw craft. His "full speed ahead" action caused an immediate sizeable wake, which in return almost capsized one of Malibu's ski boats, tied alongside the dock. Minutes later, Richard's Chris-Craft, *Rich Brew!*, was making the slight right turn down the inlet on its way to Chatterbox Falls, with Julie aboard.

Doc had made his way back to the inner floating dock from the gas dock. Standing near his harbormaster shack, he was talking to Chris. He had filled the two red gas cans for Richard's ski boat, which were now sitting on the dock in front of him. Doc and Chris briefly stopped talking while they both looked down the inlet, just as Richard's boat disappeared around the bend. Doc turned back to Chris.

"You're sure that's what she said?" he asked Chris, wanting a definite, defined answer.

"Positive. So you and Julie are—"

Doc interrupted him with the answer to his obvious question, "Yea, we are. Listen, Chris, you've got to keep this super quiet. You do understand, right? Julie and I could be in deep trouble if this gets out. You know the 'no frat' rule."

"Yea, of course. I do understand, trust me. Don't worry, Doc, I won't breathe a word about this, I promise." He looked straight at Doc and gave him an expression of honesty and assurance.

"Man, that guy Richard is such a conceited jerk. Sorry, but he is, it's the truth," Doc told Chris, feeling a little guilty about judging Richard, but confident in his description.

"Oh, I totally agree with you, Doc. He is so bossy and arrogant. I can't imagine how Julie ever—"

Quick to defend Julie, Doc interrupted Chris. "I know what you're thinking, but you know Julie, she probably felt sorry for him, in her own way. But it sounds like she is finally at the point of giving up on him, and their relationship."

"Yea, I've got to agree with you there. She certainly took me under her wing last year at Frontier Ranch when I was having my problems. She's always looking to help people improve themselves, their lives, and to believe in the message of Christ as well. That's a fact. She did with me."

Placing his hand on Chris's shoulder, Doc agreed with him. "Yes, for sure. She's an amazing gal. She is so caring and sweet." Doc paused for a moment, looking down at the two gas cans. "Hey! Don't you have an inlet cruise scheduled in a few minutes?"

Somewhat startled, Chris answered Doc, "Oh yea, that's right. I almost forgot."

"You know what? I think I'll take it for you," Doc told him, pondering an idea in his head.

"Doc, do you think that's wise? I mean, you're the boss, but Julie said that she would talk to you when—"

Again, Doc interrupted Chris. "I know. I know she said that, but . . . hmm!" He rubbed his chin with the fingers and thumb of his right hand. "I really don't like her being down there with that guy. I don't trust him. Who knows what he'll try and pull?"

Forty minutes later, Julie and Richard were standing on the floating dock at Chatterbox Falls. The float provided the yachtsmen and visitors to tie up their watercrafts. Along both sides of the dock is a number of privately owned yachts and boats, including the

Brewers' three Chris-Crafts and ski boat. Mac's houseboat was still tied securely at the farthest end of the long narrow float. Julie and Richard were near the gangplank that led up to the land where only a couple of weeks prior, Doc, Julie, and the others had gone to hike the path up to the lower falls. The two were arguing aloud. "Look, you wouldn't talk to me on the way down here," Julie said to Richard with a tone of frustration. "I agreed to visit briefly with your folks, which I did. Now it's time that you listen to what I have to say."

"Julie, again, listen to me. I know of a very romantic place up on top of the falls, where we can sit down and discuss whatever is on your mind," Richard tried to convince her, like a car salesman would do to a prospective buyer in a showroom.

"I am not interested in a romantic place, Richard. I just want to talk to you," Julie responded to him with added frustration.

"I swear to God, Julie, you'll have my undivided attention, honest! Just do this for me, please. This is important to me."

"Everything's always important to you. In fact, it's always *about* you!"

"I know I can be selfish, and I apologize. But I came all the way up here to see you, Jules. Just do this for me. I really want to take you up to the top of the falls, you're going to love it."

"See, you weren't listening to me before. I told you that I've already been up there, and yes, it's a spectacular view, I agree with you there."

"Yea, but I know a special spot, a really cool place that I'm sure you're not aware of. Fred and I found it up there last year. It's absolutely amazing! I can't wait to show it to you, please, Julie! I promise to shut up and listen to everything you want to say to me, okay?"

"Oh, Richard, you're impossible!" Julie said to him, obviously frustrated and willing to throw in the towel regarding this never-ending argument. "Okay, okay! I'll hike up the falls with you, but then, that's it. When we get up there, you're going to listen to me, right? You'd better hold to your promise, or I will just leave."

"I promise. I really do. Cross my heart." Richard made a quick *X* across his chest with his index finger. He also noded his head yes to Julie. Julie's expression was one of doubt and annoyance. They soon began to walk up the slanted gangplank in the direction of the dirt trail that would lead them to the upper falls.

Back at Malibu's inner dock area, the harbor activities were still underway. Chris was tying up a visiting thirty-foot sailboat, when suddenly from over the swimming pool area and the narrows, a dark-blue Bell helicopter made a swift entry. It buzzed loudly over the inlet waters, just off the floating dock, and up and away from the sailboat. The pilot skillfully controlled the hovering craft, which was about sixty feet in the air and near the peninsula shore, close to the angled gangplank. While the almost invisible long black rotors continued to spin rapidly, the helicopter stayed at the same elevation above the inlet, until the area of water below was safe to touch down the two sizeable landing floats on to the wet surface. Once Chris and Kyle had waved off the one ski boat nearby, beneath the copter, the aircraft began to slowly descend until it gently rested atop the water. Floating twenty-five yards off the dock, the engine began to shut down, and the two rotors started to slow down. After about a minute, the noisy machine finally went silent, as the rotors stopped their spinning. All the folks on the floating dock had their eyes glued on the helicopter, wondering why it had landed nearby and who was aboard. Small groups of teenagers and counselors were engaged in quick conversation about what the floating chopper was doing there. The incoming tide was slowly moving the craft toward the dock. When the pilot's face came into view, so did Jack Copeland's, since he was sitting in the copilot seat. With her face pressed against the back window, Mary Jo was also in view. The aircraft was soon only a dozen yards from the dock. Floating on the waters behind the sailboat, the pilot swung his door open and stepped out on to the port-side metal float. Spotting Kyle, he spoke aloud, "Hey, Kyle! Is Doc around?"

Pointing down the inlet toward Hamilton Island, Kyle shouted back to the pilot, "He's on an inlet cruise. In fact, he should be getting close to Chatterbox by now, I would imagine. What's up?" He asked with certain curiosity in his voice. By now the pilot had thrown Chris his tie-line, which was securely tied to the helicopter's port float.

"How 'bout a work crew girl by the name of Julie Copeland, eh?" the pilot asked, as he disclosed his Canadian accent. "Is she around?"

"She's down there too," Kyle answered him straightaway. "Is everything okay?"

"Oh yeah! We're just looking for them. These are her parents," the pilot pointed back at Jack and Mary Jo, who were still aboard the helicopter. Calling out to Chris, who was beginning to loop the line around a cleat, he said to him, "Oh, thanks, but I don't need you to tie us up, I think we'll head on down the inlet to find Doc and their daughter, Julie." Chris threw the line back to the pilot, as Kyle quickly introduced them to each other. With that, the pilot opened a small storage door located just under his cockpit door and swiftly pulled out a wooden paddle. With his right knee down on the flattop side of the pontoon float, he immediately began using the paddle to move the floating craft forward, away from the dock, and farther into the inlet waters. Once he felt he was in a good, clear position, he jumped back into the pilot seat and at once started the engine. The rotors quickly began to spin significantly, and the loud sound of the engine and blades revved up dramatically. The pilot lifted the aircraft back up into the air. Kyle and Chris waved, along with most of those watching from the inner dock and upper deck area. Mary Jo waved back through her backseat window, as the helicopter speedily headed down the fiord toward Chatterbox Bay, only a hundred feet off the cold dark inlet waters. Just then, Vic quickly made his way down the gangplank on to the dock and over to where Kyle and Chris were standing. They were still watching the copter as it began to veer right and soon disappeared around the bend.

"What's going on? Was that Frank piloting the chopper?" Vic was obviously curious as to why the helicopter made such a brief visit.

"It was. He was looking for Doc, but didn't really say why," Kyle answered Vic, looking a bit puzzled. "Oh, and he asked about Julie Copeland too, our new work crew girl."

"Yes, I know Julie." Vic paused briefly as he pondered the situation. "Hmm . . . that's somewhat puzzling. I wonder what it's all about." The three of them stood there for a few more minutes in additional conversation, before Kyle and Chris soon returned to their duties, and Vic left the inner dock area.

Richard and Julie had hiked their way up to the summit of the lower falls. Standing only about a dozen yards from the actual pounding water of Chatterbox, the sound was thundering and the cold wet spray of freshwater was filling the air. They were at the point of the trail that was closest to the falls. Nearby was the warning sign that Doc had spoken about a few weeks earlier to Rusty and the other hikers when he joined the group to hike the falls with Julie. It plainly read:

DANGER! DO NOT ENTER THIS AREA! ROCKS ARE EXTREMELY SLIPPERY! STAY ON THE PATH!

Julie and Richard were in a heated argument, as they shouted at each other over the loud sounds of the waterfall. "Richard, I'm not going out there!" Julie yelled at him with an angry, disturbed voice. "Read the sign! People have lost their lives doing that!"

Richard ignored her as he easily climbed over the four-foot steel railing that ran along the danger zone. "I know a spot that's safe!" Richard shouted at her. "Fred and I did it twice last summer, trust me! It's such a rush, Julie! Come on, you can do it!"

"Are you crazy! Don't go out there! Please . . . please! Can't we just sit here on the trail and talk! You promised me!"

Richard, who was still on the other side of the danger area, standing next to the wet railing, continued to holler at Julie with his demands, "Do this with me, Julie! I promise you'll have my undivided attention out there! I won't ask for anything else! Just trust me, will you!" He then reached out to her with his right hand extended over the railing. With her arms folded, she swiftly moved her head back and forth, indicating a no answer to his harsh request.

"Come on, Julie! You know I wouldn't put you in danger! Like I said, I've done this before! It's okay! You have to believe in me! You won't believe how incredible this experience is! Just do this with me! Again, I promise to listen to you!"

"How will I be able to talk to you out there, Richard!" she continued to shout over the thundering falls. "It's so loud *here*, how will I be able to converse with you out there!"

"We'll be side by side!" Richard tried again to convince her. "You can yell in my ear, I don't care!" Julie looked down in frustration, and then in a surrendering expression, she reluctantly looked up and reached her right hand out to him. As she slowly gave in to him, he helped her cross the short fence into the danger zone.

The helicopter, with Jack and Mary Jo aboard, was approaching Chatterbox Bay. Still only about a hundred feet off the water, Frank spotted the *Nefertiti* in the bay, where it was nearing the falls. The tour boat was slicing through the deep blue waters, less than two hundred yards from the dock. It began to pass by the magnificent lower falls. Frank expertly swooped the copter down toward the deep cargo boat that had at least two dozen sightseers aboard, with Doc at the helm. Closing in on the *Nefertiti*, and using an earmuff-style headset microphone device, Frank announced to his passengers, Jack and Mary Jo, "There's the *Nefertiti*!" Hearing the sounds of the chopper, and then quickly spotting the aircraft, Doc turned to watch the copter descend, as it approached him. Right away, he slowed the boat down and switched his gears into the neutral position. The watercraft began to idle off the shores of Chatterbox. Soon the helicopter dropped down upon the bay and gently floated in the water, on the starboard side of the *Nefertiti*. Fifty feet separating the two crafts, Frank turned off the engine and the rotors, and they, once again, began to spin slowly to a stop. The three occupants inside the copter removed their headsets, and without delay, Mary Jo asked Frank, "Is that Joseph—I mean, Doc?"

Before Frank could answer, Jack interrupted, "I don't see Julie."

"Yes, that's Doc at the wheel," Frank responded.

"Don't say anything, Jo. We need to talk to Julie first," Jack quickly said to her with a firm voice.

With tears in her eyes, Mary Jo was staring at Joseph and whispered to Jack from behind, "Look at him, he's so handsome." While

Frank began opening his door to climb out on to the port float again, Mary Jo continued to speak to her husband, "I don't understand, where's Julie?"

While Frank positioned himself upon the flattop of the long pontoon, Doc shouted over to him, "Hi, Frank! What's up?"

"Hello, Doc!" Frank hollered back. "Say listen, we thought that Julie Copeland, the work crew girl, was with you on this tour. These are her parents." He gestured to the copter's interior. From inside, Jack and Mary Jo wave to him.

Doc—looking surprised, confused, and even somewhat embarrassed—waved back to them and shouted out, "Oh, hi! Nice to meet you." Looking back over at Frank, he said to him, "Julie's with her friend Richard, from Spokane, over at the dock." He turned and pointed toward the three Chris-Crafts owned by the Brewer family. When he turned back, he spotted Mary Jo, her head now in the doorway in plain view, and still in tears. "Is there anything wrong?" he called out with a concerned thought.

Forcing his body closer to the open door, Jack shouted back out to Joseph, "No. Everything's okay, we'll explain later!" He then turned his head around to face Mary Jo and commented quietly to her, "What the heck is Richard doing here?"

"I haven't a clue," his wife answered him. "But it concerns me."

Just then, one of the campers aboard the tour boat pointed to the top of the falls and yelled out, "Hey, everybody! Look up there!" Everyone aboard turned sharply and focused on the falls. It appeared that two people were barely visible standing out near the edge of the falling mass of white water. Doc swiftly grabbed his binoculars stored in a padded wooden slot, attached to the right side of the helm. Using the magnified glasses, he at once realized that it was Julie and Richard standing at the edge of the cliff. The enormous river water was rushing only a few feet from them.

"Oh my God," he whispered to himself, as he lowered the binoculars.

Richard and Julie were both struggling to keep their balance, standing on the drenched moss-covered granite rock next to the falls. Stricken with fear, they both decided it would be best to sit down upon the green vegetation. They were hoping that they could grab on to the wet moss with both hands, keeping them from slipping off the big gray rock and into the rushing water. Earlier, their attempt to turn back for safety had failed, and they had no choice but to remain where they were, in frightening danger.

"It's much too wet!" Richard shouted over the thrashing, thunderous sound of the falls. "There's more water than last year. The falls are so much bigger!"

Just then, Julie, not being able to hold on to the soaked moss, the short grass slipping through her fingers, slid a short distance below Richard, into a small crevice in the granite. With her feet dangling over the rock, she could barely grip a piece of the boulder that had broken off. The massive falls were rushing only a few feet away from her.

Terrified and yelling, Julie shouted, "Help me! Richard, help me, don't let me fall!"

Doc once again spotted them with his binoculars and could see that Julie was in big trouble. Everyone aboard the *Nefertiti* was focused on the dreadful incident. Even with the naked eye, it was possible to tell a possible disaster was in the making. The helicopter had now drifted only about a dozen yards from the boat. Frank, Jack, and Mary Jo were all trying to look out the curved cockpit window to get a glimpse as to what was happening up on the falls. They had no idea that it was Julie and Richard in harm's way, and that Julie was now in frightful, imminent danger.

"Oh no!" Doc shouted. "Frank, start your engine!" Fully dressed, Doc straightaway leaped into the inlet waters toward the chopper. As he surfaced and began swimming to the helicopter, Frank jumped back into his seat and, without hesitation, turned on the craft's engine, which at once engaged the rotors. Doc climbed up on the port pontoon and reached out to the solid-blue strut that was attached to the craft's fuselage. Jack and Mary Jo were clearly confused and curious as to what Doc was doing.

"What are you doing?" Frank shouted out to Doc, his window slightly cracked open.

"She's in big trouble, Frank!" Doc yelled back, as he sat down on the flat part of the float, gripping the strut with both hands. "You've got to get me up there now, Frank!"

"Who's in trouble?" Frank asked Doc in a loud voice.

"Julie! Julie's in trouble! Get me up there, now!"

Mary Jo and Jack looked at each other with foremost concern and disbelief. All those aboard the *Nefertiti* were watching this dramatic event unfold before their eyes. The helicopter swiftly lifted off the water and headed toward the falls. Doc was strongly holding on to the copter's strut, knowing that if he were to let go of his grip, he would certainly fall to his death. Frank piloted the craft directly toward the top of the lower falls where Julie and Richard were still struggling with certain danger. Richard was trying to reach down to Julie in hopes of rescuing her from disaster, but he was obviously too frightened to risk falling himself.

"Please, Richard!" Julie pleaded with him. "My hands are slipping. I don't know how much longer I can hold on! Please help me!" she shouted up to him with an expression of desperate concern and fear.

"I'm sorry, but I can't do this. I can't reach you. I'm scared. It's too risky, we'll both fall!" He reached his right arm back up and again grabbed the soaked cold moss with both hands.

When the helicopter was only about fifty yards away from Julie and Richard, disaster struck. Julie lost her grip on the granite wall and rapidly slipped into the chilling waters of the falls. She plunged down the 120-foot drop into the churning pool of freshwater below. All those witnessing this ghastly event were stunned and frightened by the incident. Mary Jo and Jack were horrified. Doc was petrified and dismayed by this shocking occurrence.

Yelling at the top of his lungs, hoping that Frank would hear him over the loud sounds of the rotors above his head, Doc shouted out, "Drop me down to the pool, Frank! Drop me down to the pool!" he repeated. "Do it!"

Frank barely heard Doc's serious and desperate request, but without hesitation, his clear instinct kicked in, and he swiftly piloted the chopper down toward the large pool of water at the bottom of the falls. As the copter descended slowly alongside the rushing water-fall, and when the craft was just above the churning pool of frothy water, Doc let go of the pontoon strut, and feetfirst dropped into the frigid water. When Frank saw Doc entering the water below him, he immediately pulled the helicopter up and away from the falls, in fear of being too close to the violent falling white water. Taking a deep breath before entering the freshwater, Doc quickly opened his eyes beneath the water to search for Julie. The glacial, freezing water was viciously churning as Doc frantically tried to find Julie in this dark body of certain death, if he failed to locate her soon. As if by a miracle, Doc soon found Julie and, with all his strength, shoved her toward the surface. When Julie broke the surface of the water, she instinctively gasped for air and was coughing and hacking in order to breathe. She was alive. Directly in front of her, she spotted a small floating log that she was able to grab on to. After latching on to it, the force of the falls dropping into the pool began to push her toward the bank. She hurriedly fought her way toward the huge boulders surrounding the big pool of water and made her way out of danger.

Frank had landed his helicopter near an open area, close to the river of water that originated from the large pool that Julie, only moments before, had climbed out of. By the time Frank, Jack, and Mary Jo had exited the aircraft, Mac, who had monitored this entire event from the dock, made his way up to them with Mr. Brewer, Richard's father. They had followed a narrow dirt path, along the side of the river, toward the bottom of the falls. The four men continued to follow the path along the grassy terrain to reach the big rocks, in order to find Julie and Doc. Mary Jo remained at the helicopter site, too upset and distraught to hike with the men; she decided to stay back and pray for a good outcome. In the mean time, Doc had also surfaced, but not by his own merits. The churning water had fortu-nately forced him to the top of the pool, as if another miracle had taken place. Although his lifeless body had surfaced and had already begun to float toward the wet boulders, Julie was close by and was able to safely climb back into the water and pull Doc to safety. She was superficially injured with minor cuts and bruises on her legs, arms, and face, but she mustered up the strength to pull him up on to some lower rocks and sand near the shore.

When they attempted to approach the large pool area, Mac was the first one to reach Julie and Doc, since he knew the best route that led through the large boulders. Closing in on them, he soon spotted the bright-red blood staining the rocks and sand next to the two injured teenagers. Julie's clothes were torn, and some of her blood was trickling out on to her clothing and the shore. She was sitting there almost in a daze, with Joseph's head and shoulders up on her lap. He was unconscious and also had many cuts to his head and to his bare feet, which were bleeding as well.

Sobbing, Julie looked up at Mac. He knelt down beside her, and she tearfully said to him, "He's alive, Mac. He's breathing. We've go to get him to the doctor."

"Child, I can't believe *you're* alive," Mac quietly said to her, placing his hand on her shoulder. "We need to attend to your wounds."

Just then, Frank, Jack, and Mr. Brewer arrived at the scene from behind a large boulder.

Julie looked up to see her dad, and with certain surprise and shock on her face, she called out to him, "Daddy? Daddy! What are you doing here?"

Jack quickly ran to her side and knelt down, just as Mac stood up and moved slightly away from them. Her dad answered her in a voice that was a bit out of breath. "It's a long story, pumpkin. Are you all right? You're bleeding, we need to take care of that right now." As Frank, who had brought along with him an emergency first-aid kit, began to administer treatment to her wounds, Jack continued, "Your mom and I were scared to death when we realized that it was you atop the falls."

"Mom's here too?" Julie responded quickly. Before Jack had time to speak again, Julie blurted out, "We've got to help Joseph. He's unconscious. Please, Daddy, he can't die!" She began to sob again.

Jack immediately tried to calm her, "It'll be okay. He's not going to die. We're not going to let that happen, I promise."

Wiping away her tears, Julie asked her father, "Is Robin here too?"

"No, but she's fine. She's staying with the McKinleys."

Mac had knelt back down and was checking Doc's pulse, while Jack removed his sweater and placed it around Julie's shoulders. The men checked Doc for any broken bones, and once they carefully moved him off Julies lap, they bandaged their open wounds to stop the bleeding. Frank, Mac, and Mr. Brewer then carefully lifted Doc and carried him down the path toward the helicopter. Jack had his arms around his daughter and slowly helped to escort her along the dirt, winding path. On through the rocks, and then down the grassy terrain, they followed the men, who were carefully carrying Joseph to the aircraft. Tearfully, Julie looked at Jack and said, "He saved me, Dad. Joseph saved my life. He's my hero. He has to be okay."

"Trust me, sweetheart. He will be."

It was not long before the six of them reached the copter. As soon as they came into view, Mary Jo ran straight to Joseph and asked if he was going to be all right. "He's unconscious, Mary Jo, but he does have a pulse, so we can only hope for the best," Frank told her, identifying the fact that she was quite concerned and upset. She turned and scurried even farther, hurrying to check on Julie's condition. Jack was still helping her along the path toward the helicopter.

"Julie! Are you okay, sweetie?" she frantically asked her and quickly put her arm around her daughter. Now they were both helping her along the dirt footpath. Julie immediately started to sob again, while her mom tried to calm her. "You're going to be fine, honey. Don't worry," she assured her.

Trying to speak through tears of sadness and fear, Julie muffled her words. "It's Joseph I'm concerned about, Mom. He saved me, and now he's lifeless, I'm so worried!"

"I know, Julie, I know. But I'm sure the doctor at Malibu will take good care of him and make sure he's well again. I'm sure of it." Mary Jo tried to convince her injured daughter. Julie suddenly realized that she hadn't asked about Richard.

"Do we know what ever happen to Richard? He was still on the cliff when I slid down the falls."

Her dad quickly answered. "He's fine. He was able to make his way back to safety. Mac spotted him with his binoculars before he and Mr. Brewer scurried-up the path to meet up with us."

A few minutes later, the three of them reach the others, who were alongside the helicopter preparing to load Joseph aboard. Once they carefully placed him in the wide backseat of the aircraft, Frank instructed everyone to move away from the copter a short distance for safety. He was obviously anxious to board and start the rotor blades spinning. "I'll go with Frank," Jack told Mary Jo and Julie, giving them both a quick kiss before climbing aboard the chopper. "We'll make sure he's in the doctor's care in only a matter of minutes. It won't take us long to fly back to Malibu."

"Take good care of him, Jack," Mary Jo said to him, while Julie agreed with her mom by nodding her head up and down in a yes fashion.

"Oh! We will, that's for sure," Jack shouted to her, just as Frank started the loud engine and rotors. "Don't worry, it's going to be okay. At least he doesn't appear to have anything broken. Mr. Brewer, would you please—"

Instinctively knowing what Jack was about to ask, Richard's dad interrupted him by hollering, "Don't you worry, Jack. I'll bring your wife and Julie down to camp right away aboard my boat. We'll make them good and comfortable. And just so you know, when my son gets back down here to the dock from atop the falls, I'll make sure he drives the Malibu tour boat back to camp as well. Mac told me that there's really no one aboard that group qualified to pilot the *Nefertiti*, so I'll make sure my son takes care of that. That's the least he can do. He certainly has some explaining to do, I'll tell you that much!" Mr. Brewer was obviously ashamed and upset with his son regarding the entire matter. It was apparent by the tone and sound of his voice.

Frank lifted the helicopter into the air. Jack gave a quick wave to all those standing below, off to the side. The fierce wind created by the rotors violently blew the hair and clothing of the onlookers, while the copter ascended and then leaned hard to the left, as it turned and flew swiftly in the direction of Malibu. Flying between the massive mountains, a couple of hundred feet above the inlet, the speedy aircraft began to disappear around the bend.

Soon, Mr. Brewer, Mary Jo, and Julie headed for his yacht, moored at the dock. While Mr. Brewer was getting Julie and her mom settled in his boat, Mac decided to hang out on the dock for Richard to arrive. He definitely wanted to have some words with this young man regarding his dumb decision to disregard the warning signs atop Chatterbox Falls, causing Julie to almost lose her life!

CHAPTER 17

Keep the Faith,
Hope for a Miracle!

Within ten minutes, the helicopter had reached its destination, touching down upon the water, near the outside of the inner dock of Malibu. Soon the aircraft was tied to the floating dock, and numerous folks were gathering around that area. Frank and Jack disembarked the craft and were explaining to Kyle and Chris what had taken place at Chatterbox Falls and why Doc was lying injured in the back seat of the chopper. Kyle ran off to alert the doctor, and Chris scurried down the dock to the harbormaster office to retrieve a metal stretcher, a first-aid item always kept in the shack for emergencies. Vic and Ken soon were on the scene, while several people, with care, helped to reposition and transfer Doc from the helicopter on to the stretcher. By now, Malibu's loud air horn was blasting short bursts to alert the camp doctor that there was an injured person in camp. Jack and Ken positioned themselves on the back end of the stretcher, while Vic and Chris stood on the front end, ready to help. The four men cautiously lifted Doc up off the dock and began their walk up the slanted gangplank, heading for the doctor's office on Main Street. Many of the teenage campers, along with several counselors, were either following them on the short trek up the wooden walkway or they were intercepting their journey, making their way to the center of camp. Some of the young people were even crying, watching the unconscious, injured harbormaster being transported to the Medicine Man. The blast from the air horn had subsided, since Kyle was able to locate the camp's doctor. The physician got to his office just as the four men reached the front door. A few of the staff members and counselors, along with a dozen or so campers, gathered around the front of the office in sadness. There was an abundance of conversation and discussion taking place, while the stretcher, with Doc lying on it bandaged and lifeless, was being moved through the doorway and on into the doctor's office. Shutting the door behind them, Jack and Ken, with the help of Vic and Chris, carried Doc into the back room, as instructed by the doctor.

Meanwhile, back at the end of the Princess Louisa Inlet, leaving Chatterbox Bay was Mr. Brewer's yacht, with Mary Jo and Julie aboard. In the comfort of the master stateroom, Julie was lying in the queen bed, while her mother was sitting by her side. The luxury motor craft was underway, heading for the Malibu Club. In this elegant spacious cabin, decorated in nautical fashion, Mary Jo and Julie were alone in conversation.

"I have to know why you're here, Mom. I know you didn't just decide to stop by and visit me." Julie had a puzzled look and was finally having a chance to question her mom.

"Perhaps you should rest for a while first, Julie, then we'll talk," she answered with reluctance, not wanting to explain about Joseph being her son.

"No," Julie quickly responded. "I'm okay, honest. Mom, this has been one heck of a day. First, Richard shows up. Then, I fall over a huge waterfall, that nobody's ever survived from. And, the person I'm in love with saves me and is now unconscious by doing so. And then you and Dad show up . . . am I dreaming?"

"No, sweetie, you're not dreaming. Maybe I wish you were. Listen, honey, I just don't know if this is a good time to—"

Before her mom could continue, Julie abruptly interrupted her, "Please, Mom, just tell me, what's going on? I'm not a baby. You need to be upfront and honest with me."

Mary Jo paused and looked away from Julie for a moment. Then she turned back at her and placed her hands on the top of the turquoise comforter, which was keeping her daughter warm. "Julie, this is going to be very difficult for you to understand, and for you to even believe."

"Try me. Nothing more today will surprise me, believe me," she said to her mom, with a look of certainty.

"I think this will," Mary Jo instantly said to her, with confidence in her voice.

"Your dad and I are here because . . . well . . ."

"Go on, Mom, it can't be that bad, can it? It doesn't make sense that you're both here. You must have a good reason to come this far just to see me or talk to me, in person, right?"

"Yes, you're right. Julie. Listen, it's about Joseph."

"Joseph? What about Joseph? What do you even know about Joseph, other than what I wrote you in a brief letter?"

"Well . . ." Mary Jo hesitated again, as she was still having a difficult time explaining her personal truthfulness. "This is so hard. Listen, honey, Joseph is my son."

"Your son?" Julie said loudly, with shock and dismay in her tone. "What are you talking about, your son?" she asked with a stunned expression. "Now I know this is all a dream."

"Listen to me carefully, Julie. He is my son, and the fact that he is also means he is your brother. Are you grasping what I'm telling you?"

"Oh my God!" Julie responded with wide eyes, looking up at the cabin's white bulkhead and then removing her hands from underneath the blanket. She covered her eyes and shook her head in disbelief, as she continued speaking to her mother, "My brother? He can't be my brother, he just can't! This is crazy, Mom. You don't understand. And why? How do you know?" She looked straight at her mother with obvious confusion.

Now with tears in her eyes, Mary Jo reached out to her daughter's hands and held them. "He is your brother, your twin brother." Julie let go of her mom's hands and once again covered her face as she began sobbing. "I'm sorry, Julie, please let me explain."

Dropping her hands from her face, Julie quickly questioned her mom, "Explain? Explain? Are you serious! Mom, he can't be my brother. I love him. Do you understand? And he loves me. We've talked about our future together, as a couple. We've embrace and hugged many times, with intimate thoughts. Do you understand what I'm saying here? Do you?" Tears rolling down her shaken face, Julie waited for her mother to respond to her.

"Yes, I do understand, my darling daughter. I really do. But I can't change it." She started to cry again herself.

"Oh, Mother, don't cry. Please, it'll be okay." Julie suddenly realized how difficult and upsetting this is for her mother to admit. "It's just such a shock to me, Mom. Are you sure he's your son? I mean, how do you know? How did you figure this out?" With a sudden revelation and look of surprise, Julie hastily asked her mom, "Wait, Joseph said this was his mother's." She reached down inside her bloodstained white blouse and pulled out the ruby cross necklace hidden inside.

While Julie displayed the attractive piece of jewelry directly in front of her mother's face, Mary Jo, with intense emotion, blurted out, "Oh my! He really is Joseph. That necklace was mine, Julie, I totally recognize it." Examining the glimmering cross, she explained some more, "It's one of a kind. I gave it to his aunt Lois for her to someday give it to him. She agreed that she would. Oh my gosh! I never dreamed that I'd see it around your neck!" The two of them continued to look at the ruby cross necklace, as Julie's mother continued to tell her the entire story and how she discovered this amazing truth about her and Joseph.

The expensive yacht was swiftly moving through the dark waters of the renowned inlet, and the *Nefertiti* was only about two hundred yards behind the motor cruiser. Mr. Brewer, who was at the helm of the largest vessel in his fleet, had now navigated his elaborate boat in the direction of Malibu, which could now be seen in the distance. Back in the master stateroom, Mary Jo was still trying to explain to her daughter the details of how she discovered that Doc, Joseph, was her son. Julie was now sitting up with pillows propped behind her back, in the comfortable, warm bed.

Still in tears, she challenged her mother with questionable words. "So, what you're telling me, Mom, is that Daddy isn't my real dad. Joseph's dad is my real dad, and he's dead! How could you do this, Mom?"

"I'm so sorry, Julie. I truly am. Honestly, we were both going to tell you sooner than later. Listen to me, sweetie, Jack is still your father. He loves you, Julie, with all his heart. He's taken care of you since you were a toddler, and even adopted you early on."

Julie dropped her head down into her lap and again began to sob. Once she settled down and regained control of her emotions, she immediately asked her mother, "So what happened, Mom? Why did you and Joseph's dad, my real father, break up, divorce? And how old was Joseph and I? Answer me, Mom, I need to know what happened."

Mary Jo took a deep breath and began to explain her past. "Your biological father, James was his name, and I just weren't compatible, as it turned out. We got married too young, and since he was a few years older, I think I was somewhat naive and infatuated with him, instead of being in love with him." Julie's mother began to slightly cry.

"It's okay, Mom. Please continue."

"We both had different needs and interests, which caused our relationship to sour and become unhealthy. You and Joseph were only about nine months old, and because of James's business connections, and knowing people in high places, such as Oakland's City Hall, he had the upper hand when it came to custody rights. He threatened me that if I didn't agree to his terms, he would pull some strings and hire a hotshot attorney and get custody of both you and Joseph, instead of just Joseph."

"Oh my gosh!" Julie responded with anger, her hands over her mouth. "That's terrible. How mean of him."

"Well, his leverage was making me look like I was having an affair with Jack, which honestly, I wasn't. We had become friends but were certainly not in any kind of romantic relationship. James was convinced that we were, so he was telling all his cronies that I cheated on him, and that's why he felt he had the right to make the decision regarding the custody of our children. He really was a good man, Julie. I don't want you thinking ill of him, especially now that he's passed. He just had to be in control of everything." Mary Jo had stopped crying and was defending Julie and Joseph's father, to some degree. "Anyway, he demanded that he have sole custody of

Joseph and that I would have custody of you. Basically, he believed the son should be raised by the father, and the daughter be raised by the mother. Plus, I had to agree not to ever see, nor contact, Joseph, forever." She began to cry again.

"Oh, Mother, I'm so sorry. That must have been extremely hard for you. Plus, all of these years passing by. Oh my goodness!" Julie reached out and hugged her mother, as best she can, while still lying in bed.

Mary Jo regained her composure and spoke to her daughter again. "I certainly think that what James forced me to do was totally wrong and cruel. But to be entirely fair, obviously in the end, there was an attraction between your daddy—Jack—and me. It occurred a while after James and my divorce was final, but his intuition was somewhat correct, I'll give him that."

"It's okay, Mom, we'll figure it all out. I think it's important that we pray about all of this, certainly that Joseph will be completely healthy again." Julie tried to comfort her mom, but instead, the two of them showed signs of tears running down their cheeks.

The Medicine Man consisted of two rooms, the front space being smaller than the back area. It was basically a waiting room of sorts, with a couch, side table, and several chairs placed along the cedar wall, which faced the large windows looking out to Main Street. Several live, tall plants were placed along the sides of the room, and there were a couple of framed paintings depicting the surrounding inlets. They were mounted above and near the greenery. There were several photo albums upon the wooden side table, which were full of old black-and-white photographs taken at Malibu in the early years. Beyond the closed door leading into the larger rear room was the space where the doctor could attend to his patients. The room was typically clean and tidy, with white cabinets containing medical supplies and other equipment needed to mend injured or sick folks. There was an X-ray machine in the far left corner of the well-lit space, along with other standard provisions often used by physicians and emergency hospital rooms. In the opposite corner of the X-ray machine was a metal gray desk used to organize the doctor's necessary paperwork. There were four metal folding chairs available, should they be needed. Two hospital-type beds were also in the room, spaced apart, with a ceiling-to-floor sliding curtain in between them, in case privacy was necessary.

A half an hour had passed, and in the front waiting room of the Medicine Man was Doctor Morris, the camp's doctor, speaking with Jack, Vic, and Chet when Mary Jo and Julie entered the office from Main Street. Jack hurried over to them and promptly asked his daughter, "How do you feel, Julie? I want the doctor to check you over and clean up your scrapes." Julie looked at him and suddenly burst into tears. He immediately pulled her into his arms and hugged her tightly. "It's okay, pumpkin, it's okay."

She strongly hugged him back, as she whispered to him, "I love you, Daddy."

With tears in his eyes, Jack whispered back to her, "I love you too, sweetie."

Mary Jo, with tears as well, asked her husband, "How is he?"

"I'll let the doctor explain to you, honey." He introduced the doctor to her and Julie, along with Chet and Vic.

"Yes, I've met Julie," Dr. Morris said to Jack, having met Julie on the day she arrived at Malibu, waitressing the guest table, where the doctor frequently sat for meals.

"Hi, Doctor," Julie greeted him, wiping the tears from her face.

"Sounds like you were an extremely lucky lady, Julie," the doctor said to her, as he began to gaze at her numerous blood-soaked bandages taped on various parts of her body, including her left cheek. "I certainly wish meeting your dad and mom were under better circumstances."

Since Julie appeared to be okay for the moment, until the doctor could take the time to exam each of her wounds, Mary Jo straightaway asked Dr. Morris, "So, tell me about Joseph. How is he, Doctor?"

"Well, let me first explain to you that he does have a head injury. In fact, he is comatose for now, so obviously he's still unconscious.

Somehow, during the ordeal, he traumatized the head area. He probably slammed it against a rock. He also broke two ribs, which is affecting his breathing. So that is an issue and a concern of mine."

"Is he going to be all right?" Julie was quick to ask, with fear in her voice.

"Honestly, it's really hard to say just yet. I've done everything that I can do for now, since we have a limited source of supplies and equipment on hand here at Malibu. He's on an IV, in the back room," he told Mary Jo, pointing at the closed door leading to the infirmary. "I don't want to move him for at least twenty-four hours. This is an extremely critical period of time for him right now. He definitely has some swelling of the brain, and it's very doubtful that there will be any change by tomorrow, which means he'll need to be flown to Vancouver for better treatment." Mary Jo and Julie both were displaying expressions of great concern and worry. "I wish I had better news, but not right now. There are a lot of questionable concerns."

"In your professional opinion, Dr. Morris, what are his chances of recovery?" Mary Jo asked him, not sure if she truly wanted his expert opinion.

"You know, it's really difficult to tell just yet. I really don't want to mislead you or give you false hope. There are so many variables and issues that need to be addressed and investigated. I'm not saying that it's hopeless, but I'm also not saying that he's going to fully recover, or maybe worse." The doctor obviously is uncomfortable trying to explain, encourage, or place doubt, since he fumbled his words somewhat, trying desperately to satisfy Mary Jo with an honest answer.

"Worse!" Mary Jo blurted out, "What do you mean *worse?*"

"Let's just wait and see, everybody. We need to be patient and wait for the results. We need more time to give us the answers," he stated, making eye contact with all five in the room and wishing that he had not mentioned the word *worse.*

"Can we see him?" Julie asked, breaking the uncomfortable silence in the room.

"Yes, of course. But then, Julie, I want to remove your bandages so that I can check you over and make sure you're okay, understand?"

"Sure," Julie was quick to agree, since she was anxious to enter the room to see Joseph.

Jack spoked up and said to Mary Jo, "Mr. Raley has made sleeping arrangements for us for the night, Jo."

"How nice, Chet. Thank you so much."

"I want you to know, Mrs. Copeland and Mr. Copeland, that we will pray for Joseph. We know, Mary Jo, that he is your son. Jack has explained everything to us, and believe me, all of our staff and all of our work crew and counselors, we will be praying," Chet sincerely told her, as he reached both his hands out to comfort the two of them and Julie. "He is in our prayers now and until he gets well. Our Lord is a God of love and mercy, and He will heal Joseph. We believe that, don't we, Vic?"

"Yes, we do," Vic answered in his normal deep accented voice. "Joseph is a good, Christian young man, and I have heard him say to many a camper over the years, 'Keep the faith, just keep the faith.' And, folks, we will, we will keep the faith, that's for sure. Doc is extremely special to all of us." Vic politely nodded to Joseph's three concerned family members, who were appreciative of Chet's and Vic's sincerity.

Moments later, Julie and her mother entered the back room of the Medicine Man. They walked directly over to the hospital bed that Joseph was lying on. The IV bottle was hooked and hanging on a tall chrome stand, located just behind his head. The plastic clear line weaved to the side of his right shoulder, and then fed itself under his blanket, presumably releasing liquid medicine into his right arm. When Julie and Mary Jo approached Joseph's side, they could right away see the several bandages that were applied to his face by the doctor, protecting his minor cuts and scrapes. Still in a comatose state, it was clear that his breathing was abnormal and, therefore, worrisome. Julie stood close to his right side, and with tears slowly moving down her face on both cheeks, she unlatched the cross ruby necklace from around her neck. She carefully placed it around Joseph's neck by gently sliding the delicate silver chain past his pillow, and then latching the clasp, centering the cross upon his chest. Her mother watched her, as she also had tears streaming down her face.

"Joseph, it's Julie," she softly said to him, bending slightly down to be closer to his face. "I want you to know that you're going to get well, I promise. Oh, my dear wonderful brother, please trust me, okay? And guess what? Mom's here, and she loves you very much. God loves you too, and He's not going to let anything happen to you, do you hear me? He will make you well, because He cares so much about you. Just keep the faith, Joseph, remember, keep the faith. We're all praying for you, the entire camp. Thank you for saving my life. I love you so much." She then tenderly kissed his cheek while her mother looked on.

At dusk, later that day, the entire camp population had squeezed their way into Big Squawka for a special prayer meeting for Joseph Sheldon. Chet was standing on the dim-lit stage, with his head bowed in prayer. Everyone in the room either had their heads bowed or placed in their laps. Some of the campers and work crew, sitting on the long rectangle floor pads, have joined hands or were leaning on one another's shoulders, as they sat silently. Sounds of sadness, such as weeping or moaning, could be heard from time to time. Chet's prayer of healing and hope lasted for several minutes, before he asked others to join him to pray out loud for Joseph. More than a half dozen folks responded, when they asked the Almighty, the God of Love, to use his power to heal Joseph's broken mind and body. Beth was sitting on the floor, along with her roommates, in the center of the room. Tears were gracing her face, as she listened to the prayers, one by one. In the left back corner of the room, next to the dozen folding chairs, occupied by the adult guests and Jake, were Vic, Edna, and Ken, who were standing against the wall with their heads bowed, listening to the sincere prayers of so many. Chris, Kyle, Turtle, and Popeye were nearby. They too were in silent prayer. Julie, her mom, and dad were not present for the vigil. They were in the infirmary, watching over Joseph and praying for a miracle.

Later that evening, when everyone had gone to bed, and the main diesel had been turned off, the only illumination visible around camp were the small, dim-lit, emergency lights sprinkled around the resort. A new safety system installed using the small backup generator, and was now on line. Looking down the Princess Louisa Inlet, in the direction of Chatterbox Falls, the bright full moon slowly emerged above the mountain. The celestial brilliant mass instantly, and dramatically, shone its intense light upon the bare rounded rock formation of One Eye. The granite peak lit up like a giant floodlight in the darkness of night. Way beyond normal, it seemed to reflect and shine its light down upon the inlet with greater intensity than would be conceived possible.

Old Steve was slowly rowing his wooden fishing boat in the inside inlet, trolling for salmon, when witnessing this phenomenon. His face was brightly lit by the moon's reflection off the famed summit. Never, in all his years living in the inlet, had he experienced this kind of brilliance from the light of the moon. He immediately stopped rowing to ponder this curious occurrence. Suddenly, without any warning whatsoever, something happened that was not typical or common in the eyes or the minds of human thought. A focused, laser-like, vivid white light shot from the utmost top of One Eye, straight across the sky, a hundred yards above Old Steve, as he was floating silently on the dark waters of the Princess Louisa Inlet. In his amazement, he watched the beam travel in the twinkling of an eye, from the top of the mountain, over his head, and shined directly on the very tip of Malibu's tallest totem pole. The giant totem pole that was located on the upper deck, above the inner dock. The brilliant light seemed to be concentrated on the upper portion of the tall totem. The top end of the carved, colorful pole had wings spreading outward. To some extent, it resembled the silhouette of a Christian cross, standing tall, and overlooking this inspiring inlet. Since Old Steve had a good vantage point from where he was bobbing along in his tiny boat upon the inlet waters, he can see that the entire top of the totem pole was beginning to glow with concentrated illumination of white light. He was amazed and mystified.

As this incredible event was unfolding, Mac was lying in bed inside his warm houseboat, securely tied up in Chatterbox Bay. He had already fallen asleep in his dark, quiet floating home, located at the end of this extraordinary inlet. However, the concentrated, brilliant beam of moonlight, which had somehow magically reflected off One Eye, and had also instantaneously sent a ray of radiance to the top of the totem pole at Malibu, had awoken him. The light's intensity had penetrated a small window, located just above Mac's bed, and caused him to stir. He quickly sat up and peekd out through the smudged glass, looking up the inlet at this unusual glow, which was located around the bend toward the teen resort. He too was completely astonished and confused as to what it could possibly be.

High up on a ridge, hundreds of feet above the "garbage cove," used daily by Doc and Chris, Yogi, the huge brown bear, was also staring at this unusual bright light. It had mysteriously captured his attention too.

The crosslike silhouette portion of the top of the totem pole was glowing even brighter than before. Its brilliance lit up the entire deck and inner dock area of Malibu. Suddenly, the concentrated beam of light from the granite peak of One Eye vanished. Settled among some trees and facing toward the inlet, Chet and Jake's cabin was nearby the dock area, and they also had been awoken by this abnormal bright light. Sharing this rustic two-bedroom bungalow, the light had penetrated the front window and side windows with such intensity, that it caused them both to awake from the comfort of their sleep. At the same time, and close by, was another larger cabin that was housing Jack, Mary Jo, and Julie for the night. They awoke too because of the strange radiant of light penetrating the windows of their temporary dwelling. All five of them emerged from their cabins as they witnessed this extraordinary event. From the small wooden porches of their lodging, they were able to stand there and, in amazement, viewed the concentrated glow of the top section of the totem pole, standing tall above the many surrounding trees. Several counselors and campers in the guys' dorm, Sitka, were also awakened by the bright light shining into their rooms. They hustled down the hallway, through the spacious lounge area, which was surrounded by tall bay windows on two sides, and a rock fireplace against the back wall. They soon exited out onto the front planked walkway, where they stood to view the amazing sight.

While this phenomenal incident was taking place in the inner harbor, Ken was inside Haida, the home of Vic and Edna, located out by the golf course. Several candles were lit in the living room area, where Ken and Vic were engaged in a game of chess. Edna was fast asleep in the back master bedroom.

Sitting alongside one of the main bay windows of Haida, Ken and Vic quickly noticed the unusual bright light glowing from the other side of Malibu, in the vicinity of the inner dock. They were both instantaneously puzzled and curious about what it could possibly be. At once Vic woke up Edna, knowing that she would also want to investigate this curious occurrence, Vic and Ken quickly put on their boots and headed up the long wooden walkway, in the direction of the light.

The brilliant glow of light from the top of the totem pole began to create a reflection on the surface of the dark water, between the long floating dock and the fueling dock, next to shore. Amazingly enough, the image appeared to be that of the crucifixion of Christ. The light seemed to cleverly illuminate itself upon the shiny surface of the inlet saltwater, depicting this amazing picture of Jesus on the cross, as if God Himself was painting a portrait. The image moved slightly in place, when the breeze across the water stirred faintly. All those in the area who were witnessing this miraculous experience were stunned, astounded, and silent. No one could talk. Everyone was speechless. All they could do was to stare, and wonder, at this biblical image, floating on the water.

Joseph was still in a coma, lying in the hospital bed in the back room of the Medicine Man. The ruby-red cross necklace around his neck and settled upon his chest began to glow. Soon the strength and intensity of the mixed colors of red and white light illuminating from this piece of jewelry, which was shaped like a Christian cross, began to light up the entire infirmary.

Before Vic and Ken reached the inner dock area, without any warning, the glowing light from the totem pole suddenly stopped and extinguished the lighted image of Christ floating upon the inlet waters inside the harbor. The unexpected occurrence happened so fast, that it was almost as if the Good Lord Himself blew the light out. It was as if someone blew out a candle. Other than the tiny emergency lights around camp, darkness had once again prevailed. Totally startled, Chet, Jake, Jack, Mary Jo, and Julie all came together out on a stone walkway between their cabins, looking at each other in amazement and bewilderment. They move over to one another and began to talk with thoughts and questions, sharing their common, and remarkable, experience.

Several hours had passed, and back inside the Medicine Man, the doctor, who had been sleeping on a foldaway bed in the front waiting room of the makeshift medical facility, was suddenly awoken by the sound of breaking glass in the back, infirmary room. He quickly got up to investigate, and when he entered the room, he instinctively flipped on the light switch. To his amazement, he discovered Joseph standing next to his hospital bed, staring at the broken IV bottle on the floor. Before he could speak, Joseph looked up at him and, with obvious confusion, asked, "Doctor, how did I get here?" The doctor was astonished to see that not only was he awake, but the minor scrapes and cuts on his face that he had not bandaged, but only treated them with healing ointment, had vanished! His skin was smooth and healed.

"This can't be," he said to Joseph, almost in a monotone voice of shock. "I don't understand what's happened here. How do you feel, Joseph?"

"I feel fine. What's going on, Doctor?" He looked at the physician, as if he had just woken up from a deep sleep and had no idea where he was. "Where's Julie? Is she okay?" he asked, as he began to recall the frightening, tragic incident at Chatterbox Falls.

"Yes, she's all right. You must not worry about her right now, she's fine," he told Joseph in a convincing, certain tone. "Please sit down on the bed for a moment while I check something." The doctor proceeded to remove one of the larger bandages on Joseph's face, near his left sideburn and ear. When the dressing was removed, Joseph saw the stunned look on the physician's face.

"What is it? Is there a problem?" Joseph quickly asked him.

"This deep gash is completely healed."

"I told you, I feel great," Joseph responded, somewhat confused.

"Are your ribs sore?"

"Not at all, should they be?"

"Joseph, you had two broken ribs." Obviously shaken and in disbelief, the doctor continued, "This is a miracle, is what this is." He began to remove other bandages on Joseph's body, only to realize that underneath every one, his injuries had all somehow healed, completely. *How could this be?* he thought. "Listen, Joseph, can you walk okay?"

Doc took a few steps and answered, "Yes, I can walk fine."

"Oh! That's great news. There are some people who need to see you now."

"Okay, but who? Julie?"

"Yes, Julie is certainly one of them."

"What time is it anyway?" Joseph was trying to understand more of what was exactly going on, in this disorientation of mystification.

"It's 6:00 a.m."

Dawn was breaking, and back inside the rustic cabin, occupied by Jack, Mary Jo, and their daughter, Julie, all were fast asleep, after experiencing the incredible, unusual happening that had occurred in the middle of the night. The cabin was similar to Julie's room, near Nootka, that she shared with Beth and the other two work crew girls. The cedar paneling was the same, along with a variety of Canadian paintings and prints, framed and hung along the walls. However, this single dwelling cabin offered a decent-size front living room with a fireplace, seating area, and included a couch, which converted into a double bed. The room was dark, with heavy green curtains drawn across the two bay windows, facing the Princess Louisa Inlet. Julie was sleeping on the couch made into a portable bed, when there was a knock at the front door. Several hard knocks later, Julie stirred and awoke, hollering out to the person on the front porch, "Hang on, I'll be right there." Fumbling for the light switch to illuminate the room, she immediately grabbed her robe that was lying atop the backside of one of the two green leather chairs in the center of the room, facing the fireplace. Just then, her dad, Jack, and her mom entered the front room from the back master bedroom. Obviously, still somewhat half asleep, Jack whispered to Julie, "Who is it?"

"You got me, I don't know who it is," she, without hesitation, whispered back to him. Jack walked over to the front solid-wooden door and opened it.

Standing there, the doctor apologized to Jack by swiftly saying to him, "I am so sorry to wake you so early, but this is important and can't wait."

"That's okay," Jack responded quickly to him, "come on in."

"Is it about Joseph?" Julie asked with a quick tone of concern. "Is he okay? Did he wake up?"

"As a matter of fact . . ." The doctor motioned to Joseph to move into the doorway and into the light.

When the illuminated room shined upon his face, Julie was overjoyed and yelled out, "Joseph! Oh, Joseph!" Without any hesitation, she quickly gave him a hug, as he hugged her back with great enthusiasm. Once they let go of each other's grasp, she stood back and glanced up and down at him from head to toe and back. Seeing that he was absent of all bandages on his face, she said, "Look at you . . . Look, Mom, he doesn't have a scratch on him."

Mary Jo and Jack inspected him by carefully studying his face and hands and wondering what had happened to the wounds that they had seen on him only the day before. Julie noticed that he was still wearing the ruby cross necklace around his neck, as it hovered about his chest area. But what caught her eye, more than just the necklace itself, was the fact that the cross was no longer the color red. The delicate piece of jewelry was now pure white. She stepped toward Joseph and, in amazement, held up the necklace for her mom and dad to see. There was a silent pause when Mary Jo, with sudden tears of joy, moved closer to her son, Joseph, and announced to everyone, "It's from the Light. He's been touched by God, I know it. It is a miracle."

Jack stepped closer to examine the necklace, and he too had a look of awe on his face.

"Mrs. Copeland, Mr. Copeland, excuse me, can someone explain to me what's going on here? This is all very confusing," Joseph asked them with clear perplexity.

Now it was Jack's turn to speak up, as he looked directly into Joseph's eyes and said with assured acceptance, "John 8:12, son, 'I am the light of the world: he that followeth me shall not walk in darkness, but shall have the light of life.'" The five of them standing there, just inside the open doorway, were looking at one another. It was quite obvious that Joseph was still quite confused, as he scratched his head with his unbandaged right hand.

"I'm going to leave the four of you alone," the doctor said, after a moment of silence. "You have a lot to talk about." He then, without saying another word, turned and exited the room, shutting the door behind him. As he stepped off the wide weathered wooden porch, he said to himself in a whisper, "Unbelievable . . . wow!" Quickly he disappeared into the darkness, heading back toward Main Street.

Minutes later, Popeye was walking along a narrow boardwalk, which weaved its path up from his residence near the gas dock, alongside slabs of granite rock, through tall pines, and in front of Jack and Mary Jo's cabin. He was headed for the dining room kitchen, ready to join the kitchen crew, who were already there preparing the morning breakfast for the camp. Just as he walked in front of the cabin's porch, he heard the blaring sound of Doc's voice, penetrating through the closed front door and windows.

"My sister? No way! Mother?"

With a baffling expression, Popeye stopped for a brief moment and looked toward the cabin door. It was obvious that he was quite perplexed about hearing Doc's voice and what he said. Seconds later, shaking his head in confusion, he continued his short journey toward the dining room kitchen.

Later, that same morning, at precisely nine o'clock, the doors to the dining room were open, a steady flow of campers, guests, counselors, and staff began to sit at the dozens of round tables, set with silver wear, napkins, clear plastic pitchers of milk, orange juice, and water. The canned rock-and-roll music filling the spacious room was blaring quite loud, as to make sure the camp's residents were all awake and ready to start a grand day. There was an immense amount of conversation going on about the so-called miraculous event that had happened ten, or so, hours prior, down in the inner dock area. Much of the talk, and questions, were about the state of Doc's health, and the surprise that Julie Copeland was his twin—that they were brother and sister. The information was quickly spread through the camp like wildfire, starting with the few who had talked to Jack and Mary Jo, as well as Julie, when Joseph was taken to the Medicine Man for treatment the day before. The decision had been promptly made not to keep this news quiet. There was no reason not to share it. Why keep it a secret? The only kept secret for now was that there were only a few folks who knew of Doc's wellness.

Once everyone had taken their seats in the dining room, Chet stepped up on to the small platform and rang the brass bell several times to get the attention of the crowd. The music ended, without delay, when he began to speak into the microphone. "Listen up, everyone. Hey! Before we give thanks for our food this morning, I know that you're all anxious to hear about the amazing event that took place here last night at Malibu. Even though it was witnessed only by a handful of us, most of you have heard the story about the miraculous bright light down in the harbor, and the image it produced out on the inlet waters. But before we talk about that in depth, I also know that all of you have been concerned about Doc, and his condition, which I would like to address now. Instead of having the doctor come up on stage and explain what's going on, I'm going to invite Julie Copeland, our work crew waitress, who is certainly involved in all of this, to share the latest news. Julie." Chet extended his right arm and hand out to Julie, who was hidden behind the massive stone fireplace, next to the beverage area.

She promptly appeared and directly walked to the stage and joined Chet at the microphone. The room was so quiet, one would think it was empty. No one spoke a word, as they all waited for Julie to address them with her story. She had two insignificant-sized Band-Aids on her face, along with several scrapes on her bare arms, but otherwise, she looked healthy and happy. Taking a moment to scan the crowd, and taking a deep breath, she spoke clearly into the microphone.

"I have some wonderful news to share with all of you concerning Doc. The incident, the event that took place last night here at Malibu, is not only miraculous, but self-rewarding for me and for all of us. Let me explain. Not only did I learn yesterday that Doc is my twin brother, but it's my belief that last night the Lord used His mighty power and grace to give Doc, Joseph, a gift. The gift of allowing him to continue his life here on this earth. Through the spirit of Christ and the glory of God, Joseph has been completely healed."

Without hesitation, Julie turned toward the back area of the fireplace and extended her hand. "Joseph!" Doc right away walked out from behind the stone structure, and with a broad smile, he waved to the assembled camp, stepping up on to the stage to join Julie and Chet. He had no signs of any injuries, nor did he even have one bandage or scrape. His skin was completely clear of any blemishes; he was entirely healed. The entire gathering of everyone in the dining room broke into a thunderous cheer. With a look of wonder and happiness, they all watched Doc and Julie embrace each other with heartfelt love, as they kissed each other on the cheek. Chet stood by on the stage as others began to filter out from behind the floor-to-ceiling stone fireplace. Vic, Edna, Ken, Chris, Beth, Kyle, Turtle, the doctor, Chet, and Popeye all emerged from this somewhat behind-the-scene area of the dining room. They walked over to the stage, clapping and smiling. Soon, the entire camp joined in and began to clap, whistle, and holler out shouts of joy, while they stood by their chairs. Joseph and Julie, standing up on the platform, overlooked this sign of contentment among all those present. They both continued their smiles of appreciation during this time of bliss and delight. At least a full minute went by before the gathered group quieted and sat back down in their chairs. Joseph approached the microphone. With poise and sensitivity, he spoke directly and clearly into the sound system, which could easily be heard throughout the room.

"Thank you. Thank you, everyone. Thank you for your faith and for your prayers. I really don't know what to say about all of this. I think I'm still in a bit of shock to find out that God touched me and healed me last night. I really don't know why I was chosen. Why He picked me, my life, to perform one of His loving miracles upon. Although I'm certainly grateful and humbled, I must be honest and say that I'm also somewhat embarrassed as to this great act of love He has given me." Doc gestured at Julie with his hand and arm and said, "I think it's also a miracle that my sister, Julie, is as well as she is, after her extremely frightening fall from Chatterbox. I feel so blessed to have been able to save her, but I truly believe it happened by the hand of God that she too survived and is with us today."

Everyone in the dining room applauded loudly, while Julie instantly broke into a giant smile, dimples and all. When the room quieted again, Doc continued, "I can say to all of you that I sincerely believe that our Lord has a plan for each of us and that we're all walking miracles of life. Obviously, for whatever reason, I've been blessed and given a second chance on this earth. The only thing that I can figure is, perhaps, He spared my life because He wanted me to know my family—my sister, Julie, and my mother. I thought my mother was dead." Joseph began to lose his composure and started to cry and looked over at Julie. She immediately put her arm around his waist to quickly comfort him. When he gained control of his feelings, he turned toward Mary Jo and Jack, who were also behind the immense fireplace, and gestured for them to join him and Julie up on stage. Again, speaking into the microphone, he said, "Everyone, please meet and welcome my mother and her husband, Julie's dad: Mary Jo and Jack Copeland."

When the two of them proudly stepped out from behind the stone wall, happiness filled Julie's eyes with tears of joy. Mary Jo and Jack smiled when they anxiously joined Joseph and Julie on the wooden riser. The four of them embraced one another, and Joseph kissed his mother on the cheek. Obviously, overjoyed by all the love surrounding him in this moment of happiness, Joseph turned back to the mass of folks in the well-lit room and waved with a heartfelt smile. His white cross necklace around his neck could easily be seen, against his dark-blue Malibu T-shirt he was wearing.

CHAPTER 18

Saying a Temporary Goodbye

Two weeks had passed since that glorious, exciting morning at breakfast time in the Malibu dining room. Once again the *Malibu Princess* was tied up along the outer dock, and campers were boarding the small ship, after experiencing one of the best weeks of their lives at Malibu. The *Nefertiti*, full of luggage, was tied alongside the wide floating dock, ready for the work crew boys to unload. But at the moment, they were busy unloading freight from the belly of the ship, and stacking it on the dock. Chris was helping, while Vic was supervising the dozen or so guys who were all working hard, and fast, to get the job done quickly. Once the freight was unloaded, they could move all the suitcases into the area of the ship where the cargo had been. Doc was near the bottom of the portable stairs that were used to board the ship. He was talking to his sister, Julie, who was about to embark. She had fulfilled her time at Malibu on work crew, and it was now time for her to leave.

"Well, I guess this is it, Joseph," she reluctantly said to him, knowing that her time had ran out at Malibu. "I'll soon be heading back home to Spokane."

"According to the letter I just read from Mom, she can't wait to see you, so that's a good thing." He tried to soften her scheduled and unwanted departure.

"She can't wait to see you too, my handsome brother. And I can't wait for you to meet your little sister, Robin, and to see our house. Oh! And I can't wait to show you off to all my friends in Spokane." She winked at him and smiled.

"I can't wait for you to meet my aunt Lois, at some point in time." Joseph chimed in. "Well, I guess I'd better go." She took a moment to look around, glancing up at the wooden boardwalk above the slanted gangplank, and then out into the Jervis Inlet. "Gosh! I'm going to miss this place." She then looked back at Joseph. "Not to mention you," she said to him in a melancholy tone.

"I'll miss you too, Julie, trust me. In fact, I'll miss you a bunch, that's for sure. You are such a special lady, a special sister."

"So I guess this means I'm no longer your princess, huh?"

"Oh, yes, you are! You'll always be my princess. In fact, speaking of that, I want you to have this." Doc removed his white cross necklace from around his neck and directly, and carefully, placed it over Julie's head.

"Joseph, what are you doing?" Julie asked with a puzzled expression. "This belongs to you. It's your miracle cross." She began to remove the necklace back over her head.

At once, Joseph gently stopped her from removing the necklace by softly grabbing her arms and slowly moving them back down to her side. "No, it needs to be worn by a princess, and that is you! I gave it to you, and I want you to have it. Case closed." He winked at her, as she understood his thoughtfulness and sincere desire for her to hold on to the precious cross necklace.

"Thank you," she quietly said to him, giving him a hug, and then whispered in his ear, "I love you, little brother."

After their quick embrace, Joseph looked at her and asked, "Little brother? What do you mean *little brother?*"

Answering him with another smile, she said, "Mom told me that I was born two minutes before you. I'm older than you, so there."

"Oh brother! Or I guess I should say, 'oh sister!' Go on, get out of here!" He laughed and gestured for her to head up the steps, but all in good humor. She laughed as well, and with her fiddle case in hand, she turned and ran up the metal stairs leading to the ship.

Chris looked over at Doc and Julie when she was climbing the steps. He ran over to Doc and waved up to Julie, just before she was about to disappear into the ship's interior.

"Take care, Julie!" Chris shouted up to her. "Don't forget, you and Doc have to come down to Hollywood for a visit! I really want you to meet my dad!" he proudly announced.

"And your mom!" Julie shouted back, giving him one of her darling smiles and, once again, showing off her charming dimples, with all of her bandages removed.

Minutes later, and before the *Malibu Princess* was ready to depart from the dock, one of the work crew boys, near the *Nefertiti*, was trying to fix a busted freight box by tying twine around it. Vic and Chris were also nearby working while the cargo was being loaded by the work crew into the open workboat. The boy fixing the heavy cardboard box shouted out to Chris, "Hey, Chris! Can I borrow your knife for a second?"

Chris, who was standing near the water's edge on the dock, helping to move boxes into the boat, hollered back, "Oh, sure." Without hesitation, he quickly pulled his knife out of its leather sheath, attached to his belt. He then tried to carefully toss it over in the direction of his work crew mate, planning for it to land on the wooded planked dock, just in front of his friend. He certainly did not want his buddy to have to catch the knife with the blade exposed. His aim was bad, and the custom, loaned, buck knife hit the deck and bounced off into the inlet with a splash. The cold saltwater was dark and deep. The knife was gone forever. All the work crew guys who were in the immediate vicinity, along with Vic and Doc, witnessed this misfortune. In a brief moment of disbelief, Chris just stood there with a stunned, shaken, and then sheepish expression on his face, dropping his head in distress.

"Christian!" Vic shouted at him, in his deepest voice and in obvious anger and displeasure.

Doc quickly jumped in with his sense of humor, even though he knew that Chris was now in trouble with him, and certainly with Vic. He promptly hollered over to Chris, "Say there, Mr. Christian, Captain Bligh is calling you!"

Everyone, except Vic, began laughing loudly, knowing that Doc was referring to the classic novel *Mutiny on the Bounty*. Chris could only shake his head in worry. Retribution was sure to come.

SPECIAL
ACKNOWLEDGEMENT

The story of *Doc and the Princess* would not exist if it was not for the wonderful nonprofit organization, **Young Life**. This Christian ministry based organization was founded by Jim Rayburn in 1941. Young Life operates globally with different focuses. They reach out to middle school, high school, and college-aged kids in all 50 of the United States as well as more than 90 countries around the world. As noted in their website (younglife.org), they *"invite kids to follow Christ, care for them regardless of their response, and change lives in the process."* As of 2016, Young Life was impacting the lives of an estimated 2,000,000 kids worldwide. In the USA alone, there were 1,243 areas of ministry. The number of volunteer leaders in 2016 in the USA was 32,480. And each year, more than 100,000 kids around the world spend a week, or a weekend, at camp.

Attending Young Life Club when I was a sophomore in high school and experiencing Malibu as a camper in 1962, I embraced the Christian faith and that summer welcomed Jesus Christ into my life. Working at the Malibu Club the following year on work crew, and resident staff, I began to realize just how special and unique this amazing camp was. During the times I worked at Malibu, over a span of 50 years, I witnessed hundreds of kids committing their lives to Jesus.

I truly believe that Young Life's camp, the Malibu Club in Canada, is on Holy ground. The emotions and closeness I feel towards the Lord when I am anywhere on the property is remarkable. There is no mystery to the spectacular scenery and beauty of Malibu, God's extraordinary creation. The enchantment and miracles happen with the interaction of the people at Malibu ~ the campers, counselors, work crew, staff, adult guests, and management. That is the constant reason, *"Malibu, Canada, sure does shine, all of the time!"*

David Siegle

ACKNOWLEDGEMENTS

A heartfelt thank you to my family for continued encouragement to write this story. I also wish to express my gratitude to Wendy Love, Ken Smith, Cherrie Smith, and especially, **Leslie Siegle**, for initially working with me in the first editing phase of *Doc and the Princess*. And I wish to convey my appreciation and praise to **Christian Faith Publishing** for their expert editing and professional publication of this book.

I also want to acknowledge the hundreds of individuals with whom I met during my many years of service at the **Malibu Club**. Many of which were campers that I only briefly got to spend time with. Others were on work crew, staff, counselors, or in management. Over scores of summers I embraced many friendships that are dear to me. The story of *Doc and the Princess* would not have materialized if it were not for the many lives and personalities that touched my heart. Let truth be known that even though this tale is fiction, there are a number of persons in this book that are actually real. Some of the colorful characters, such as: Vic, Edna, Mac, and Old Steve, are portrayed in the novel as who they really were. I use the word 'were', because they have passed-on now into the Kingdom of Heaven. Their friendship and comradeship were important to me, therefore, I am pleased that I am able to share a glimpse into their lives for you, the reader.

CREDIT TO

- **The history of the Northwest "Seashelt Indians":**
  Pender Harbour ONLINE ~ www.penderharbour.org/html/sechelt_indians.html *Canadian Genealogy* ~ www.canadiangenealogy.net/indians/seechelt
  True Ghost Tales ~ www.trueghosttales.com/native-americans-ghosts-and-evil-spirits.php
- **"Historical knowledge and descriptions"** of the Malibu Club and surrounding inlets: Book titled, Young Life's MALIBU by Elsie Campbell, 1984
- **"Indian Story"** about the weather:
  AAA Native Arts.com ~ www.aaanativearts.com/article1019.html
- **Information and stories about "twins" (siblings):**
  About.com ~ *Twins & Multiples* ~ http://multiples.about.com/od/funfacts/a/twintelepathy.htm
  http://multiples.about.com/od/funfacts/tp/10thingsabouttwins.htm
- **About "Job's Daughters:**
  Job's Daughters International ~ http://www.iojd.org/AboutUs/AboutUs.htm

RECOMMENDED BOOKS
BY DAVID SIEGLE

"Should you be interested in reading more about Young Life, the Malibu Club, or the Princess Louisa Inlet, I recommend the following books":

Young Life's MALIBU, by Elsie Campbell, 1984

Mac and the Princess ~ The story of Princess Louisa Inlet, by Bruce Calhoun, 1976

THROUGH THE RAPIDS ~ The History of Princess Louisa Inlet, by Charles William Hitz, 2003

MALIBU ~ a celebration of faith, by Andrew Stone and Allan de la Plante, 2003

MADE for THIS: The Young Life Story, by Jeff Chesemore, 2015

ABOUT THE AUTHOR

David Siegle was a resident staff member at the Malibu Club in Canada for four summers in the mid-1960s. He served as the resort's harbormaster and was active in the program. After serving in the United States Navy in Vietnam, during the late 1960s, he returned to Malibu in 1970 as program director for July. In the past fifteen years, he continued to work at Malibu, now and again.

David was a volunteer Young Life leader in several cities in Northern California in the 1960–70s. He retired in 2002 as an event producer for sporting, music, military, and corporate events in California. His resume also includes working in the motion picture film industry. He is also proud to be an Eagle Scout.

Having a passion for connecting with the youth on a personal and spiritual level is what drove him to write *Doc and the Princess*. He shares, "I wanted to share with young people, and others, my amazing experience working and witnessing my Christian faith at this unique, remarkable, Young Life camp—Malibu!"